You are Invited to Attend Readings
by Authors Featured in

The Archipelago
Conjunctions: 27

The Miami Book Fair International will host readings by Fred
D'Aguiar, Adrian Castro, Bob Shacochis, Antonio Benítez-
Rojo, Cristina García, and Rosario Ferré, along with Robert
Antoni and Bradford Morrow presenting the work of other
writers from the issue, as well as a unique tribute to Manno
Charlemagne, musician and mayor of Port-au-Prince, Haiti.

MIAMI BOOK FAIR
INTERNATIONAL

For one incredible week, experience the nation's
most exciting literary climate, including nearly 300 national
and international exhibitors, readings, and lectures.

MIAMI
BOOK FAIR
INTERNATIONAL

November 17-24, 1996
Street Fair: November 22-24
at
Miami-Dade County Community College
Wolfson Campus
300 N.E. Second Avenue,
Miami, Florida 33132
Phone (305) 237-3258   Fax (305) 237-3645

CONJUNCTIONS

Bi-Annual Volumes of New Writing

Edited by
Bradford Morrow

Contributing Editors
Walter Abish
Chinua Achebe
John Ashbery
Mei-mei Berssenbrugge
Guy Davenport
Elizabeth Frank
William H. Gass
John Guare
Susan Howe
Robert Kelly
Ann Lauterbach
Patrick McGrath
Nathaniel Tarn
Quincy Troupe
John Edgar Wideman

published by Bard College

EDITOR: Bradford Morrow
MANAGING EDITOR: Michael Bergstein
SENIOR EDITORS: Martine Bellen, Ben Marcus, Pat Sims
ART EDITOR: Anthony McCall
ASSOCIATE EDITOR: Thalia Field
INTERNET ADVISOR: Michael Neff
EDITORIAL ASSISTANTS: Sage Jacobs, Katherine Moore, Paulina
  Nissenblatt, Charles Peirce, Nathanael Schwartz

CONJUNCTIONS is published in the Spring and Fall of each year by
Bard College, Annandale-on-Hudson, NY 12504. This issue is made
possible in part with the generous funding of the Lannan Foundation,
the J.M. Kaplan Fund, Inc., the National Endowment for the Arts and
the New York State Council on the Arts.

SUBSCRIPTIONS: Send subscription order to CONJUNCTIONS, Bard
College, Annandale-on-Hudson, NY 12504. Single year (two volumes):
$18.00 for individuals; $25.00 for institutions and overseas. Two years
(four volumes): $32.00 for individuals; $45.00 for institutions and
overseas. Patron subscription (lifetime): $500.00. Overseas subscribers
please make payment by International Money Order. Back issues available at $12.00 per copy. For subscription and advertising information,
call 914-758-1539 or fax 914-758-2660.

Editorial communications should be sent to 33 West 9th Street, New
York, NY 10011. Unsolicited manuscripts cannot be returned unless
accompanied by a stamped, self-addressed envelope.

Printers: Edwards Brothers.
Typesetter: Bill White, Typeworks.

ISSN 0278-2324
ISBN 0-941964-43-4

Manufactured in the United States of America.

TABLE OF CONTENTS

THE ARCHIPELAGO: *New Writing From and About the Caribbean*
Edited by Robert Antoni and Bradford Morrow

Drawing tailpiece to Editors' Note, "Los Ingredientes," by José Bedia. Courtesy Peter Menéndez Gallery.

EDITORS' NOTE

THE ARCHIPELAGO AROSE out of a conversation between friends. Any literary formulations grew naturally *from* the friendship, as we began, during a series of exuberant dialogues to address simple yet impossible questions such as *What is the Caribbean?* and *What are its literatures?*

The history of that crescent of islands between Miami and Caracas seems to us archetypal and intimate, deeply expressive of human experience in all its spectrum of possibility. In this part of the world, so many cultures and languages have converged, clashed, synthesized and resynthesized — a continuing process further complicated and enriched by their latter-day dispersion to every corner of the globe. We see the Caribbean as as much a state of mind, of history and politics, as of place. Its literatures — so kinetic and imaginative — are among the purest of its memories and documents. *The Archipelago* is our attempt to celebrate a small part of that vast experience.

We have only begun here to touch upon the region's richnesses and profundities of linguistic expression. So much more, we realize, awaits exploration. Nor did we want to reprise other Caribbean anthologies that focused on more specific aspects of the area in terms of language (Francophone, Dutch, Portuguese) and genre (West Indian folktales, for instance). At the same time, we are pleased to be the first to bring together three generations of writers — from the original Magical Realists to their youngest descendants. Eminent elders like Wilson Harris and Juan Bosch have never appeared together with Gabriel García Márquez and Derek Walcott; who again have rarely if ever appeared with young writers like Cristina García and Lorna Goodison, Marlene Nourbese Philip and Edwidge Danticat, as well as others collected here. (Our intention to represent the region's expansiveness is further expressed by the "Polishness" of Derek Walcott and the "Caribbeanness" of Adam Zagajewski.) The variety of voices that speak in *The Archipelago* will surely convince you, as it has us, that the Caribbean is one of the most fertile new grounds of twentieth-century literature.

Many people have helped us along the way. We would like to express heartfelt thanks to Ana Pineda, Carmen Balcells, Carina Pons, Susan Bergholz, Mervin Morris, Fred D'Aguiar, Mark McMorris, Forrest Gander, Sandra Paquet, Mitch Kaplan, José Bedia, Peter

Menéndez, Fred Snitzer, Zaida del Río, Senel Paz, Thalia Field, Martine Bellen, Melanie Fleishman, Nathaniel Mackey, Minna Procter, Eliot Weinberger. Special thanks also to the translators Esther Allen, Clare Cavanagh, Thomas Christensen, Mark Dow, Edith Grossman, Suzanne Jill Levine, James Maraniss, Anabella Paiz and Mark Schafer.

— Robert Antoni & Bradford Morrow
August 7, 1996
Miami/New York City

Los ingredientes (naturales, vegetales, animales y minerales)

Caribe Mágico
Gabriel García Márquez

— Translated from Spanish by Edith Grossman

SURINAM — AS FEW IN the world know — is an independent nation on the Caribbean, a Dutch colony until a few years ago. It has 163,820 square kilometers of territory and a little over 384,000 inhabitants of many backgrounds: East Indians, local Indians, Indonesians, Africans, Chinese and Europeans. Its capital, Paramaribo (in Spanish we pronounce it with the accent on the "i," while the natives stress the third "a"), is a dismal, clamorous city, its spirit more Asian than American, where four languages and numerous indigenous dialects are spoken in addition to the official language, Dutch. Six religions — Hinduism, Catholicism, Islam and the Moravian, Dutch Reform and Lutheran churches — have their adherents. At the moment Surinam is ruled by a regime of young military men about whom very little is known, even in neighboring countries, and chances are no one would pay attention to the place if not for the fact that once a week it is a scheduled stop for a Dutch airline that flies from Amsterdam to Caracas.

I've known about Surinam ever since I was very young, not because of Surinam itself (in those days it was called Dutch Guiana) but because it bordered French Guiana, whose capital, Cayenne, had once been the site of the infamous penal colony known in life and in death as Devil's Island. The few who managed to escape that hell — and they could as easily have been brutal criminals as political idealists — fled to the many islands of the Antilles to wait until they could return to Europe, or else changed their names and settled in Venezuela and along the Caribbean coast of Colombia. The most famous of these was Henri Charrier, author of *Papillon*, who prospered in Caracas as a promoter of restaurants and other, shadier enterprises, and who died a few years ago on the crest of an ephemeral literary glory as merited as it was undeserved. The glory, in fact, should have gone to another French

9

fugitive, René Belbenoit, who described the horrors of Devil's Island long before *Papillon*, though today he has no place in any nation's literature and his name cannot be found in encyclopedias. Belbenoit had been a journalist in France before he was sentenced to life in prison for a crime no contemporary reporter has been able to discover; he found refuge in the United States, where he continued to practice his profession until he died at an honorable old age.

Other fugitives came to the Colombian town on the Caribbean coast where I was born, during the time of the "banana fever," when cigars were lit not with matches but with five peso bills. A few assimilated and became very respectable citizens who were distinguished by their heavy accents and hermetic pasts. One, Roger Chantal, whose only trade when he arrived was pulling teeth without anesthetic, mysteriously became a millionaire overnight. He celebrated with a Babylonian fiesta (in an improbable town that had little reason to envy Babylon), drank until he could no longer stand and shouted in his jubilant collapse: *Je suis l'homme le plus riche du monde.* In his delirium he displayed philanthropic qualities no one had seen in him before, and donated to the church a life-size plaster saint that was enthroned with a three-day bacchanalia. On an ordinary Tuesday three secret agents arrived on the eleven o'clock train and headed straight for his house. Chantal was not there, but the agents made a meticulous search in the presence of his native-born wife, who offered no resistance until they attempted to open the enormous armoire in the bedroom. That was when the agents smashed the mirrors and found more than a million dollars in phony bills hidden between the glass and the wood. Roger Chantal was never heard of again. Later, the legend was born that the million counterfeit dollars had been spirited into the country inside the plaster saint, which no customs agent had been curious enough to inspect.

This all came back to me in a rush just before Christmas 1957, when I had an hour stopover in Paramaribo. In those days the airport consisted of a flattened earth runway and a palm hut whose central wooden post held a telephone like the ones in cowboy movies, whose handle had to be cranked many times, and with a great deal of force, before an operator came on the line. The heat was scorching, and the heavy, dust-choked air carried the smell of sleeping caymans that identifies the Caribbean when you come there from another world. On a stool propped against the telephone post sat a young black woman, very beautiful and well built, with a many-colored turban like the ones used by women in certain African countries. She was pregnant, almost at term, and in silence she smoked a cigarette as I've seen it done only in the Caribbean: she held the lit end inside her mouth and puffed smoke out the other end as if it were a ship's smokestack. She was the only human being in the airport.

After fifteen minutes a decrepit jeep drove up in a cloud of burning dust, and a black man in shorts and a pith helmet climbed out carrying the papers that would send the plane on its way. As he handled the documents he spoke on the phone, shouting in Dutch. Twelve hours earlier I had been on a waterfront terrace in Lisbon, facing the enormous Portuguese sea, watching flocks of gulls that came into the port taverns to escape the icy wind. At that time, Europe was a worn, snow-covered land, the days had no more than five hours of light and it was impossible to imagine the reality of a world of burning sun and overripe guavas, like the one where we had just landed. And yet the only enduring image of this experience, the one I still preserve intact, was of the beautiful, imperturbable black woman whose lap held a basket of ginger root to sell to the passengers.

Now, on another trip from Lisbon to Caracas, with another stopover in Paramaribo, my first impression was that we had landed in the wrong city. Today the airport terminal is a building with bright lights, huge glass windows, subdued air conditioning, the odor of children's medicine and the same canned music that is repeated without mercy in all the public spaces of the world. There are as many well-stocked duty-free shops selling luxury goods as in Japan, and in the crowded cafeteria one finds a lively mix of the country's seven races, six religions and countless languages. The change seemed one of several centuries, not twenty years.

My teacher, Juan Bosch, the author of a monumental history of the Caribbean, among many other works, once said in private that our magic world is similar to the unconquerable plants that come back to life beneath the concrete, breaking through and destroying it, to bloom again in the same spot. I understood this as never before when I walked through an unexpected door in the Paramaribo airport and found an impassive row of old women, all of them black, all of them wearing many-colored turbans and all of them smoking with the lit end inside their mouths. They were selling

11

fruit and local handicrafts, but none of them made the slightest effort to attract buyers. Only one, not the oldest, was selling ginger root. I recognized her right away. Without really knowing where to begin or what to do about my discovery, I bought a handful of roots. As I did so, I recalled her condition the first time and asked straight out how her son was. She did not even glance at me. "I had a daughter, not a son," she said, "and at the age of twenty-two she's just given me my first grandchild."

Signs
Derek Walcott

— for Adam Zagajewski

I.

Europe completed its silhouette in the nineteenth century
with steaming train-stations, gas-lamps, encyclopedias,
the expanding waists of empires, the grocer's inventory
of the novel, its structure as a beehive with ideas,
fiction that echoed city-blocks of long paragraphs
with parenthetical doorways, with crowds on the margin
waiting to cross, and slate doves on ledges gurgled epigraphs
for the next chapter where mediaeval cobbles begin
the labyrinth of a contorted plot; leisurely heresies
over coffee in steamed cafes, too chilly outdoors,
opposite the gilt doors of the opera, two green bronze horses
guarding a locked square like bookends, the odours
of a decaying century drift from autumnal gardens
with the smell of old books chained in the National Library.
Cross a small bridge into our time, and the past hardens
into statues of gesturing generals, a magnified cemetery
devoted to the great dead, the linden perspective hazes
into a mist that goes with the clopping horses
of carriages, of a range that was Dickens's and Balzac's
until the grand vision narrows back into ghostly houses
where a plume of smoke rises from distant chimney stacks.

II.

Far from streets seething like novels with their century's sorrow
of charcoal sketches by Kollwitz, the emigre's pain
in feeling his language translated, the synthetic aura
of an alien syntax, an altered construction that will drain
the specific of detail, of damp: creaks of sunlight
on a window-ledge, under a barn door in the hay country
of boyhood, the linen of cafes in an academic light,
in short the fiction of Europe that turns into theatre
over this dry place where there are no ruins only an echo
of what you have read. It is only much later
they will become real: canals, churches, willows, filthy snow.
This is the envy we finally commit, this happens
to us readers, distant devourers, that its pages whiten
our minds like pavements, or fields where a pen's
tracks mark the snow. We become one of those, then,
who convert the scarves of cirrus at dusk to a diva's
adieu from an opera balcony, ceilings of cherubs, cornucopias
disgorging stone bounty, the setting for a believer's
conviction in healing music; then huge clouds pass,
enormous cumuli rumble in trucks like barrels of newsprint and the faith of redemptive art begins to leave us
as we turn back the old engravings, the etched views
that are smudged with terror in dark cobbles and eaves.

Derek Walcott

III.

The cobbled streets keep to themselves, their gables leaning
to whisper to one another, the walls are scraped of signs
condemning the star of David; there are no grey faces screening
themselves (like the moon drawing a cloud's thin curtains
at the tramp of jackboots, or the shattered store-glass that rains
diamonds on the pavement). Now there is a punishing silence
since they took the old tenants away. There are sins
whose truth no streets dare pronounce, much less the meaning
of why they occurred, then they are various repetitions
of the same sins, blood washed from cobbles, 'the cleaning.'
And now there is the romance, the movie-setting
for History's enormous soap-opera, the old houses,
the cobbles, the shattered shops, the deliberate forgetting
that changes into drama, even Buchenwald and Auschwitz.
The braille of wet cobbled alleys, the street lamps punctuating
some boulevard's interminable sentence, autumn leaves
blown past the closed opera-house, the soot-eyed crowd waiting
in a bread-line, or near a train line, the camera grieves
for us all now, it moves with the habit of conscience
around the theatrical corners of the old town,
replastering the right paraphernalia, swastikas, signs
of the coming cleansing, until the ancient tongue
that forbade graven images, seems, at last, to make sense.

15

IV.

That cloud was Europe, dissolving past the thorn branches
of the lignum vitae, the tree of life, but a thunderhead remains
over these islands in crests of arrested avalanches
like a blizzard on a screen in the snow-speckled campaigns,
the same old news just changing its borders and policies,
beyond which wolves founder with red berries for eyes,
and their unheard howling trails off in wisps of smoke
like the frozen smoke over bridges. The barge of Poland
is an agony floating downstream with remote, magisterial
scansion, St. Petersburg's minarets a cloud. Then clouds
are forgotten like battles. Like snow in spring. Also evil.
All that seems so marmoreal is only a veil;
play Timon then, and curse all endeavour as vile,
and the combers will continue to crest, to no avail.
Your shadow stays with you startling the quick crabs
that stiffen until you pass. That cloud means spring
to the Babylonian willows of Amsterdam budding again
like crowds in Pissarro along a wet boulevard's branches,
and the drizzle that sweeps its small wires enshrouds
Notre Dame. In the distance the word Cracow
sounds like artillery; then Serbia. Then snow that clouds
walls riddled with bullet-holes, that like cotton-wool, close.

The Room I Work In
Adam Zagajewski

— Translated from Polish by Clare Cavanagh
— for Derek Walcott

The room I work in is as square
as half a pair of dice.
It holds a wooden table
with a stubborn peasant's profile,
a sluggish armchair and a teapot's
pouting Hapsburg lip.
From the window I see a few skinny trees,
wispy clouds and toddlers,
always happy and loud.
Sometimes a windshield glints in the distance
or, higher up, an airplane's silver husk.
Clearly others aren't wasting time
while I work, seeking adventures
on earth or in the air.
My room is in a building with many floors;
the dead dwell in the cellar. They toss and turn,
waiting for someone to reveal their belated dreams.
Future conspirators, still unborn, with imaginations
light as a poor man's gold,
meet in secret on the roof and sing.
Triumphant armies march the corridors
accompanied by drums; while at night
defeated legions flit by quietly,
bearing the white blood of the fallen.
The room I work in is a camera obscura.
And what is my work —
waiting motionless,
turning pages, patient meditation,
passivities not pleasing
to that judge with the greedy gaze.

17

Adam Zagajewski

I write as slowly as if I'll live two hundred years.
I seek images that don't exist,
and if they do they're crumpled and concealed
like summer clothes in the winter,
when frost stings the mouth.
I dream of absolute concentration; if I found it
I'd surely stop breathing.
Maybe it's good I get so little done.
But after all I hear the first snow hissing,
the frail melody of daylight,
and the city's ominous rumble.
I drink from a small spring,
my thirst is greater than the sea.

A Natural History
Cristina García

A SIGUAPA STYGIAN

MY NAME IS IGNACIO AGÜERO and I was born in the late afternoon
of October 4, 1904, the same day, my mother informed me later,
that the first president of the republic, Estrada Palma, arrived in
Pinar del Río for a parade and a banquet and a long night of
speeches at the governor's mansion. Cuba had gained its independence two years before and despite the Platt Amendment,
which permitted the Americans to interfere in our country from
the day it was born, the citizens of Pinar del Río poured into the
streets to welcome the president.

A brass band played on a wooden platform decorated with ribbons and carnations, and children scampered about in their Sunday
finery, clutching pinwheels and balloons. Angry cigar workers
pressed through the crowd, shaking placards protesting the high
foreign tariffs levied on tobacco. My father, Reinaldo Ureña, a
lector who read to the cigar workers in their factory, marched
among them.

Back at our whitewashed cement house, shaded by the crown of
a graceful frangipani, my mother was readying herself for the fes-
tivities when she felt the first of my violent kicks deep inside her.
She sat down at the edge of the bed and slowly rubbed her stomach,
humming a Mozart sonata whose soothing effect on me she had
previously noted. Instead the kicking intensified, followed by a
series of rhythmic contractions. Mamá was all alone. She would
miss the parade and the suckling pig and the ballroom lit with
candelabras.

No sooner had she settled back on her matrimonial bed than
Mamá spotted the shadow on the far wall. Straight ahead, standing
guard between the open shutters of the bedroom window, was a
Siguapa Stygian owl. My mother did not know its official name
then, only that it was a bird of ill omen, earless and black and unmistakable. It was doubly bad luck to see one during the day since

19

they were known to fly about late at night, stealing people's souls and striking them deaf.

Hoo-hoo, hoo-hoo, it called to her as she breathed a voluminous breath that caught her very center. She grabbed the etched glass lamp on the nightstand and threw it with all her might, but it fell short of the owl's luminous eyes. Suddenly, the pain inside her spread upward and downward like two opposing tidal waves and despite her fear or because of it, she delivered a nine-pound four-ounce baby boy.

The owl remained still on its perch until the placenta spilled forth in a rush of blood. Then with a dark flap of its wings it swooped forward, plucked the sodden organ from the floor, and flew with it like a rumor out the window once more.

Later, my mother learned that the bird had flown low over the president's parade with her placenta, scattering the crowd and raining birthing blood. Even President Palma, trembling with fear, crossed himself twice before jumping headlong into a flowering Angel's trumpet bush, his crisp linen suit spattered with Mamá's blood.

Word of the incident quickly spread throughout Cuba. Mamá told me that for once the priests' and the *santeros'* interpretations were in accord: the island was headed for doom. Since then, the Siguapa Stygians are no longer so common in Cuba, killed over the years by superstitious country folk and the disappearance of the vast, unlit woods that once had concealed them.

From the start, my mother blamed the Siguapa Stygian for my tin ear, although she was grateful it hadn't flown off with my hearing altogether. Both my parents were accomplished musicians, and, as a child, I studied the piano, the violin, the flute and the oboe, but I never coaxed more than rudimentary sounds from any of them. This was a heartbreak for my parents, who had hoped we might one day form a trio.

Pinar del Río was a steamy backwater in those days. Its cultural amenities included a theater with a red tile roof, where my mother and father and I attended an occasional concert, and a natural sciences museum — a dusty back room in a deteriorated municipal building — that had on exhibit a rare cork palm, a species indigenous to Cuba that can be traced back two hundred and fifty million years.

The Sierra de los Organos loomed to the northwest, and though the mountains were far off, they managed to stamp the town with their somber mood. Tobacco fields stretched in every direction: on the vales, on the hillsides, on the mountain tops and on the sheer sides of the *mogotes,* limestone bluffs which the workers ascended and descended by means of ropes. Although there were pineapple fields nearby and orange groves and acres of sugarcane, nothing competed with the supremacy of tobacco.

My father, as the *lector* of El Cid Cigar Manufacturers Company, was revered for his intellect and his splendid renditions of the works of Cervantes, Dickens and Victor Hugo. For two hours every morning and then again after lunch, Papá read aloud from an assortment of newspapers, novels, political treatises and collections of poetry. While the workers occasionally voted on what they wanted my father to read, more often than not they left the choice to him, a testament to their utmost confidence in his taste. For twenty-one years (not counting strikes, holidays and illnesses), Papá stood at his lectern and read to the hundred or so workers seated below him. Most of them smoked continuously as they listened to him, stripping and sorting and rolling the finest tobacco in the world.

Papá had a deep, sonorous voice, cured to huskiness over the years by the sheer volume of smoke he inhaled. Although he nursed his throat regularly with honey and lemon, he refused to yield to the temptations of the microphone which, he was convinced, distorted the robust timbre of his voice. In the afternoons, when he customarily read from novels, townspeople gathered outside the factory with their rocking chairs and embroidery to listen to the intriguing tales that drifted through the open windows.

My father was particularly proud of the literary name that was imprinted on the factory's cedar boxes and its gilded cigar rings. Once a year, an occasion for which he would dress up in a jacket and waistcoat and his patent leather spats, my father read in its entirety *El Cid,* that great medieval epic poem, moving even the stolid factory director to tears.

What most people did not know was that my father was also a superb violinist. Many who heard his serenades from the street or in the nearby square assumed that the music came from my father's phonograph, prized by the town as evidence of its collective sophistication. Papá did not discourage this assumption. The violin was a link to his past, to his own father, who had lived like a pauper in the hills of Galicia carving fine, sturdy fiddles that nobody bought. My father's father had grown demented in his last years, convinced that he was descended from the great violin makers of Cremona, which had bestowed upon the world the successive geniuses of Nicolò Amati and Antonio Stradivari.

I have often wondered why someone of Papá's talent never sought to make a larger impression on the world, why he had so whittled down his dreams, for dreams he must have had to abandon Spain. It seems to me now that Papá had exhausted his lifetime's supply of adventure on his one voyage across the Atlantic. The hardships of that trip must have sated him, cured him completely of any further scheming. By the time he'd arrived in Cuba, my father wanted nothing more than to reclaim the stability he'd so recklessly left behind.

During brief nostalgic lapses, Papá recreated his favorite dishes from Spain. He made his own sausages, complaining that the local *chorizos* slept on his palate, and he taught himself to bake perfect *empanadas,* plump with spiced ground beef. When he cooked codfish and white bean stew, his eyes watered in happy relief. One winter, he planted a dwarf olive tree in our backyard, but despite his painstaking care, the sapling never bore fruit. My mother, seeing how homesick Papá was for the verdent hills of Galicia, often encouraged him to return for a visit. But Papá shook his head and said, "My fate was decided a long time ago."

That is not to say that my father was a melancholy man, not at all. Most days he awoke with an exaggerated sense of purpose. His readings engrossed him enormously, and as he strode to work, his throat fairly rumbled with anticipation over what the morning newspapers might bring.

It was my mother who was the moodier of the two. Her name was Soledad and she knew better than anyone the meaning of solitude: that the beginning already implies the end, and that at the end we understand only the vague dimensions of our ignorance. As you get older, you question the utility of your life.

Years later, I learned that Mamá had had a child out of wedlock long before I was born, a little girl named Olivia who'd drowned when the Guamá River overflowed one rainy September. I remember my mother was always saddest in September, and to this day it seems to me the bleakest of months.

TREE DUCKS

My father liked to boast that he'd arrived in Cuba with ten pesos in one pocket, a volume of verse by the great Romantic poets in another and his handmade violin. For one month he played his caprices and sonatinas, collecting coins on the streets of Havana, interspersing his concerts with the more mundane requests of passersby. One day, a young widow spat at him on the Paseo Prado. Her husband had been killed in the Spanish-American War and she could not stand to hear Papá's Castilian accent.

The desk clerk at my father's *pensión* recommended that he become a *lector* on account of his orotund voice. A week later, Papá got a job in a cigar factory in the Vuelta Abajo region of Pinar del Río. His first day on the platform, perspiring with nervousness and encircled by cigar smoke and the scrutinous eyes of a hundred workers, he began to read:

> "In a village of La Mancha the name of which I have no desire to recall, there lived not so long ago one of those gentlemen who always have a lance in the rack, an ancient buckler, a skinny nag and a greyhound for the chase . . ."

As a boy, I often wondered how Papá had endured those first months away from home, surrounded by strangers, a refined misfit among coarser men, a man whose first purchase in Cuba, after much sacrifice and diligent saving, was a gramophone and a thick black record of the *Witches' Dance Variations* by Paganini.

In time, my father met Soledad Varela, a local flutist ten years his senior. It was a Sunday afternoon and they were attending a concert by a chamber music quartet from Havana. In fact, they were the only ones in the audience. Mamá sat in her wide-brimmed straw hat. Papá smoothed the Panama in his lap. She liked the way his mouth moved, his unseemly moustache. He liked the way she held her silence, unafraid, weighing her words like silver on her tongue.

It turned out they had much to say to one another, about the muddy-sounding flute and the violin tuned half a note too high. They continued their conversation after the concert, beginning a three-day courtship that ended in Pinar del Río's town hall. Mamá was thirty-one years old and by then had refused proposals of marriage from suitors women half her age would have coveted. But in

Reinaldo Agüero of Galicia, a newcomer not long off the boat, she had found her match.

From my parents' first meeting, my future was born and the very moment I am living was predetermined. From my parents' first meeting, two more people walk the planet in search of solace, two more people with Papá's first loneliness echoing in our breasts.

Music is my earliest memory, earlier than sight or smell or touch, earlier than consciousness itself. My parents spent many evenings playing duets, for which they were technically suited, if not temperamentally. Papá worshipped the magnificent *Carnaval de Venice*, while Mamá preferred the stateliness of Beethoven's adagios or the more restrained brilliance of Tchaikovsky's *Danse Russe*. I remember how the mood of our house was colored by the music in it, as if the notes themselves could brush the air with paint.

Although I was not musical in any conventional sense, I could, at an early age, accurately imitate the calls of every bird in the woods around Pinar del Río. Our neighbor, Secundino Robreño, used to coax me into the forest to help him secure doves for his poultry cart. I warbled with such proficiency that within moments, dozens of birds dropped from the trees to welcome his shotgun. Secundino repaid me with sticky candies from his pockets, usually less than fresh, or a handful of spent bullets.

During one of our expeditions, I discovered the nest of a tree duck in a hollow stump north of town. Inside were four eggs and, fortunately, no mother *yaguasa* in sight. Secundino offered me twenty cents apiece for the eggs, a fantastic sum at the time, but I refused him and decided to raise the fledglings myself. I gathered the eggs carefully, placing one in each trouser pocket, and held the other two in my cupped hands. On the way home, balancing on the balls of my feet, I whistled the *yaguasa's* one-note song to soothe the unborn chicks.

In those days, people used to gather tree duck eggs for profit. The nests could be found in clumps of regal bromeliads or in the crooks of trees upholstered with thick Spanish moss. Common folk and fanciers alike used to raise the *yaguasas* among their own domestic poultry because they broke up barnyard quarrels and whistled at the approach of strangers. Tree ducks, I daresay, were an avian blend of bouncer and rural guard.

My *yaguasas* grew to be quite elegant, with lovely long necks and the hauteur of fine geese. Of course they were excellent watch ducks, too. In fact, my mother credited them with saving my father's life during a particularly fractious strike at the cigar factory.

Early one morning, two men I did not recognize knocked on our front door. The taller one carried a tree limb studded with nails. The shorter one, unshaven, had pineapple fists. It was apparent they had come to teach my father a lesson for his leading role in the strike.

No sooner did Papá come to the door than my ducks raced from the backyard, whistling and squawking and scattering feathers. They attacked the men with the resolve of old hens, viciously pecking and scratching them until the thugs stumbled away in a daze. No one ever came to disturb our peace again.

Sadly, the once-abundant *yaguasas* have disappeared along with the island's lowland forests. With luck, one might still spot a few in the remotest regions of the Zapata and the other lesser swamps. At night, they fly out to visit the palm groves of cultivated plantations and eat the *palmiches,* the clustered fruit of the royal palms.

Neither of my parents had any inclination toward ornithology, so it was all the more remarkable that they encouraged in me a preoccupation so far removed from their own. They indulged me with frequent drives into the countryside for my field observations. On one trip near Bailén, I spotted a pair of sandhill cranes, already quite rare when I was a boy. They were digging in the scorched earth of what was probably their former breeding grounds, digging with their bills for roots or beetle larvae in land that had been cleared to plant more sugarcane.

On another trip to the Lomas de los Acostas, I caught my first sight of a red-tailed hawk. It was known locally as the *gavilán del monte* by the peasants who lived in the huts high on the open savanna hills. *"Gavilanes del monte! Gavilanes del monte!"* the women cried from ridge to ridge when they spotted the hawks. Then they turned to warn their own chickens, who scurried, terrified, into their coops.

Every spring and fall, I searched the trees for the many migrant birds that lingered in Cuba en route to and from South America. I studied their migrations and imagined flying in their immense flocks, darkening the unreachable parts of the sky. They would travel at night, billions of them, at altitudes too high to be easily observed, taking their cues from the sun and the stars, wind directions and the magnetic fields of the earth. That, I decided, was how I'd fancy travelling.

During the winter of 1914, a record number of American redstarts and black-throated blue warblers nested in Cuba. The trees around our house positively shook with their commotion, disturbing my father, who had fallen ill with yellow fever. His temperature soared, he vomited continuously and could barely lift his head from the pillow. After several days, jaundice set in. Still, the birds continued to bicker and sing.

My mother and I took turns reading aloud *The Meditations of Marcus Aurelius*, to which Papá had frequently turned when troubled: "Think of the universal substance, of which thou hast a very small portion; and of universal time, of which a short and indivisible interval has been assigned to thee; and of that which is fixed by destiny, and how small a part of it thou art."

Mamá soothed Papá's fever with cold cloths and held his hands for hours, as if trying to transmit through her fingertips the vitality of her own life. She made Papá codfish and white bean stew and gave him black Spanish olives to suck. Slowly, his health improved, although it left him in a permanently weakened state.

On his first day back to the cigar factory, Papá's step was plodding and tedious, and I was certain he could not walk the entire mile to the outskirts of town. I accompanied him, bracing his elbow. Friends greeted him along the way, ignoring the sweat that rolled from beneath his hat, and this seemed to encourage him.

When at last we arrived at the factory and Papá, with great difficulty, climbed the three steps to his platform, the room erupted with hoarse cheers. "A-GÜE-RO! A-GÜE-RO!" the workers chanted, clapping and stamping their feet to the rhythm of our name.

"Please, *hijo*," my father finally turned to me, his voice barely audible. He raised his palm to the crowd and the room became silent, muted by smoke and the sweet smell of cedar. "Read for me today."

He handed me a heavy book, its red leather faded, its spine broken from so many readings, and I took his place at the lectern. I turned to the first page. The smoky air made my eyes water. Words scattered before me like a frightened school of fish.

The workers strained toward me. My voice was small, hesitant. Down below, a paper fan fluttered. I reached the second paragraph, and stopped.

"Go on, Ignacio," my father whispered.

CONJUNCTIONS Give a subscription to yourself and a friend!

Your subscription:

Name _____

Address _____

City _____

State _____ Zip _____

☐ One year (2 issues) **$18**
☐ Two years (4 issues) **$32**
☐ Renewal ☐ New order

All foreign and institutional orders $25 per year, payable in U.S. funds.

☐ Payment enclosed ☐ Bill me   Charge my: ☐ Mastercard ☐ Visa

Account number _____   Expiration date _____

Signature _____

Gift subscription (with a gift card from you enclosed):

Name _____

Address _____

City _____

State _____ Zip _____

☐ One year (2 issues) **$18**
☐ Two years (4 issues) **$32**
☐ Renewal ☐ New order

"There was a king with a large jaw and a queen with a plain face, on the throne of England; there was a king with a large jaw and a queen with a fair face, on the throne of France. In both countries it was clearer than crystal to the lords of the State preserves of loaves and fishes that things in general were settled forever."

THE LEATHERBACK

My parents celebrated my fourteenth birthday the way they did every important event in our lives, with ceremony and fanfare. Papá baked me an almond torte with marzipan parrots he'd ordered from a sweet shop in Havana, then the two of them serenaded me for an hour like a pair of mariachis. Mamá sang in her squeaky, scratchy way, so unlike her mellifluous speaking voice, and Papá slowly forced out his baritone until "Happy Birthday to You" sounded more like a speech than a song.

I'd expected a gift but none so spectacular as the full-color, single-volume British encyclopedia: *Birds of the World.* One thousand forty-three pages in all. Years later, this exquisite volume was stolen from my office at the University of Havana. The illustrations turned up in markets throughout Cuba, framed in cheap wood and sold for pennies to *guajiros* as decorations for their homes. I know this because I bought several of the illustrations myself in Guardalavaca and Morón.

After dinner, my father and I walked through the balmy streets of Pinar del Río, stopping here and there to greet a friend or admire the binoculars in the window of the new camera shop. This aimless strolling went on for an hour or more, unusual for my purposeful father. It seemed that Mamá had instructed Papá to discuss with me the ways of nature — me, a keen observer of the animal kingdom since I could walk! Papá coughed and strained uncomfortably with his words until I found myself waving my hands the way he did when he was impatient or anxious.

"De acuerdo," he said. "But in case your mother asks you, tell her we've spoken."

Since his bout with yellow fever, Papá often asked me to substitute for him at the cigar factory. I was no longer so nervous before a crowd and the cigar workers complimented me on my voice — not nearly as sonorous as my father's, they said, but high and distinct as chimes. It was not what I wanted to hear, but I accepted their praise just the same.

On one such day, I organized the morning's reading: two local newspapers, a movie magazine, the latest newsletter from the International Cigar Workers' Union and Papá's favorite recipe for Galician-style scallop pie. My father had taken to sharing his culinary expertise with the cigar rollers, who greatly appreciated his cooking tips. Once when Papá had tried to demonstrate how to prepare the perfect *torta a la española* on a portable burner, the director stopped him mid-lesson for creating a fire hazard. A banner reading NO COOKING ON THE PREMISES still hung, frayed and yellowed with smoke, in the back of the hall. In the afternoon, I would continue with the Spanish translation of *La Bête Humaine*, which Papá had begun the week before.

After lunch, a new employee walked through the factory doors. She was the very image of a voluptuous carnival reveler I'd once admired in a nineteenth-century engraving. The young woman, who wore a gingham dress and a starched white kerchief, took a seat in the front row and removed a circular blade from her purse. The foreman brought her a large pile of tobacco leaves. She was a *despalilladora*, whose specialty it was to strip the stems from the leaves.

Up on the platform, all my old nervousness returned. I felt as if the *despalilladora* alone sat below me, judging me with her lustrous eyes. I cleared my throat and began to read:

"At eleven fifteen, dead on time, the man on duty at the Europe bridge gave the regulation two blasts on the horn to signal the approach of the express train from Le Havre as it emerged from the Batignolles tunnel . . ."

I felt exceedingly hot, stifled, but there was no window I could open, no place I could turn for air. I noticed that the *despalilladora* did not smoke cigars but that she inhaled the smoke deeply, with satisfaction, as if the wisps encircling her were fresh breezes from the sea.

". . . soon the turntables clanked as the train entered the station with a short note on the whistle, squealing on the brakes, steaming and running with water from the

driving rain that had been pouring down all the way from
Rouen . . ."

A distressing prickliness spread through my body, starting in
my chest, where my heart knocked loudly, then to all my extremi-
ties at once. In an instant, my skin was coated with sweat and
every vein in my body jumped with blood. Down below, the *despalilladora* stared at me, her eyebrows raised in concern, her circular blade poised in midair.

I awoke flat on my back in the offices of El Cid's general manager.
My mother stood above me, passing a hand over my forehead. It
smelled good, of vanilla, of the creamy soaps she used. She helped
me sit up, straightened my collar and tie, then looked me full in
the face.

"You're in love, Ignacito," Mamá whispered so no one else could
hear, and held me tight against her.

Nothing came of my obsession, which lasted the better part of a
year, except that I missed many days of school spying on Teresita
Castillo. My sentiments, opulent with insecurities, bred in me a
humorlessness so severe as to border on pathos. How could I laugh
when I feared more than anything being laughed at myself?

I learned that Teresita had recently married and moved to Pinar
del Río from another part of the Viñales Valley. Her husband,
Rodolfo, a slight man with an unexpected, sinewy strength, drove
a truck for a box factory and was gone for days at a time on cross-
country deliveries. I imagined saving Teresita from this unworthy
mite, offering her a life by my side, but I had just then started high
school.

Each time Teresita and I met — never by chance since I knew her
schedule down to the minute and occasioned to see her several
times daily — she asked about my health, as if I were somehow
sickly or prone to fainting spells. This ate at me more viciously
than any acid, which in my despair, I also thought of swallowing.
If I could not win Teresita's love, I would settle for her pity. Pity,
I'd learned from reading so many of Papá's novels, often proved a
fertile, if shallow, soil for romance.

Such foolish thoughts, such a foolish heart! It would be almost
comical if looking back I did not feel a twinge of the anguish I'd
once felt.

My mother was kindest to me during this time, which is to say she left me alone, asked me no questions and made certain I ate despite my distraction. Papá was less comforting. He lost patience when I pestered him for details about my beloved. I wanted to hear only superlatives about Teresita Castillo. That she was the best *despalilladora* in the factory, the quickest and most efficient with her knife. That she was the kindest of all the cigar workers, the most generous of heart. But my father would not condescend to tell me what I wished to hear.

During the time I was in love with Teresita, Papá did not ask me to read for him at the factory. My mother must have ensured this with gently pointed threats.

Shortly before Easter, Teresita confided to me that she had an infestation of bats in her roof. What marvelous luck! Of course I knew all about her bats from my constant spying, but I did not let on. Most Cubans in those days were quite tolerant of bats — a simple fact of life, after all. This was very unlike the attitude prevalent among Americans and even a few Europeans who erroneously credited bats with all manner of antisocial behavior. Still, the number of bats in Teresita's house had grown immoderate and the stench too pronounced to ignore.

I arrived at Teresita's house just before nightfall, dressed in my father's borrowed waistcoat and jacket, looking more appropriate for a state dinner than a mass extermination. She invited me in, wisely ignoring my appearance, and offered me something to drink.

"A whiskey, if you have it. Or a cognac. *Por favor.*" I immediately regretted this.

"Would a little rum do?" she asked me, straight-faced. I wanted to kiss her in gratitude.

"Yes, yes. Thank you."

I took small, burning gulps of the liquor.

"This is about the time they begin stirring," Teresita said. I stared at her, uncomprehending, my face and chest on fire. "The bats," she emphasized. "Can't you hear them?"

In fact, the bats were squeaking and scuttling above us with a rapidly intensifying clamor. A moment later, the sounds melded into what sounded like the buzz of a gigantic beehive.

"There they go!" Teresita announced above the din. "*¡Mira!*"

Outside the window, a stream of bats poured into the air, forming a huge gray-black whirlpool. Around and around they went as hundreds more took flight, circling at high speeds before flying off in every direction.

"Tedarida murina," I said. "They're the best flyers on the island." I wanted to tell Teresita that the bats were the second-most plentiful in Cuba after *molossus tropidorhynchus,* that they occupied much the same position among their kind as swifts do among birds, that their long narrow wings rowed through the air so rapidly that the bats oscillated from side to side, that their habitat extended to Jamaica, Santo Domingo and Puerto Rico.

Reluctantly, I told her how to plug the roost openings with straw and cement, where to place the rat poison for maximum fatalities, what to do about the persistent stink. It made me sad to tell her all this. On my way home an hour later, still slightly drunk from the rum, my love for Teresita Castillo began to fade.

That summer, partly to console me for love's failure, my parents drove me to the south coast of Cuba for my first solitary expedition. From there, I connected with a steamer that ferried me across the Batabanó Gulf to Nueva Gerona, the capital of the Isle of Pines. Before I boarded the ship, Papá handed me a wicker hamper laden with foods he'd prepared himself: shrimp tartlets, fresh bread with anchovy paste, lamb sausages and a still-warm seafood stew. It occupied twice the space of the satchel I carried for my entire trip.

As I crossed the turquoise waters of the gulf, past archipelagos of tiny islands with fanciful names, I thought of what the first explorers must have felt at the sight of a new horizon, at the roar of possibilities in their heads. How they imagined the vast riches that awaited them, all there for the taking with only a musket and a strong pair of hands.

On the steamer, an American woman with two young children befriended me. She had been living on the Isle of Pines since 1913, when her husband had bought a grapefruit plantation. On warm summer nights, she sighed, the aroma of citrus coated every particle of air. Señora Crane recommended I visit the Punta del Este caves. They had recently been discovered by survivors of a shipwreck, she explained, and contained paintings from pre-Columbian times. In the biggest cave, pictographs of red and black concentric circles were connected by arrows pointing east.

In my exalted state and the Isle of Pines's unforgiving heat, I found it impossible to sleep. I calmed myself with nightly swims along the northern beaches, brilliant with black sands. It was on my fifth night, lazily floating in the ocean, that something mammoth swam by me, grazing my leg. I panicked, quickly calculating the odds of a shark coming so close to shore. That afternoon, I had cut my foot on a hunk of marble at Bibijuagua Beach, and the wound was still raw.

Cautiously, I paddled my way toward shore, keeping my injured foot above the water as best I could. I reached the beach, breathing so hard I thought my lungs would collapse.

It was then I saw her. Her ridged back and the enormity of her flippers made identification easy, especially in the moonlight. She was over eight feet long, a half-ton of slow magnificence. The leatherback turned her wrinkled, spotted neck and gazed at me, as if gauging my trustworthiness. I could see her eyes clearly, the inverse widow's peak of her beak. She proceeded up the beach, dragging herself with her front flippers, stopping every few feet to rest. In her wake, she left a long wide ridge of sand.

It was exceptionally rare to see a great leatherback on our shores. The turtles breed primarily off the Gulf of Guinea in West Africa and lay their eggs in the shallow waters around Ceylon. Even then I knew that a leatherback turned up in Cuba no more than once every several years, and almost never to spawn.

When the leatherback found a nesting site, she sunk herself deep into the sand, rotating several times until she had shaped her hollow. Again she faced me, as if warning me to come no closer. Then she continued to dig her egg pit, using one flipper and then the other, curling the edges inward to force up more sand.

After what seemed interminable digging, the giantess brought her hind flippers together, craned her neck forward and began to sway slightly to a private rhythm, finally laying her eggs in the sand. When she was done, the exhausted mother filled in her pit. She patted the sand until she erased all traces of her nest, then wearily made her way back to the sea.

All night I searched the waves for a sign of her, but only the steady surf answered my scrutiny.

At dawn, a fat scavenging gull dropped onto the leatherback's buried nest. I cursed the bird and threw a fistful of sand at it. A moment later, more gulls appeared, suspended in formation overhead, and a stray dog nosed its way down the beach.

What choice did I have? I sat on the leatherback's nest all that day and all the next night, guarding the eggs from predators, guarding the eggs for her. I imagined her babies racing for the surf later that summer, and I still wonder sometimes how many of that hatch survived. Perhaps only one or two. Those turtles would be fully grown by now, parents themselves, idly traversing the seven seas.

THE NATURE OF PARASITES

The Great War had been over for a year when I left Pinar del Río for the University of Havana. It was the days of the "Dance of the Millions," when the price for sugar had soared so high that many Cubans became millionaires overnight. The rich erected marble palaces along the Prado and other fashionable neighborhoods of the capital and in the late afternoons, they could be seen cruising their fancy foreign cars up and down the Malecón.

It was a time of unseemly extravagance, and it had little to do with me, a sixteen-year-old scholarship student from *el campo*. Few in Pinar del Río had benefited from the sugar boom. At El Cid, where my father continued to read at his lectern, half the cigar workers had lost their jobs to falling tobacco prices. Those who remained were fearful of losing them to the new cigar rolling machines from America.

Papá, as usual, was involved in union policy and wrote editorials for the *Boletín de Torcedor*, the cigar worker union's newspaper, extolling the glories of revolutionary Russia. What relation this had to the workers' daily concerns was a mystery to me, and Papá and I argued frequently over what we considered each other's misguided politics.

By then, Mamá had developed arthritis, which curtailed the hours she could teach flute, and I saw in her reddened joints the nascent disfigurements that would plague her last years.

It was understood that I would work while I was at college, and within a few days I found a job that suited me perfectly: night usher in a movie house on Avenida Galiano. It was a garish theater, in keeping with the times, and I was required to wear a uniform festooned with enough braids and tassels to command an entire battalion. The work itself was easy and the perpetual darkness accustomed me to working at night, an invaluable advantage when I began to research bats in earnest.

Most nights, after guiding patrons to their seats, I joined the projectionist in his fetid cubicle, where I studied as best I could. The movies, mercifully, were silent in those days, although I still had to contend with the melodrama of the organ. Occasionally, I would peek through the projectionist's window when the music rose to a crescendo, but I never understood those who would choose to sit through this dark make-believe when the whole world was waiting outside.

In the spring of my freshman year, the renowned Dr. Samuel Forrest of Harvard University came to Havana to teach a course on tropical zoology. Word spread quickly of his need for a field assistant, and the best graduate students signed up for an interview. Although I hardly expected to capture such a coveted position, I, too, signed up to meet the great man.

The next week, a dozen hopeful young men milled outside his office. For three hours we waited as one shaken student after another emerged from his interrogation. "What does he want?" those of us who had remained outside asked. But the only clue came from one exceedingly frustrated student: "He wants your opinion on the universe!"

"Please sit down," Dr. Forrest said wearily when it was finally my turn. He was quite obese and his eyes, blue as a quail dove's features, were accentuated by a high lineless forehead and woolly mutton chops.

"Could you tell me, please, Señor Agüero, which of our brethren in the animal kingdom you most admire?"

I thought at first I'd misheard Dr. Forrest, or that he was in a mood to test my humor. Why else would he ask me so facile a question? He looked up from his notes and blinked impassively, hardly expecting, it seemed, a remotely suitable response.

There were many creatures I was particularly fond of: the tree ducks that had saved my father's life; the regal hawks of Cuba, circling their inspiration beyond the mountain tops; and of course, my lovely leatherback who one humid night on the Isle of Pines entrusted her eggs to my care. Instinctively, I knew not to mention her to Dr. Forrest, to hide my sentimentality at all costs.

"Parasites," I offered.

"Parasites?" Dr. Forrest seemed surprised. He smiled tightly, out of amusement or disdain I was not yet certain.

"Yes, sir. I believe they are the most original of all animals."

"Go on," he said, serious now, as if he were trying to gauge my audacity.

"Consider intestinal worms, or beetles, or even fleas for that matter." I grew bolder. "A good parasite must exploit a host that is larger, stronger and faster than it with minimal disturbance. Every fiber, every function of its being is inscribed with this necessity . . ."

" — of quiet boorishness." Dr. Forrest smiled more broadly.

"Precisely," I laughed.

He leaned forward in his chair, tugging his left mutton chop. I continued, encouraged by Dr. Forrest's unwavering attention.

"The difference between us and lower life forms, I believe, comes down to the fact that humans have developed a variety of receptacles and containers for their needs, and animals have not. It seems to me that building vases or suitcases or skillets indicates a unique human ability to plan for the future, to predict the behavior of matter in ways wholly distinct from animals. A bee, after all, has been constructing its same tiny cell for one hundred million years."

"Very interesting," Dr. Forrest said. "And now a personal question, if you don't mind, Señor Agüero. Are you a Catholic?"

"No," I answered quickly. In fact, I'd been trained by Papá to be suspicious of all organized religion. Only later did my father come to realize that politics, too, could be a form of religion in extremis.

Then Dr. Forrest stood up and thrust a fleshy hand toward mine. "This concludes our interview, Señor Agüero. It will be a pleasure working with you."

That night, I quit my job at the movie theater.

For the next six months, I accompanied Dr. Forrest as he crisscrossed the island by boat and train and horseback. Everywhere we went, Dr. Forrest bemoaned the ruin of Cuba's lowland forests. Although the island could not support the luxuriant *foresta real* of Central or South America, he said, its vast areas of calcareous soil once sustained a heavy and varied sylvan growth. The only true forest remaining in Cuba then was in the higher mountain ranges of Oriente province, to this day so steep and inaccessible as to offer refuge to many treasured species.

Sadly, it was mostly in the cities and their environs that we could appreciate the charms of the island's tropical flora — the broad groves of royal palms, the great red-green mango trees offering the densest of shades and every variety of exotic flower. Although there continued to exist large areas of granatic and serpentine savanna lands in Cuba, these were unfit for agriculture. With their groves of jata and cana palms, these regions were home to only a relatively meager bird and animal population.

I remember well our first trip into the heart of the Zapata Swamp, the relentless rustle and hum of its invisible creatures, the air thick as pudding in our lungs. I followed Dr. Forrest as he eased one foot in front of the other across the surface of sawgrass and bulrushes, the formidable mass threatening to engulf us at any moment.

On another trip, Dr. Forrest asked me to collect ordinary house bats at an abandoned cavalry barracks outside Matanzas. Dr. Forrest intended to preserve a series of their embryos so that he might study the early development of their teeth. Protected with heavy gloves, I managed to fill two sacks with live bats and return to the Hotel El Mundo, where I left my restless cargo in the bathtub.

"After we have had our luncheon," Dr. Forrest said in his proper, drawling Spanish, "we shall kill the bats and search for their embryos."

During our meal, Dr. Forrest was expounding on the finer implications of Freud's theories when a terrible clattering and commotion came from the hotel kitchen. In an instant, the chef, two assistants and a waiter came storming through the swinging doors pursued by a swarm of *molossus tropidorhynchus*. Dazed by the light, the bats buzzed and dropped over the banquet tables, splattering soup and sending the cutlery flying.

"Naturen expellas furca, tamen usque recurret," Dr. Forrest said, shrugging off the incident. He was fond of philosophizing in Latin.

On another expedition, camping in the back country of Sancti Spíritus, Dr. Forrest was pleased to catch an iguana for our dinner. Now I knew that in Central America, where Dr. Forrest had spent a considerable portion of his career, iguana meat was considered a delicacy. But I found my repugnance difficult to overcome. You see, when iguanas are hung to dry, a brown gurry like coffee grinds runs from their mouths, reminding me of my father's yellow fever vomit.

That night, Dr. Forrest roasted the iguana over a camp fire and offered me a slab from its back liberally sprinkled with salt. I could hardly refuse. I swallowed the meat whole, barely allowing it to slide down my throat. Then I excused myself, hid behind a white ixora and disgorged my meal on its splendid snowball blossoms.

Despite these and numerous other mishaps, Dr. Forrest always treated me as a friend and a competent colleague. In time, and with his patient encouragement, I became one. My debt to him is immeasurable. The modest successes I enjoyed under his guidance nurtured my confidence as a scientist.

Dr. Forrest had begun his vocation in the latter half of the nineteenth century, when great scientific advances had kindled the enthusiasms of thousands. Darwin's theory of evolution. Mendel's law of heredity. The identification of light as an electromagnetic phenomenon. The law of the conservation of energy. The development of the spectroscope. When Dr. Forrest came of age, it was science, not politics or economics, that held the key to conquering the universe. Science was his mission, and soon enough, it became mine as well.

Perhaps my most satisfying discovery under Dr. Forrest's tutelage came toward the end of his stay in Cuba. It started one May evening at the University of Havana library, where I came across a page of field notes tucked inside a 1907 edition of *National Geographic* magazine. The notes, which had no date or name attached, were written in a clear, minuscule hand and stated that in the scrub between the Morro Castle and the little fishing town of Cojímar a deep pool could be found containing shrimp that "looked as if they had been boiled." This struck me as curious because all the cave shrimp I had studied with Dr. Forrest were pallid. Only deep-sea shrimp sported the dark red color the notes described.

The next day, I set off in search of the mysterious shrimp. The morning air was warm and I walked briskly to hasten the adventure. I felt rather ridiculous relying on the anonymous notes, but Dr. Forrest had taught me that no expedition was ever futile. Over the years, he had happily followed many a *campesino*—he counted them among the finest observers of nature—with only a vague promise of observing something new. Dr. Forrest dismissed no clue or wild tale without first investigating the matter personally.

I hurried to the edge of the harbor and hired a rowboat to take me across the bay to Morro Castle. I landed at the steps on the shore near the Battery of the Twelve Apostles, then trudged through the coastal forest of beach grape trees until I came to a broad area of bare rock. In the middle was an open basin of the purest water where, it appeared, the roof of a cave had fallen in.

Cristina García

The depth and crookedness of the channel made it difficult to see beyond a foot or two.

I stirred the water with the long-handled net I had brought and before long, tiny crimson shrimp came out of their hiding places and swam closer to the surface. The shrimp were striking, their wispy legs tipped in white, as if they had accidentally stepped in paint. Over and over, I dipped my net, but the creatures were nearly impossible to catch. After several arduous hours, I finally secured twenty specimens.

That evening, Dr. Forrest seemed impressed with my shrimp. He sent them off to a Miss Barbara J. Winthrop, an authority on crustacea at the United States National Museum in Maryland. Before long she wrote back, identifying the shrimp as a new genus. She had also taken the liberty of suggesting a name for them: *Forrestia agueri.*

From Jonestown
Wilson Harris

NOTE

FRANCISCO BONE WANDERS for seven years in the great Forest of South America after the 'tragedy of Jonestown.'

He arrives in New Amsterdam where he begins to write his Dream-book.

That book has been writing itself in his subconscious and unconscious within the seven years that seem an age (or several ages) in his wanderings.

He starts the book on a Dateless Day in 1985 and on completing it in the 1990s sends it to W.H. to be edited.

The extracts from the Dream-book that follow this Note are firstly a piece taken from the letter to W.H. and secondly a passage from Bone's wanderings before he comes to New Amsterdam.

Bone implies that the book he sends is as much the product of his hand as it is the record of a living ghost written on leaves, on the bark of trees, on re-traceries of broken yet archetypal fabric of place-in-person, person-in-place, fiction-in-history, history-in-fiction, through which Bone seeks to assemble an approach to the mystery of survival across overlapping pasts and presents and futures that deepen and change the textualities of the imagination.

Francisco Bone is haunted by a collective and variable seminality instinctive to animals and virgins of spirit within chasms of reality.

Trinity Street
New Amsterdam

Dateless Day

Dear W.H.,

I have learnt of your sympathies for voyagers of the Imagination and trust therefore that you will undertake the task of editing the enclosed manuscript or book.

I am the only survivor of the 'tragedy of Jonestown', which occurred — as many people know — in late November 1978 in a remote forest in Guyana.

The Longman *Chronicle of America* tells of the 'tragedy of Jonestown' and of the scene of 'indescribable horror' which met the eyes of reporters from every corner of the globe when they arrived in stricken Jonestown after the self-inflicted holocaust engineered by a charismatic cult leader, the Reverend Jim Jones.

In my archetypal fiction I call Jim Jones Jonah Jones. All of the characters appearing in the book are fictional and archetypal. In this way I have sought to explore overlapping layers and environments and theatres of legend and history that one may associate with Jonestown.

Not all drank Coca-Cola laced with cyanide. Some were shot like cattle. Men, women and children.

Francisco Bone is a disguised name that I employ for myself. I suffered the most severe and disabling trauma on the Day of the Dead (as I see and continue to see in my mind's eye the bodies in a Clearing or town centre in Jonestown on November 18). The shock was so great — I blamed myself for not taking risks to avert the holocaust — that though I was wounded a numbness concealed for some time the physical injury that I suffered. The consequences of such 'numbness' occupy different proportions of the Dream-book.

When I escaped I dreamt I was dead and gained some comfort from rhymes of self-mockery, from handsome skeletons, all of which helped to promote the theme of Carnival Lord Death in the Book when eventually I began to write it. One such self-mocking poem — which I came upon when I arrived in New Amsterdam before I had started writing — is the first epigraph that I use. That poem helped me to offset the hell of Memory theatre for a while and to join strolling players on a village Amsterdam green. I relished the Jest that I associated with eighteenth-century Dutch plantation owners who superimposed structures and promenades upon the bank of the Berbice River in the vicinity of New Amsterdam. When I arrived in 1985 to write my Dream-book I strolled on a promenade called *village Amsterdam green* that ran from the township to a mental hospital. Patients and townsfolk tended to stroll arm in arm dressed in masks of Bone at Carnival time. I sought a pleasant hole to simulate the grave into which I should have fallen on the Day of the Dead. Why me? Why did I survive? It was this thought that drove me to write . . . Questions as much

40

as thought! No easy answers.

I feared to write in — and be written by — a demanding book that asserts itself in Dream and questions itself from time to time (even as I question the meaning of survival) as you will see as you read. One overcomes the fear of Dreams, I suspect, for I did not stop writing or being written into what I wrote . . .

I was obsessed — let me confess — by cities and settlements in the Central and South Americas that are an enigma to many scholars. I dreamt of their abandonment, their bird masks, their animal masks . . . Did their inhabitants rebel against the priests, did obscure holocausts occur, civil strife, famine, plague? Was Jonestown the latest manifestation of the breakdown of populations within the hidden flexibilities and inflexibilities of pre-Columbian civilizations? The Maya were certainly one of the great civilizations of ancient America and the fate of their cities — such as Palenque, Chichén Itzá, Tikal, Bonampak — has left unanswered questions. Teotihuacán in Mexico raises similar enigmas. The unsolved disappearance of the Caribs in British Guiana is another riddle of precipitate breakdown. And there are many others . . .

HOME. Home is as elusive as it is real in Memory theatre. I remembered the Cave of the Moon into which I had fled from Jonestown on the Night of the Day of the Dead. It seemed home in a high cliff or bank from which a Waterfall fell beneath me into the Jonestown river. Was that Waterfall beneath me or did it spring from an opposite cliff or bank into which my Shadow reached as if it sought to bridge a chasm in creation? My stomach was hollow and I fed Bone with bread and rice and tinned fruit, tinned vegetables that I had stored in the Cave. Bone ate ravenously. So much so I was tempted to leap down the ladder of the Waterfall onto a rock far below shaped like a loaf of bread. Bone was universal me. I was universal Bone.

The holocaust is a vision of famine, the famine of the Soul imprinted on breath as much as bread that living skeletons bite or choke upon or devour . . .

I wanted to leap and forget everything that had happened . . .

But then I saw the faint outline of a body on the rock or loaf of bread. I broke my visionary teeth upon it. My pleasant rice and fruit in the Cave seemed straw for cattle.

Bone is tough, a spirited survivor in the wilderness of civilization.

Was it Deacon lying there far below?

Had he collapsed there and died after shooting Jones? Or was he asleep forever in the wake of the procession that he had led as a child?

His head lay on rock or seeming wood as mine had lain upon a pillow of stone. I resisted the temptation to fling myself down beside him and began instead to contemplate the construction of a Virgin Ship made of wood, of bread, stone, everything, times past and present and future.

Such a Ship begins to create itself upon a land and a sea of Limbo memory, Limbo chameleon memories upon which diminutive survivors such as myself feed in order to clothe themselves with the terrors of history that one may still convert into rare however flawed consciousness, indestructible hope. Such was my Limbo initiation into the writing of my Dream-book. I was to wander far and wide — uncertain of the steps I took — before I came to lodgings in Trinity Street, New Amsterdam.

Home is multi-dimensional space. And Limbo is the chameleon of home into which one reaches self-deceptively and endlessly in order to face truth when one comes abreast of the masquerades of the past that one has sustained voluntarily or involuntarily.

I left the Cave of the Moon and adventured into Limbo where I came upon the handsome, beautifully dressed grave-digger who had profited from the burial of the dead in Jonestown which he supervised.

'Did you bury them all?' I said, 'in a mass grave?'

In asking the question I could not help recalling Deacon and his child's heroic, monstrous incarceration of common-or-garden folk who were nevertheless giants and dwarfs, weak and strong, in the Eye of Mr. Mageye's Camera. *They would return to judge me, to put me on trial.* Why me? Why not Deacon? Such are the paradoxes of judgement day, dateless day, theatre of Limbo — within the unacknowledged interstices of Purgatory, Hell and Heaven — when one is recast to answer for another, when the embattled folk are recast into embodiments of self, oneself's trial is theirs, they are judges arisen from the living and the dead. One may know then under their terrible hand — considerate and inconsiderate hand — a flicker of the injustices inflicted by others upon their peers and subjects across the ages.

The grave-digger eyed me with a quizzical look: as if he were weighing every stitch I wore. My Nemesis Hat had deposited a few threads on my mother's grave, on Mr. Mageye's grave and on the Moon when Marie danced. The Hat or Bag was lighter now. It could be weighed on the scales of future pasts, past futures, radiating out from an apparitional core of composite self.

'Lost a few threads, Francisco,' he confirmed. 'Each could be auctioned no doubt for a bite of bread. I fancy sweet bread myself. Made from currants and lemon, Demerara sugar and rich flour. I found quite a store in Jonestown. We split it between ourselves, me and the Inspector and that Doctor-God chap who is popular with the peasants of Port Mourant. They say he cares for the sick who lie on pallets on the floor. All well and good but your shirt and trousers are in tatters. A disgrace! Those would fetch nothing at all in the marketplace. I can see clean through to Bone, Francisco. Ah! but there's your shoes. I like those. Jolly good leather. I pulled off quite a few like yours from the heels of the dead in Jonestown. Gave me quite a turn. It was as if they were ready to run, to sprint. Well you can do it for them, Francisco. Just as well you got away, Bone. You're worth but a bite or two of meat and potatoes to me. Imagine my having to cart you into the grave for virtually nothing. I'm glad you got away.'

He laid out at least five hundred watches in the Limbo forest. He tied them to the branches of trees. He laid out earrings, women's purses and men's linen shirts, men's vests, short pants and long pants and baby clothes.

A curious business, a curious self-addictive satire, a curious mockery and self-mockery rooted in despair, it was that the gravedigger conducted in charting his evolution into millionaire Carnival Lord Death.

The robes on his back had been borrowed from the dead and the living. The baby clothes seemed dead baby clothes too small for the giant of Death. Who knows how small or large Death is? He possessed a scarf, on the other hand, around his neck that had been mine. I had wrapped it around my hand when blood oozed from the wound I received and left it on the bushes beside the Clearing. Nothing! I felt nothing at all when I lost two fingers from Deacon's random bullet . . . Carnival Lord Death wore the bloodstained scarf now with style that was a wonderful gloss upon numbness.

What was bizarre and charismatic in his style was the strangely lifeless but majestic, ritualistic folds of his dress. He possessed the aplomb of an astronaut on the Moon in Limbo theatre.

This was fascinating stuff. Charismatic aplomb was in fashion.

43

Tradition bouncing on surfaces but bereft of depth, Brain shorn of mind or philosophy, life shorn of unpredictable Spirit or originality.

The array of goods — far beyond the range I have described — confirmed his majestic skills as an entrepreneur par excellence of Limbo Land.

But there were other considerations and moral fables in Carnival Lord Death's pitiless barter of the numb word, numb lips, numb ears and eyes for treasures that he pulled from the pockets of the living and the dead, from their running feet, or reluctant hands, from their frames and bodies, to adorn his kingdom.

The quality of Justice! What sort of Justice did Carnival Lord Death administer? He was a just man: as just as any man could be in the Mask of Death. What are the foundations of Justice as the twentieth century draws to a close?

I looked around but there was no help from Mr. Mageye in this instance. Carnival Lord Death loomed over me as I uttered a silent prayer; an unorthodox prayer that was more an awkward statement than a request for enlightenment.

'To feel nothing,' I dreamt inwardly, 'except the possession of privileged immunity to famine or to hell, to feel nothing but a licence that is granted in Carnival jump-ups and crusades, in an age of the mechanical death of the soul, *is* justice. Justice is the tautology of the death of the soul. Justice is the prosecution of spare-parts methodologies, spare-parts bodies. Or so it seems everywhere. I know for mechanical ornamentation, buttocks and breasts and all, in pleasure palaces, is the structure of a wound that forgets it is a wound.

'God forgive me (as I pray awkwardly) but I know. I was shot in Jonestown and lost all feeling in my hand. It became a tool, an insensible tool.

'Perhaps Lord Death (you are in my prayer, for who knows what Carnival omens Death employs in an age of the death of the soul in the machine?), were you to permit me to reach up and unloose the scarf around your neck, feeling would invade my absent fingers at last which were blown like cigarette ends in the wind.

'The scarf or noose is mine. That very rich scarf that you wear. Poor man's, beggar man's, thief's, scarf of kings! It sings of soul's blood and the genesis of pain all over again. It sings of an apparitional or phantom grasp of reality that may resurrect the elusive lineaments of the Soul.

'And this brings me to the mystery of injustice that the Soul expresses in my wounds. To suffer injustice is to see the Soul within every small creature that cries out for pity against pitilessness. Can we fathom the enduring, insubstantial cry of pity? Pity's sake can neither be bought nor sold. Compassion is beyond price.'

Another form of prayer it was that involved me not in a plea for justice but enduring, creative capacity to suffer the mystery of injustice if the Soul were to live, phenomenal fellow-feeling, despite predatory games and uniform insensibility to crisis . . .

I feared Carnival Lord Death but he appeared to acknowledge — in some recess of himself — the mystery of prayer and he returned the scarf to me.

'You poor devil Francisco,' he said, 'if it gives you some comfort have the bloody scarf. It went well with my daring dress. I came upon the eighteenth-century attire I now wear in Jones's house . . .'

I wanted to tell him that this too was mine. I had loaned it to Jones for a fancy-dress occasion in Jonestown. It was a kind of heirloom or legacy that I had been given by my mother.

The travail for me in the grave-digger's evolution into a capitalist and into Carnival Lord Death lay in the chasm it illumined between mechanical Justice and the extraordinary numinosity of Injustice and in every trial one is called upon to endure at the bar of time. How to come abreast of the past one believes one has forfeited or killed is more self-searching than knowledge of current affairs. For if one fails to come abreast of dead time (or what seems to be dead time) a Predator in the future will destroy us. And time past, the living texture and spirituality in time past, would have become too weak to stand at our side and assist us.

Limbo Justice involved an equation between numbness and immunity to hell. To be just then in Limbo Land was to serve one's vested interests absolutely, whether pleasure or profit, to sublimate or suppress or eclipse one's wounds in favour of strengthening a wall between oneself and the inferno that rules elsewhere in many dimensions of one's age.

Injustice, on the other hand, bore on a coming abreast of wounds one had suffered in the past through which one knows pain in oneself and others, pain of mind that revives the Soul of Compassion beyond all machineries of the law of Death or of the state of embalmed institutions.

Without the mystery of Injustice — when one suffers with others to whom the world is unjust — the soul would vanish entirely and leave behind the mechanical futility of knowledge in the besieged

Brain in the crumbling Body . . .

I had never meditated on morality in this light and I needed to emphasize and reemphasize, rehearse and rehearse again, what I had learnt from my encounter with the capitalist Carnival Lord Death.

I needed a Dream-book that would take nothing for granted within the prayer I had attempted to address to an unfathomable Creator of worlds and universes. I needed to embrace 'pity's sake' though such an embrace of the Word made me infinitely vulnerable.

I was now convinced that Limbo Land was a trap from which it was unlikely I would ever escape to view the open cities of Paradise. I had failed in building a new Rome in Jonestown's web of abandoned and lost cities arching back into pre-Columbian mists of time.

All well and good to have escaped from the holocaust into Limbo Land but a variety of enormous and subtle dangers now encompassed me. Foremost amongst these was the menace of the Predator who lurked in the giant forests of Day and Night.

I was infinitely vulnerable. How could I withstand such a menace? In a sense I felt easier with the grave-digger now — when I ran into him in my wanderings after the Day of the Dead and prior to my arrival in Trinity Street — I accepted his new role (with the death of the conventional Church) as Lord Death. Perhaps he and I possessed a secret understanding about the omens of Carnival.

Nothing, however, could forfeit or erase the scent — the backwards, forwards scent — of the Predator. I knew I was hunted, pursued or stalked in Limbo Land. Stalked as a commodity to be devoured by mighty institutions, great Banks, great systems that ransacked and devoured privacy: but such systems were but one feature in the unnameable menace of the Predator.

I wondered, *as my mind tended to lapse and to lose reflection in the bark of a tree to which I clung, in shed leaves of memory here and there or cracked branches or trees into which I occasionally climbed (as my Carib or African or Arawak ancestors — runaway European antecedents as well — had done in the sixteenth century when slavery and persecution ruled the Americas)*, whether the Predator was Carnival Lord Death after all despite our secret treaty or understanding. A part of that understanding was to inform him of flying or running strangers in Limbo Land.

I had no intention of doing so but I humoured him, especially when he assured me that the Inspector would take me to see the

Prisoner or Old God of Devil's Isle who claimed to be the father of the Virgin of the Wilderness, Marie of Port Mourant.

BUT NO! The Predator was older than Death itself. The Predator possessed a curious weight that lay beneath gravity's Skull, beneath every falling or fallen creature, a curious *violence* that subsisted on nuclear deadlock, or perversity, or cosmic devastation, on meteorites colliding with Jupiter, on the manipulation of elegant mathematics into spectacles of beauty that kill, random bullets in space, or from space, that strike the Earth from time to time. The Predator's craft and skill and range in Limbo Land was immense and I felt his breath (unlike the breath of resurrectionary organs of Compassion) rearrange the grain of the hair on the back of my neck.

The tickling sensation of the hair on my neck and head aroused in me a contrary sensation to absolute fear that the Predator sought to instill in me. I broke my Nemesis Hat or Bag into two containers. One I retained as a Hat and this I replaced on my head. The other I adopted as a Bag. I retraced my steps in Limbo Land and collected the fallen leaves of memory from cracked branches or trees into which I had climbed. They possessed the numinous texture of a book and I promised the three Virgins (Jonestown, Albuoystown, Port Mourant) that I would write a Dream-book should I gain Trinity Street in New Amsterdam . . .

How much did I know, how much remember — within composite epic — of ages prior to Death, ages in which the Predator's regime of violence seemed both immanent and transient, ages in which nevertheless the Womb of Virgin Space seemed shorn of violence, shorn of intercourse with reality that was violent?

Within that implicit and terrifying opposition how wounded were the parameters of genesis — the genesis of the Imagination to cope with terror and grace — how wounded the Virgin herself as she broke into a trinity of Masks, the three Maries?

I scanned each leaf as I placed it in my Bag. A variety of inscriptions appeared upon leaf after leaf. Faint light-year vistas . . . Were they progeny of the Virgin driven by a quest to minimize violence in a world in which Death had appeared? Were they progeny of the Predator to augment or absolutize violence in a world in which Death had appeared?

Such vistas lay beyond absolute translation into certainty.

They were resources of uncanny drama, resources of uncanny rehearsals of the genesis or unfinished genesis of the Imagination . . .

47

The Scorpion Constellation shone in the eyes of the Tiger mask of the sun. Which blinded which, who whom, it was difficult to say. The Scavenger swooped. The Eagle dealt the Jaguar a blow on the Moon and on the walls of abandoned Maya cities. But all such manifestations were curiously hieroglyphic: self-deceptive and true within the partialities of genesis. They bore on the mystery of injustice that runs hand in hand with the resurrection of the Soul of Compassion for all wounded creatures whether born of the Predator or of the Virgin.

A further complication lay in another well-nigh indescribable imprint, a huntsman who seemed to stand within the Womb of Virgin space. I sensed that he had no illusions about the might of the Predator. As I listened to the whisper or rustle of each leaf within my phantom fingers I dreamt that I heard his voice seeking to instill the strangest wisdom everywhere, into creature and constellation, however prone these were to linkages with the Predator, into heroes and angels, however prone these were to linkages with monsters. I sensed his tread at Night in the footprint of the Predator.

The gathering menace broke into a Storm and I felt it was useless running from the Predator any longer. My desire had been to destroy him by hook or by crook. So much so that unconsciously, subconsciously, I was driven to contemplate poisoning the air everywhere that he breathed, the seas and oceans and lakes and rivers in which he swam, the environments and places that clothed him. 'Kill him even if it means killing yourself,' Carnival Lord Death had said to me. Death's freedoms encompassed the advocacy of Suicide. 'Walk with a Bomb of environmental disasters under your shirt to blow up the globe.'

But the huntsman in the footfall of the Predator — close on the heels of the Predator — possessed a different tune.

'Leap,' he said (in the gathering menace of the Storm), 'into my net and help me to hold the heart of the Predator at bay within rhythms of profoundest self-confessional, self-judgemental creativity. The leap into space I grant is dangerous. It is a kind of surrender to an unfathomable caring Presence that seems absent in a cruel age. It is the leap of the unfinished genesis of the Imagination that may bring to light unpredictable resources in an open universe that nets, in some paradoxical way, creature and creation. LEAP . . .'

But I was unable to do so. Nevertheless, my desire to poison or slay the Predator loosed its grip on my unconscious, unconscious motivation, motivation of disaster. I settled myself on a tree-platform instead and created a pillow with the Bag of memory leaves and pages. The Storm blew a further volume of leaves upon me. The Predator knew of my lofty hiding place. He knew of my inner Dream-pillow or book. He knew of the outer volume that the Storm had granted me, the raining blanket of leaves in circulation, cross-circulation, rehearsal, re-visionary momentum . . . I was lost. I was convinced I was lost. It was finished. I lay in the Predator's bed and he knew.

And then the huntsman threw his net. I knew without knowing how I knew that the net fastened itself upon the limbs of the Predator even as it appeared to release me, leaving me still to leap . . .

'I cannot leap,' I said. 'Not now. But thank you huntsman for saving me from madness, from being devoured by an appetite for violence that grows everywhere.'

I wondered in a flash of lightning whether the huntsman would now seize and destroy the Predator forever. I listened and my heart virtually ceased to beat. BUT NO. The huntsman held the Beast at bay, he lifted him in his net. And I was privileged to gain, with another flash, a glimpse of terrifying beauty. I was bewildered, confused. Heartrending grief arose in me at the sight of such stripes of beauty. Such was the inimitable hide of the Predator. As the huntsman turned in the lightning Storm with the Beast in his net I dreamt I was free to surrender myself at last, *not to leap now* but to contemplate surrendering myself to an omen of Beauty that I needed to turn inside out for hidden graces, hidden sorrows, in creatures one despised because they appeared to lack the might, the power, the charisma, of the Predator.

The Storm passed and as the Moon descended on my tree-platform it shed a striped visor over my Nemesis Hat: an astronaut-knight above Limbo Land. One version of Limbo seemed charred, another version appeared to have been pierced to the heart, still another glowed, intricate, lovely, beauty translated into inside-out, marvellous graces and sorrows. It was the vulnerability of the Earth, planet Earth, that made me weep.

Once again I wanted to leap but instead I flung my visor into space. Skin and Bone throbbed where the shield had grazed my countenance and I was conscious all at once of punctures on my head and neck and shoulders. Holes had been imprinted there. The subtlest holes into which futuristic nails would lodge as if they were new bones to uphold another Mask of flesh and blood in Memory theatre. Perhaps the huntsman's net in its range and sweep — as it bore the Predator away — had inflicted wounds from which new bone would grow to uphold the Mask when it came . . . I was confused and bewildered by the prospect . . .

Dawn light brought me to the ground again. No visionary leap this! Problematic descent, problematic feet . . . I felt faint and leaned against the trunk of the tree. I placed the Bag of leaves over my shoulder and set out for New Amsterdam.

Problematic feet implied problematic stages of implicit surrender to the huntsman's net. But the hiatuses and gaps in Memory theatre remained to be reconnoitred afresh in my Dream-book, the fears, the uncertainties, of pilgrimage, of departure, arrival. Who was I? Where was I?

Were there perverse resurrections, death-dealing regimes and crushing labour, that one would need to re-vision and come abreast of, in order to break a numbness and paralysis of the Imagination everywhere?

Were there amazing truths and unfinished genesis and resurrectionary consciousness that one would glimpse through the Wheel of civilizations within the turning globe in the Womb of space?

Hospitals, El Dorado, colonial possession, Dutch, French, British within a web of ancient vanished empires in the Americas, apparitions of the dead-in-the-living (of all races) in the wake of imperial Limbo and Jonestown, banqueting halls, circuses, would haunt me as I wrote. Yet from their debris I became a diminutive cosmic architect of a Virgin Ship and of Memory theatre. All were stages for initiations into my trial at the bar of time.

Six Poems
Olive Senior

g
o
g o u r d
r
d
hollowed dried
calabash humble took-took
how simple you look. But what
lies beneath that crusty exterior?
Such stories they tell! They say O packy,
in your youth (before history), as cosmic
container, you ordered divination, ritual
sounds, incantations, you were tomb, you were
womb, you were heavenly home, the birthplace of
life here on earth. Yet broken (they say) you
caused the first Flood. Indiscretion could release
from inside you again the scorpion of darkness that
once covered the world. The cosmic snake (it is said)
strains to hold you together for what chaos would ensue
if heaven and earth parted! They say there are those
who've been taught certain secrets: how to harness the
power of your magical enclosure by the ordering of sound
— a gift from orehu the spirit of water who brought the
first calabash and the stones for the ritual, who taught
how to fashion the heavenly rattle, the sacred Mbaraká,
that can summon the spirits and resound cross the abyss
— like the houngan's asson or the shaman's maraka. Yet
hollowed dried calabash, humble took-took, we've walked
far from that water, from those mystical shores. If
all we can manage is to rattle our stones, our
beads or our bones in your dried-out container,
in shak-shak or maracca, will our voices
be heard? If we dance to your rhythm,
knock-knock on your skin, will we
hear from within, no matter
how faintly, your
wholeness
resound?

hollowed
dried
calabash
humble
took-took

how simple

you look

51

Olive Senior

SHANGO: GOD OF THUNDER

He come here all the time
sharp-dresser
womanizer
sweet-mouth
smooth-talker
— but don't pull his tongue
is trouble
you asking
his tongue quick
like lightning
zigzagging
hear him nuh:
I SPEAK ONLY ONCE!

He well arrogant
is true but don't question
take cover
when his face turn dark
like is thunder
rolling
like is stone
falling
from on high
from the sky
is like rain

Just as suddenly
is sunshine breaking
is like water
in his sweet-mouth
again

Is so everything
swift with him
he don't stand
no nonsense (though
he likes to be
one of the boys)
he'll roll in here

on his steed
(plenty horsepower
there) ride in
like a warrior
of old (you expect
him to be waving
some primitive tool
like a hatchet)
When he comes in
no matter what tune playing
they rev up the drums
as if he own them
to play that zigzag
syncopated beat
that he like

Everybody rushing
to salute him
do his bidding
for there's no telling
the state of his mind:
I SPEAK ONLY ONCE!

The girls like him
(though they say
he have three wife already)
he sweet-mouth them yes
have his way
give plenty children

If they want him to stay
they must do as he say
he prefers
hanging around
with the boys
anyway
woman must know her place
plus he swear
is only son
he can father

I tell you something:
If you want
to get anywhere
with him
act
like you tough
that is what he respect
work yu brains
not sweat but cunning
win the fight
learn sweet-talking
be smooth

Just remember
he alone can strike
with his tongue
zigzagging
like lightning

Hear him nuh:
IS ONLY ONCE I SPEAK!

OYA: GODDESS OF THE WIND

You inhale
    Earth holds its breath
You exhale
    Cities tumble
You sigh
    We are born
You whisper
    The Hallelujah Chorus rises
You hiss
    Lightning forks
You sneeze
    Thunder rolls
You belch
    Oceans churn
You break wind

Forests wither
You puff your cheeks out
    Bellows roar
You chuckle
    Angel-trumpets bloom
You enter the marketplace
    We trade glances
You whistle
    We dance
You sweep
    We fly
You yawn
    Death rattles

Terrible Goddess,
no need to show your face.
As long as we breathe
we know you are there.

OLOKUN: GOD OF THE DEEP OCEAN

1.

In the waiting room
beneath the sea
lies mythical Atlantis
or sacred Guinée

Who knows
save Olokun
master of the deep

guardian of
profoundest
mystery.

2.

Shall we ask him?

Shall we ask him
where the world tree
is anchored?

Shall we ask him
for the portal
to the sun?

Shall we ask the tally
of the bodies
thrown down to him

on the crossing
of the dread
Middle Passage?

Shall we ask him
for secrets read
in the bones

of the dead, the souls
he has guided
to his keep?

Will he reconnect
the chains of
ancestral linkages?

Send
unfathomable answers
from the deep?

3.

Divine Olokun
accept the tribute
of your rivers

the waters of your seas
give back wealth
as you please

guard us from our innermost
thoughts; keep us
from too deep probing

but if we cannot
contain ourselves and
we plunge

descending
like our ancestors
that long passage

to knowing,
from your realm
can we ascend again

in other times
in other bodies
to the plenitude of being?

YEMOJA: MOTHER OF WATERS

Mother of origins, guardian
    of passages;
generator of new life in flood
    waters, orgasm,
birth waters, baptism:

Summon your children
haul the rain down

white water: blue water
The circle comes round

Always something
cooking in your pot
Always something
blueing in your vat
Always something
Growing in your belly
Always something
moving on the waters

From Caribbean shore
to far-off Angola, she'll
spread out her blue cloth
let us cross over —

Summon your children
haul the rain down

sweet water: salt water
the circle comes round

Always something
cooking in your pot
Always something
blueing in your vat
Always something
growing in your belly
Always something
moving on the waters

If faithful to Yemoja
mother of waters, fear not
O mariner, she'll
smooth out your waves —

Summon your children
haul the rain down

fresh water: salt water
the circle comes round

Always something
cooking in your pot
Always something
blueing in your vat
Always something
growing in your belly
Always something
moving on the waters

Life starts in her waters
and ends with her calling
Don't pull me, my Mother,
till I'm ready to go —

Summon your children
haul the rain down

ground water: rain water
the circle comes round

Always something
cooking in your pot
Always something
blueing in your vat
Always something
growing in your belly
Always something
moving on the waters

Renewal is water, in
drought is our death,
we dissolve into dust and
are washed to the sea —

Summon your children
haul the rain down

white water: blue water
the circle comes round

Always something
cooking in your pot
Always something
blueing in your vat
Always something
growing in your belly
Always something
moving on the waters.

GUÉDÉ: LORD OF THE DEAD

By the sign of the crossroads
beat two turns of the drum
turn and beat again
put the pepper in the rum

lay out the cassava bread.
I might come. If I'm not busy.
Don't complain. You think
I'm just a trickster, playing

the cocksman, joking around,
working brain. Remember: is you
waiting on me, not the other
way: today you here, tomorrow

you gone — if I say. Pray
I don't come dressed in top hat
and tails, dark glasses
on mi face, puffing big Havana,

strutting round the place.
If you realize what's good
for you no matter who else
you expecting you'll still

turn and beat the drum
put out the pepper rum, pile up
the cassava bammy, maybe a chicken
or two for company

and pray I don't get more hungry
than that

this very night.

The Wolf, the Forest and the New Man
Senel Paz

— Translated from Spanish by Thomas Christensen
With illustrations by Zaida del Río

ISMAEL AND I SAID GOOD-BYE to each other, and we left the bar—
sorry, David, it's two already—but I still needed to talk, to be with
someone, so I started to go to a movie, but then changed my mind
just as I got to the ticket window, and I thought maybe I'd give
Vivian a call, but I changed my mind again just as I got to the
phone booth, and I said to myself, you know, David, the best thing
would be to wait for the bus at the Coppelia, in the Ice Palace.
And then . . . Diego.

The Ice Palace, as my faggot friend calls it. I call him faggot as a
term of affection—he wouldn't have it any other way. He's got a
theory. "*Homosexual* is when you like it to a point but you've got
it under control," he says, "or when your social—which is to say,
political—position has got you so uptight it dries your balls." I can
almost hear him, beside me at his balcony doorway, a cup of tea
in his hand. "But those like me, who at the hint of a prick lose
their composure—or should I say we turn a bit cheeky—we're
faggots, David, *fag-gots*, there's no denying!"

We met there, at the Coppelia, on one of those days when, once
lunch was done, you didn't know which way the wind would be
blowing. Murmuring "Excuse me," he appeared at my table and sat
down across from me with his bags, purses, umbrellas, rolls of
paper and cup of ice cream. I glanced at him: there wasn't much
doubt which way he was swinging. He rejected chocolate and
selected strawberry.

We were in the middle of the ice cream shop, close enough to
the university so that at any moment I might see some of my
friends. They would ask me which girl I had come to the Coppelia
with, why I didn't bring her around to the dorm and introduce her.
No harm intended, but fuck, I always give a poor account of myself, and what's more I'm never more uncomfortable than when

I'm innocent, so joking would grow into suspicion, and the next thing you know they'd be going David's always a little mysterious, David's close-mouthed, Have you heard the way he says "Prick-shit!" David doesn't have a girlfriend since Vivian left him, Oh, she left him? Why did she leave him? and then the only smart thing would be to leave the ice cream behind and head out whistling, whichever way the wind was blowing. But in that period I didn't do the smart thing the way I once did, when so many smart things had made my life such a pile of shit. . . . I felt a cow was licking my face. It was the lascivious look of the new guy — I knew that's the sort he was! — and my stomach cramped up like it was con-stipated. In small towns gays have no defense, they're everybody's laughingstock so they avoid showing themselves in public; but in Havana, or so I'd heard, it was different, they had their little tricks. If I poked him in the chin the next time he gave me that look, if I put him on the ground vomiting strawberries, he would wail loud enough for everyone to hear: "Oh, baby, what did you do that for? I swear I wasn't looking at anyone, oh oh oh!" So let him lick all he wanted, I wouldn't tumble for that gambit. And when he saw that his stunt wasn't getting results, he spread open one of his bundles on the table. I had to repress a smile because I knew this was another ploy, and I wasn't inclined to bite. I just gave a side-ways glance and saw that they were books, foreign books, and the topmost one, that particular one, being on top, caught my eye: *Seix Barral, Biblioteca Breve, Mario Vargas Llosa, La Guerra del Fin del Mundo.* Oh! *The War of the End of the World,* that book, none other! Vargas Llosa was a reactionary, talking up the Cuban and Socialist menace wherever he went, but I was mad to read his latest novel, so to see it there — faggots are always the first to get their hands on everything! "If you don't mind, I'm going to pack up," he said, and he put the books away in a bag with enormous straps, which hung from his neck. "Motherfucker," I thought, "this character has more pouches than a kangaroo."

"I've got more pouches than a kangaroo," said he with a little smile. "This material is too explosive to exhibit in public. Our police are literate. But if you're interested, I'll show it to you . . . elsewhere." I moved my red Young Communists Union I.D. from one pocket to another: so he would understand that my interests as a reader did not imply any intimacy between us; or would he prefer that I called one of his literate policemen? He was oblivious to this message. He looked at me with another little smile and occupied himself with collecting a tip of ice cream with the tip of his spoon, which he raised to the tip of his tongue. "Exquisite, isn't it? It's the only thing they make right in this country. Pretty soon the Russians will get it in their heads to have us give them the recipe, and we'll just give it away."

Why should anyone have to put up with that kind of thing from a faggot? I filled my mouth with ice cream and started to chew. He let a few moments pass. "I know you. I've often seen you passing by here with a paper under your arm. How do you like Galiano Street?" I was silent. "A friend of mine, who will go nameless, also knows you: he ran into you in some provincial setting I can't remember, and he said you were from Las Villas, like Carlos Loveira." He let out a little cry: he had discovered an almost whole strawberry in the ice cream. "Today's my lucky day — one treat after another!" I was silent. "They talk about easterners and habaneros, but you people from Las Villas are the ones who are really full of yourselves. How silly." He tried to get the strawberry to stay on his spoon, but it didn't want to. I had finished my ice cream, and now I didn't know what to do, because that's another of my problems: I don't know how to begin or end conversations, I listen to everything anyone says to me even if I could care less. "You're interested in Vargas Llosa, comrade military youth?" he said, pushing the strawberry with a finger. "Would you like to read him? They're never going to publish him here. Goytisolo just sent me the one you saw, his latest novel, from Spain." He continued to look at me. I began to count: once I reached fifty I would get up and hit the road. He let me get to thirty-nine. Raising the spoon to his mouth and savoring the comment more than the fruit, he said, "If you come over to my place and let me open your fly button by button, I'll give it to you, *Thorvald*."

If he knew the effect that name would have on me, Diego would have sheathed the barb. That was a poke I couldn't endure. The blood rose to my face, the veins in my neck swelled up, I felt dizzy, my eyes clouded over. Four years before, my high school literature teacher — who was not just a lit teacher but also a frustrated theater director — got a golden opportunity when the school failed to get a first place in the scholarship competitions because of low marks for cultural accomplishment. She went to the principal and convinced him, first, that Rita and I had exceptional histrionic potential, and, second, that with her sure hand she could bring it out in *A Doll's House,* a work that, as Martí has said, señor principal, should be seen by everyone in the Republic; even though it is foreign, it is ideologically incisive, and it even appeared in the Ministry's revised study program last summer. Delighted, the principal agreed (it was a golden opportunity), and as for Rita, well, although her stage fright kept her from answering roll in class, she was secretly deeply in love with me. But for my part, I gave out a resounding *no!* I had altogether too elevated a concept of manliness to deck myself out as an actor, and my friends were even worse. The principal chose the most direct path of persuasion: he told me it was an assignment — an assignment, Alvarez David, made possible by the Revolution, thanks to which you, the son of poor campesinos, have been allowed to study, for the main stage of battle in the fight against imperialism isn't the stage of a theater play, take my word, it's in all those countries of Latin America where young people of your age encounter repression every day. All we are asking is for you to portray one of Ibsen's characters. So I accepted. Not because I had no choice — I was convinced. He was right. I learned my role in a week, and Rita's too, since her secret love for me was so constricting that she blanked out whenever I came near her. She was one of those pale, helpless, faithful girls (usually orphans) who so often fell for me, and whom I, out of sympathy and because I didn't want them to end up traumatized, would make my girlfriends. The night of the play, the same night Diego discovered me and pegged me for life, her stage fright was compounded by her fear of the public, her nervousness about being judged and most of all her nervousness about the final scene when she would be in my arms — or at least in the arms of the nineteenth-century character whom I played in the suit dreamt up by the literature teacher. Finally she couldn't do another thing, and she clammed up in the middle of the stage, looking at me with the eyes of a decapitated sheep. The teacher held her breath, the principal ground his teeth and the audience closed its eyes. It was I, the actor on assignment, who kept his equanimity in that difficult moment of Theater and the Homeland. "You are troubled and silent, Nora," I said, approaching with the hope of reviving her with a little kick or a pat. "Yet I know we must talk. Shall I sit with you? We have to have a long talk." Nothing. Rita was seriously gone, and the play had to continue as Thorvald's self-critical monologue until finally the literature teacher took charge, lowered a couple of screens and, to the rhythms of *Swan Lake* — the only music in the projection room — started showing slides of workers and soldiers, proclamations of the First Congress of Education and Culture, and poems by Juana de Ibarbourou, Mirta Aguirre and their ilk; and as a result (so she later claimed) the piece acquired meaning and relevance that Ibsen's text, by itself, lacked. "It was the most embarrassing moment I have witnessed in my life," Diego confessed to me later. "All I could do was try to bury myself in my seat; half the audience started to pray for you, and someone mentioned short-circuiting the wiring. And that red and green jacket that looked like an African flag! We were moved by your control, the innocent way you made yourself ridiculous. That's why we were so effusive with our applause." Which was the worst thing, the pity in their applause. As I stood listening in the glare of the spotlights, I wished with all my heart that total amnesia would affect each and every one of those present and that never, never, never—do you hear me, God?—would I ever meet any of them, anyone who would recognize me. What's more, I promised myself to think twice the next time I was given an assignment, never to masturbate and to pursue a scientific-technical career, which was exactly what the country needed. And so I did, except for the part about the scientific-technical career, and as for masturbation God had to put that down to despair and inexperience; but He, for his part, failed me—he forgot his word and put me at the Coppelia on a day when I didn't have my wits about me, face to face with some character who thought he could blackmail me with that debacle.

"No, no, it's a joke," Diego insisted, seeing me on the verge of apoplexy. "Forgive me, it was just a joke, of course, to lighten things up. Here, drink, have some water. Do you want to go to the emergency room at Calixto?" "No!" I said, getting up and making a momentous decision. "Let's go to your place, look at the books, talk them over and forget about the rest." It was sheer nervousness. He gaped at me. "Let's go!" But it was one thing to shed his bags and another to reassemble them, so that while he was doing so he had time to collect himself as well. "First I have a few things I want to say because I don't want you to claim I didn't make things clear. You're one of those people whose naiveté is dangerous. I, first of all, am a faggot. And, second, I am religious. Third, I've had some trouble with the powers that be—they think there's no place for me in this country, but it's not so; I was born here: I am, before anything else, a patriot and a Lezamian—a devotee of the writer Lezama Lima—and I'm not leaving even if they stick a candle up my ass. Fourth, I was arrested as a gay activist, a member of the

UMAP. Fifth, my neighbors are keeping an eye on me, and they keep records of everyone who visits. Do you still want to come?" "Yes," replied the son of poor campesinos in a hoarse voice I hardly recognized.

The apartment, hereafter The Lair, since it did not escape the habanero custom of baptizing their residences when they are small and self-standing (I was already familiar with The Locker, The Closet, The Asteroids, The Alternative, The Don't Ask Where), consisted of a single room and a bath, part of which had been transformed into a kitchen. The roof, about a mile from the floor, was decorated in the corners and the middle with those cowpies habaneros call soffits, and like the walls and the furniture it was painted white, while the trim and molding, the kitchen fixtures, the bedclothes and all the rest were red. Everything was white or red except Diego, who was dressed in tones from black to the palest gray, with white socks and pink glasses and handkerchief. That day almost the entire space was taken up with wooden saints, all with downcast faces. "These carvings are a treat," he explained as we entered, to make clear that this was a matter of art, not religion. "Germán, the artist, is a genius. They will cause an uproar in our plastic arts such as you won't want to see. A cultural attaché from one of the embassies is already interested, and yesterday we got a call from the correspondent of the Spanish press, the EFE." I knew little about art, but not long afterwards, when the Culture functionary announced that the statues failed to transmit a positive message, I thought he was right, and I said so to Diego. "Let Radio Reloj transmit it!" he screamed. "This is art. And it's not for me, David, you must understand that. It's for Germán. When this hits Santiago de Cuba it'll blow sky high—he'll probably be fired."

But the problems with Germán's exposition came later. Today I was in the middle of The Lair, surrounded by saints with upset stomachs and convinced that I had entered the wrong place. Once I got the book, I'd beat it. "Sit down," he said, "I'll make some tea to help us get comfortable." He went to close the door. "No!" I stopped him. "As you wish—this will facilitate my neighbors' work. Have a seat in this armchair. It's special, I don't offer it to just anyone." He went to the bathroom and I heard his voice over the sound of the toilet: "I use it exclusively for reading John Donne and Cavafy, although Cavafy is an indulgence of mine. He should be read in a Viennese chair or a banquette against a wall." Diego reappeared, explaining that John Donne was an English poet totally

68

unknown to us, and as the only one who had a translation of his work, he never tired of introducing him to young people. "There will come a time when his fame will reach all the way to the Bar Los Dos Hermanos, I assure you. But sit down, kid." I sank so far into the John Donne armchair that my ass was lower than my knees, but I soon made myself quite comfortable. "Shall I put on some music? I've got everything. First pressings of María Melibrán, Teresa Stratas, Renata Tebaldi and Callas, of course. Those are my favorites. Those and Celina González. Which do you prefer?" "I don't know who Celina González is," I said honestly, and Diego doubled up with laughter. Habaneros think that anyone from the interior spends his days in rustic folk dancing. "Okay, well. You have the honor of being the first to hear a recording of Callas that I just received from Florence, her interpretation of *La Traviata*, from 1955, in La Scala of Milan . . . Florence in Italy, you know." He put on the record and went to the kitchen. "What do they call you? My name is Diego. They always make the joke 'Dig it, Diego.' It's like Antonio, they call him Tony Tony. What about you?" "Juan Carlos Rondón, at your service." He stuck his head out. "Liar. You'll be pure Las Villas till your dying day. Your name is David. I know everything about everyone. Well, everyone of any interest. You, for instance, write." When he came in with the tea service he stumbled and spilled milk on me. He wouldn't be satisfied until I agreed to remove my shirt, which he quickly washed and hung on the balcony beside a Spanish shawl that he also brought out from the bath. He sat down in front of me and set a box of chocolates on my knees. "At last we can talk in peace. You pick a subject, anything is fine with me." Instead of responding, I hung my head and stared at the floor. "Nothing occurs to you? Oh well, I know, I'll tell you the story of how I became a faggot."

It happened when he was twelve, a boarding student in a religious school. One afternoon, he doesn't remember why, he was supposed to light a candle, and he couldn't find any matches, so he went up to the students' dormitory on the upper floor, where he accidentally came out into the baths. There, naked under a shower, was one of the players on the school's basketball team, all soaped up and singing "We love each other so, why must you go? Oh, please, don't say no . . ." "He was a redhead with curly hair," he recalled with a sigh, "between fourteen and fifteen. A shaft of light, more worthy of the rosettes of Notre Dame than the skylights of our school, Hermanos Maristas, shone down on his back, casting shifting colors over his foam-covered body." The boy, he added, was aroused, clutching his penis (the object of his song), and Diego was mesmerized, unable to avert his gaze from that demigod who stared at him and let himself be stared at. No words were spoken: the boy took him by the arms, turned him around against the wall and possessed him. "I returned to the dormitory with the candle out," he said, "but glowing from within, palpitating with new knowledge of worldly pleasure." Destiny, however, reserved for Diego a bitter surprise. Two days later, going to get another candle, he learned that his violator had died of a blow to the head: he was trying to get a ball that had fallen between the hooves of the mule used to bring coal for the school, and the mule, insensible to his charms, clobbered him a good one. "Ever since," Diego concluded, looking at me, "my life has been nothing but the search for the ideal of that basketball player. . . . You are rather like him."

It was obvious that he was a master of the technique of getting the attention of recruits and students, and of making them feel comfortable, as he later admitted. This involved getting us to hear or see what we didn't want to hear or see — which, he said, produced excellent results with Communists. But that's as far as it went this time. I had come, like the others, I had sat in the special armchair, like them, but unlike them I had fixed my gaze on the floor and refused to break it. He had thought of showing me the porno magazine that he kept for difficult cases, or offering me the bottle of Chivas Regal in which he always kept a few fingers of nondescript rum, but he held back because that wasn't what he wanted from me; finally he started to get hungry and, not wanting to share his food, he began to wonder how he would bring the visit to a close. He sat silent and pensive. He later confessed that he had sought this meeting ever since he had first seen me as Thorvald in the play. He had even dreamt about me, and several times he had been on the point of hailing me in Galiano Street, for from the beginning he had a presentiment of our friendship. But that day, mute and rigid in the middle of The Lair, I was so uptight that he began to think that as usual he had been the dupe of an illusion, of his habit of attributing sensitivity and talent to baby-faced types. I really surprised him, and he was distraught at having misjudged me. I was his latest diversion, his one last chance before deciding that it was all a crock of shit, that God had been mistaken and Karl Marx even more so, because this "new man" in whom he placed so much hope was nothing but a poetic conceit, a joke,

socialist propaganda — if there was a new man in Havana it wouldn't
be one of those fine, strapping Special Commandos, but rather
someone like me, someone who could play the fool, and he had to
meet one someday and bring him to The Lair, offer him tea and
conversation, shit yes, conversation, he didn't have a one-track
mind, as he explained to me in another of his perorations. "I'm
going," I said finally, getting up, and I looked at him — we looked
at each other. He spoke without rising. "David, come back sometime. Today I don't think I was able to explain. Perhaps to you I
seemed superficial. Like everyone who talks a lot, I say a lot of
nonsense. It's because I'm nervous, but I felt different talking to
you. Talking is important, and a dialogue even more so. Please
don't be afraid to come back. I know how to show respect, I can
control myself as well as anyone, I can give you a lot of help, lend
you books, get you ballet tickets, I'm a good friend of Alicia Alonso,
I'd like to take you to the Loynazes' someday too, around five
o'clock, that's a privilege only I can bestow. And maybe I'll fix you
a lunch *à la Lezama*, now that's something I don't offer just anyone. I know that the generosity of faggots is a two-edged sword, as
Lezama himself says somewhere, but not in this case. You know
why I want to talk with you? It's a feeling I have. I think we're
going to understand each other, despite our differences. I know

71

the Revolution has accomplished some good things, but for me it has brought many bad things as well, about which I have my own ideas. Maybe they're wrong, that could be. I'd like to discuss these things, to have a chance to explain. I listen to reason, I can change my opinion. But I've never managed to have a talk with a revolutionary. You only talk with each other; it doesn't matter to you what others might think. Do come back. I'll leave to the side the faggot question, I swear. Here, take *The War of the End of the World*, and look, *Three Trapped Tigers* too, you won't find this one in the street either." "No!" I cried so loudly it startled him. "Why, David, what is it?" "No!" I left, slamming the door behind me.

Good, I told myself in the street, the sound of the slammed door still ringing in my ears: I didn't borrow the books or take them as gifts either. And my Spirit, which the whole time had been worried within me, relaxed, and it began to take a certain pride in this young fellow who in the end didn't weaken. That's what was expected of me, the young Communist who would demand the floor in meetings and (though not expressing myself very well) speak my mind, whom Bruno had already called on twice. So much for my Spirit, but my Conscience was not having such an easy time of it, and before I reached the corner it was demanding an explanation: why, David Alvarez, if you were really a man, would you go to the house of a homosexual; if you were really a revolutionary, why would you go to the house of a counterrevolutionary; and if you were an atheist, why would you go to the house of a believer? All while I kept walking, got on the bus and got pushed to the back with the crowd. How could you let him make cracks about the Revolution (your Revolution, David) in front of you, and champion his sickness and corruption without your walking out? Didn't having the I.D. card in your pocket mean anything, or was that just a place to tuck it away? Who are you really, kid? Don't you know you're just a frightened little parrot the Revolution pulled from the muck and took to study in Havana?

But if there's one thing I have learned in life, it's not to answer my Conscience in crisis situations. Instead, I surprised it by going down to the university, hurrying up the staircase looking for Bruno, finding him in a corner, and asking him what I should do, to whom should one report when one discovers someone receiving foreign books, speaking ill of the Revolution and following religion. Take that, Conscience! The affair seemed so important to Bruno that he took off his glasses and took me to see another comrade, and as soon as I saw the other comrade I could tell I was going to put my foot in it again. Like Diego, he had a clear and penetrating gaze, as if people with clear and penetrating gazes were joining forces that day to fuck me over. He led me into his office, pointed to a seat that wasn't any kind of Viennese shit and told me to sing out. I explained that we revolutionaries must be ever-vigilant, our guard raised high; and that therefore (being ever-vigilant, my guard raised high) I had met Diego, accompanied him to his house and discovered what I now knew. I was soon suspicious of his foreign books and his fancy talk. Did he understand? Either he didn't understand or my story didn't have much punch. He yawned once and even flipped the pages of a book while pretending to listen. Which is another of my problems: I lose my cool when someone is bored with what I'm saying, and I begin to wring my hands and start heaping on details. "This character is a counterrevolutionary," I stressed. "He has had contact with the cultural attaché of an embassy, and he is attempting to influence young people." "So you're saying," I expected the comrade to say, "that you went to the home of a counterrevolutionary, religious faggot just because one must be ever-vigilant?" "Precisely." But that's not what he said. He fixed me with his clear and penetrating gaze, and a chill ran down my spine as I guessed what he was going to say. "What a miserable asshole you are, kid, you little opportunist." But that's not what he said either. He smiled, and said in what seemed to me a condescending, ironic, but sympathetic tone, "Yes, we must be ever-vigilant. It's David, right? The enemy appears where one least expects him, David. Find out what embassy he has had contact with, note what questions he asks about military movements and the positions of leaders, and then we'll see. This is an assignment: you're a spy now, all right?" That was Ismael. We would become friends, almost like brothers, and one day I would offer him a lunch *à la Lezama*, because there had been a literature teacher in his past as well.

I marched down the staircase to a military tune, feeling like a movie star pressing forward beneath an unfurled flag waving its solitary star. When I reached the dorm I had a deep, hot bath, lots of hot water splashing over me until I felt that the last of the day's trials had been washed away and I could sleep. But to really end the day on an up note I decided to study a little, and I got into bed. Which was my mistake. From the bed I looked out at the beautiful, calm, deep blue sea, and it had a terrible effect on me. Inside me, besides my Conscience and my Spirit, there lived my Counter-conscience, which remains to this day a terrible son of a bitch, and it began to stir and awaken and ask its own questions; and from my Counterconscience there's no escape. Just one of its questions can carry me up to the twenty-fourth floor and fling me into space. I dropped the book and, standing in front of the bathroom mirror, said, "Prickshit!" And I promised the guy who was looking back at me that I was going to give him a break, that under no circumstances would I return to that person's home, not him or any other Diego, I swear.

I wasn't true to my word, nor was Diego true to his. "We homosexuals fall into a more elaborate and interesting classification than I told you the other day. That is, *homosexuals*, properly termed — this word is used because even at its worst it retains some degree of respect; *faggots* — also popular — and *queens*, for whom the lowest expression is the *drag queens*. This scale reflects the subject's degree of disposition to social responsibility or queerness. When the balance inclines to social responsibility, we are in the presence of a homosexual. There are those — I count myself among them — for whom sex occupies *a* place in their life but not *the* place in their life. Like heroes or political activists, we balance Duty and Sex. The cause to which we dedicate ourselves comes first. My cause is our nation's culture, to which I dedicate the better part of my intellect and my time. I'm not boasting when I say that my study of Cuban women poets of the nineteenth century, my census of fences and grills of Oficios, Compostieia, Sol and Muralla streets, and my exhaustive collection of maps of the island beginning with Columbus are indispensable for the study of this country. Someday I'll show you my inventory of seventeenth- and eighteenth-century buildings, each one accompanied by a pen drawing of the exterior and main interior parts, which will be vital for any future restoration projects. All this — along with my papers, among which the most important are seven unpublished texts by Lezama — is the fruit of many sleepless nights, love, like my comparative study of buggers' jargon from the Port and the Central Park. I mean, if you see me out on the balcony where that Spanish shawl is waving, a pen in my hand, revising my text on the poetry of the sisters Juana and Dulce María Borrero, I won't abandon the job even if I see the most portentous mulatto of Marianao pass by, even if he exposes his balls when he spots me. Homosexuals of this category don't waste time on sex, nothing can sway us from our work. The belief that we're corruptible and treacherous by nature is completely erroneous and offensive. No, sir, we are as steady and patriotic as anyone! Between a fairy and a Cuban, we'll take the Cuban every time. Our intelligence and productivity warrant a respect we are always denied. Marxists and Christians, mark my words, will continue to be hobbled until they recognize our place and accept us as allies, since more often than they admit we share a common attitude toward social responsibility. *Faggots* don't require any special explanation, since they occupy the midpoint between the two extremes: you'll see if you consider *queens*, who are easy to understand. They always have a phallus on their mind, and it's behind all their actions. Wasting time is their basic characteristic. If the time they devoted to flirting in parks and public baths were dedicated to socially useful work we could achieve what you call Communism and we paradise. The most wayward of all are the ones called *drag queens*. I loathe them for their fatuity and vacuity, and because their lack of discretion and tact has made such simple and necessary things as painting one's toenails into acts of rebellion. They provoke and wound the popular sensibility, not so much by their affectation as by their tastelessness — they're always giggling for no reason and talking about things they know nothing about. The repulsion is even greater when the queen is black, because among us blacks are a symbol of virility. And if these poor people live in Guanabacoa, Buenavista or interior towns, their life becomes hell, because the people in those places are still extremely intolerant. This typology can also be applied to heterosexuals of either sex. Straight men of the lowest type, corresponding to the drag queens whose chief characteristic is wasting time and lust for perpetual fornication, are the *lechers,* who on their way to mail a letter, say, can even lay their hands on one of us without a loss of virility, just because they can't contain themselves. Among women, the scale terminates in prostitutes, of course — not the ones who work the hotels in the tourist section or labor out of self-interest (of whom we have few, just as the official propaganda says) but rather those who offer themselves just for the pleasure of putting out, as the saying goes. So, face it, we've got them all — queens and lechers and drag artists — in this paradise beneath the stars, and in saying so I do no more than echo an English writer who said: 'The disagreeable things of this world cannot be eliminated by looking away from them.'"

So, through our conversations on this and other topics, we became friends, and we got in the habit of spending afternoons together, drinking tea in the cups he said were so valuable, and making our Sunday lunches (for which we reserved the most interesting topics) into something sacred. I walked barefoot around The Lair, took off my shirt and raided the refrigerator whenever I felt like it, which was something that for a timid rural type shows better than anything that one has reached a point of absolute confidence and ease. Diego insisted on reading my work, and when I finally dared to give him something he made me wait two weeks before commenting on it; finally he put it on the table. "I'm going to be frank, get ready. This doesn't work. Why choose these elevated words instead of the words people really use? This shows too much reading of *Mir* and *Progresso*. You'll have to start over from the beginning, because you do have talent." And so he took my education in hand. "Read," he said, giving me the book *Sugar and Society in the Antilles,* and I read. "Read *A Study of Taunting,"* and I read. "Read *American and Cuban Literary Style,"* and I read. "Read *Cuban Counterpoint: Tobacco and Sugar,"* and I read. "Hide this one under the cover of the review *Verde Olivo* and don't leave it lying around; it's *El Monte,* the black Bible, you know? For poetry, read *The Poetry of Cuba.* Now here's something that's like goldwork: a complete collection of *Orígenes,* which they don't even have in the Rodríguez-Feo. You'll go through these one at a time. And here — but this is for afterward, everything we're doing is just leading up to this — is the work of the Master, poetry and prose. Look, put your hand on it, caress it, absorb its wisdom. One day, some evening in November, when the Havana light is most beautiful, we'll walk past his house in Trocadero Street. We'll be coming from the Prado, on the other side of the street, talking with a carefree air. You'll be in something blue, a color that suits you, and we'll imagine that the Master is alive, that he's even then looking through his blinds at us. You'll smell his tobacco, hear his labored breathing. He'll say: 'Look at this queen with his boy, look how he struggles to make him his pupil instead of just slipping a nice ten-peso bill into his jacket.' Don't take offense, that's just the way he is. I know he will appreciate my work and recognize your sensitivity and intelligence and, although there will be misunderstandings, he will be especially pleased by your revolutionary status. That day he will be grateful for his assignment of reading parts of his work for half an hour to the Bureaucrats of the Cultural

Council consigned to the realm of Persephone—a large crowd, for sure."

On maps spread out on the floor, we marked the most interesting buildings and squares of Old Havana, the church windows that have to be seen, the subtlest ironwork, the columns cited by Carpentier, the ruins of three-hundred-year-old walls. He prepared a precise itinerary for me that I traced to the letter, and I returned all excited to comment on what I had seen in the intimacy of his apartment, shut within its walls of lime and stone, drinking cider, oriental prú or chirimoya pulp and listening to Saumell, Caturla, Lecuona, the Trio Matamoros or—not too loud, because of the neighbors—Celia Cruz and the Sonora Matancera. As for the ballet, which was his strength, I didn't miss a one. He always got me tickets, no matter how difficult they were to obtain, and in really important cases, he even gave me his own invitation. If we met each other when we got to the theater or when we left, we didn't greet each other but pretended not to see one another, and we never sat together. To avoid meeting, I would stay in the hall during the intermissions, counting the songs in the program listings. "What I find most remarkable about our friendship," he would say, "is that I know about as much about you as I did when we met. Tell me something, love: your first sexual experience, when you came for the first time, what your erotic dreams are like. Don't try to deny it: with those eyes of yours, you must burn like a torch. And tell me why"—he renewed his attack, sensing that I was tensing up—"if we're like brothers, you never let me see you naked. I tell you, I can't keep in mind the figure of a man whose prick I haven't seen. So, let me guess, yours must be tender as a dove; though I must say, there are boys of your type, sensitive and spiritual, who, when they get undressed, nonetheless reveal quite a load."

For the lunch *à la Lezama* he made me wear a tie and jacket. Bruno lent me the jacket and made me pay him ten pesos, thinking I was taking a girl to the Tropicana. The exceptional quality of the meal, as I later realized Lezama himself says in *Paradiso*, was given by the lace tablecloth, neither white nor red, but a cream color, on which was scattered the perfection of the chinaware with a green ring that followed the contours of all the pieces, a green ring delimited by golden filets. Diego uncovered the tureen in which a thick plantain soup was steaming. "I've decided to rejuvenate you," he said with a mysterious smile. "And take you back to your early childhood. That's why I've added a little tapioca to the soup . . ." "What is this?" "Yuca, kid, don't interrupt me. . . . I've put in some popcorn to float on top because there are so many things that we liked as children and yet will never enjoy again. But don't get worried, it's not so-called Western soup, because some gourmets as soon as they see corn, imagine covered wagons migrating west across the Sioux prairies at the beginning of the last century. And here I must look to the young people's table," he interrupted his strange recitation, which I approved with a stupid smile, pretending to follow the game. "Let us swap," he resumed, taking away the dishes after we had eaten the wonderful soup, "the sparky canary for a lazy prawn," and the second course appeared, a fluffy soufflé of shellfish, the surface adorned by pairs of prawns forming a circle, their claws spread over the steam coming from the clump like white coral. Part of the soufflé also was a fish called emperor and lobsters showing the livid surprise with which their shells had caught the lantern's inquisition burning their bulging-out eyes. I couldn't find the words to praise the soufflé, and that linguistic incapacity of mine turned out to be the highest praise of all. "After a dish of such impressive appearance, with flowing colors like those of a flambée, nearing the baroque but still gothic, owing to the baking and the allegories sketched by the prawns, we want to calm the rhythm of the meal with a beet salad that has received a spatula lick of mayonnaise, crossed with Lübeck asparagus — now pay attention, Juan Carlos Rondón, because we are reaching the climax of the ceremony." As he cut a beet, he dropped it onto the tablecloth. He couldn't resist a fastidious gesture, and he tried to rectify the error, but the beet kept bleeding, until it fell apart where he had skewered it — half was stuck to the fork and half fell back on the tablecloth, so that three isles of bleeding showed up among the rosettes. Embarrassed, I opened my mouth, but he looked at me with satisfaction: "They have remained perfect," he said. "Those three stains actually give the relief of splendor to the meal." And, half declaiming, he added: "In the light, in the resistant patience of craftmanship, in the omens, in the way the threads absorbed the vegetable blood, the three stains open up in somber expectancy." He smiled, delighted to reveal the secret to me: "You are participating in the family lunch that doña Augusta offers in the pages of *Paradiso*, chapter seven. After this, you can say you have eaten like a real Cuban, and enter forever into the brotherhood of the adorers of the Master (lacking only knowledge of his work)." We continued with roast turkey, followed by ice cream *à la Lezama,* for which he offered me the recipe so in my turn I could give it to my mother. "Now Baldovina should bring the fruit-bowl, but since she's not here I'll get it for her. I apologize for the apples and pears, for which I have substituted mangos and guavas, which are actually not bad at all with tangerines and grapes. Afterward we will have coffee on the balcony while I recite to you poems by the unpopular Zenea, and we'll skip the cigars that neither of us enjoy. But first," he added with sudden inspiration, when his gaze alighted on the Spanish shawl, "some flamenco dances," and he amused me with some frenzied stamping, then suddenly stopped. "I hate it," he said, hurling the scarf away. "I don't know if you will ever forgive me, David." I felt the same way, and I suddenly began to feel ill, because while

I was enjoying the lunch I couldn't avoid some of my neurons hovering outside the feast, ever-vigilant, not tasting a single morsel, realizing that the lobsters, prawns, Lübeck asparagus and grapes could only be obtained in special stores for diplomats and thus constituted proof of his relations with foreigners, which, in my role as spy, I would have to report to the comrade (no longer Ismael).

Still, time passed happily by, until one Saturday when I arrived for tea and Diego only half opened the door. "You can't come in. I have someone here whose face I don't want you to see. I'm having the time of my life. Please, come back another time." I went away, but only across the street, in order to see the face he didn't want me to see. Soon Diego came out alone. I noticed he was nervous, looking up and down the street, and he quickly turned the corner. I hurried after him in time to see him get into a diplomatic car concealed in a passageway. I had to hide behind a pillar as they pulled out with a roar. Diego in a diplomatic car! A sharp sorrow seized my chest. My God, it was all true! Bruno was right and Ismael was wrong when he said that these people's cases must be considered one at a time. No. One really must be ever-vigilant: faggots are traitors by nature, by original sin. No more duplicity for me. I could forget the matter and be happy: mine had been a pure class instinct. But I could not achieve happiness; instead I felt sad. Such sadness when a friend betrays you, oh, such sadness and such rage in discovering that you've been stupid again, that another has used you as he wished. Such sadness when you have to admit the hardliners were right, and you're nothing but a great sentimental asshole, ready to make friends with just anyone. I got to Malecón when, as often happens, nature itself took up my mood: all of a sudden the sky clouded over, thunder sounded louder and louder, and it began to feel more and more like rain. My steps carried me straight to the university, looking for Ismael, but I had the presence of mind — or whatever it was, since for me presence of mind is a rare luxury — to realize that I could not endure a third encounter with him, with his clear and penetrating gaze, and I stopped in my tracks. The second time had been after the lunch *à la Lezama*, when I had to put my mind at rest to keep it from bursting. "I was wrong," I told him, "this fellow is actually a good person, just a poor devil, and it's not worth the trouble to keep watching him." "But didn't you say he's a counterrevolutionary?" he commented wryly. "Of course, we have to realize that his experience of the Revolution has not been like ours. It's difficult to follow someone who wants you to stop being the way you are in order to be accepted. In short . . ." I said nothing, I wasn't yet comfortable enough with Ismael to talk to him as I would have liked. "He is the way he is, according to his own thinking. He has an inner freedom that I, as a military man, can only envy." Ismael looked at me and smiled. What was different between the clear and penetrating gazes of Diego and Ismael (to finish up with you, Ismael, since this isn't your story) is that Diego's was limited to pointing things out, while Ismael's urged you, if you didn't like things, to act on them and change them. That's why he was the best of the three of us. He would be talking to me about something, and then as we parted he would put a hand on my shoulder, and tell me we should get together again sometime. I realized that he was releasing me from my spying assignment, and that was the beginning of our friendship. What would he think now, when I told him what I had just discovered? I went back to Diego's house, determined to wait for him as long as necessary. It was pouring when he returned by taxi. I went up to his door and went in before he could shut it. "Well, my boyfriend's gone," he teased. "But look at that face! Don't tell me you're jealous." "I saw you get into a diplomatic car." He wasn't expecting that. He looked at me, the color draining from his face, and dropped into a chair, head lowered. When he looked up a moment later, he seemed ten years older. "Come on, I'm waiting." Now would come the confessions, the repenting, the requests for pardon, revealing the name of the counterrevolutionary group he was a part of, and I would go straight to the police. "I was going to tell you, David, but I didn't want it to be so soon. I'm leaving."

For us Cubans, *I'm leaving*, in the tone that Diego had spoken it, had a terrible connotation. It meant leaving the country forever, erasing yourself from its memory and it from yours, and — like it or not — it meant treason. That is something one knows from the start: it's included in the price of passage. Once you have it in your hand you can never convince anyone that you didn't want it. That can't be your case, Diego. What are you going to do away from Havana, from its hot, messy streets, the clamor of the habaneros. What will you do in some other city, Diego, love, where Lezama had not been born, and Alicia didn't dance her farewell performance every Friday night? A city without bureaucrats or hardliners to criticize, without a David to love you. "It's not for the reason you imagine," he said. "You know that for me politics is a pig in a poke. It's because of Germán's exposition. You're not very observant, you didn't notice the stir it made. It turned out it wasn't him they fired, it was me. Germán worked out something with them, he rented a room and came to work in Havana as a craftsman. I realize I went too far in defense of his work, that I was insubordinate and reckless, that I took advantage of my position. So what? Now, with that censure in my file I'll never find any work, except in agriculture or construction, and you tell me, what am I going to do with a brick in my hand, where would I put it? It's a simple labor censure, but who's going to hire me with that on my record, who would take a chance on me? It's unjust, I know it; I have the law on my side, and in the end they will have to see reason and exonerate me. But what can I do? Fight? No. I'm weak, and your world is not for the weak. On the contrary, you act as if we don't exist, as if we were here solely to mortify you and collude against you. For you life is easy: you don't suffer from Oedipus complexes, you don't worry about beauty, you never had a favorite cat that your father quartered before your eyes just to make a man of you. I know you can be a faggot and still be strong, there are lots of examples. That is clear. But not in my case. I'm weak, I'm worried about growing old, I can't wait ten or fifteen years for you to reconsider, as confident as I am that the Revolution will in the end correct its errors. I'm thirty. I've got another twenty useful years at most. I want to do things, to live, make plans, stop and look at myself in the mirror at Las Meninas, give a lecture on the poetry of Flor and Dulce María Loynaz. Don't I have that right? If I were a good Catholic and believed in an afterlife it wouldn't matter, but your materialism is contagious after all these years. This is life, there is no other. Or at least, there better not be another, you know what I mean? They don't want me here, why turn my cheek any longer; besides, I like being the way I am, to put on a little plumage now and then. Tell me, who do I harm, if they're my feathers?"

His remaining days were not all sad. Indeed, sometimes he seemed euphoric, flittering about among old papers and packets. We drank rum and listened to music. "Before they come to take inventory, take my typewriter, the electric stove, this can opener. Your mama will find it useful. These are my studies on architecture and city planning: a lot, aren't there? And they are good. If I don't have enough time, send them anonymously to the City Museum. Here are recollections of Federico García Lorca's visit to Cuba. There's a very detailed itinerary, along with photographs of people and places with my annotations; I couldn't identify this black man. I want you to keep that anthology of poems about Almendares, and add to it if you like, although the Almendares isn't really poetry material anymore. See this photo: it's me in the literacy campaign. And these are ones of my family; them I'm taking. Check out this gorgeous uncle of mine; he choked on a stuffed potato. Here I am with my mother, see how good-looking she is. Look around, what else do you want me to leave you? I already gave you the papers. Send the articles you consider most palatable to *Revolución y Cultura*, maybe someone will appreciate them there; if you choose topics from the last century they will be better received. Send the rest to the National Library, you know to whom. Don't lose that contact, take him a smoke occasionally, but don't take offense if he says something suggestive — he won't go beyond that. I'll also leave you my ballet contact. And these, David Alvarez, the cups in which we have drunk so much tea, I want to leave on deposit with you. Someday, if the opportunity presents itself, mail them to me. As I told you, they are Sèvres porcelain. But that's not the reason why they're valuable — they belonged to the Loynaz del Castillo family, and they are a gift. Okay, I'm going to tell you the truth, I stole them. My records and books are already gone, your lot took them away, and these that remain are to throw the inventory takers off the scent. Let me have a poster of Fidel with Camilo, a small Cuban flag, the photos of Martí in Jamaica and of Mella in his hat; quick, they have to go in the diplomatic bag with my photos of Alicia in *Giselle* and my collection of Cuban bills and coins. Do you want this umbrella for your mama, or this cap?"

I accepted everything in silence, but sometimes I felt a surge of hope and gave things back. "Diego, what if we write to someone? Think: who could it be? Or I'll go request an interview for you with some functionary while you wait outside." He just looked mournfully at me and didn't take the bait. "Don't you know a lawyer? There must be some of those little weasels still around. Or some closeted gay who occupies an important post? You've done a lot of people favors. I'll graduate in July; by October I'll be working. I can give you fifty pesos a month." Seeing that his eyes were tearing up, I stopped, but he always found a way to recover. "I'm going to give you one last bit of advice: pay more attention to your clothes. You're no Alain Delon, but you do have your charms and an air of mystery that, say what they will, always opens doors." Then I was the one who didn't know what to say; I lowered my head and rearranged his packages, preparing to take them away. "No, not those, no, no, don't open those! Those are Lezama's unpublished texts! Don't look at me like that. I swear that I will never misuse them. I know I swore I'd never leave, too, and I'm leaving, but that's different. I'll never bargain with them or give them to anybody who could use them politically. I swear. By my mother, by the basketball player, by you, just go. If I can make it through this tempest without them, I'll return them. Don't look at me like that! Do you think I don't understand my responsibility? But if I'm very threatened, I might need them. You're making me feel bad. Pour me a drink and go."

The closer the time for departure came, the more he languished. He slept badly and grew thin. I stayed with him as much as possible but he said little to me, and sometimes he hardly seemed to know I was there. Curled up in the John Donne armchair with a book of poems or a crucifix in his hands, because his religious leanings had intensified, he seemed pale and lifeless. Maria Callas kept him company, singing soft and low. One day he looked at me with particular interest (you will always be with me, Diego, I'll never forget that look of yours): "Tell me the truth, David," he asked, "do you love me? Has my friendship been useful to you? Was I disrespectful? Do you think I harmed the Revolution?" Maria Callas stopped singing. "Our friendship has been correct, and I respect you." He smiled. "Don't change the subject. I wasn't speaking of respect but of love between friends. Please don't be afraid of those words anymore." Which was what I also wanted to say but I have this difficulty, and since I was sure of my respect and the fact that I had changed, that I was somehow different because of our friendship, that I was more the person I had always wanted to be, I added, "I'd like to invite you to breakfast tomorrow at El Conejito. I'll go early and wait in line. You can come just before twelve. I'll pay. Or would you rather I came to get you and we went together?" "No, David, that's all right. Everything is fine as it is." "Diego, I insist. I know what I'm saying." "All right, but not El Conejito. In Europe I am going to be a vegetarian." And if what I wanted, or needed, was to display myself with him, if that was what would put me at peace with myself, well, he certainly obliged. He arrived at the restaurant at 11:45, just as the throng was milling up to the door, beneath a Japanese parasol, in an outfit that would stand out from two blocks away. He called out both my surnames from across the street, waving his arm, which was covered with bracelets. Coming up to me, he kissed me on the cheek, and he began to describe an expensive outfit he had just seen in a window display that would really just suit me — but to his surprise and mine and everyone's in line I rushed to the defense of another line of fashion with an enthusiasm that put his to shame, because when we timid souls really let loose, we become brilliant. At lunch, we celebrated the success of his technique for unbuttoning Communists; turning to my literary development, he added new titles to my reading list. "Don't forget the Countess of Merlin, you must look into her. Between that woman and you, you'll produce an encounter that will be talked about." We finished with dessert in Coppelia, and then a bottle of Stolichnaya at The Lair. It was wonderful, until we stopped drinking. "I needed that red vodka to tell you two last things, David. I left the most difficult for the end. I think, David, that you lack a bit of initiative. You must be more decisive. Your role is not that of the spectator but that of the actor. I assure you that this time you will acquit yourself better than you did in *A Doll's House*. Don't stop being a revolutionary. You might say, who am I to speak to you this way? But I do have the right; as I told you before, I am a patriot and a Lezamian. The Revolution needs people like you, not because of the Yankees, but because the food, the bureaucracy, the type of propaganda you people make and the arrogance with which you do so could put an end to it, and only people like you can prevent that. It won't be easy for you, you'll need spirit. Now, the other thing I have to tell you, we'll see if I can, because this makes me want to hide my face with shame . . . pour me some more vodka . . . remember when we met at the Coppelia? I behaved badly that day. None of that was casual. I was out with Germán, and when we saw you, we made a bet that I could get you to The Lair and get you into bed. The bet was in foreign currency, and I accepted it to motivate me to approach you, because I was always inhibited by a paralyzing respect for you. And when I spilled the milk on you, that was part of the plan. Your shirt together with the Spanish shawl on the balcony would be the signal of my triumph. Germán, naturally, spread it around everywhere, and even more now that he hates me. In some circles, since recently I've devoted myself exclusively to you, they call me the Red Queen, but others say that my leaving is just a feint, that I'm actually a spy for the West. Don't worry too much about this, when this kind of uncertainty clings to a man, far from damning him, it gives him mystery, and there are plenty of women

85

who will fall into your arms, attracted by the notion of restoring you to the straight and narrow. . . . Can you forgive me?" I was silent, which he interpreted as meaning that I could forgive him. "See, I'm not so good as you think. Would you have been capable of something like that, behind my back?" We looked at each other. "Well, I am going to make the last tea. Afterward you must go away and never return. I want no good-byes." And that was that. When I got to the street, I found a file of scouts blocking my way. Their uniforms looked freshly pressed and they all were carrying bunches of flowers; and though scouts with flowers have always been a rather corny symbol of the future, inseparable from those slogans that encourage us to "fight for a better world," still, they pleased me (perhaps for that very reason), and when I stopped to look at one of them he stuck out his tongue at me; and right then I told myself (I told myself, I didn't promise) that the next Diego who crossed my path I would defend heart and soul, even if nobody understood me, and I told myself that I was not going to feel alienated from my Spirit and my Conscience because of that; no, just the opposite: if I understood things rightly, this would be fighting for a better world for you, scout, and for me. So I want to end this by thanking you, Diego, for all that you did for me, for coming to the Coppelia and asking for ice cream the way you did. Because I rejected chocolate and selected strawberry.

The description of the lunch *à la Lezama* quotes from Lezama Lima's *Paradiso*, and the translator wishes to acknowledge passages from the fine translation by Gregory Rabassa of *Paradiso* by José Lezama Lima, copyright © 1968 by Ediciones Era, S.A., translation copyright © 1974 by Farrar, Straus & Giroux, Inc.

Mac Arthur's Life
Ian McDonald

What happen to old Mac Arthur
I wonder. They call he Barnyard
When he young, Slim Boy, Hot Cock,
All about town he run, crowing, mounting,
Sunlight and morning, stain-sky and night.
It so sweet, why he should bother about anything else
How a man like he could always find women?
He never pay but he always get. Something, boy,
Something in this world, people don't want lonely.
But he get old and begin to fall in trenches
Women ease he for a while, then drink.
Like he could always find women, he could always find
           drink.

He eye soft, people like he
He never pick up a stone to pelt.
The years go by so quick, life waste, life done.
The last I see Slim Boy he look groggy
And like he trying something new, I don't know.
Mass finish at Sacred Heart, I see he in a pew
Sink on the knee, head bend, one hand shaking.
But that was years ago, I don't know after.

Two Poems
Kamau Brathwaite

1
Bird Rising

Until it come to the time for the great myriad bird the Mithurii .
    to begin its ascent
its challenge against the earth . the paradoxical oracle of wind . the
    wings beating
unchaining. out. boarding as seamen might say . the great breast
    ruffled & rising
as in all the great legends

and this happening here before me under me now wonderfully
    surrounding me
the white silver louvered feather shift & chevron stretching out
    across the sunlight
the great terrible beauty & beating we have always heard about
beating beating upward & forward . the planks of its shape
    shivering at first like a ship

like a dhow . then spheering down into smooth as we scool
    up. wards

Now the first hills at the darker mountains of english . the sea
    below all shard
& silver like our shadow . the beacon topaz eyes unblinking even
    through all the shudder
the wings now stretched across all space openly & awesomely . so
    that we are not beating

any. more but ahh sailing something like singing . because at last
     I have been able

to use all the wounds in the language . as long as I lay them out
     softly & carefully
like these unfluttering feathers of song . like the sea below
     turning into a grey ball of wine
without fishes or sperm . like the darkness no longer lingering
     above us
but we moving towards it as part of its fuse & its future . the àxé
     & ayisha of sails

one last time in our ears . the earth gone a long time now from
     green spur arrogance
of john crow mountain. strange
not even the memory of a veiled carefree river in these high
     places . too far up now
for sunsets through all this rain & distance in our eyes. in our
     sleep. in our silence

the metaphor at last afloat almost alight in the darkness

2

Descending Gardens

From this high bough of glistance . stretch of air .
spinning in splendour down daylight arriving under the moon .
the dark broken into the ice of stars slowly losing their lustre

the great bird circling down through the high cloud
buffeting & like ploughing once more into a memory of like
     that water
we had almost forgotten .

slippering sipple over the white roof of rain .
seeing where it starts its sprinkle . the wind louder

now more buffeting of cloud . the fusilage of feathers shuddering
    into great plumages

coigns . valleys . canyons of what is now blue space

the sea at last recognized . remembered like a blue awhile .
more like a wheel now . still distant & dreaming between
    thunders .
the whales at last almost here with their wrinkled centuries of
    skin .

more blue . some green . widening out of their indigo . the great
    old ancient legendary
wings slanting & flattening out towards this new world our planet
as the eyes . all that night still unblinking . smelling earth. nest.
    rock. song. crying .

the forthcoming distance of ages . returning to what might be
    agony. stone. walls. weather-
falls . even beaches unrolling their blankets & reefs . the white
    water . people walking
into their various businesses . boys leaping into that blue crack of
    ocean .

gallileos of gardens all looking up. upwards towards us from
    where they have carved their
speckled squares & circles . flowers even birds tree-
top flamingoes . can you believe it .

animal eyes looking evening towards our arrival . our shadow at
    last travelling over the
brown lineage of ploughed land . cloudless of rain . loud in our
    praises .
raising even rising the voices of grasses .

lambs of withholding . forgiving . no
anger . blackbelly sheep . feeling stronger & stronger . no
longer that stranger of space in the new spoken language of
    certain .

Kamau Brathwaite

renewed in the vigour of this smooth unexpected returning .
    doorways at last so it seems
without danger . opening onto the raindrops of Dream Chad's long
    line of clotheslines
long line of headlights along the causeway . each one rainbow &
    full of the sun

of the morning

Consuelo's Letter
Julia Alvarez

THE OLD WOMAN CONSUELO, what a dream she had last night! She tossed and turned this way and that as if the dream were a large fish she were trying to haul in — without success. Finally she gave a great roll to one side and her little granddaughter Wendy let out a yelp that woke Consuelo up. *¡Dios santo!* She ran her hand over her face, wiping off sleep, and maybe it was in doing so that she lost a part of the dream which all the next day she was trying to recall.

In the dream Consuelo was counseling her daughter Ruth about her predicament. Consuelo had not seen her daughter since five years ago, when Ruth had come by the village with the surprise of a baby she had given birth to in the capital. Along with the infant, the daughter had brought an envelope of money. She counted out over two thousand pesos to leave with the grandmother. The rest was for a plan that Ruth would not tell the old woman about. "You'll just worry, Mamá," she had said, and then, throwing her arms around the old woman, she added, "Ay, Mamá, our lives are going to be so much better, you'll see."

And everything that had actually happened was also so in the dream. Ruth had made it to Puerto Rico on a rowboat, then on to Nueva York where she worked at a restaurant at night and at a private home as a maid during the day. Every month, Ruth sent home money along with a letter someone in the village read to Consuelo. Every few months the Codetel man came running through town. "International call!" Consuelo would be out of breath by the time she arrived at the telephone trailer to hear her daughter's small voice trapped in the wires. "How are you, Mamá? And my baby Wendy?" Consuelo would curse herself later, for she would fall into that mute bashfulness she always suffered in the presence of important people and their machines. Words to her were like the fine china at the big houses she had worked in, something she felt better if the mistress were handling.

Then, just as with her own Ruth, the dream Ruth had gotten

married. It was not a true marriage, she had explained in a letter, but one of convenience in order to get her residency. Consuelo prayed every night to el Gran Poder de Dios and la Virgencita to turn this mock marriage into a true one for her daughter's sake. He is a good man, the daughter had admitted. A Puerto Rican who wants to help a woman of a neighbor island. Hmmm. Then the letter that occasioned the dream had arrived. Even though she could not read the words, Consuelo studied the dark angry marks that were so different from the smoother roll of her daughter's usual handwriting. The man — it turned out — would not give Ruth a divorce. He was saying he was in love with her. If she tried to leave him, he was going to turn her in to the immigration police. What should she do? *¡Ay, Mamá, aconséjame!* It was the first time Consuelo's daughter had asked for her advice.

How she wished she could sit her daughter down and tell her what to do. Use your head, she would say. Here is a good man who says he loves you, *m'ija,* why even hesitate? You can have a fine life! It is within your grasp! Next time her daughter called, Consuelo would have her advice all prepared. For days as she washed or swept or cooked, Consuelo practiced saying the words, the little granddaughter looking up surprised to hear the taciturn old woman speaking to herself.

Then the shock of last night's dream! It was as if her daughter were by her side listening. But what Consuelo was saying was not what she had planned to say — that much she remembered. Her daughter was nodding her head, for Consuelo was speaking wonderful words that flowed out of her mouth as if language were a stream filled with silver fish flashing in the water. Everything she said was so wise that Consuelo wept in her own dream to hear herself speak such true words.

But the devil take her for forgetting what it was that she was saying! When she had run her hand over her face, she had wiped the words away. All morning, she tried to recall what it was she had said to her daughter in the dream . . . and once or twice . . . as she swept out the house . . . as she braided the child's hair into its three pigtails . . . as she pounded the coffee beans and the green smell of the mountains wafted up to her, why there it was, the tail of it, quick! grab it! But no, it inched just out of her reach.

And then, she could almost hear it, a far-off voice. She crossed the yard to María's house after it. Almost a year ago, María's youngest boy had drowned in Don Mundín's swimming pool.

María had stopped working in the big house, and even after the period of mourning, she continued to dress in black and to hold on to her grief as if it were the boy himself she were clutching to her side.

"I have had such a dream," Consuelo began. María had placed a cane chair under the samán tree for the old woman. She sat by, cleaning the noon rice in a hollow board on her lap. The child, accustomed only to the company of the old woman, hid her face in her grandmother's lap when María's boys beckoned to her to come look at the leaping lizard they had caught. "In the dream I was speaking to my Ruth. But this one woke me, and I cleaned my face before remembering, and there went the words." The old woman made the same gesture as María, flinging the rice chaff out beyond the shade of the samán tree.

"My Ruth has written for my advice," Consuelo went on. Among her own people and out of the sight and presence of the rich and their machines, the old woman found it much easier to speak her mind. "In the dream, the words came to me. But I have forgotten what it was I said to her."

María combed her fingers through the pile of rice as if the lost words could be found there. "You must go down to the river early in the morning," she began. With her long, sad face and her sure words, she was like the priest when he came up the mountain once a month to preach to the campesinos how to live their lives.

"You must wash your face three times, making a sign of the cross after each washing."

The old woman was listening carefully, her hands folded as if she were praying. The child at her side looked up at the old woman and then folded her small hands.

"And the words will come to you, and then immediately you must go to the Codetel and call your daughter —"

Just the thought of speaking into that black funnel stopped the words in Consuelo's throat. She took a deep breath and made the sign of the cross and the words blurted out. "I do not have a number for my daughter. She is always the one who calls."

María stood up and shook out her skirt. She called the child to her side and asked again how old the child was and whether she was going to school to learn her letters. The child shook her head and held up five fingers but then thought better of it and held up another five. Consuelo watched the playful conversation. A tender look had come on the grieving woman's face. It was as if she had forgotten the dream altogether.

María sat back down. The interlude with the child seemed to have put a new thought in her head. "You have gotten letters; there is an address on the envelopes, no?"

"I do not know," Consuelo shrugged. "There are marks on the envelopes."

"You must bring me the letters," María concluded. "And if there is an address, then a letter must be written with the words of advice that will come to you by the river tomorrow."

"Who shall write this letter?" Consuelo worried. She knew María could read letters, but Consuelo had never seen her write them. And once written, how would the letter be sent to the daughter?

"My hand is not good," María confessed, "but there is Paquita." Consuelo could see the same caution on María's face that she herself was feeling. The letter writer in town, Paquita Montenegro, always broadcast your business as if you were paying her, not just to write your letter, but to tell everyone about it. Consuelo did not want the whole village to know that Ruth had paid a man to marry her and was now wanting to divorce him. There was already enough talk about how Consuelo's good-looking daughter had come by the money to end up in Nueva York.

"I am thinking now," María said, interrupting the old woman's thoughts. "A woman has come to the big house. Don Mundín's relation. She is from there. She will help you write this letter and then she will see to it that your daughter receives it."

At these words, Consuelo could feel her old bones lock with fright. Before she would talk about her daughter's problem to a stranger, she would rather pay Paquita the forty pesos to write the letter and blab its contents to everyone. Again she found it hard to get the words out. "Ay, but to bother the lady . . . what if . . . I could not . . . ." Her voice died away.

But now María seemed more determined than ever. "What do you mean? They bother us enough when they want." Consuelo could see the face of the boy surfacing in the mother's face — before it was washed away by a look of terrible anger. "Sergio will take you tomorrow after the words come to you in the river." The younger woman grabbed the old woman's hand. "It will go well. You will see."

Consuelo did not know if it was the fierceness in María's eyes, but the look struck deep inside her, flushing out the words that she had spoken in the dream! Right then and there, she knew exactly what it was she must say in the letter this stranger would write to her daughter.

Just as Sergio had reported on their walk over to the big house, Don Mundín's relation was so easy. She was standing at the door, waiting for them — as if they were important guests she had been expecting. She was not the usual run of rich ladies, calling your name until they wore it down to nothing but the sound of an order. All her life, Consuelo had worked for many such fine ladies who kept everything under lock and key as if their homes were warehouses in which to store valuable things.

But this lady addressed her as Doña Consuelo and asked to be called Yo. "It's my baby name and it stuck," she explained. And what a little lady she was — you could fit two or three of her inside Ruth and still have room for little Wendy. She was dressed in pants and a jersey shirt, all in white like someone about to make her first communion. She spoke easily and gaily, words just sputtering from her lips. "So, Doña Consuelo, Sergio says you need help with a letter?"

Consuelo prepared to say something.

"What a pretty little girl!" The lady crouched down, crooning until the child was beside herself with fear and excitement. Before Consuelo knew it, the child's pockets were full of Don Mundín's mints and the lady had promised that before they left, she would take the child out to see the swimming pool shaped like a kidney bean. No one seemed to have informed the lady that only last summer in that pool, María and Sergio had lost their boy, no bigger than this little girl.

"We do not want . . . ," Consuelo began. "We ask pardon for the molestation." Her heart was beating so loud she could not hear herself thinking.

"No bother at all. Come in and sit down. Not on that old bench." And the lady pulled Consuelo by the hand just as little Wendy did when she wanted the old woman to come attend to something. Consuelo felt her heart slowing to a calmer rhythm.

Soon, they were settled in the soft chairs of the living room, drinking Coca-Colas from fancy fluted glasses. Every time Consuelo took a sip of the syrupy liquid, the ice tinkled against the glass in a way that made her feel distracted. She kept reminding the child to hold her glass with both hands as she herself was doing.

But the lady did not seem fazed by all the breakable things

97

around her. She propped her glass on the arm of the couch, and went on speaking, waving her hand within inches of the vase beside her. Consuelo pulled the packet of letters from the sack and waited for a pause in which she could insert her request. But the lady spoke on, a whole stream of words whose sense Consuelo could not always follow. How beautiful the mountains were, how she had come for a month to see if she couldn't get some writing done, how she had noticed that so many families in the village were headed by single mothers —

"The child is my granddaughter," Consuelo informed her. She did not want the lady to get the wrong idea that in her old age Consuelo had been going behind the palms with a man.

"Ay, I didn't mean that!" The lady laughed, slapping the air with her hand. Her eye fell on the packet of letters in the old woman's lap. "But let's get to your letter. Sergio told me about your daughter. . . ." And off she was again, telling Consuelo all about Ruth going to Puerto Rico in a rowboat, about Ruth living in New York, working hard at two jobs. It did spare Consuelo the trouble of having to tell the story from the very start.

A silence followed the lady's coming to the end of what she knew. Now it was Consuelo's turn. She began haltingly. Each time she stopped, at a loss for words, the lady's eager look reassured her. Consuelo told how Ruth had married a Puerto Rican man, how she had done so for her residency, how the man had fallen in love. As she spoke, the lady kept nodding as if she knew exactly what it was that Consuelo's Ruth had been going through.

"But now she has written for my advice." Consuelo patted the packet of letters on her lap. "And in my dream it came what I should say to her."

"How wonderful!" the lady exclaimed, so that Consuelo felt momentarily baffled as to what exactly the lady felt was so extraordinary. "I mean that your dreams tell you things," the lady added. "I've tried, but I can never make sense of them. Like before I got divorced, I asked my dreams if I should leave my husband. So I dreamed a little dog bites my leg. Now what's that supposed to mean?"

Consuelo could not say for sure. But she urged the lady to visit María, who would know what to make of the little dog.

The lady waved the suggestion away. "I've got two therapist sisters who are full of theories about the little dog." She laughed, and her eyes had a faraway look as if she could see all the way home to the two sisters giving the little dog a bone.

Consuelo eased the topmost letter from the packet in her lap and watched as the lady read through this last letter Ruth had written. She seemed to have no trouble with the writing — Ruth had a pretty hand — but as her eyes descended on the page, she began shaking her head. "Oh my God!" she finally said, and looked up at Consuelo. "I don't believe this!"

"We must write to my daughter," Consuelo agreed.

"We sure should!" the lady said, pulling over the coffee table so that it was right in front of her. On it lay a tablet of clean paper and a pretty silver pen that gleamed like a piece of jewelry. The lady looked over at Consuelo. "How do you want to start?"

Consuelo had never written a letter, so she could not say. She glanced back at the woman for help.

"My dear daughter Ruth," the lady suggested, and at Consuelo's nod, she wrote out the words quickly as if it took no effort at all. The child came forward on the couch to look at the lady's hand dancing across the paper. The lady smiled and offered the child some sheets as well as a colored pencil. "You want to draw?" she asked. The child nodded shyly. She knelt on the floor in front of the table and looked down at the clean sheet of paper the lady had placed before her. Finally, the child picked up her colored pencil, but she did not make a mark.

"Okay, so far we've got, *My dear daughter Ruth,*" the lady said, "What else?"

"*My dear daughter Ruth,*" Consuelo repeated. And the ring and skip of those words were like a rhyme the child often said to herself skipping in a ray of sunshine. "*I have received your letter and in my dream came these words which this good lady is helping me to write down here with all due respect to el Gran Poder de Dios and gratitude to la Virgencita without whose aid nothing can be done.*" It was just as it had been in her dream: the words came tumbling from her tongue!

But the lady was looking at her, perplexed. "It's kind of hard . . . you haven't really . . ." Now she was the one at a loss for words. "It's not a sentence," she said at last, and then she must have seen that Consuelo had no idea what she meant because she added, "Let's say one thing at a time, okay?"

Consuelo nodded. "You're the one who knows," she said politely. It was a phrase she had been taught to say when asked by the rich for an opinion.

"No, no, it's your letter." The lady smiled sadly. She looked down at the paper as if it would tell her what to do. "Never mind, it's fine," the lady said, and she marked a whole half page in her quicksilver hand and turned the paper over. "Okay, let 'em come!" She whooped as if she were urging lazy cows across the evening pasture.

"My daughter, you must think of your future and the future of your child for as you yourself know marriage is a holy vow—" Consuelo stopped briefly to catch her breath, and for a moment, she could not go on. She had begun to wonder if these indeed were the words she had spoken in her dream or had she confused them with what she herself had wanted to say to her daughter?

"And so my daughter, honor this man, and he will stop beating you if you do not provoke him for as the good priest has taught us we women are subject to the wisdom and judgment of our fathers and of our husbands if they are good enough to stay with us."

The lady lay the pen on top of the paper and folded her arms. She looked over at Consuelo and shook her head. Her face had the stony gravity of María's face. "I'm sorry. I can't write that."

Consuelo's hand flew to her mouth. Maybe she had misspoken? Maybe this young woman, skinny as a nun at Lent, maybe she could tell that Consuelo was not speaking the correct words. For a second time, the words of her dream seemed to have fled her memory. "My daughter will make another foolish choice," Consuelo pleaded. She indicated the child with her chin in order to present proof of Ruth's errors without giving the child the evil eye by saying so. The little granddaughter, who had been studying her blank sheet for a while, bore down on her pencil and made a mark.

The lady bit her lips as if to keep back the words that were always so ready on her tongue. But a few slipped out, full of emotion. "How can you advise your daughter to stay with a man who beats her?"

"The man would not beat her if she did as she was told. She should think of her future. I have always advised her to think of her future." Again, Consuelo felt the words she was speaking were not the wonderful words of the dream that had drawn agreement even from the stubborn Ruth. In a much smaller voice, she concluded, "She has always been too willful."

"Good for her!" The lady gave a sharp nod. "She needs a strong will. Look at all she's done. Risked her life at sea . . . supported herself on two jobs . . . sent money home every month." She was counting out the reasons on her fingers like the shopkeeper counting out the money you owed him.

Consuelo found herself nodding. This woman had an eye that could see the finest points like the eyes of the child, who could thread a needle in the evening light.

"If I were you, I definitely would not advise her to stay with a man who abuses her," the lady was saying, "but, I mean, you write what you want."

But Consuelo did not know how to write. The brute of a man who had been her father had beat her good and hard whenever he found her wasting time like the child now bent over her sheet of paper. "You have reason," she said to the lady. "Let us say so to my Ruth."

She had meant for the lady's words to be added to the ones that had already been written. But the lady crumpled the sheet in her hand, and commenced a new letter. The child retrieved the crushed letter, unfolded it and ironed it out with the flat of her small hand.

"My dear Ruth," the lady began, *"I have thought long and hard about what you have written to me.* Does that sound all right?" The lady looked up.

"Sí, señora." Consuelo sat back in the soft chair. This indeed was a better start.

"You have proven yourself a strong and resourceful woman and I am very proud of you."

"I am very proud of her," Consuelo agreed. Her eyes were filling with tears at the true sound of these words of praise for her daughter.

"You entered upon a clear agreement with this man, and now he refuses to honor it. How can you trust him if he so badly abuses your trust?"

"That is so," Consuelo said, nodding deeply. She thought of Ruth's father, stealing into the servants' quarters in the middle of the night, reeking of rum, helping himself to what he wanted. The next morning, Consuelo was up at dawn preparing the silver tray so it would be ready when the mistress rang the bell in her bedroom.

"A man who strikes a woman does not deserve to be with her," the lady wrote.

"A man who lifts a hand," Consuelo echoed. *"Ay, my poor Ruth . . . you should not suffer so. . . ."* Again Consuelo felt the words knotting in her throat, but this time, it was not from

101

bashfulness, but from the strength of her emotion.

"And so, Ruth, you must find a way to get help. There are agencies in the city that you can call. Do not lose heart. Do not let yourself get trapped in a situation where you are not free to speak your own mind."

And as the lady spoke and wrote these words, Consuelo could feel her dream rising to the surface of her memory. And it seemed to her that these were the very words she had spoken that Ruth had been so moved to hear. "Yes," she kept urging the lady. "Yes, that is so."

As the lady was addressing the envelope, the child held up the sheet she had filled with little crosses, copying the lady's hand. Consuelo felt a flush of tender pride to see that the child was so apt. And the lady was pleased as well. "You wrote your mami, too!" she congratulated, and she folded the child's letter in the envelope along with Consuelo's letter.

From Dancing on Her Knees
Nilo Cruz

Characters:
FRANCINE, a man in his mid-thirties, cross-dresser, born in 1954
RAMONA, a woman in her early fifties (1930–1983)
FEDERICO, a man in his mid-forties (1938–1983)
ROSARIO DEL CIELO, an angel or caretaker; a woman in her
    mid-twenties
ANUNCIO, an angel or caretaker, a man in his mid-twenties
MATTHIAS, a man in his late thirties; he used to live around the
    late 1800s

*Time and place: Late eighties. November the 2nd, All Souls'
Day. Miami Beach, Florida.*

*(Setting: There is sand on the floor and a few scattered big
trunks. To the right of the stage there is an altar with a
white cloth; on top there are old photographs, candles,
flowers and other paraphernalia. By the altar there is a
wooden chair. To the left of the stage there stands another
wooden chair. A large backdrop of blue and white painted
cabanas against a blue sky frames the stage.)*

Note: The Caretakers are the angels of death, at other times
informers, spies and loving spirits who have a good time
while doing their job. They must be playful and have fun
while on duty.

MY ALTAR OF SOULS
Prologue

*(FRANCINE plays a bolero and is dancing with a photo she
holds in her hand. She makes her way to the altar and kneels
down by a box of photographs. She takes a cloth and begins
to polish the frame of the picture.)*

103

FRANCINE. Been listening to our old music, Evaristo. Pulled out all those old records . . . Couldn't help myself. Things have to be dusted. Aired. (*As if she hears him.*) I KNOW . . . I KNOW . . . I CAN HEAR YOU FROM UP THERE . . . YOU DON'T WANT ME TO GET MELANCHOLIC. But things inside the chest have to be dusted too. Have to take a broom and sweep the heart. Brush and scrub the whole thing. — No regrets, I tell you. I wear an emotional girdle, Evaristo. A bustier, to keep my heart contained. Not a tear shed when I listen to those old songs. Maybe one . . . two . . . three . . . four tears . . . Ay, five! . . . Can't help it . . . — YES, I CAN JUST HEAR YOU FROM UP THERE. (*Upwards in a louder voice.*) "THERE SHE GOES AGAIN. SHE'S TURNING INTO AN AQUARIUM OF TEARS." I DON'T GIVE A HOOT WHAT YOU SAY TO ME! BUT THINGS COME UNDONE, *COÑO* . . . They get to me. (*Starts to light some of the candles.*)

Do you like my altar, Evaristo? Is it all right if I place this picture next to yours? My uncle Alejandro Luján and his wife Iluminada . . . I know you won't mind. Such a beautiful couple those two . . . But what misfortune . . . He choked on a chicken bone. It got stuck in his throat and he died. Two weeks later, Iluminada, his wife, dies after him. *Yes,* she was running after a rooster in the middle of the field and got struck down by lightning. Some people say it was fate. I say it was love. Yes, LOVE, Evaristo! — I can sense you don't believe me. She couldn't bear to live without her husband. — That story gets to me. But I'm not asking you to love me like that. Please, don't get any ideas! I don't want to get struck down by lightning. Just to know that you can hear me in the sky is a consolation . . . Just to know that maybe you'll come down for All Souls' Day makes me happy. See how I sprinkled petals on the floor so all my loved ones could make their way back to the world. To my altar. Is it all right if I place this picture of Federico and Ramona on this other side? I know you won't say no to that. That must've been another love story. Nobody can outdo those two when it comes to dancing the tango and the rumba. Not even you and I. Ay no, Evaristo . . . This is getting to me, and I know you don't like that. WHAT YOU SHOULD DO IS COME AFTER ME WITH A SHOE, A BELT! THROW A BUCKET OF RAIN AT ME, A PIECE OF THE SKY, DUST FROM A STAR, OR COME THROUGH

THAT DOOR AS YOU SHOULD FOR ALL SOULS' AND MAKE YOUR PRESENCE KNOWN TO ME. — Would you come to me for All Souls' Day? *(More contained.)* I'm sorry, Evaristo. Sometimes I tell myself, Francine, you must learn to speak the language of the other side. You must learn to speak with your mouth shut. In silence. But can you hear me if I speak with no voice? Can you hear my voice from under my skin? . . . From under my face . . . My eyes . . . From under my bones and my knees? Like this. *(Kneels down.)*

(Lights fade.)

COMING BACK TO WHAT THEY LEFT BEHIND

Scene 1

(Early morning lights. Mambo music plays. RAMONA, FEDERICO *and* FRANCINE *dance. They each take turns doing their best steps on the center of the stage.* RAMONA *runs to a chair and sits. She does her dancing steps from this position. The* CARETAKERS *stand to the left of the upstage area. The woman sits on the man's shoulders, looking through a pair of opera glasses. Music plays under dialogue.)*

RAMONA. Yes . . . Francine . . . Look at me, Francine . . . Federico, look here, I'm dancing sitting down . . . Pah . . . rah . . . ran . . . panh . . . Oh, I can tell Fedo is in a good mood. Do your steps.

FEDERICO. *(Does a dance step.)*

RAMONA. That's it, Fedo . . . Do your steps. Celebrate your soul. *(*FEDO *demonstrates his best steps.)* Celebrate your spirit, Federico.

FEDERICO. Se acabó.

RAMONA. Tomorrow is All Souls' Day. Oh, I can feel light entering me, as if someone has lit a candle in front of me to light my way.

FEDERICO. See, you want to dance sitting down, but you won't dance with me. Why don't you dance with me?

RAMONA. I'm not dancing anymore. Dance with Francine . . .

105

FRANCINE. Dance with him, Ramona . . . I want to see you two dance.

FEDERICO. She won't dance with me. She won't come near me . . .

RAMONA. He knows why I won't dance with him. He knows why . . .

FEDERICO. Bah! In limbo. Still stuck in the past. Tell her to wake up. To snap out of it.

RAMONA. Tell him to touch me, to pinch me so he can see how awake I am. Just touch me, Federico. — Ha! He knows I'll bite his hand.

FEDERICO. Turn up the music! And turn it up loud!

RAMONA. No! I don't need for you to listen to me. I don't want to talk to you. I can talk to Francine. Francine, are you enjoying yourself?

FRANCINE. Well, all of a sudden, I don't know what to say . . . It's as if I have lost a book of instructions and I can't assemble myself. You two right here. The two dancers I admire the most. — And me here stupefied, wishing I lived in a better place. Wishing I had hired a mariachi band to play Mexican ballads.

RAMONA. Oh, but it's all coming back to me, Francine . . . The smell of things. The fragrance of memories. You'll have to take me to the Barcelona Hotel. I want to go up on the roof. And you'll have to take him too . . . Tell him to go upstairs and smell the pigeon shit on the roof. There's something about that smell mixed with feathers that will remind him of the past.

FEDERICO. See, still in limbo. Mad. Drunk. Who wants to go back to an old roof and smell shit! Talking about pigeon shit . . . (*To* RAMONA.) How many drinks have you had?

RAMONA. I'm not drunk. Don't insinuate that I'm drunk. — I know what I'm saying, Francine. When he goes upstairs to that roof, it will all come back to him. Tinn . . . Like a Chinese bell . . . He'll remember the past . . . Embracing and rolling on the pigeon shit. Practicing our steps up there on the roof. I had a firm body then. Strong legs. I could jump high. I was a gazelle. My legs were my pride and my butt. I had a round butt. He used to say that my butt was so round it emanated a halo, like Saturn.

106

FEDERICO. And you never gave it to me.

RAMONA. Vulgar!!! That's one thing you'll never get from me.

FRANCINE. Ay! Ramona, why not give him everything?

RAMONA. Bah! You give him a finger and he takes your whole hand.

FRANCINE. Why not give him the moon!

FEDERICO. *La luna* . . .

RAMONA. What moon and what moon! Oh, I forgot you like all that.

FRANCINE. Oh, you two should go upstairs and dance on the roof like before. When was the last time you danced? [*There is a pause.*]

RAMONA. Ask him . . . He can tell you . . . He can tell you all about it.

FRANCINE. Where was it, Federico? Where did you dance?

RAMONA. Why don't you tell her all about it, Fedo? [*Pause.*] Why don't you say something?

FEDERICO. [*To* RAMONA.] You like to bother me, don't you?

RAMONA. Does it make you uncomfortable to talk about it? Does it bother you to talk about the cruise ship you took me to dance on?

FEDERICO. Why would it bother me? [Still looking at RAMONA but talking to FRANCINE.] It was a dance floor in the middle of the sea, Francine . . .

RAMONA. In the middle of a bathtub. In the middle of nowhere, with nothing but sharks and drowsy seasick tourists.

FEDERICO. [*Towards* RAMONA.] Uh-huh — . . . Drowsy seasick tourists . . . The ship with the blinking lights and round mirror ball and the passengers guzzling down their drinks, stuffing themselves with food then vomiting over the railing. How do you like that, Francine?

RAMONA. You're an oaf. A scumball. He does that to pester me.

107

FEDERICO. (*Enacts introduction to the dance.*) Punparanh . . . pan . . . pah . . . Welcome aboard the Transmarine ship, Francine . . . I'm Federico San Miguel and she's Ramona Soniat.

RAMONA. You're a fool! Someone should cut off your tongue!

FEDERICO. Punparan . . . pan . . . pah . . . She traveled the world dancing the cancan, until she met the great Federico in Havana . . .

RAMONA. Bah! My disgrace!

FEDERICO. . . . Kin . . . kon . . . koon . . . Pa . . . rah . . . ra . . . rah . . . Together they dance the tango, the rrrrumba, the mambo, the pachanga . . . What a pachanga, Caballero! *Tremendo tumbao* . . . Pim . . . pam . . . panh . . . — What do you have to say to that, enh! What do you have to say!

FRANCINE. Oh, it sounds adventurous, Ramona. What country did the cruise ship sail to?

RAMONA. (*Turns away. Fans herself.*) That's it . . . It didn't go anywhere. It sailed around the harbor.

FEDERICO. She always looks for the drama in things.

RAMONA. — Well you didn't care! You didn't care! I have dignity! I have dignity, you hear!

FEDERICO. I'm a performer. I can dance anywhere.

RAMONA. I'm not a performer. I'm a dancer.

FEDERICO. Enh, once I had my costume on I was a different man. Completely transformed.

RAMONA. Yes, a buffoon. A fool. I'm not wasting my day on this! Let's go for a walk, Francine.

FRANCINE. That was the past, Ramona. It's all behind you now! Don't let it get to you.

FEDERICO. That's right. Life is about the foot you have in front of you, not the one behind. The one behind is just there to give you impulse. The one behind is the past. I always say . . . I always say to myself . . . Federico . . . Don't step out of bed with your two feet . . . One foot at a time . . . Now take your step . . . Your

left foot . . . Step with your left foot, like the Egyptian statues . . .
Sculpted with their left foot in front.

RAMONA. Well you got out of bed on the wrong foot and tripped
over your shoes when you danced in your cruise ship . . . Let's
go, Francine, he's not going to spoil my day. Let's go out for a
walk on the beach.

FEDERICO. Aren't you going to invite me? *(Slight pause.)*

FRANCINE. *(Looks at both of them.)* Of course you're being invited.
I just don't want you two fighting. You should enjoy your time
here.

RAMONA. Forgive us, Francine. Forgive him. He's forgotten what
it is like to be living in the world. That rum he used to drink
distilled his manners.

FEDERICO. Oh, I have manners, my cappuccino.

RAMONA. Yes, I taught you manners. You should've seen him
when we met, Francine. Feral. Undomesticated. A beast.

FEDERICO. What? . . . What? . . . You fell at my feet. Tell me you
didn't fall at my feet when we met.

RAMONA. *(Fans herself.)* Bah, you were the one who was after me.
From the moment I got to Havana from Paris, you were after
my skirt. Went to see me dance every night at the Copa.

FRANCINE. *(Applauds.)* Ah! This is what I like. It's like starting
all over again, isn't it?

RAMONA. Bah! Look at him smiling. He thinks he's funny. Look
at those teeth of his. He's a goat that chews and eats everything.
He used to eat my pearl earrings, Francine.

FRANCINE. Oomph! A man who eats pearls!

RAMONA. Oh, it was terrible, Francine. He would swallow them.
I couldn't wear pearls.

FEDERICO. I bought you lots of pearls.

RAMONA. Bah! From Taiwan.

FEDERICO. They were round and per-fect.

RAMONA. Well, I never liked pearls from Taiwan.

FEDERICO. What did you want me to do? Did you want me to scuba dive into the toilet and save your pearls from my shit?

RAMONA. See, he's vulgar.

FRANCINE. Oh, you two! Look at this picture I have of you dancing a waltz. (*Takes photo from altar.*) Why can't it be like this? Look at you dancing. Look at those smiles. You're here for such a short time, why fight? Look at this other picture I have of you two dancing the tango. And look at this one of me imitating you, Ramona. This is when Evaristo and I used to do our Federico and Ramona show. Didn't I capture your essence, Ramona? Look at this photo.

RAMONA. You do resemble me a little.

FRANCINE. Oh, it was something. I used to love doing an impersonation of you.

FEDERICO. You look exactly like Ramona in that photo.

RAMONA. And so does her partner, Federico. He looks exactly like you.

FRANCINE. That's what everybody used to say. That took three hours of makeup and preparation. Almost the same time that it takes for heart surgery. And look at this picture of La Argentina. I liked doing an impersonation of her too. That took four hours of makeup. Thank God I'm bad at arithmetic; I don't want to think of all those hours I've spent in front of a mirror. — But you were my favorite, Ramona. Look at this other picture I stole from the library. (*Reads from card.*) La Argentina, a unique figure in the history of dance. Hers was a career of strange contrasts, glorious triumphs and bitter disappointments.

RAMONA. Exactly like me. That part describes me. Bitter disappointments. (*Looks at* FEDERICO.) Continue reading, Francine.

FRANCINE. Stripped bare the Spanish dances of the mannerisms and vulgarities . . .

RAMONA. Federico?

FEDERICO. I heard it . . . I heard it . . .

RAMONA. You need to hear it again. Read it again, Francine.

FRANCINE. Stripped bare the Spanish dances of the mannerisms and vulgarities . . .

RAMONA. Vulgarities. That's the word.

FEDERICO. You're insane, Ramona . . . You're insane. You're the one who pesters. I'm the one who's leaving . . . You're insane . . . You're the goat around here. (*Exits yelling the lines.*) . . . A crazy goat . . . A crazy goat . . . A loon . . . *Loca* . . . Crazy . . . A crazy goat . . . *Loca . . . Loca . . . Loca . . . Una chiva loca . . . chiva loca . . .*

RAMONA. (*After a pause.*) He knows what I'm talking about . . . He'll remember the past, the good years when I used to dance with him . . . (RAMONA *fans herself.* FRANCINE *does the same. Lights change. Spotlight on the* CARETAKERS. *She is sitting on his shoulders looking through a pair of binoculars.*)

ROSARIO DEL CIELO. What do you know about what is a little and and what is a lot?

ANUNCIO. A lot is you sitting on my shoulders . . .

ROSARIO DEL CIELO. I can see them better from here.

ANUNCIO. Aren't you getting a little carried away with all this?

ROSARIO DEL CIELO. Move me to the right.

ANUNCIO. (*Walks to right side.*) Did you hear what I said?

ROSARIO DEL CIELO. Stop. This is good. I said stop. Put me down. Everything seems so familiar to me — the houses, floors, chairs. They say that the secret to life is in the belly button. That's what differentiates humans from angels. Wouldn't you like to have a belly button? One of those little holes in the belly. And wouldn't you like for me to have long eye lashes like Francine?

ANUNCIO. Hunh! I can tell you're falling for it.

ROSARIO DEL CIELO. Falling for what?

ANUNCIO. The world. Material things, like fake eyelashes and belly buttons.

ROSARIO DEL CIELO. Those are the tiniest things a person can have.

ANUNCIO. It's still something.

ROSARIO DEL CIELO. Is that why you called me a whore, because I told you I wanted a pair of earrings like Francine's?

ANUNCIO. You were so busy looking at Francine, you didn't even hear what I said.

ROSARIO DEL CIELO. You're a moron. You don't even know what a whore is.

ANUNCIO. Give me the glass. Give me the thing.

ROSARIO DEL CIELO. I'm not giving you anything.

ANUNCIO. See, you've turned wild and reckless since we got here. Like a . . . Like a . . . Not even human . . . Like a wild beast. An animal, capable of doing something violent.

ROSARIO DEL CIELO. You were the one who used to say, Save yourself for All Souls' Day. Save yourself until we get down there. When we get there we could have a taste of life. You said we could act as people and be ordinary. And now we're here for All Souls' Day and nothing. Nothing.

ANUNCIO. All right, so that's what I told you. But all in due time. All in due time . . . You have to be patient, Rosario.

ROSARIO DEL CIELO. There's not much time. The holiday doesn't last forever. I feel like shouting at them. Going over there.

ANUNCIO. Are you crazy?!

ROSARIO DEL CIELO. Move back. Quick. Fast.

ANUNCIO. What's going on?

ROSARIO DEL CIELO. Federico is putting on his hat. Francine is also putting on a hat.

ANUNCIO. Let's get the bicycle. They're going out.

ROSARIO DEL CIELO. Wait a minute! Move back, jerk . . . I don't want them to see us. Back. Back up . . .

(*Lights change.* RAMONA *and* FRANCINE *are fanning themselves.* FEDERICO *is dressed elegantly in a white suit and two-tone shoes. He wears a Panama hat.*)

112

FEDERICO. Well, that's the way things are. I keep repeating myself. These clothes. This hat. These shoes. We are here today and gone tomorrow . . . I keep repeating it to myself. Gone out there . . . Gone out there tomorrow in the distance. And all those wasted days. All those days I spent talking at the barber shop. Wasted. Gone. All that time gone in conversations and hair spilled on the floor. The scissors clipping away. The barber's blade shaving my face. How I spent my life in idle conversations. But that's the way things are, I keep repeating it to myself. — That's why if we're here for so little time, we should do something special. We should go flying on the Goodyear blimp, Ramona. What do you say to that? My Ramona. My beloved Ramona.

RAMONA. Well, I prefer to take a taxi and let it take us around the city. Isn't that a better idea? Where we can see people, life.

FRANCINE. We can also go for a picnic. I can make ham sandwiches, with mustard, lettuce and tomatoes.

FEDERICO. *(Raises his arm.)* I vote for a ride on the Goodyear blimp.

FRANCINE. *(Raises her arm.)* Well, I vote for a ride on the blimp too.

RAMONA. I vote for a ride in a car. I'm not flying on a blimp. That's out of the question. If we're here for a short time, I don't want to spend my day on a zeppelin.

FRANCINE. It could be romantic, being up there in the clouds.

FEDERICO. See, Francine says the blimp is romantic.

RAMONA. I don't. You can do that with your time if you like, Federico. And you can do that with your time, Francine. I want my shoes to stay on the ground. I want to walk on the earth. I don't want to look out the window of a blimp and look at little houses, like in a monopoly game. I want to be inside houses with people — life. If you want to ride the blimp, you can ride the blimp with Francine. Francine, do you want to ride the zeppelin with Federico?

FRANCINE. I will be delighted. That is, if you don't mind me going with him, and he would like company.

FEDERICO. I wanted to go for a ride with you, Ramona. Why don't you ask me if I want to ride the blimp with Francine?

113

FRANCINE. What's the matter, you don't want to be seen with me? He probably doesn't want to be seen with someone like me. Ha!

FEDERICO. I didn't say that! Did you hear me say that?

RAMONA. You didn't. But I know you. And so does she. She knows your type.

FEDERICO. Type? What type am I? What type am I, Francine?

FRANCINE. In the ice cream category, the pasta category or the fruit category?

FEDERICO. Don't talk smart to me or I'll cut off your tongue!

RAMONA. You do something to her and I'll tear you to pieces!

FEDERICO. She's getting fresh with me. She's got to respect me, I'm a man!

RAMONA. And so is she.

FRANCINE. Yes, don't forget that!

FEDERICO. She . . . She's not a man . . . Not in that getup. Not in that dress.

FRANCINE. Good, you fell for it!

RAMONA. Forgive him, Francine. Don't mind him. I won't let him touch you with a finger.

FRANCINE. I don't mind if he touches me. I'm not as delicate as he thinks I am. He doesn't know me. I'm a mystery to him. An intriguing mystery. Well, that takes care of that! He can fly on the big old blimp by himself. Let him go up there alone in a balloon. You and I can go out and have some fun. So what are we going to do? What do you want to do?

RAMONA. You're right, he chose too much for me in life. Now I'll choose.

FRANCINE. Yes, that's a woman.

FEDERICO. (*Mimicking.*) Yes, that's a woman. — She'll make a scarecrow out of you.

FRANCINE. Yes, a scarecrow, that will scare you away. Suaaahh . . . Suaaahhh . . . A drunk spirit she doesn't need to follow.

FEDERICO. I'm going to cut off your tongue. *Bruja!* Witch!

RAMONA. Stop it, Federico. Stop it.

FEDERICO. You choose what you want to do, Ramona. Choose. I'm waiting.

FRANCINE. We can go to the movies.

RAMONA. I want to see real people. Life.

FRANCINE. Then we can go to the theatre.

RAMONA. I want to see trees, birds, nature.

FEDERICO. We can go to the zoo.

FRANCINE. You both can go to the zoo. I'm not going to the zoo. Well, maybe you two want to decide what you want to do alone. After all you should decide, it's your holiday. I'll leave you two. I'm going to my mailbox for my unemployment check. (FRANCINE *exits.*)

FEDERICO. (*After a pause.*) Everything's gone to the dogs, Ramona. You talk about us making fools of ourselves in the cruise ship, and look at who you have doing an impersonation of you.

RAMONA. If you so much as open your mouth one more time and offend Francine, I'm leaving.

FEDERICO. So you don't mind a scarecrow like her doing an impersonation of you.

RAMONA. I can't control what other people do.

FEDERICO. It's demeaning.

RAMONA. There's nothing I can do. And there's nothing you can do about it. I didn't sign a contract for her to do an impersonation of me. You were the one who signed a contract and sold my feet, our dance. And all for nothing! Nothing! To dance on a cruise ship.

FEDERICO. You're never going to forgive me, enh? Why can't it be like before?

RAMONA. Of course it will never be like before. We've gone through this already.

115

FEDERICO. I thought that maybe now that we've come back . . .

RAMONA. You're free. You're free to do whatever you want to do. You can go out there . . . Go out there and drink and dance with somebody else.

FEDERICO. Suppose . . .

RAMONA. I won't fall into the trap of supposing. (*Pause.*) It was like selling our bodies . . . You taking my legs from me and selling them. That's what you did. How can I forget so easily?

FEDERICO. But I love you, Ramona. I love you.

(*The* CARETAKERS *enter dancing. A mambo plays.*)

ROSARIO DEL CIELO. If we were in Mexico we would be having a party! We would be strolling down the streets to the graveyards dancing and singing with the dead. What do you have to say to that, enh? What do you have to say?!

ANUNCIO. Punparanh . . . pan . . . pah! And I'd be there with my guitar singing Mexican ballads dancing the rumba, doing the mambo and the guaracha, for the Day of the Dead. What do you have to say to that, enh? Are you enjoying your stay, Federico and Ramona?

FEDERICO. Yes, we are.

RAMONA. Yes, of course we are.

ANUNCIO. Well, we thought we might just drop in to see how you're getting along.

FEDERICO. We're fine. We're fine.

RAMONA. Yes . . . We're fine.

ANUNCIO. Well, we're just doing our job. Just doing our job, being the good angels that we are. Come on and dance with us. You two need to dance. You need to dance like before. Dance with her, Federico.

ROSARIO DEL CIELO. Yes, come and dance with us. You must dance with us. (ANUNCIO *brings them together and forces them to dance. The mambo plays again. Then stops.*)

ANUNCIO. Mira . . . before we get carried away. We thought we might just remind you of the rules for All Souls' Day.

FEDERICO. We know the rules. We know the rules . . .

ANUNCIO. Yes, you must ascend after sundown on November the second, and all worldly possessions must be left behind. Please, don't take a bottle with you . . .

FEDERICO. We know . . . We know . . . We've been told . . .

ANUNCIO. Well, you've been drinking. Alcohol makes people forget. Isn't that why people drink? Remember Evangelina . . .

ROSARIO DEL CIELO. I remember Evangelina . . . She came down for All Souls' Day. Had a good time. Drank as much as she could before ascending to the blue. Poor thing, forgot all the rules of the holiday. Climbed all the way to the sky with her wedding gown. Wanted to take her dress for keepsake. When she got to the heavenly gates we had to toss the white thing back to earth. (*Mambo plays. Then stops.*)

ANUNCIO. (*Joins* FEDERICO *to dance.*) Remember that couple Abelino and Georgina . . .

ROSARIO DEL CIELO. Yes, I remember Abelino and Georgina. Stubborn souls, tried to linger after the holiday.

ANUNCIO. Uh-huh . . . hardheaded souls. They bought wigs and sunglasses, bought designer clothes, changed their names, took an airplane to Portugal and didn't return to the sky after All Souls' Day.

ROSARIO DEL CIELO. Yep, six months later they were found by an angel at a cafe in Lisbon, drinking cappuccinos and having a good time. And you remember what happened when they were returned to their place?

ANUNCIO. Uh-huh . . . Pufff . . . Pan . . . Pin . . . Pon . . . Poom . . . Rakatakatah . . . into the woosssssh . . . *Se jodieron.* Never saw the blue firmament again . . . What a pity!

ROSARIO DEL CIELO. Yes, what a pity!

RAMONA. I'm not listening to this anymore. (*Clave percussion sounds.* RAMONA *and* FEDERICO *walk around the stage in different directions.* ANUNCIO *follows* FEDERICO, *imitating all his movements.* ROSARIO DEL CIELO *follows* RAMONA.) Cursed angels!

Demons. Tell them we don't need anybody following us. They scare me, Federico.

FEDERICO. (*With open arms dramatically.*) But I'm here, Ramona, and I love you.

RAMONA. Tell me that I'm sober, Federico!

CARETAKERS. (*Dramatically.*) Tell me that I'm sober, Federico!

RAMONA. (*Moving away from* ROSARIO.) Tell me that I'm alive. Tell me that they're apparitions. Figments of my imagination.

ROSARIO DEL CIELO. Where should we wait for you, when the holiday is over?

ANUNCIO. (*To* FEDERICO.) Yes, November the second, at sundown. Where should I wait for you?

RAMONA. We're nothing, Federico. We're nothing. Still in limbo. This body. These clothes. It's all a lie.

FEDERICO. (*Joins* RAMONA *to dance.*) Oh, no it's not. Hold me tight. (*Both couples dance throughout the rest of the dialogue.*)

ANUNCIO. I'll be waiting behind the stack of chairs, by the beach umbrellas.

FEDERICO. Listen without listening. Let's go in the water.

ROSARIO DEL CIELO. I'll wait behind the cabana. By the leftover bottles of suntan lotion.

ANUNCIO. I'll wait for you on the diving board of the empty swimming pool, jumping on the trampoline.

ROSARIO DEL CIELO. I'll wait after sundown, on the empty balconies, watering geraniums and begonias, brushing my hair against the veranda.

ANUNCIO. And I'll be swimming in the empty swimming pool. And I'll be waving at the seagoing ships. Waiting after sundown on November the second. (*In a menacing purr.*) RRRRRrrrrrrrrrr-rrrrrrrrr . . . rrrrrrrrrrrrrrrrrrrrrrrrrrrrrrrrrrrrrrrrrrrrrrrrrrr . . . (*Simultaneously.*)

ROSARIO DEL CIELO. (*Hissing.*) Ssssssssssssssssssssssssssssssssssss-sss . . .

ANUNCIO. Rrrrrrrrrrrrrrrrrrrrrrrrrrrrrrrrrrrrrrrrr . . . rrrrrrrrrrrrrrrrrrr-
rrrrr . . .

FEDERICO. Sssssssssssssssss . . . Sssssssssssssssss . . .

RAMONA. Ssss . . . Ssss . . . ssss . . . Sssss . . .

FEDERICO. Sssssssssssss . . . Ssssssssss . . .

(FRANCINE *enters.*)

FRANCINE. Let's go out before I burn to cinders in these clothes.
Ay, did I interrupt something?

RAMONA. No . . . dancing, Francine.

FEDERICO. Just practicing.

RAMONA. Dusting off our steps.

FEDERICO. Yes, it's been so long. Kind of rusty. Trying to find our
center of gravity.

FRANCINE. Oh, I know about gravity. When Evaristo and I used to
do our show, we would do that. I used to imagine your arms,
Ramona . . . Imagine your face . . . How you use your neck . . .
How you turn your neck when you dance, like the stem of a
tulip.

RAMONA. Francine, you're making me blush . . .

FRANCINE. Of course I don't have your neck. But I pretend I do.
My Adam's apple is what spoils it. I always have to hide it be-
hind a high-collar dress. A feather boa. It's like an elevator. Ay!
Up and down. Up and down. My skeleton doesn't do me justice.
But I call you in my mind, I say, Ramona, give me your legs . . .
Your strength, Ramona . . . Possess me with your spell . . . (*Does
a dance pose.*)

FEDERICO. I'm going out for a smoke.

RAMONA. Fedo, we're ready to leave.

FEDERICO. I'll be back. I'll be back. (FEDERICO *walks away.*)

FRANCINE. I offend him, don't I?

RAMONA. Nonsense. Why do you say such things?

FRANCINE. I know people are offended by the likes of me. It's a given. Kids scream at me when I walk the streets . . . Dogs bark at my perfume and my bracelets. And men complain about my feet and my neck. And old ladies do the sign of the cross when I pass them by. And on top of that I'm poor and wretched . . . Living in a cabana of an empty hotel.

RAMONA. Don't say that, Francine.

FRANCINE. Well, I may perfume my reality, but I don't disinfect myself from the truth.

RAMONA. You can't pay Federico any mind. He's always been like that. But you don't offend me. You keep me alive on the stage. How can I be offended? You bring me back memories. That you do. You have a good stage presence. Come here and stand by my side.

FRANCINE. What do you want me to do?

RAMONA. Something I learned in life. I want to share a secret with you. Something my dance teacher taught me. How to call the dance, Francine. How to envision the sea roaring out there, and let it come to you as the dance. Duende. You see, how I hold my head. It's as if I'm standing on a port, but my eyes are always looking out at the sea. Because the dance must be here in your legs. On the port. But your eyes are out there where the sea brings and takes away the dance. Like this. Look at me. I'm already calling the dance . . . It comes to me when I call it. *(They both dance.)* Good, you're getting it. That's it, Francine.

FRANCINE. I never learned to dance. Not in a school. I learned by watching people's feet. Watching people's knees and hips. A step here, step there. My father didn't want me to dance. He liked dancing. He liked for me to dance. But not on a stage. He would not have it. Not under lights in a cabaret.

RAMONA. That's it, Francine . . . You're getting it.

FRANCINE. I learned by practicing in the bathroom, with a towel under my feet, not to make noise. When I first saw you on a stage, I was eight. It was in Acapulco. My father said, "If no one wants to stay home and watch over the boy, we'll take him with us." And no one was willing to stay. So my family took me to a cabaret, and they crowded themselves around me to get me through the door. Then when I was inside the cabaret, they hid me under the table like a bandit. A *terrorista*. When the lights came down, the curtains went up, I lifted the tablecloth and there you were with Federico, and me under the table. And the lights from the stage come up . . . They come up over me, like a reflector, and you and Federico dance on the stage. And I'm happy as can be under the table watching how the two of you fly up in the air dancing. *(Pause.)* And I know, I know from that moment on that I want to be like you and Fedo. That I want to be a dancer. *(Points to altar.)* When I saw that photograph, where you two are standing in front of the Aladdin Hotel, I knew this place was special to you. If you don't mind me telling you, I read what you wrote behind the photograph.

RAMONA. What did I write? That was a long time ago. I forgot what I wrote.

FRANCINE. Ah! "Meet me here every year whether together or separate at the Aladdin Hotel, room 22. The blue room."

RAMONA. I remember now. I was crazy in love with Federico. Every year we would come to Miami and dance at the Aladdin, the Barcelona Hotel. Yes, the room with the white curtains. Room 22, like two swans.

(Music and change of light.)

A LOST WIFE AND FINDING ALUMINUM
PAPER ON THE BEACH

Scene 5

(Music plays. MATTHIAS *stands to the center of the stage. He holds a locket and a photograph. The* CARETAKERS *stand behind him.)*

MATTHIAS. I can assure you this is not my wife. She must be somewhere in the world and she hasn't found her way back to me. I can sense you are trying to help me, but this is not her.

ROSARIO DEL CIELO. No. This is your wife. There was an explosion in your town. Your wife was working at the soap factory. The whole place went up in smoke. And in the smoke she disappeared. Years later your wife materializes in this body, this face. And her name is now Francine.

MATTHIAS. My wife never dressed this way. She never wore feathers. She was a simple woman. I know my wife. I can hear her still. She used to say, "Matthias, if I don't sing, I die." She liked singing. She sang in church. I can still hear her songs. We had a wise old dog. The dog was deaf and didn't bark. But the animal would prick up his ears when she sang. I can still smell her food. She used to keep a good table. Perhaps she climbed her way back to me and didn't find me. For many years I have stayed put in one place. I just have to make my way back to where I was.

ANUNCIO. It's all a mumbo-jumbo to you, isn't it?

MATTHIAS. I don't know what is this you say. (*Pulls out a locket.*) This is my wife. These are her initials, I.M.V.U. . . . Ida Maria Von Unruh. Born January 14, 1873.

ROSARIO DEL CIELO. (*Simultaneously.*) Born January 14, 1873.

MATTHIAS. You know this!?

ROSARIO DEL CIELO. Of course . . .

MATTHIAS. I can assure you . . .

ANUNCIO. Go find her . . . Go before she goes away . . .

MATTHIAS. I can assure you . . .

ANUNCIO. No. We can assure you that you'll find her walking on the beach. You'll find her.

(MATTHIAS *takes the picture and starts to walk away.* ROSARIO *looks through opera glasses.*)

ANUNCIO. Francine doesn't have a clue of the things that can come her way on All Souls' Day.

ROSARIO DEL CIELO. Anuncio, I have something to tell you.

ANUNCIO. What? (*Pause.*) What is it?

ROSARIO DEL CIELO. I don't know if it means good or bad, noble or base . . . I want to stay one more day, Anuncio.

ANUNCIO. I thought you were back to your old self.

ROSARIO DEL CIELO. I am . . . I am . . . Would you do it for me? Would you let me have it my way for once?

ANUNCIO. Let you have it your way? Let you have it your way? And what are we going to say when we get back up there? What excuse are we going to come up with?

ROSARIO DEL CIELO. We can always say . . . I'll say we lost the glass.

ANUNCIO. You'll say you lost the glass! Lost the glass! You better come up with something better than that.

ROSARIO DEL CIELO. Sometimes it pays to be naive, innocent. (*Kisses him.*) One more day in the world . . . Life . . .

ANUNCIO. No.

ROSARIO DEL CIELO. Just one more day . . . (*Stands behind him and caresses his chest and neck.*)

ANUNCIO. No, Rosario . . .

ROSARIO DEL CIELO. (*Turns him around and kisses him around the neck.*) Yes . . . One more day in the world.

ANUNCIO. No, Rosario . . .

ROSARIO DEL CIELO. (*Kisses him passionately.*) Yes . . .

ANUNCIO. No, Rosario. Don't do this to me.

ROSARIO DEL CIELO. Yes, Anuncio . . . Just one more day. Me in this body and you in your body . . .

ANUNCIO. Rosario, you know what it takes, don't you? . . . You know what to do . . .

ROSARIO DEL CIELO. One more day, Anuncio.

ANUNCIO. (*He is pressing himself against her now.*) Ave Maria Purisima!

ROSARIO DEL CIELO. One more day . . . Yes . . .

ANUNCIO. Not a month . . . Not a year . . . Just one more day . . .

ROSARIO DEL CIELO. Yes . . . Yes . . . One more day . . .

ANUNCIO. (*In ecstasy.*) Yes ... Yes ... One more day ... One more day ... (Lights change. FRANCINE *enters wearing sunglasses.* MATTHIAS *follows her.*)

MATTHIAS. *Warten Sie ... Warten Sie ...* The lady will hurt her skin if she continues walking in the burning sun without a parasol. May I give you this? (*Gives her a parasol.*)

FRANCINE. Thank you. You are very kind.

MATTHIAS. What is your name?

FRANCINE. Francine.

MATTHIAS. Oh, Francine. I am Matthias.

FRANCINE. Pleased to meet you.

MATTHIAS. I am pleased to meet you too. In my country the sun doesn't burn this much. In Germany the sun is gentle and soothing. We have a different kind of sun. I mean ... Yes ... the same sun but less splendor. At this time of the year the birds fly south. It is very beautiful to see them flying in flocks. Yes, thousands of them flying south. I'm not surprised if some of them come here. But how can one tell the birds that fly in from Germany and the ones that fly in from Paris? ...

FRANCINE. You are making me laugh.

MATTHIAS. Well, yes ... It is the truth. Maybe some of the birds from my country come here. I don't blame them for flying to this part of the world. It is a beautiful place, with beautiful women.

FRANCINE. Oh, yes ...

MATTHIAS. Well, it is my Ida Maria.

FRANCINE. You called me Ida. That's not my name.

MATTHIAS. Ida Maria Von Unruh is a beautiful name.

FRANCINE. Yes it is, but it's not my name.

MATTHIAS. But Francine is also a beautiful name.

FRANCINE. Thank you.

MATTHIAS. I found this silver paper. It was flying in the air. Yes, someone must have lost it. It is good paper, of much value. It can be utilized for mirror making. With a piece of glass, many small mirrors can be made. Yes, and one would need a small diamond for cutting the glass.

FRANCINE. How do you say mirror in your language?

MATTHIAS. *Spiegel.*

FRANCINE. *Spiegel. Spiegel.* Like the magazine.

MATTHIAS. I don't know this magazine.

FRANCINE. And sea? How do you say sea?

MATTHIAS. *Meer.*

FRANCINE. *Meer.* And love?

MATTHIAS. *Liebe.*

FRANCINE. Say it again.

MATTHIAS. *Liebe.*

FRANCINE. And kiss?

MATTHIAS. You mean kissing? Like this. (*Purses his lips.*)

FRANCINE. Yes. Kiss.

MATTHIAS. Ah, yes . . . Yes . . . *Küssen.*

FRANCINE. Say it again.

MATTHIAS. *Küssen.*

FRANCINE. I wanted to kiss you. (*Kisses him on the lips.*)

MATTHIAS. You have kissed me.

FRANCINE. Yes. And now I must leave. Tell me how to say good-bye. Say good-bye in your language. I must leave.

MATTHIAS. But you have kissed me, Ida.

FRANCINE. I'm not Ida . . .

MATTHIAS. Why must you leave?

FRANCINE. Because . . . Because I have a husband and five children.

MATTHIAS. But the kiss. It means something.

FRANCINE. No. You have a wife and I have a husband and children. I kissed you because . . . Because I have never kissed German lips.

MATTHIAS. But it is not proper to kiss and walk away.

FRANCINE. Blondes have always been my disgrace. You will be my disgrace. Good-bye. (*Runs from him. He follows her.*)

MATTHIAS. But Ida . . . But . . . Francine . . . Francine . . . (*In a loud voice.*) Ida Maria . . . Ida . . . Francine . . .

ROSARIO DEL CIELO. Something tells me that there's more than what you tell me. Is he calling her Ida? Give me the glass. This was my plan.

ANUNCIO. Shshsshshhhhhhhhhhh . . . Nothing's happening yet. He's running after her.

ROSARIO DEL CIELO. He is? Give me the glass.

ANUNCIO. No. Now it's my turn. There is Federico and Ramona walking on the sand. They're coming this way. Back! Back!

RAMONA. Don't go swimming, Federico.

FEDERICO. Of course I'm going to go swimming.

RAMONA. Play ball with me. It scares me when you go swimming far out. Sometimes I think you're never coming back. (*They throw the ball to each other.*)

FEDERICO. Where do you want me to swim—by the shore with the children?

RAMONA. Yes. I don't like it when you go swimming underwater and I don't see you come up for air. You're not a frogman.

ANUNCIO. (*Takes the ball from* RAMONA *and throws it to* ROSARIO.) There's time-keeping. There's punch the clock.

ROSARIO DEL CIELO. There's time in time out . . .

ANUNCIO. Ring, ring . . . All Souls' . . . No more souls . . .

ROSARIO DEL CIELO. Did you say the end of the holiday?

RAMONA. Tell them something, Fedo. Tell them something.

ANUNCIO. Yes. Speak to me underwater. Let's go in the water.

RAMONA. No!!!!

FEDERICO. Allow me to make a deal with you.

ANUNCIO. A deal? What kind of a deal?

RAMONA. Yes, I'm listening, Federico. What kind of a deal?

FEDERICO. Leave it to me, Ramona. Please! (*To* CARETAKERS.) I know Ramona and I must go back. We . . . We are planning . . .

ROSARIO DEL CIELO. You can't overextend your stay, dear, All Souls' Day will be over in a few hours.

FEDERICO. Well, I was thinking. We plan to go back, you see. We promise.

RAMONA. You better not say something stupid, Federico.

FEDERICO. Ramona, please! Leave it to me!

ANUNCIO. What a pity! What a pity! I keep singing to myself. What a pity!

ROSARIO DEL CIELO. There's the dance floor. Bygone days. Empty by. Dancing by . . . (*A bright idea.*) Should we have a picnic in the empty swimming pool?

ANUNCIO. Poon Paranh . . . Poon Paranh . . . Should we have a pachanga!

ROSARIO DEL CIELO. Poon Paranh . . . Poon Paranh . . . Shall we dance?

(MATTHIAS *enters running after* FRANCINE.)

MATTHIAS. Francine . . . Francine . . . I must talk to you . . .

FRANCINE. No, I won't talk. I can't talk.

MATTHIAS. Francine, please! I would like for you to know who I am. Where are you going to go?

FRANCINE. (*Covers her ears.*) I won't listen to you. Go away and start following someone else.

RAMONA. Francine . . . Francine . . .

ANUNCIO. If you kiss him your teeth will fall out.

ROSARIO DEL CIELO. Oh! Oh! Oh! They have fallen out. Your teeth! Pick them up and make me a bracelet.

FRANCINE. I have my teeth.

MATTHIAS. Yes, she has her teeth.

FRANCINE. Ramona . . . Ramona, who are these people?

ROSARIO DEL CIELO. Guardian angels, Francine.

ANUNCIO. Sometimes you see us . . .

ROSARIO DEL CIELO. Sometimes you don't.

ANUNCIO. We came to guard your guests . . .

ROSARIO DEL CIELO. Federico and Ramona.

RAMONA. Demons!

FEDERICO. Ramona, please!

ROSARIO DEL CIELO. Fallen teeth. Your teeth fallen on my door-steps.

FRANCINE. What about fallen teeth? What is she saying about my teeth?

ANUNCIO. (*To* MATTHIAS.) Will you love her without her teeth?

MATTHIAS. What are you two talking about? She has her teeth . . .

FRANCINE. (*Feels her teeth.*) Yes, I have my teeth.

ROSARIO DEL CIELO. (*Rings a little bell.*) There's a show. There's a show. Let's have a dance competition . . . (*Goes to trunk and takes out large printed numbers for dance competition and gives them to* MATTHIAS, FEDERICO *and* ANUNCIO.)

ANUNCIO. Yes, two more seconds before the dance competition!

MATTHIAS. What dance competition?

ROSARIO DEL CIELO. Come with me. Behave. Do as I do.

ANUNCIO. And what will the couples win in the dance competition? Will it be a refrigerator, an ashtray from a hotel, a beach towel or a pair of socks? Or . . . ?

ROSARIO DEL CIELO. One more day. One more day of life after All Souls' Day!

ANUNCIO. Ahhhíííí! Rin . . . koon . . . koon. *Otro dia pa' goza!* What do you have to say to that? What do you have to say?

MATTHIAS. What did he say? Tell me what he said.

ANUNCIO. You win the dance competition, you get to wear your hat one more day.

MATTHIAS. But . . . But . . . I don't know how to dance. I don't know. Francine . . . Francine, would you dance with me? Please dance with me. I don't know how to dance. But I will try . . . For one more day I will try to dance with all my heart.

FRANCINE. I'm not dancing with anybody. This is all a mistake. I don't need to dance for another day. Federico, tell them something. Tell them that I'm not a part of this, that I'm alive . . . — I'm alive, you hear. I don't need to dance.

FEDERICO. She doesn't need to dance.

ANUNCIO. *(Blows the whistle.)* You stay out of this or you won't be able to compete!

ROSARIO DEL CIELO. That's what happens, Francine, when you play with the other side.

ANUNCIO. Ahah . . . *Con los muertos no se juega.*

FRANCINE. Oh, I have to tell myself that this isn't happening! This isn't happening, Francine. It's all a mistake.

ROSARIO DEL CIELO. What do you mean, Francine?

ANUNCIO. Bah, she wanted the whole sky to come down for All Souls' Day, and here it is. Come dance . . . Music, Maestro!

(ROSARIO *takes* MATTHIAS *by the hand to dance,* FEDERICO *takes* RAMONA. ANUNCIO *takes* FRANCINE *to dance. A danzón plays. In the middle of the dance the music is lowered but still heard under the dialogue.)*

FRANCINE. I have to tell myself that this isn't happening. That it is all a mistake. That it's all a dream. See what you got me into, Evaristo. *(Looks up.)*

MATTHIAS. It's not a mistake, Francine. I thought I came down to the wrong country, but that wasn't a mistake because I found you.

ROSARIO DEL CIELO. Keep to the dance. Keep to the dance.

RAMONA. Speak to me in another language, Federico. So they won't know what you say.

ANUNCIO AND ROSARIO DEL CIELO. Speak to me in another language, Federico.

FEDERICO. *De aqui no salimos.*

ANUNCIO. *Que dijiste? Mira a ver lo que hablas.*

RAMONA. French, Fedo. French . . .

FEDERICO. *Oui,* Ramona. *Oui.*

ROSARIO DEL CIELO. *Ça suffit. Ça suffit. Qu'est-ce que tu marmonnes?*

FRANCINE. *Español,* Ramona. Try Spanish so I can understand what you say. So you can explain to me who these freaks are.

ANUNCIO. *Dimelo cantando.*

MATTHIAS. If you speak Spanish I won't understand what you say, Francine.

FRANCINE. I don't want to talk to you. I told you I don't want to talk to you.

MATTHIAS. But why won't you talk to me? What have I done to you?

FRANCINE. Start following someone else.

ANUNCIO. *(Blows a whistle. Music stops.)* No more talking on the dance floor or everybody will be disqualified from the dance competition.

MATTHIAS. Please, I have a request . . . I would like to dance . . . I would like to dance with Francine.

FRANCINE. No. I'm not dancing . . . I'm not dancing with him.

ANUNCIO. Granted. Request granted. You can dance with Francine. (*Blows the whistle.*) Let's have couple Number 5 to the dance floor.

FRANCINE. (*Starts to leave.*) I'm leaving, I can't take this anymore.

ANUNCIO. (*Blows the whistle.*) If you don't cooperate your teeth will fall out.

ROSARIO DEL CIELO. You win the competition, you get one more day after All Souls' Day and maybe your love will come down to visit. (*There is a pause.* FRANCINE *reflects and stays.* ROSARIO *takes* FRANCINE *by the hand and brings her to* MATTHIAS.)

ANUNCIO. Next the tango. Couple Number 5 to the dance floor. FEDERICO *and* RAMONA *place themselves in position to dance. A tango plays. They both dance passionately. When they are done doing their best steps* ANUNCIO *blows the whistle.*)

FEDERICO. (*With anger.*) We didn't finish. We didn't finish.

ANUNCIO. Too bad. That's enough! Competitors Number 5. That's enough! (*Blows whistle.*) That was couple Number 5 dancing to a tango. (*A rumba plays.*) Couple Number 7 to the dance floor.

ROSARIO DEL CIELO. — Oh, that's me. That's me. Right here. (*Takes a dance pose.*)

ANUNCIO. Of course that's us, *mi* Rosario del Cielo.

MATTHIAS. But ... but ... (ANUNCIO *gives the whistle to* MATTHIAS.)

ANUNCIO. Let's see if you can outdo this tumbao, Federico. (ANUNCIO *and* ROSARIO *throw themselves into the dance. They are like fire on the stage dancing.* ANUNCIO *shows his best steps, makes remarks and taunts* FEDERICO *and* RAMONA *as he dances with* ROSARIO.) What do you have to say to this! *Goza! Echale limón. Mojito ... Tirate ... Tirate ... Rrrrrriiiiiiiiiiiii ... Cogelo ... Cometelo ...*

ROSARIO DEL CIELO. Ramona, Rrrrrrriiiiiiiiiii! (FEDERICO *and* RAMONA *throw themselves on the dance floor to compete against* ANUNCIO *and* ROSARIO. FEDERICO *and* ANUNCIO *compete with each other on the dance floor, then the two women struggle in the dance. The dance is at its peak now and* MATTHIAS *blows the whistle. There is silence. He covers his head as if the dancers are going to kill him for blowing the whistle.)*

MATTHIAS. I beg your pardon. I don't mean to stumble on like this in the middle of your dance, but perhaps you should stop now. You are getting carried away. No good will come of this if you continue on . . . Forgive me, I don't know how to do those steps, and my shoes are old but I would like to dance too. And I believe it is my turn to dance with Francine. (*Looks at* FRANCINE *lovingly.*)

ANUNCIO. Go ahead . . . Go ahead, the dance floor is yours.

FRANCINE. I'm not dancing with anybody. I'm getting out of here. (FRANCINE *starts to walk away.*)

MATTHIAS. Francine, where are you going? Where are you going?

FRANCINE. Far from you . . . Far from all of this. I've had enough. (*Makes her way out.*)

MATTHIAS. But Francine. Francine . . . Francine . . . Please come back. Come back . . . (*Runs after her. There is a pause. The* CARE-TAKERS *walk around the stage following* FEDERICO *and* RAMONA. *They parade the stage as couples. Percussion sounds.*)

ANUNCIO. She'll have dreams . . . She'll have dreams of falling teeth . . . And you . . . You. (*Sings a Spanish lament song.*)
Deja de soñar . . .
No sueñes mas . . .

Deja de soñar . . .
No existe el mar . . .

ROSARIO DEL CIELO. Did you read the travel section this Sunday?

ANUNCIO. No, I didn't read the travel section.

ROSARIO DEL CIELO. You can go on a car ride and crash into a wall like Federico and Ramona, and you die wounded like a bullfighter.

ANUNCIO. And you die drunk. Too drunk to go to heaven, too drunk to go to hell. Too drunk to come back to life. Because you can't find your way through anything. What a limbo!

ROSARIO DEL CIELO. Yes, what a limbo! They lied their way to the sky.

ANUNCIO. Yes. Trying to pass as Islamic. So they can wander through earth and sky with a dreamlike body for forty days. Did they think it was for forty years? More than forty days, suspended in the celestial sphere, between death and eternity.

RAMONA. And you . . . You piece . . .

FEDERICO. Ramona, please!

RAMONA. No, Federico. They're not going to insult me. Not these chimney cleaners of hell.

ANUNCIO. And you thought you could come back unguarded on All Souls' Day. Without us. Without caretakers. Without caring angels.

RAMONA. Bah! Scum. Fallen angels. Dregs of hell.

ANUNCIO. Sssssssssssssssssss . . . (*Sound of thunder.*) What a mess! Enough to dance the pachanga. What a pachanga! Bin ban boom! Traca taca tah! Charges! Read the charges! Tin . . . boon bao . . .

ROSARIO DEL CIELO. She was still drinking bourbons in the sky and smoking cigarettes.

ANUNCIO. Tracataca tah . . . More charges!

ROSARIO DEL CIELO. And him smoking Cuban cigars.

ANUNCIO. Splashing themselves with cheap cologne so angels couldn't smell their worldly habits. Ha! Tracatah . . . More charges.

ROSARIO DEL CIELO. Defying death.

ANUNCIO. Tracatah . . . Fuckin' on rooftops . . .

ROSARIO DEL CIELO. More charges.

ANUNCIO. Idle conversations . . .

ROSARIO DEL CIELO. Tracatah . . . More charges . . .

ANUNCIO. Denying hell, heaven. Eternal life . . . Tanga ro . . . ro . . . roh . . . tan . . . bin . . . ban . . . beh . . . kirikirikí . . .

ROSARIO DEL CIELO. What's the verdict?

ANUNCIO. We'll . . . We'll . . . Nobody won the dance competition, but we'll give them another day. But only because we want to

133

stay longer, enh . . . Tomorrow we'll come with the black car, and you'll go back. And the neighbors will say, what a hullabaloo!

ROSARIO DEL CIELO. What a hullabaloo! (*Sound of thunder. Then silence.*)

ANUNCIO. What a hullabaloo! (*They exit.*)

RAMONA. Fedo, it's finished. It's finished. Gone. Let's not delude ourselves. We can't go on like this. Can't stay in this limbo forever. It's time to go give in. And I can't see myself living in the world. Where everything is thrown away, disposed after use. We come from another time, Fedo. Old days when life was different. Where objects were cared for. They were saved, a bed, a chair. Handkerchiefs were mended, shoes were resoled. I always felt closer to you when I used to mend your socks. And wasn't it the same for you, when you used to go to the hosiery store and buy me stockings? How you cared that my legs would have stockings. Would you do that for me now? No. You would probably leave me barefoot, like a vagrant.

FEDERICO. No, I wouldn't.

RAMONA. Fedo, it's time to give in.

FEDERICO. No, we're alive. For me, you're alive, Ramona. You've never died, and we're not going anywhere. This is how I like to exist. And this is how you like to exist: skin, bone and hair. Height, width and length . . . Pants, shoes, shirt and hat . . . We're not going to be submissive. We're here, *carajo,* and we're staying.

(*Change of light.*)

Two Stories
Juan Bosch

— *Translated from Spanish by Mark Schafer*

THE MASTERS

WHEN CRISTINO WAS NO LONGER GOOD for anything, not even for milking cows, *don* Pío called him over and said that he was going to give him a present.

"I'm giving you half a peso for the road. You're in very poor health and can't go on working. Come back if you get better."

Cristino held out a trembling yellow hand.

"Thank you, *don*. I'd get goin' this very instant, but I'm runnin' a fever."

"You can stay here tonight if you want and make yourself some verbena tea. It'll do you good."

Cristino had removed his hat and his plentiful hair, long and black, fell against his neck. Beneath his pronounced cheekbones, a scrappy beard made his face look dirty.

"That's fine, *don* Pío. God bless you."

He climbed slowly down the stairs, covering his head once again with the old black felt hat. When he came to the last step, he paused for a moment and began to look at the cows and calves.

"That bull calf sure is frisky," he remarked in a low voice.

This was a calf he had cured a few days earlier. It had been suffering from worms in the gut and was now frolicking and leaping about.

Don Pío went out onto the balcony and paused to look at the cattle as well. *Don* Pío was short and chubby with small darting eyes. Cristino had been working with him for three years. He paid Cristino one peso a week for milking the cows, which he did in the early hours of the morning, and for the household chores and taking care of the calves. The man had turned out to be hard-working and easy-going but had fallen sick and *don* Pío did not like to support sick people in his house.

Don Pío looked into the distance. Far from the house, a thicket concealed the course of a brook, and above the thicket, clouds of mosquitos. *Don* Pío had arranged for wire screen to be placed on all the windows and doors in the house, but the laborers' hut had neither doors nor windows: it didn't even have walls. Cristino moved around down on the first step and *don* Pío decided to offer him one last recommendation.

"When you get home, treat that malady, Cristino."

"Oh yes, of course, *don* Pío. Thank you very much," he heard the man respond.

The sun was boiling in every tiny leaf on the plain. From the hills of Terrero to those of San Francisco, out of sight to the north, everything sparkled under the sun. On the edge of the fields, far in the distance, were two cows. One could barely pick them out, but Cristino knew every single head of cattle.

"Look, *don*," he said. "That dappled one you can pick out over there must've calved last night or in the mornin', 'cause I don't see no belly on it."

Don Pío walked around on the balcony.

"You think so, Cristino? I can't see it clearly."

"Lean a little this away and you will."

Cristino was cold and his head was starting to hurt, but he kept his eyes on the animal.

"Take a little walk and herd it over this way, Cristino," he heard *don* Pío say.

"I'd go after it in a flash, 'cept I'm feeling pretty sick."

"The fever?"

"Uh-huh. It's creepin' up."

"Pay it no mind. You're an old hand at this, Cristino. Go and get me the calf."

Cristino wrapped his two emaciated arms around his chest. He felt how the coldness was taking over his body. He looked up. All that sun, the bull calf . . .

"Are you going to get me the calf?" the voice insisted.

All that sun and his legs, shaking under his own weight, and his bare feet covered in dust.

"Are you going to get the calf for me, Cristino?"

He had to say something, but his tongue was thick in his mouth. He squeezed his arms tighter around his chest. He was wearing a dirty striped shirt made of a fabric so thin it offered him no protection at all.

From above came the sound of footsteps and Cristino thought that *don* Pío was about to come down. That scared Cristino.

"I sure am, *don*," he said. "I'm gonna go. Just wait for the cold that's in me to leave."

"The sun will get it out. Do me a favor, Cristino. See to it that the cow doesn't wander off and that I don't lose the bull calf."

Cristino continued shaking but began to stand up.

"Yes, I'm goin', *don*," he said.

"It's over by the bend in the brook now," *don* Pío announced from the balcony.

One step after another, his arms folded over his chest, hunched over so as not to lose any heat, the peon started to cross the plain. *Don* Pío watched him walk off. A woman slipped out onto the balcony and stood beside *don* Pío.

"What a beautiful day, Pío!" she remarked in a lilting voice.

The man did not respond. He pointed to Cristino, who was walking clumsily away as if he were bumping into things.

"He didn't want to go after the dappled cow that calved last night. And I just gave him half a peso for the road."

He was silent for a half a minute and looked at the woman, who seemed to be asking for an explanation.

"They're ungrateful, Herminia," he said. "You treat them well, and all for nothing."

She expressed her agreement in her eyes.

"I've told you that a thousand times, Pío," she said.

And the two of them stood there, watching Cristino, who was now nothing more than a smudge on the green of the plain.

IN A HOVEL

The woman didn't dare to think. When she thought she heard the footfalls of animals, she raced to the door, her eyes nervous. Then she returned to the room and stood there a long while, submerged in a kind of lethargy.

The hovel was a squalid wreck. It was black with age and inside, they lived between dirt and soot. As soon as the rains came it would be uninhabitable. She knew this and also knew that she couldn't leave, for, besides this shack, she didn't have a piece of palm thatching to her name.

Again the sound of voices. She ran to the door, fearful that it might not be anyone passing by. She waited a short while; waited longer; longer still. Nothing! Nothing but the rocky yellow road. It was the wind blowing in front of the hovel, the damned wind blowing off the hillside, causing the pine trees on the rise and the apple trees down below to moan. Or perhaps it was the river flowing at the bottom of the cliff, behind the hovel.

One of the sick little children called out and she, undone, wanting to cry but lacking the tears to do so, went in to have a look at him.

"Mama, was it Daddy? Was it Daddy, Mama?"

She didn't dare answer. She touched the boy's forehead and felt it burn.

"Was it Daddy, Mama?"

"No," she said. "Your Daddy, he'll be comin' later."

The boy closed his eyes and turned on his side. Even in the darkness of the room, his skin was visibly pale.

"I seen him, Mama. He come and brung me a new pair of pants."

The woman could not listen any longer. She was about to topple over like one of those old tree trunks that rot from the inside and suddenly, one day, they fall. It was the delirium of his fever that was making his son talk like that and she had nothing with which to buy him medicine.

The boy seemed to doze off and the mother rose to her feet to take a look at the other one. She found him lying down peacefully. He was nothing but skin and bones and he whistled as he breathed, but he wasn't moving around or complaining; he just looked at her with his big eyes. Ever since he was born, he had been a quiet one.

The dingy room stunk of rotten cloth. The mother — skinny, with sunken temples, a dirty rag around her head and wearing an old striped dress — was not aware of the smell, for she had grown accustomed to it, but the fact that her children could not get well in such a place told her something. She thought that when her husband returned, if he ever got out of jail, he would find nothing but crosses planted next to the wooden posts of the hovel, its boards and roof long gone. Without understanding why, she put herself in Teo's place and suffered.

It pained her to imagine Teo arriving and there being no one to greet him. The last time he had been in the hovel — just two days before he gave himself up — the small farm was still clean, and the corn, beans and tobacco swayed in the breeze that blew off the hillside. But Teo gave himself up, for they told him he could argue his own defense and that he wouldn't be in jail for long. She was unable to keep working because she felt sick, and the children — the girl child and the two boys — were so small they couldn't keep the farm clean or go to the woods to chop down the wood necessary to fix the stockade fences. Then the rainy season began, that damned rainy season, and the water fell and fell and fell, night and day, without a break, one, two, three weeks in a row until the torrents had left the road covered with rocks and mud and had carried off whole sections of the fence and filled the farm with small pebbles and the dirt floor of the hovel grew moss and the roof thatching began to rot.

But it was better not to remember such things. Now she was waiting. She had sent the girl child to Naranjal, an hour's walk, down the hill. She had instructed the girl to gather half a dozen eggs she could find in nesting places in the woods and which she could trade for rice and salt. The girl had left early in the day and hadn't returned. Her mother was eyeing the road, filled with anxiety.

She heard footsteps. This time it was no illusion: someone was approaching on horseback. She went out and stood beneath the overhang of the hovel, the muscles in her neck tense and her eyes hard. She looked toward the rise. The feeling that she was not getting enough air made her flare her nostrils. Suddenly, she saw a palm hat rising and gathered that a man was coming up the hill. Her first impulse was to go back inside, but something held her there, as if she were nailed to the spot. Beneath the hat an indistinct face appeared, then the shoulders and chest, and finally the horse. The woman watched the man approach and still was not thinking a thing. When the man was just steps away, she looked him in the eyes and sensed, more than knew, that the stranger wanted something.

A vague yet bitter series of images flashed through the woman's head: her daughter, the eggs, the sick boys, Teo. All of it was suddenly erased by the sound of the man's voice.

"Greetings," he said.

"Give me something, anything at all."

The man measured her up with his eyes without dismounting. She was a skinny and dirty woman with the look of a lunatic in her eyes. She was undoubtedly alone and also, without a doubt, wanted a man.

"Give me anything at all," she insisted.

And suddenly, the idea penetrated her tormented head that this man was on his way back from La Vega, and if he had gone to sell something, he would be carrying money. Perhaps food, medicine. Furthermore, she understood that he was a man and that he was looking at her as a woman.

"Get down," she said, filled with shame.

The man leapt to the ground.

"All I have is half a peso," he ventured.

Calm, now, and collected, she said: "That's fine. Come in."

The man abandoned his suspicion and seemed to experience a sudden happiness. He took the horse's bridle and bent down to tie it to the base of the hovel. The woman went inside. Suddenly, having survived the worst moment, she felt that she was dying, that she couldn't walk, that Teo was arriving, that the boys weren't sick. She felt like crying and wished that she were dead.

The man entered the hovel, asking: "In here?"

She shut her eyes and motioned for him to be silent. Feeling an anguish larger even than her soul, she walked over to the door of the room. She stuck her head in and saw that the children were sleeping. Then she turned to the stranger and noticed that he stunk of horse sweat. The man saw that the woman's eyes had a hard shine to them, like the eyes of the dead.

"Uh huh. In here," she said.

The man came over to where she stood, breathing sonorously, and at that moment she heard someone sobbing outside. She turned around. Her gaze cut like a knife. She rushed outside as quickly as she could, a bundle of nerves. There was the girl, huddling beneath the overhang, crying, her eyes swollen. She was small, her skin burnt by the sun, nothing but skin and bones.

"What happened, Minina?" her mother asked.

The girl continued sobbing and wouldn't speak. Her mother lost patience.

"Tell me now!"

"In the river . . . ," the little girl said. "Crossin' the river . . . The paper got wet and nothin's left but this."

In her small fist, she held all the rice she had managed to save. She continued crying, her head pressed against her chest, leaning against the boards of the hovel.

The mother felt she could not go on any longer. She went inside and was unable to focus her eyes on a single thing. She had completely forgotten about the man and when she saw him, had to make an effort to piece together the situation.

"The girl's back. My girl . . . Get out," she said.

She felt very tired and moved over to the door. With blurred vision, she watched the man slip out, untie the bridle and mount his horse; then her eyes followed him as he rode off. The sun was burning down upon the traveller and ahead of him, a breeze lowed. She was thinking: "Half a peso, half a peso lost."

"Mama," called the boy from inside. "Wasn't that Daddy? Wasn't Daddy here?"

Wiping her hand across her forehead that burned like iron in the sun, she stood there, saying: "No, son. Your Daddy, he'll be comin' later, in a short while."

Five Songs
Manno Charlemagne

— Translated from Haitian Creole by Mark Dow

LAMAYÒT

I.
Lan fè grimas se drapo nou pote
An madigra se konsa'n evolye
Pou kanaval nou poko rasazye
Men mèkredi lè sann gen pou'l rive
Nou pran patri nou pase'l anba pye
Nou vann peyi pou bèl kay lot kote
Pou mwen nou pa menm madigra'k malmaske
Vin wè pou'n ta devan lan defile

II.
Antan ke moun ak responsabilite
Ki vle lite ak tout lisidite
M'ouvri-on dra blan pou sa'k gen lonètte
Vini kouche woule montre salte
Pat met anyen sou do soudevlopman
Pa chèche mo pou'n fè fuit annavan
De syèk de sa nou te moun konsekan
Lan goumen kont zot pou'n endepandan

(Refrain)
Potoprens a la kote-w tande
Madigra mache lan cha blende
Madigra m pa pè-w se moun ou ye
Se premye fwa'm tap wè sa rive
Madigra bay tèt li on grad souple
Pou'l fè'm pè se lè sa-a'm pral pyafe
Lamayòt m pa pè-w m pa pè-w m pa pè-w
Lamayòt m pa pè-w se moun ou ye

142

Manno Charlemagne

MARDI GRAS MAN

I.

That grinning mask is the flag you carry—
That's what your Mardi Gras has become.
Carnival hasn't satisfied you yet,
And Ash Wednesday is almost here.
You take the country and you walk all over it,
You sell it for a nice house across the sea.
But I see through your Mardi Gras disguise—
Let's see what happens if you lead the parade.

II.

As long as there are those who will take responsibility,
Who want to fight with lucidity,
I'll open a white sheet for the honest ones—
Come lie in it, roll in it, confess your sins.
Don't put the blame on underdevelopment,
Don't look for words to hide behind.
Two centuries ago we were important people
Because we fought other people to make ourselves free.

(Refrain)

In Port-au-Prince you hear all kinds of things . . .
Mardi Gras Man's parade float is an armored car.
Mardi Gras Man, I'm not afraid of you, you're only a person.
It was the first time I saw how this works,
The Mardi Gras Man gives himself a military rank
To scare me, but it excites me—
Masked Man, I'm not afraid of you, I'm not afraid of you,
        I'm not afraid of you,
Masked Man, I'm not afraid of you, you're only a person.

LA FIMEN

I.

Sa ki kache k pran pay mouye
Ranyon pise k poko seche
Pa fè difè pou fè manje
Touse sa yo ka fè n touse
Sin wè lan figin dlo koule
Se pa kriye n ape kriye
Nou son la konsyans ki kanpe
Ki mache k ap analize
Van la fimen'k vle mechanste

II.

La pèsonn kanzo plizyè fwa
L a sou le lyè an de twa pa
Sou bitasyon pa'l li sèl wa
Pa ti oungan tankou lika
Ti jan mari ti nikola
Ki ta ka fè l mache opa
La pèsonn konn sa sa vle di
La vi k detri pou bay lavi
Pa ka pèdi sa pap pèdi

III.

La pèsonn konnen la viktwa
Pou respè lavi pou le dwa
Se bagay ki gen gwo konba
Li konnen byen ke ti moura
Si w lan bat bravo e sava
Pa gen moun ki gen dout sou sa
M pa kwè la pèsonn sezi
Pou sa k te rive a minui
Se nuit ki ale jou pral vini

(Refrain)
La fimen di m lan ki zorèy ou tande
La fimen se mètrès kay ki komande
La fimen pa kite la pèsonn fache
Pou l ouvè pot la pou li fout fose w ale

Manno Charlemagne

SMOKE

I.
The one in hiding who takes wet leaves,
Pissed-in mattress-stuffing that's not yet dry,
Is not making a fire to cook,
But to make us cough.
If you see tears running down our faces,
Our crying is not crying.
We are the conscience that stands up,
That moves on and analyzes
The puff of smoke that's up to no good.

II.
The people have been initiated many times,
They're through that place in just two or three steps.
On their land, they are the only king,
Little vodou priests like Lika,
Little Jan or Little Nikola,
Cannot make them march in step.
The people know what this means:
The life that is destroyed to give life
Can't be lost, it will not be lost.

III.
The people know that the victory
Of respect for life and of right
Is something you have to fight for.
They know very well that you may die
If you just applaud and stand by,
No one has any doubt about that.
I don't think the people were surprised
By what happened at midnight:
The day always follows the night.

(Refrain)
Smoke, listen closely.
Smoke, the mistress of the house is the one who gives the orders.
Smoke, don't let the people get angry
Or they'll open the door and, dammit, you're gone.

145

Manno Charlemagne

MON FRÈRE

Tu voudrais que je chante encore
le doux chant des p'tits oiseaux pour te plaire
même quand j'entends des cris de morts
qui sortent de nos cachots putrides
que je chante l'eau claire
des ruisseaux, des rivières
devant l'Artibonite
rouge du sang de nos frères
tu te dis pacifique
tu te dis apolitique, mon frère

T'aime bien les chanteurs de charme
ça plait bien aux belles dames
quand elles tombent dans les pommes
ça ne fait de mal à personne
quand le chanteur se tremousse
devant l'Amerique qui glousse
les idoles ça donnent des thrills
ça fait oublier les missiles
Salvadore et Haïti
la Grenade et compagnie, mon frère

Quand le show business fait des sous
on n'est plus raciste du tout, mon frère
on aime le rock, on aime le blues
on discothèque, on joue sa perte
on s'en lave les mains
on est de bons p'tits citoyens
et dans le sable les autruches
dorment du sommeil du juste
pendant que le grand aigle
se joue à devorer les faibles
les faibles, les faibles, les faibles

Manno Charlemagne

MY BROTHER

You would like me to sing yet again
the sweet song about the little birds to please you
even as I hear the cries of the dead
coming from our filthy prison cells
you'd like me to sing of the clear water
of the streams and rivers
of the Artibonite
red with the blood of our brothers
you call yourself a pacifist
you call yourself apolitical, my brother

You really like the romantic crooners
it pleases the beautiful women
who love to faint
it doesn't hurt anyone
when the singer shakes it
in front of a clucking America
idols supply the thrills
which make us forget about the missiles
El Salvador and Haiti
Grenada and company, my brother

When show business makes big bucks
you're no longer racist, my brother
you like rock, you like blues
you dance, you play at losing yourself
you wash your hands of it
you're all good little citizens
and in the sand the ostriches
sleep the sleep of the just
while the great eagle plays
at devouring the weak ones
the weak ones, the weak ones, the weak ones

OGANIZASYON MONDYAL

Oganizasyon mondyal yo pa pou nou yo ye
Sa la pou ede volè yo piye, devore
Lè pep ki nan di pran fizi yo
Konnen yo bouke

Lamedsin entènasyonal sa met ko-l sou kote
Yo fè reyinyon, yo pale, yo ranse
Devan vè chanpay, bon diven k enpote
Se la sa rete
Lè pep anba zam tout peyi, tout kote
Mwen renmen tande zot k ap analize
Lè l pa konsène
Lè l pa konsène

Tout sa yon moun pa vle tande
Se verite li ye
Reyaksonè sou devlope yo sa pi danjere
Lè entere yo menase, se yo k toujou rele
Tout fos entèvansyonis yo pou pep ki soulve

Laklas dominan entelijan ke li ye
An prensip konnen ke l an minorite
Li konn kijan pou l jwè
Pozisyon de klas li se sa ki konte
La fè lenposib, l a kraze, l a brize
Pou l elimine ti moun ki nan ze

N ap goumen jouk mayi mi, jouk tan nou libere
Pran konfyans nan lit lòt pèp yo ki pa pè tonbe
Delivrans yo se jefo yo lan san ki ap koule
Grenn doktè ta vle preskri
Yo voye sa jete

N ap voye yon sali pou tout pèp k ap lite
Anpil konpliman pou tout moun ki tonbe
Pou koz libète
Pou chen Ayisyen k ap di yo kiltive
K ape fè komès ak mizè refijye
Lan inivèsite, nou voye yon plot krache

INTERNATIONAL ORGANIZATIONS

The international organizations are not for us;
They're there to help the thieves plunder and devour.
When people who are suffering arm themselves,
Know that they are exhausted.

International medicine stays on the sidelines.
They hold meetings, they sit and they bullshit
With a glass of champagne, a nice imported wine
And that's it.
When people are under the gun all over the world,
Don't give me all that analysis
When you really don't give a damn.

What people don't want to hear
Is the truth.
Underdeveloped reactionaries are the most dangerous of all —
When their interests are threatened, they're always the ones
Who call for intervention against the people who are rising up.

The dominant class is very clever:
In principle they know they are the minority,
They know how to play it,
Their class position is what counts.
They'll do the impossible, they'll rampage
To eliminate the child in the womb.

We will fight until the corn is ripe, until we are free.
We take heart from the struggles of other peoples who are not afraid to die.
Their deliverance is their efforts, is in their blood that is shed.
As for the pills the doctors would like to prescribe,
They throw them away.

We salute all peoples who are fighting,
We honor all those who have died
For the cause of freedom.
As for those Haitian dogs who say they are cultured
While making a living at their universities
From the suffering of refugees,
We spit in your face.

Manno Charlemagne

LAN MALÈ M YE

Pèp ayisyen nou si milyon
sou chak san mil gen youn ki byen
sa fè si mil ki gen lajan
eske se bondye k vle l konsa
pou n jwenn repons la, nou sèl wa
m pa kwè lan bib la lekri sa
depi lan ansyen testaman
esklav toujou goumen kont wa
yo lite pou yo kase chenn
yo te goumen kont fararon
nou menm peyizan ayisyen
ki pa konn li, se sa yo di
yon rekòt diri se pa de
ni se pa twa, men l pa piti

Sou chak sen mil entelektyèl
kat mil nef san lan komokyèl
yon bann tyoul ki san ren, k san fyèl
yo bliye si pèp se sèl fòs
fè mès pou meriken antre
vin pran peyi, mèsi mouche
kontrebann plis la charite
se pou sa k san figi se vre
san lonè, san la diyite
nou twouve sa byen malere
pou yon bann moun ki kiltive
ki al lekòl ki konn a b c
kòlonn vètebral yo pliye
ak yon kwi kote yo pase

La rivyè k move se malè
inyon pa l sa fèt nan lanmè
pou nou sa son w bagay ki klè
pou le zòm sa se bel pawòl
sitou lò l vle jye yon gwo wòl
sa bo chantè ke wosiyòl
l ap toujou pale de linyon
kan w wè l ta anvi prezidan
desann kanton lan bel machinn

150

bay lajan pou de kout vaksinn
vye frè pa pran lan mannigans
se sa yo rele la twonpans
kite visye lan pòtoprens
toujou vann tèt yo pou anyen

(Refrain)
Si mil moun o ki gen lajan
malgre tout vye zam o
yo jwenn chak fwa
ey lè nou vle chanje sa
pa vle di anyen a dye y
devan yon pèp o
le jou l vle sa chanje
lan malè m ye
fo m soti la
pa tafya koudyay ey
ni kandida, k ap wète m la
la vi k pou chanje a dye
pou w alemye
se pou m revandike

I AM IN MISERY

We are six million Haitians —
out of every hundred thousand, there's one who lives well,
that makes six thousand who have money.
Is it God who wanted it that way?
You are the king as far as that answer's concerned,
I don't think it's written in the Bible.
Ever since the old testament
slaves have always fought against kings,
they struggle to break their chains,
they fought against pharaoh.
You yourselves Haitian peasants,
who cannot read, that's what they say,
one rice harvest isn't two
and it isn't three, but it is something.

151

Out of every five thousand intellectuals
four thousand nine hundred are full of shit,
a bunch of gutless, spineless pimps,
they forget that the people are the only power,
say a mass for the Americans to come in,
come take the country, thank you, sir.
Contraband plus charity
is for those with no face, it's true,
with no honor, with no dignity.
It really is a pity
for a group of people who are cultured,
who went to school, who know their abc's,
to bend their backs
with a beggar's bowl wherever they go.

The angry river is trouble,
its union is with the sea,
for us that is clear.
For the man it's pretty words,
especially when he wants to play a big role,
he's a better singer than the nightingale.
He's always talking about union,
when you see how he wants to be president,
comes down to the neighborhood in a nice car,
pays a couple of rara bands to play their bamboo horns,
brothers, don't get scammed,
that's what they call the big sham.
Let the thieves in Port-au-Prince
keep selling themselves for nothing.

(Refrain)
Six thousand people who have money —
in spite of all the old weapons
they find every time
we want to change that,
it doesn't mean a damn thing
to the people
the day they want it to change.
I have to get out
of this misery I'm in,
neither tafia street parties

152

nor candidates can get me out of it.
To change this life,
to make an improvement,
it's up to me to stand up and fight.

Note:
Gage Averill provided extremely generous and invaluable contributions to all the translations.
Francine Chouinard co-wrote "Mon Frère."
Rose-Anne Auguste co-wrote "Lan Malè M Ye."
Manno Charlemagne participated in early versions of the English.
Gregg Ellis co-translated "Mon Frère."
Thanks also to Rose-Anne Auguste, Karen Brown, Gina Cunningham, Peter Eves, Katherine Kean, Fresnel Laurent, Felix Morisseau-Leroy, Guy Nozin, Jan Sebon and Tap Tap. —M.D.

NOTES ON THE SONGS

Lamayòt: This song was written in 1989, the first year Carnival was held in Port-au-Prince after the fall of Duvalier in 1986. For three years, Carnival had been banned by the military authorities because it combines songs of political critique with exuberant lower-class crowds, an unstable mix for the elite in politically unstable periods. *Lamayòt* is an individual masque (i.e., not part of a large Carnival group). The *Lamayòt* carries a box in which he has hidden something odd, humorous, gross or obscene, and he charges people to look inside, or even to buy one of the contents. Parents will sometimes scare their children by telling them that the *Lamayòt* will put them in his box. The refrain *"Madigra m pa pè w se moun ou ye"* is also found in a 1960s Carnival song by Nemours Jean-Baptiste.

La Fimen: The line in the second stanza, "The people have been initiated many times," literally says, "The people have undergone the fire ritual (*kanzo*) many times." In a song in which Manno implies that the elite and army have lit a smoking (not burning) fire to blind and confuse people, the *kanzo* serves as a contrasting kind of fire, one that purifies and that tests people's faith and determination.

153

Manno Charlemagne

When a *gwo nèg* (big shot) rides by in the street, the *ti-nèg* (little people) are supposed to line the street and *bat bravo* (pay collective tribute by applauding), as in the third stanza here. It is one of those many rituals of power that define hierarchy and the social order in Haiti.

Mon Frère: The Haitian term *"twoubadou"* (troubadour) includes singer-songwriters of conscience like Manno, but it also encompasses the quaint ensembles that play old *méringues* about the beauty of Haiti as well as Creole versions of Cuban trio songs. In the first stanza of this song, Manno contrasts himself to these quaint *twoubadou* ensembles. The song that he refers to in the second line is "Choucoune," one of the best-known romantic *méringues*, with a chorus that starts "Ti-zwazo" (or Little Birds). This is the same song that is sung in English as "Yellow Bird." In the second stanza, Manno tells us of another kind of singer that he *isn't:* commercial singers in Haiti are routinely classified into "chanteurs de charm" (romantic crooners) and "chanteurs de choq" (hard rockers).

Oganizasyon Mondyal: The former dictatorship, in an effort to skim off more profits from the country, let foreign aid groups provide all of the infrastructure, health, education and agricultural development that the Haitian government should have been providing. The resulting foreign aid bureaucracy has been compared to a shadow government that too often works in the interests of the Haitian import-export elite and against those of the peasants and the poor. One translation of the title, "World Organization," anticipates George Bush's kinder, gentler "New World Order."

Lan Malè M Ye: In the last stanza and the refrain, Manno tells Haitians not to be persuaded by the institution of the *koudyay*. Derived from the French phrase *"coup de jaille"* (spontaneous bursting-forth), the *koudyay* became a military celebration in Haiti, and eventually any street party "hosted" by an important person.

— Gage Averill

Manno Charlemagne performing at Tap Tap Haitian Restaurant in Miami Beach, 1994. Wall painting by Jan Sebon. Photograph by Peter Eves.

Manno Charlemagne

SELF-CRITICISM & SONG:
A PROFILE OF MANNO CHARLEMAGNE
Mark Dow

When we were translating his song "La Fimen," Manno Charlemagne pointed out that he pronounces *"minuit"* in French, instead
of the Haitian Creole *"minwi":* "I pronounce it like a fucking
bourgeois" in Port-au-Prince. He said he was just being honest
about himself.

"Dear me, think of it! Niggers speaking French," said Secretary
of State William Jennings Bryan at the start of the first U.S. occupation of Haiti in 1915. Seventy years later, racist notions about
Haitians and their language persist. Anthropologist Robert Lawless has documented two centuries of misconceptions about the
Haitians' "primitive language." He notes that it should be called
"Haitian," not even "Haitian Creole." The language, he tells us, is
not a *patois,* and asks, "Would a journalist feel obliged to describe
English as a mixture of Anglo and Saxon and Norman-French and
some of almost every other European language?" Demeaning the
Haitians' language remains an element in the stereotypes that
would dehumanize the people. As the United States began its
second occupation, the *New York Times* referred to then President
Aristide, who was also a priest, as "[t]he slight, left-wing Roman
Catholic cleric with the Creole accent and exotic metaphors." A
CNN correspondent observed that while Aristide's followers considered him also mystical, he had come to appear "almost European"
in his dealings with Washington. It was only in 1987 that Haiti's
constitution recognized Creole as the country's official language,
and it is no accident that Creole literacy was a major element of
President Aristide's program. Government business has been conducted in French to maintain the division between the educated
elite (what Lawless calls "a very small pseudobilingual ruling class")
and the illiterate majority. Aristide made history when he delivered
his inaugural address in Haitian Creole.

Born in Port-au-Prince in 1948, Charlemagne spent his adoles-
cence in the "popular" neighborhoods that would later vote over-
whelmingly for Aristide and would, in return, suffer brutal military
reprisals. When he recalls his childhood, Charlemagne describes
the mix of politics, music and street language he absorbed in those
neighborhoods. "I was raised in a *lakou*," he says. "A *lakou* in the
Haitian countryside means several houses that connect to each

156

other. . . . I lived in an 'urban *lakou'* in Port-au-Prince. That means you have the Abel family, the Odé family, the Charlemagne family, etcetera. When Odé had a problem with my mother, I could hear them arguing. I could hear the dirty words they used. And I also learned from the workers, streetworkers, those macho guys who came from the countryside to Port-au-Prince. They are the ones who built the roads in Haiti. When they are digging, they are singing songs, dirty songs. So I was a specialist in dirty songs. I was the one who brought those songs to my school, helping rich kids who were raised behind high walls to know what was happening outside. I was their teacher. I was also singing church songs. I went to the Catholic schools, I was raised by the priests, so you might hear that Gregorian thing when I'm singing. Eight years old, six years, learning things from Jesus, from my school and from the street. I always prefer the street."

Manno, as he is widely known — and his last name is "Chalmay" in Haitian — came to musical maturity in the *"kilti libète,"* or freedom culture, of the 1970s, described by Gage Averill: "The *kilti libète* groups' choice of acoustic music set them apart from commercial, middle-class *mini-djaz*. Their model drew from a tradition of *twoubadou* (troubadour) music, a guitar-based tradition that owes a debt to Cuban *sones* and *boleros* as well as to older Haitian rural song traditions. In many cases, the groups rewrote and radicalized peasant songs, transforming them into weapons to use against the dictatorship." In 1986, after the overthrow of Jean-Claude Duvalier's dictatorship, Charlemagne returned from six years in exile and became an essential part of a cultural renaissance that included a rejuvenation of roots-based music. He was arrested twice after the 1991 coup d'état that overthrew Aristide, Haiti's first democratically elected president and a personal friend of Charlemagne. Finding refuge in the Argentine embassy in Port-au-Prince, Manno was able to leave Haiti with the help of former U.S. Attorney General Ramsey Clark and a group of Hollywood stars led by director Jonathan Demme.

One morning last November, Port-au-Prince Mayor Joseph Emmanuel Charlemagne sat brooding about the assassination of Israeli Prime Minister Yitzhak Rabin. Charlemagne was sitting on the balcony of his room at the Hotel Oloffson, made famous by Graham Greene's *The Comedians*. According to a story that may be apocryphal, when Charlemagne returned to Haiti in 1994 after the three-year coup, he found that people with nowhere else to live had moved into his Port-au-Prince home — and had now put up a banner welcoming him back. Since they had nowhere else to go, according to the story, Charlemagne let them stay, and he moved into the hotel.

As Charlemagne spoke about the Rabin assassination, it became clear that his mind was not on the intricacies of Middle East politics. And he was certainly not participating in the grotesque public transformation of Rabin into a martyr for peace. On the contrary, Charlemagne instinctively understood that Rabin's "peace agreements" were simply a strategy change from the days of breaking young Palestinians' bones. The 1986 song "Oganizasyon Mondyal" (International Organizations) is a clear indictment of international "aid" in Haiti. And it was appropriate to translate it, as we did, for a September 1994 concert in Miami Beach denouncing the second U.S. occupation of Haiti. But Charlemagne wrote the song in the aftermath of the massacre of Palestinians at Sabra and Shatilla in southern Lebanon. "I saw [United Nations Secretary General] Javier Peres de Cuellar think, by drinking a glass of wine with King Hussein of Jordan, he can resolve that problem," Charlemagne said. Then, alluding to the so-called "peace process" under way since the secret Oslo agreements, Charlemagne added, "Now, what happened? See, I was right."

But Charlemagne was thinking of the Rabin assassination in a larger context: in his next breath he lamented the growing strength of reactionaries in France. He was upset, at the most personal level, by the increasing power of the right in all its forms. And, in his new position as mayor, he was also worried about Haiti, and about himself. Over the next few days, the phones kept ringing, and many of the calls brought unconfirmed reports of killings in various parts of Haiti — the kinds of killings that made Charlemagne and other activists fearful about a growing boldness by anti-democratic forces, and the kinds of killings that would not be important enough for the media to cover. For now, the media wasn't in Haiti. Why should they be? On the one hand, there weren't photo-op bodies on the streets within a short distance of the main Port-au-Prince hotels. And on the other hand, the State Department wasn't saying that there was news.

Within days, Charlemagne's foreboding proved justified. The police discovered a large weapons cache in the Port-au-Prince home of former dictator Lt. General Prosper Avril. Avril himself escaped to the safety of the Columbian embassy — "right over there," Charlemagne gestured from his balcony railing. He seemed in those few words to be outraged, disgusted and afraid. And obsessed: he wanted to get Avril, he wanted to speak with an American attorney and friend due in town any day about how to get Avril. When the attorney showed up and said, "How are you?" the mayor replied, "I'm fighting." The Avril situation wasn't the only danger, but it was emblematic. About a week later, the mayor and some of his staff and security people were working late at the Hôtel de Ville, or city hall. Gunmen appeared and opened fire on the building with automatic weapons. Charlemagne said later that this was meant to scare him, not to kill him. He also said that he saw National Police and U.N. vehicles (which would have been under U.S. command) drive by and keep on going.

That same week brought the assassination of Jean-Hubert Feuille, deputy of Parliament and a cousin and close ally of Aristide. Some interpreted this as a clear warning to those who would continue efforts at economic and social reforms. At his cousin's funeral, Aristide delivered a powerful, angry eulogy in which he demanded that disarmament be enacted in earnest, *"total et legal,"* not just in the slums but in the big houses of the wealthy. And he encouraged the people to work with the new police force to expose hidden arms. The North American press finally found news in Haiti: Aristide's speech was thoroughly misrepresented as a call for violence from his supporters. His indictment of the international community for failing to disarm supporters of the military was not taken seriously.

It is important to remember that the occupying American forces had made a lot of noise about disarmament without doing much disarming. And that also should not be surprising. The United States has supported the military and paramilitary repression of democracy in Haiti since it first occupied the country early this century (1915–1934) and created an army designed to repress its own citizens. More recently, the U.S. had actively opposed Aristide's presidential candidacy, opposed his populist efforts at reform during his seven months in office (creating a front organization, for example, to work with the Haitian business community in opposing Aristide's efforts to raise the minimum wage) and continued to work secretly with the Haitian military — and train them — during the charade of Washington-brokered negotiations to return Aristide to office. Moreover, as journalist Allan Nairn has documented in detail, the U.S. financed the paramilitary organization FRAPH during Aristide's exile as a counterweight to Aristide's supporters in Haiti. FRAPH is responsible for thousands of cases of rape, torture and murder of Aristide supporters. And as Nairn also discovered, U.S. defense personnel were inside Haitian military headquarters when the coup against Aristide took place on the night of September 29, 1991.

Manno's "La Fimen" (Smoke), the title cut on his most recent album (1994), is about that *koudeta* (coup d'état). He told me that his intention in this song—which he admits is "a beautiful song, which took me some time to write"—is not only "to accuse the army . . . to accuse [the one] who tries to do something in secret," but also to "minimize the idea of the coup." It is this second intention, I think, which is the perfect example of the kind of independent thinking that angers many of Manno's potential (and former) political allies, and which also points to the sense of complexity that makes so many of his songs into poems rather than political tracts set to music. A few years ago, a Haitian newspaper editor said that Charlemagne "does not make metaphors. If he sees a murder, he calls the man a murderer." The editor was right about the directness, but wrong about the poetry. *"M pa kwè la pèsonn sezi/Pou sa k te rive a minui/Se nuit ki ale jou pral vini"*: "I don't think the people were surprised/By what happened at midnight/It's night that goes, day is coming." In these lines Manno is minimizing the idea of the coup, not only by saying no one was surprised (as no one is surprised that day follows night) but by offering hope for change (night gives way to day) in the same image.

"This was the very prototype of the Chilean coup," Manno told me in August 1994. "The difference is that in Chile the U.S. used generals, and in Haiti they used the majors. The U.S. had used majors in the Haitian army to eliminate people when there was a danger of a popular uprising against Avril when Avril was in Taipei [in 1990]. The majors still control the country today. . . . So they trained those majors, and then saved them for something interesting—they used them to overthrow Aristide." In the song Charlemagne says no one was surprised by the coup, but he has said in an interview that the progressive community let down its guard and allowed itself to be victimized: "People saw the election of Aristide as an end instead of a beginning. For the first time the *progressiste* community in Haiti had the power, and we were drugged. After working so hard to overthrow Duvalier, the

160

movement started to become weak. When Aristide took power, people were resting. . . . They thought the fight was over after February 7, 1991 [Aristide's inauguration]. And the coup happened."

If all this detail seems a bit esoteric, that's only because it is unfamiliar. There is nothing inherently mysterious about these political machinations, in spite of North American journalists' propensity for the word "murky" when reporting Haitian politics. Certainly there are complications and intricacies, but they are made murky by the press's complicity with U.S. propaganda about its role in the world. Because of our grade-school indoctrination, there are things we can't easily see that the illiterate Haitians know as a matter of life and death:

Si ayiti pa forè
Ou jwenn tout bèt ladann l
Ou jwenn lyon, ou jwenn tig
Ou jwenn chat, ou jwenn rat
Ou jwenn menm leyopa

"If Haiti is not a forest/you still find all kinds of creatures there./ You find lions, you find tigers/You find cats, you find rats/You even find leopards." This list of animals isn't about some *Serpent and the Rainbow* melodrama, which we have been conditioned to associate with Haiti. In a song combining his own lyrics from 1974 with a 1986 resistance song from the town of Gonaïves against Baby Doc Duvalier and his wife, Michelle Bennet, Charlemagne is singing about the U.S. role, which we have been conditioned *not* to be aware of. The Leopards were an elite, U.S.-trained battalion in the Haitian army:

Ki leyopa souple?
Yon bann fòv malmaske
Si gen nenpòt ti bwi
Ti bwi tankou latòti
Leyopa pran kouri, wi.

Which leopards, please?
A bunch of thinly disguised beasts.
If there's any little noise,
even the noise of a tortoise,
the leopards run away, yes.

161

Manno Charlemagne

Here two crucial Charlemagne strains come together: the constant effort to unmask the hidden perpetrators, the hidden realities and the victory over fear that comes with the unmasking. These songs call for resistance, but they also demand and offer analysis. In "Ayiti Pa Forè" he also sings, *"M pat gen bon pwofesè/Ki pou te montre m koulè/Ki pou te ka fè m wè klè"*: "I didn't have good teachers/To show me the colors/To make me see clearly." Elsewhere he sings sarcastically, *"Banm yon ti limyè, mèt/Banm yon ti limyè pou m wè sa k ap pase"*: "Give me a little light, boss/Give me a little light so I can see what's happening." He could have been singing to the *New York Times*'s Rick Bragg, who "explained" the relations between Haiti's wealthy elite and the military on the eve of the occupation and noted, "Poor Haitians cannot understand all this."

"Lamayòt" in the present selection of songs is an excellent example of seeing through masks and overcoming fear. Here Avril enters the picture again. Manno wrote the song in exile (in Boston) in October 1989, just before the November arrests by Avril of activists Evans Paul, Jean Auguste Mezieu and Marineau Etienne. These men were tortured by the Avril regime and then put on Haitian television as a gruesome warning, and they became known as the "Prisoners of All Saints' Day." Manno describes the refrain of the song as introspective; he's thinking over what he has seen. I use the ellipsis in the line "In Port-au-Prince you hear all kinds of things . . ." to try to give a sense of this contemplation. And I should note here something that is applicable throughout these transcribed versions: these are songs, and when Manno sings them, his melodies and his guitar and his voice are hauntingly beautiful.

What I hear in his voice is crucial to my reading. *"Madigra bay tèt li on grad souple/Pou'l fè'm pè se lè sa-a'm pral pyafe/Lamayòt m pa pè-w m pa pè-w m pa pè-w/Lamayòt m pa pè-w se moun ou ye"*: "The Mardi Gras man gives himself a military rank/To scare me, but it excites me—/Lamayòt, I'm not afraid of you, I'm not afraid of you, I'm not afraid of you/Lamayòt, I'm not afraid of you, you're only a person." In an earlier version, I omitted the repetitions, thinking they were unnecessary on paper. Then I listened to the song again (it's also on the album *La Fimen*), and felt the repetitions were essential to the mood, the singer explaining things to himself, seeing them for what they are, and then as both warrior and child, getting excited at what is meant to scare him, repeating

162

the phrase to calm himself, and also to prod himself into battle. Manno once told me: "I was raised by my aunt, not my mother. And both of them are singers. I didn't know who my father was until I was thirty-seven years old, and it turns out that when I knew my father's family, they're all musicians, too. And I feel I had some psychological problems because of not knowing my father, some 'child problems.' If you listen to my songs, you can feel it." In "Lamayòt" you can feel it.

On a more explicit level, too, "Lamayòt" is about self-criticism, what Manno in his richly imperfect English calls "auto-critic." Of the line, "Don't put the blame on [the word] 'underdevelopment,'" Manno says he is "talking with my fellow leftists." The false nationalism of the abused flag in the opening line becomes the white sheet in the second stanza, which Manno offers to those who want to "fight with lucidity"; I rendered *"montre salte,"* literally "show [your] dirt" or "dirtiness" as "confess your sins." Manno approved: the Bible says wash your sins, he said, in my language it means come and make your auto-critic. After he wrote the song for Evans Paul and the others, Manno says, he discovered that they weren't so clean after all. In the margins of his transcription of the song, he listed Paul and others who he claims were involved in meetings with senior U.S. officials leading up to the 1991 coup. "And I wrote the song for that fucker," he said. Paul was the mayor of Port-au-Prince when Aristide was overthrown, and after Aristide's return, many observers felt Paul was being groomed by the United States to succeed him. He was running for reelection to the mayor's office when Manno decided to enter the race in the summer of 1995. (Paul has also been a playwright and founded a Port-au-Prince theatre company in the eighties; he is commonly known as K-Plim, an abbreviation for "literary sage.")

I'm not at all sure that the personal/political animosity is what made Manno decide to run. So what did? When I asked him, he didn't really answer. He said that when he saw his pictures on walls around the capital, he realized that it was for real. But then he tells me that he paid for those posters himself. He also said, "I'm a student man," meaning that his activist work had long been with students, and that students had pushed him to enter the race. Finally, he tells me a joke that had aired on the radio about the candidates' campaign slogans. For Paul: he's the incumbent. For Frank Romain (Port-au-Prince mayor under Baby Doc):

he's a *makout* (or Tonton Macoute). For Manno Charlemagne: *"Pourquoi pas?"*

Graffiti also appeared on Port-au-Prince walls during the campaign saying *"Manno Charlemagne li pwòp"*: he's clean. Self-criticism is a cleansing rite, and Manno will often indicate his approval for someone by saying "He's clean." Before the return of Aristide, Manno was frustrated with the exile community's obsession with returning him. He felt that negotiations with Washington could not ultimately benefit Haiti, and he made enemies among former supporters when he said on Haitian radio in Miami that Aristide would not return. Explaining himself later, he said, "[The people] have to know, Aristide *was* their man. There can be others, there can be, there will be someone else, some other person, clean person, to help guide the movement."

Rose-Anne Auguste was with the student organization FENEH when she co-wrote *"Lan Malè M Ye"* with Manno in 1987, on the eve of elections which the U.S.-sponsored military stopped with an election-day massacre. Auguste operates a community health clinic in Karfou Fey, one of the "popular neighborhoods" or slums of Port-au-Prince, which were Aristide strongholds. She courageously opened the clinic during the coup years, and since the U.S. occupation has refused to accept funding from the U.S. Agency for International Development. When I spoke with her on the balcony of the clinic, patients waited below, under a gazebo, watching a video about AIDS prevention prepared by Paul Farmer (Farmer, author of the indispensable *The Uses of Haiti*, is an assistant professor of medicine at Harvard and runs a clinic in rural Haiti). Auguste told me that she respects Manno's strategy though she disagreed with his decision to run for office with the country under occupation. *"Se nèg ki renmen batay,"* she said. "He's a man who loves to fight." *"Yo pa ka achte l fasilman,"* she added. "They can't buy him easily," and that is why the job is dangerous.

In fact, back in November, Manno could not stop talking about those in the government whom he accused of buying or being bought. He talked to anyone who would listen about the *"vòlè,"* the thieves, just as he has in his songs for years. Now, in the opinion of one longtime Haitian activist and former political prisoner, Manno was incensed because he was seeing up close what he had known about for years. Manno often drives himself around the city, and when pedestrians recognize him at a stoplight or stuck in traffic, they start to gather around the car. Again and again I saw Manno respond by rolling down the windows to talk to people. Sometimes he asked them what they wanted. Other times he just started in with whatever was on his own mind, and often that was the *vòlè*. He went on the radio to denounce particular people in the National Palace, that is, in the Aristide government, who were profiting from drug trafficking or who had unexplained large bank accounts of U.S. dollars, and he criticized Aristide himself for knowing about these people and tolerating them. One person told me she felt Manno was brave and doing the right thing, another felt he was making a mistake by lashing out instead of organizing. But he could not help himself.

At the National Palace for the swearing-in of a new prime minister, Manno said he felt like *"une mouche dans ver du lait,"* a fly in a glass of milk. He seemed physically uncomfortable in his suit, among the dignitaries of whom he was now one. Last night, he tells me, playing music at the Oloffson, I was relaxed. Here I have to shake hands with people I hate. I can't keep doing this — "I'm a natural guy." In the same week he told me, "I'm starting to enjoy this job" and also that he felt "morally tired." At his office downtown, he can spend a whole day without sitting at his desk, moving from one constituent to another. They were coming to see him personally. "You see that guy," he says of a young man, maybe eighteen, "he should go to school . . ." Another young man talks to the *majistra* about getting materials for a construction job. "He's the best carpenter around," says the mayor. An old man outside wonders when he will be paid — he's been sweeping the streets since the former mayor's office hired him, and he hasn't been paid in four months. The current mayor is obviously embarrassed by the indignity of the situation. "I know that guy since I was a little kid," he says. And of a woman who has come asking for money for a prescription, he explains, "Her son is dying from malaria."

But that is not the whole picture. In April, a major human rights organization in Haiti condemned the mayor's office for its agents' use of violence in clearing *ti marchand* or small vendors, mostly women, from their longstanding but illegal spots on the streets and sidewalks of the capitol. The group compared the arbitrary use of violence and authority to FRAPH tactics. The next month, the mayor announced that, because the new police are incompetent, he would arm his own people to patrol the city; the Interior Ministry said that such a force would be unconstitutional.

Manno Charlemagne

In a characteristic blend of ego and humility, Manno Charlemagne once told an interviewer, "I'm not supreme. There are a lot
of people they say came from heaven and dropped to earth. I am
the child of a woman, a poor woman who suffered but who felt
the necessity for me to help others." One hopes that in the pressure
of the current situation, Manno's respect for democracy, complexity and self-criticism will prevail.

*Campaign Poster, Port-au-Prince, 1995. Slogan reads: "His back
is wider than a winnowing tray." Photograph by Mark Dow.*

The Day You See Me Fall
Is Not the Day I Die
Bob Shacochis

VOUDOU RHYTHMS

"THE FICTION WRITER." A greeting in the field, the Chinook that brought in the brass whipping dust on the edge of town.

These were the first words Colonel Mark Boyatt ever said to me, a dismissive double entendre, however good-natured the delivery, a cutting acknowledgement and many-layered joke to let me know I was on his radar screen, to test my own mettle perhaps, and I had to laughingly bend to the colonel's sense of gamesmanship, his easy half-smile and sly charm. Except for the spark of mischief in his eyes, Boyatt looked like a soft-spoken Jesuit prefect, a man given to the ascetic disciplines of transcendent contemplation, yet he was the field commander of the Special Forces — the legendary Green Berets — in Operation Uphold Democracy, and his men controlled ninety-five percent of the Haitian countryside.

Yes, I told Boyatt, I am the fiction writer, and if I had had the presence of mind at the time — this was February 1995, the middle of the story I am about to recount — I would have in turn acknowledged the colonel's own considerable talent for creating fictions — mysteries, intrigues, secret and elusive victories — imaginary worlds meant to reinvent the vital political landscape of places like Haiti.

But we had not come to Haiti to practice the same art, the colonel and I: he, a lesser god of war in the pantheon of a superpower, had come to shape events; I, duly appointed correspondent, booted and vested citizen scribe, had come to bear witness to those efforts, honorable and otherwise, to chronicle the modern exploits of Americans in the Third World, particularly the Caribbean, as I often had in my fictions and in my reportage. I had come to write about the Americans who, for the second time this century, had invaded and occupied the world's first black republic, but the story, mostly the story of soldiers, the Special Forces, which is not fiction, does not begin with them but with drums — with Haitian drummers—on the Champs Mars, the expansive and somewhat tawdry patchwork park that spreads out beyond the grandiose National Palace, an architectural wedding cake, in downtown Port-au-Prince.

Handmade drums, *voudou* drums, heartbeat drums with a rising pulse as furious as hurricane-driven rain, drums that never fluctuate, ease to a simmer or beg patience, rhythms that never seduce but command, take possession, spraying like Uzis, like a deafening cascade of rocks on the tin roofs of oppression, and eventually, because these drums are war drums, they'll bring us back to the colonel, all in good time.

The tyrants wanted everyone happy, the first carnival after the coup d'état; they wanted celebration—and when it was not forthcoming, set about to manufacture it themselves—because the cancer that had metastasized in Haitian society had been cut away, gouged out with less than surgical precision, the disease called Lavalas was in regression, the tumorous and malignant Aristide removed and the status quo revived. No single social event was more important to the Haitian people, high or low, elite or peasant, than carnival, and carnival was the government's responsibility, a once-only chance to exercise its deformed sense of noblesse oblige, but when the tyrants sent the musicians to Champs Mars to inaugurate the seasonal jubilation, inconceivably, no one came, maybe a few hundred people, but in Haiti during carnival that was no one.

There were many reasons for the people's absence, but the foremost problem, the putschists determined, was the music—the music wasn't working. The regime had hired *compas* bands, when what they really needed to attract a crowd was a *racine* band, but *racine* was Aristide's music, roots music, the music of the masses, *racine* was the sound of uprising and revolution, a regime-sponsored *racine* band would be analogous to Bob Marley playing for the Republican National Convention, but now nobody could stomach *compas*, its simple melodies and trivial lyrics were like a funeral dirge for democracy, they hated the putschists so much that now nobody even wanted to listen to it except the attachés, the killers, the Macoutes—the ones who when they danced, danced in blood.

To control a country as fucked up as Haiti, you had to wrap your hands around the throat of everything, the language, the music, especially the songs and the potent rhythms of the songs, because in the people's centuries-old war against the tyrants, drums were weapons, words were lethal ammunition, and so the generals decided they had to get a *racine* band out on the Champs Mars, the quicker the better. During pre-Carnival celebrations in January, they summoned Richard Morse, a young Haitian-American musician who ran the Hotel Oloffson, to the Ministry of the Interior — the administrative headquarters for Haiti's brutish police and new paramilitary security forces. The duty officer directed Richard to a large room already crammed with about fifty or sixty red-eyed assassins, it must have been payday for the assassins, and Richard's thinking, *God, what's going on, these guys have probably been killing people all week and they're waiting to get paid and here I am.*

For about ten minutes he stood there, not saying a thing, watching himself being watched, until finally one of the vultures said, *Get RAM a chair* — RAM was the name of Richard's band — and so they sat him down and then a lieutenant sauntered in and told him he wanted Richard to do a concert and Richard said, *Fine.*

The lieutenant said, *If a crowd doesn't show up I'm going to arrest you.*

Richard returned to the hotel, gathered the band for a debate, talked to the staff, got on the phone and asked everybody he knew and trusted — Should we or shouldn't we? Pro-Lavalas musicians were being shot, disappeared, bands were going underground, going into exile, the troubador Manno Charlemagne was living like a prisoner at the Venezuelan embassy. In Haiti there was never a good answer, never a right answer, the entire scene was complicated to the point of dysfunction. To play for the Ministry of the Interior meant he would be associated, in the collective eye, with the coup leaders, and yet to refuse would be a fundamentally suicidal response, so Richard kept soliciting advice until the most logical thing somebody said was do the gig, but keep your mouth shut. *Play your songs, don't say anything and get the hell out.*

That night as RAM stood on the stage in the band shell on Champs Mars, there were people as far as they could see, ten thousand people, and cars all the way down to the palace. When they started playing, anybody in the audience who raised his arms into the air to dance was swarmed by plainclothes cops and dragged away; two songs into the gig and Richard had counted a dozen arrests. *Good God*, he thought, *I'd hate to leave this party and have them think I'm part of all this.* The stage was surrounded by

FAHD — the Haitian army — a company of helmeted, well-armed soldiers, and two more truckloads of troops were parked on the street. The intensity escalated deep into the red zone: suddenly everything was quiet, everything was bad, the crowd's riveted on Richard, the lead singer, the man out front, wondering what he would do next as he stepped back over to the microphone.

"Well, up until now I haven't said anything." He listened to his voice, his New York–accented Creole, reverberate, booming throughout the park, echoing beyond the palace, the Holiday Inn where the Macoutes and the journalists congregated, filtering down into the slums where most of his band members lived. "Join us," he said, signaling to the female vocalists, who began, a cappella, to deliver the band's first of many subversions throughout the years of the regime — an old ballad, a traditional part of Haiti's oral culture of resistance. *Kote moun yo, pas way moun yo.* Thirty seconds later, realizing what the band was singing — a parable, in a sort of peasant code, about Aristide — the soldiers pulled the plug.

The sun had gone down long ago; now there's no power, no stage lights, and it's pitch black in the park. Behind Richard on stage a row of drummers hunkered over their hand-made congas, RAM's *voudou* rhythms section; he turned to command them to keep drumming, full force, a spontaneous decision that would evolve into a strategy, a method of survival, and be repeated again and again in the difficult years ahead whenever the lights went out and the horror descended, and by the time Richard turned back around — fifteen seconds — thousands of people had disappeared into the night. The girls took up the song again, their voices clear and strong in the darkness, the drums were drumming, you could hear their thunderous report throughout the terrified city as RAM played on, drums and vocals, as if nothing was happening, as if this wasn't a nightmare and the dream was still alive.

Petro drums — the rhythms of Haiti's ethos, which was *maroonage*; the rhythms of the new world, Haitian-born among Indians and slaves; the rhythms of the ghost of Boukman and *voudou* and insurrection. Not *rada*, the rhythm of ancient Africa, the mythic Guinee, the lost land beyond the sea, because *rada* rhythms had proved impotent against the French, *rada*'s power had dwindled in the Middle Passage.

But *petro* — *petro* lived. *Petro* was the percussive language of blackout and embargo, when you heard *petro* drums what you heard, what you knew you were hearing, was war. *Petro* was the rhythm of war.

Drums and vocals — *Kote moun yo, pas way moun yo. Where are the people? We don't see them?* Meaning, Lavalas. Meaning, Aristide. Meaning, the uncounted multitudes who had disappeared into the sea.

When the lights came back on, a fragile miracle, the people left cowering in the shadows were astounded to see that RAM — unlike the countless thousands who, since the coup six months earlier, were already dead or missing — had been unharmed, that Richard was still alive, and not a shot had been fired.

Richard Morse counted governments, not years, to measure his time in Haiti since 1987 when he had taken a lease on the Oloffson, the most famous hotel in the Caribbean. Fifteen, sixteen? He had to stop and think about it, because the governments went up and down like tin ducks in a shooting gallery, here at the boneyard carnival that was Haiti. It was mad, and it was unspeakably weird, and it was always bloody during the island's seemingly endless struggle toward the light. He had come down by himself from New Jersey in September 1985, a tall, twenty-eight-year-old sleepy-eyed, surly-faced Princeton grad, his mother a renowned Haitian dancer and his Anglo father a Latin American scholar at Yale — a kid who had grown up in houses with many, many rooms. He had been playing bass in a New Wave band that worked the downtown clubs in Manhattan and really didn't know what he was doing — pursuing a vague desire for different rhythms, something like that — when he landed in Port-au-Prince, and suddenly they're shooting people everywhere, there's a mass uprising — the *dechoukaj*, or uprooting of all things Duvalier — by February, Baskethead — Baby Doc — is aboard a United States Air Force jet headed for France, twenty-nine years of vampirism and dictatorship out the window . . . and then back in again, now in the guise of narcotraffickers and military clowns, six months later. Still, a true metamorphosis had taken place during the *dechoukaj*, not from totalitarianism to democracy, but from the bondage of the spirit to the release of the imagination. Though it had been their fate to exist in purgatory, boiling and on fire for hundreds of years, the Haitians had finally done what providence and history and their own rulers would not do: they had created themselves as human beings. Haiti's improvisation had been in its singers, not its song.

171

Overnight the country seemed intoxicated with possibility, and Richard attached himself to the Hotel Oloffson, a whitewashed, multi-tiered tropiGothic monstrosity nestled in its own private jungle in a high-walled enclave in downtown Port-au-Prince. The Oloffson, by its very architecture and ceiling fan ambiance, created an indelible vision of faded authority and exotic intrigue, but it was built atop a history that didn't quite match the Kiplingesque groove of the white man's burden, and though its exteriors suggested a certain nostalgia *noire* for imperial glory, any such nostalgia would have been severely misplaced. Instead, the Oloffson was a native hybrid, a reproduction that became authentic through the grind and twist of desperate events. In *The Comedians*, Graham Greene's novel about the Duvalier era, Greene described the grotesque impression the Oloffson, alias the Hotel Trianon, made on one's senses — "You expected a witch to open the door to you or a manic butler, with the bat dangling from the chandelier behind him" — and *New Yorker* cartoonist Charles Addams, a frequent guest, modeled his trademark haunted houses after the hotel. A folly, a travel writer once wrote, "of spires, crotchets, finials and conical towers," the structure was the grandiose vision of the Sam family, which had constructed the mansion at the end of the 19th century and inhabited it until 1915, when the family's dubious contribution to the nation, President Guillaume Sam, was dragged out of his office into the street, shot, his body torn apart by a mob, and the pieces paraded around town skewered on the ends of poles. Waving the Monroe Doctrine and growling about Germany's increasing influence in the West Indies, the U.S. Marines seized the occasion as an excuse to invade and, the next day, into the capital they marched, leasing the Sam family residence — the future Hotel Oloffson — as a hospital until they left, nineteen years later, serenaded by Richard's maternal grandfather, Auguste, a popular singer still remembered for the songs he composed to taunt the American soldiers and their iron-fisted occupation.

Haiti, back in the early seventies when Baskethead inherited the palace from his ghoulish father, enjoyed a relatively brief but unprofitable tenure as an off-the-path destination for the rich and famous — Jackie Onassis, for instance, who became a major collector of Haitian artwork — but once the *dechoukaj* flamed over the countryside, once Club Med closed its doors in 1986, the *blancs* — foreigners, white people — wouldn't come anymore, not as tourists anyway. For a generation, for generations, there had been the killings, the state-sponsored violence, the crushing and ubiquitous poverty, the incomprehensible polyglot of Creole; the Centers for Disease Control in Atlanta made matters worse with a bogus AIDS alert. Hollywood and the missionaries and the Duvaliers demonized *voudou*, an ancient theocratic view of the universe based on animism. In 1986, I came across the stationery of one of the island's evangelical missions — *Haiti*, it read, *6½ million souls in witchcraft and Catholicism*. There was the racial dynamic to boot, a permanent and insurmountable barrier to the majority of whites and so the trade, never more than a golden trickle, dried up, and Haiti, as was its common fate, fell off the map of civilization.

The Oloffson survived by serving as a sort of crashhouse for bohemian reporters — journotrash — and aid entrepreneurs, some checking in for the sole purpose of carousing with the highly literate chameleon Aubelain Jolicoeur, the hotel's most curious and enduring artifact — aging spy, former Duvalierist apparatchik, dapper gallant and gossip columnist for Haiti's only daily newspaper, *Le Nouvelliste*, the spry Jolicoeur transformed only slightly by Graham Greene into the fictional Petit Pierre. Greene enhanced his reputation, Jolicoeur wrote in 1991, upon the occasion of the novelist's death, "to such an extent that some fans kneel at my feet or kiss my hand in meeting a man living his own legend."

Year after year you could sit on the Oloffson's airy veranda and observe Jolicoeur, his spidery body impeccably suited, a silk ascot at his throat, mount the hotel's diamond vee of steps to hold soirees in the wicker and rattan drawing room, adulating the women attracted to the gleam of his bald head and gold-knobbed cane, stroking the *femmes* with flowery prose, prying himself away from their heavenly perfumes to play backgammon with cronies from the CIA. Jolicoeur had been a fixture at the hotel for decades, just as the foreign correspondents had returned on their annual migrations, year after year, dining on the veranda at twilight, their collegial discourse interrupted by rude bursts of automatic weapon fire down the street at the national palace where, in the long march toward democracy after the *dechoukaj*, still another coup unfolded, each journalist hesitating with fork in mid-air, wondering, *Didn't I order a double?*

Bartender, *s'il vous plaît*. Barbancourt, *encore*.

When Richard signed a fifteen-year lease on the Oloffson in No-

Bob Shacochis

vember 1987, the country had fallen apart again, driving from Petionville, the elite suburbs up the mountain, down to Port-au-Prince after sundown was considered insane — random shootings, burning tires, vigilante roadblocks, bodies in the street — but he was operating on the theory that if there were elections and they went well, there'd be democracy and tourists would come to the hotel. And if the elections didn't go well, the rooms would fill up with journalists. But the elections, prematurely foisted upon a population ill-prepared (but forever yearning) for such an exercise by the Reagan administration, were catastrophic — voters (and journalists) slaughtered as they queued up at polling stations, and everyone bugged out, even Blair, Richard's girlfriend from Princeton, the entire nation was reeling from one near-death experience to another, everybody's head was filled with a kaleidoscopic blur of violent images, the Americans kept pushing elections, Band-Aids in the trauma unit, and by the time Richard convinced Blair to come back, he was no longer the naive newcomer but a player, working part-time at the El Rancho for Joe Namphy, whose brother Henri, a general in the army, was president and in deep shit with Washington for letting the Macoutes shoot up the elections. The White House wanted Namphy out, so the Haitian military was in the market for a stooge and Richard swung the deal, matchmaker between an old family friend, Leslie Manigat, a professor with human rights credentials, and the Duvalierist generals. This happened on the second of January, 1988, and in two weeks Manigat was in the palace, where he held on until a night in June, just by coincidence Richard's birthday, when the military yanked him with a coup d'état. As the sun went down gunfire erupted all over town, Richard's phone started ringing, people calling to say Manigat had been arrested, Manigat had been shot, Manigat was in an ambulance, Manigat's fucked, *what are you going to do?* Die? Blair went over the edge, shrieking at him, *I told you not to get involved in politics! I told you not to get involved!* and when she stopped screaming she packed her bags and left for good.

Happy birthday.

In 1989, George Bush wanted to try the democracy thing again and guarantee the result, which was meant to be a foregone conclusion. The White House's preferred and handsomely financed candidate, Marc Bazin, an economist and former World Bank executive, was slotted to ascend to the national palace under the sunny skies of

174

Haiti's first free and fair election, to be overseen by Jimmy Carter, whose own bias for Bazin was stupidly transparent. Indeed, the subsequent election — in 1990, just as Richard was forming his band — was a triumph for democracy but for the fact that the Haitian people, by an overwhelming and euphoric majority, chose for their new president not Bazin but Jean-Bertrand Aristide, a young leftist priest from the slums given to anti-American rhetoric, a disciple of both Christ and liberation theology whom the FAHD couldn't seem to assassinate, try as they might, though they burned down his church and hacked to death his congregation. Inaugurated in February 1991, for a five-year term, Aristide lasted only seven months before the military pitched him into exile and took to murdering anyone who even dared to mention his name — Titid, little Aristide, Haiti's messiah. President Bush, underwriter of the island's nascent democracy, swiftly announced the coup would not stand, then just as quickly receded into embarrassed silence when informed by his staff that his own crew in Port-au-Prince not only had foreknowledge of the putsch, but had allowed it to advance with a wink and a nod.

Ironically, early on in the coup, as the terror began to coalesce into a system, RAM prospered, the band had more hits on the radio than anybody else but people were afraid to come to their concerts, afraid to be identified with *racine*, with the politics of the *petro* rhythms. Until the mandarins woke up to the band's agenda, they were constantly being showcased on the government-run radio and television stations, but then the generals began to review and censor their tapes, the military would send attachés out to the Oloffson to interview Richard: *What do you think about what's happening here? What do you think of this situation?*

Uh . . . what situation?

Military coup d'état, and the attachés would take Richard's hand and make him pat the guns tucked into their hip pockets; they wanted payoffs and Richard would give them RAM T-shirts and twenty bucks.

After the fiasco on Champs Mars the regime at last understood where RAM stood in their cosmology and the band was blacklisted by the government. Then film director Jonathan Demme's searing documentary on the coup, *Killing the Dream,* was picked up in Port-au-Prince via satellite and the generals couldn't believe it, there was this crazy motherfucker from RAM sitting in his office at the Oloffson, saying the coup looked planned, the elite families were involved, they raised the blood money, saying the military had tried to make it look like Aristide was a man who had to be stopped for the good of the nation because Aristide was a lunatic, a man who talked poetically about the beauty of necklacing, a man who gave a speech advocating crimes against humanity and so the military claimed they had no choice but to whip up a coup on the spur of the moment. Aghast, the generals watched the documentary, this American guy sitting over at the Oloffson and pointing his finger at every single one of them. After that it seemed that every time Richard picked up the phone somebody was calling in a death threat, and eventually he was even "arrested," called down to police headquarters to be interrogated by Evans Francois, brother of Michel Francois, police chief and prime coup leader, who carefully explained to Richard that there were a lot of people in Port-au-Prince who would be only too happy to waste him for fifty cents.

Inexplicably, Francois let him walk; what Richard hadn't yet figured out was that he and RAM, by their very defiance, were proving to be valuable assets to the tyrants, windowdressing for their faux-democratic posturing — freedom of the press, freedom of speech; subterfuge for the idiot Americans who were trying to bargain their way back toward some gloss of decency and moral rectitude without having to actually go the distance with Aristide — but there were limits to these dangerous luxuries, and Richard Morse, for whatever reason — fantasies of immunity? — seemed particularly slow to get the message.

RAM cut a record, their first album, and out it came: *Aibobo*, a *voudou* term equivalent to Hallelujah or Amen. A song on the album — "Fey" — Richard knew would create a scandal, so he positioned it at the end of the tape, released a politically innocuous single — "Ibo Lele," which Demme would later include on the soundtrack of *Philadelphia* — and let the album slowly work its way into the market. By the time the de factos discovered "Fey" it was too late, the song was all over the airwaves, people were singing it in the street and the regime started closing down radio stations — but only outside of Port-au-Prince — and raising the ante on Richard by threatening his wife, Lunise, a stunningly beautiful former dancer in a troupe who had so infatuated Richard as the embodiment of the rhythms that he had married her and made her the lead female vocalist in RAM. This was 1993, the tension was vile, unbearable, Aristide's lone champion in the ruling class, a wealthy businessman named Izmarie, was hauled out of church one Sunday morning and assassinated in the street, the UN-brokered Governor's Island agreement was being hammered out in New York, Aristide was supposed to come back in October, "Fey"'s getting played and the rumors were flying: Lunise has been kidnapped, Lunise has been killed. A taxi driver, not realizing who she was, told her, *Yeah, that lady from RAM is hiding in Petionville somewhere.*

The band — slum kids mostly, Lavalas diehards — had grown to believe nothing bad was going to happen because Richard had this envelope, these force fields — white guy, American guy — which protected them from harm. But the phone was ringing constantly, friends calling to find out if he was dead, *Just checking to see if you're alive, Rich,* and what the fuck was he supposed to do? Go away? Go where? Grad school? Some pick-up job back in Jersey? He had Lunise, two kids, the hotel, the band, he had become some strange variation of *voudou* impresario, so wrapped up in the rhythms they existed within him at the cellular level, they percolated in his blood, and the alternatives were incomprehensible. Life or death — was that what it was, were those the options? What if the options, the true options, were really democracy or repression? He was trying not to get anyone shot, but if you started retreating, where did you stop? Where were the Haitians themselves going to stop, because just about everybody he knew would jump overboard off this festering, floundering slave ship of a nation, its hull bored through with the worm holes of corruption, if they could. Like, *Fuck it, let's just get out of here, two hundred years is enough, let's just go somewhere else.*

But ultimately it would be to the regime's advantage if he left. All the parasites and bloodsuckers who fought without mercy for Haiti to remain in the Dark Ages — they wanted him to leave. He understood that, but he had roots in Haiti, old and new, he had insights that maybe Haiti needed, he believed in free enterprise and capitalism and opportunity, the whole package, and he provided a little beacon of hope, he thought, for some people who had nothing else to cling to. But his family, Lunise and the babies — risking their lives was his biggest fear. If anybody hurt them he was going to mobilize, urban guerrilla warfare, not a long-term thing, just find the assholes responsible and go down blazing, but he didn't even know if that's really what he would do, he prayed it would never come to that, but it was getting close, it was getting very close.

CRACKDOWN

The summer of '93 Aristide was coming back, Aristide was not coming back, the Americans were bringing him home — Yes? No? — Clinton had checkmated the tyrants at Governor's Island but he wouldn't act, the embassy was perilously divided over whether the negotiations were too hard on the Haitian military or too hard on Aristide; the CIA, in collusion with elements in the Defense and State Departments, was openly working to subvert the White House's stated policy, launching a smear campaign against Titid's mental health, vowing the bug-eyed little priest would *never* again set foot on Haitian soil and, most damagingly, functioning as the behind-the-scenes architect of FRAPH, a paramilitary terrorist organization run by a media-slick, cocaine guzzling madman named Emanuel Constant, whose job it was to develop an effective counterforce to Aristide's base of popular support. The United Nations dispatched the USS *Harlan County* to enforce the Governor's Island agreement, two hundred soldiers aboard, mostly American, Special Forces masquerading as medics and engineers, but FRAPH chased it away, Constant bursting into international headlines when he and his thugs unexpectedly succeeded (with the CIA's prodding) in transforming a staged media event — a "nationalist" protest against foreign intervention — into an indelible American humiliation by preventing the ship, whose captain panicked, from docking.

Two days later, intoxicated by their victory over the colossus to the north, the generals assassinated Guy Malary, the pro-Aristide minister of justice, and the wholesale killing began again, the murder rates astronomical, people dropping like flies, nothing working in the embargo-suffocated country but state-sponsored terrorism despite the presence of OAS human rights observers, who had Richard wondering what they were doing to earn their six grand a month, other than hanging out at the Oloffson, glued to the chairs on the veranda. The capital seemed to be operating on ever more poisonous energy, people were visibly stiff with tension, RAM started doing regular Thursday night gigs in the hotel, setting up in the acoustically rich cavernous rear half of the main room, its back wall actually the bare limestone face of the hillside, and the house was packed, everybody coming to blow off steam — the bourgeoisie were there, the MREs — Morally Repugnant Elites, so called by embassy wags; these beautiful, beautiful women from up the mountain in Petionville, La Boule, Kenscoff, valium and coke and handguns tucked into their purses; the attachés came, the Macoutes, even some low-profile Lavalas, foreign legionnaires from France, the spooks from Central Intelligence, FAHD in the foreign press, military guys from the embassy in their civvies, and of course the human rights observers until one night, after the attachés started smashing bottles and smacking around one of the band members, the OAS banned the observers from the Oloffson. Attachés coming to an American-run business, beating up Haitians, making them bleed, and the people supposedly there to monitor human rights violations were being pulled out. If that was happening at the Oloffson, Richard dreaded to think what sort of awfulness was washing over the rest of the country.

"Fey," meanwhile, wouldn't go away, stations were still slipping it onto the air, the band would hear stories of people singing "Fey" in crowds and the police coming out of nowhere, swinging their batons — apparently the regime, in their duplicity, would permit RAM to sing "Fey," at least for the time being, but no one else could. The violence swelled and inflated, one long crescendo of wretchedness into 1994, the embargo was crucifying everyone in the country, destroying what little was left of the economy while up on the Dom Rep border, the army extorted bags of money from the contrabandistas; Cedras had been making such fools out of the Americans that everyone thought Clinton had no choice but to slap him down, but the anticipated early summer invasion never materialized, the island was infused with despair and knotted with fear, hordes of people were flinging themselves into the sea, the army was sexually assaulting the wives and daughters of Lavalas supporters (a campaign of intimidation that inspired a counter-terrorism expert at the embassy, Ellen Cosgrove, to compose a memo arguing that the military regime's use of rape as a political weapon was greatly exaggerated by the press and no big deal anyway since, according to Cosgrove's keen analytical eye, rape itself seemed innate to Haitian culture, somehow a quasi-acceptable form of expressing one's Haitianness).

RAM kept playing at the hotel, the attachés would come around, liquor up and flaunt themselves, then disappear after midnight headed for the slums, and in the mornings the bodies would be there on the streets, strategically placed at intersections, trussed and mutilated and fly-blown, the regime's version of Thought for the Day. The Champs Mars became the frontier, the band members were terrified to cross it at night, on Thursday nights they'd sleep on the floor of the hotel, or sometimes journalists would take them home, speeding through the deserted streets. If they had their way they would have left, the airports were closing at the end of July and they wanted out. RAM had been invited to perform at the New Music Seminar in New York, but if they went the airport would have shut down behind them, and Richard said no, he had a hotel to run, he didn't want to get stuck in New York with the band being daddy to eighteen people, and he couldn't bear the defeat, knowing the Duvalierists and Macoutes and the elites would love it if everyone left — everyone with an education, anyone with an open mind, anyone who lived in the twentieth century. We'll stay, he told the group, and see this thing through to the end.

The band never got invited anywhere anymore but then in July, a well-connected club owner in Jacmel, the once beautiful colonial port on the southern coast, asked them to do a concert and Richard naively agreed, not knowing that the police had broken up a party at the club for playing the tape — playing "Fey" — which had so pissed off the host that he called a friend in the military, a colonel in Jacmel, and received permission to bring down the band, thereby setting up a confrontation between the army and the police. Two nights before the gig, however, the club owner had second thoughts, hopped in his car and drove two hours to Port-au-Prince, found Richard at the Oloffson, nervously reassured him he wanted the band to come to Jacmel but look, don't play "Fey." He didn't explain why but he didn't really need to, but Richard was noncommittal, agreeing only to maybe not play the song.

The morning of the concert, a tap-tap was supposed to collect them at nine but didn't arrive until five in the afternoon; no one was willing to come pick them up, Richard would learn later, because for two weeks the police in Jacmel had been boasting about how they would bust up the concert. The band loaded up the equipment and off they went, headed south toward the coast through the scoured mountains, the driver oddly silent, the driver stopping at the first military checkpoint even though it appeared they were being waved through, and then a soldier was shouting at them to get out of the van.

While they were frisked, Richard kept thinking, *All right, this is normal, we're out in the provinces, crackdowns are the local sport, no big fucking deal. Hey, we're going to a party, right?* At the out-skirts of Jacmel, there was another checkpoint and somebody—a sergeant in the police force—was waiting for them, a guy dressed all in black whose wild eyes reminded Richard of a horse pulling at the bit, about to bolt, go berserk, sweat streamed down the man's face as he ordered them out of the tap-tap, the guy was acting crazy so Richard walked away, usually in these situations with Haitians there was always a little something you could do, something that cooled everyone out but the fellow wouldn't calm down, he wanted all the equipment off the vehicle, Richard tried to reason with him, which only made matters worse, Lunise started to speak and the guy spun around, yelling at Lunise to shut her mouth. He got into their suitcases, everything was a mess when he finished, barking at them to get the fuck out of here, and Richard said to himself, *I'm going to remember you, pal, I'm going to deal with you later.*

At the club, a place called the Samba, they dropped off the gear and walked through the impenetrable darkness of town—Jacmel hasn't had electricity since the townspeople can remember—look-ing for somewhere to eat, and the market ladies, the *marchands* on the street silhouetted by the buttery glow of their oil lamps, were saying, *They came, they came,* and Richard assumed they were simply glad the band was here, when in fact the women couldn't believe the band had come because, according to the plan, they were all about to die.

The nightclub, lit by its own generator, had an enormous dance floor, the size of an Olympic swimming pool, rimmed with chairs occupied by about three hundred people, stone-faced and severely sober. The band filed on stage, kicked off the set and . . . nothing, total impassivity. It was customary for Richard to remain back-stage until the third song when he would amble out like a Corsican pirate, scrutinizing the audience with his heavy-lidded eyes, his skull wrapped in an *houngan's* scarlet scarf, a skinny rat-tail braid of his wiry hair flopping down between his shoulder blades. For Haitians, he was an odd sight, his appearance usually stirred things up, but here at the Samba it was junior high school, whatever you do you can't find the right thing to get people going. Richard stared at the three-sided crowd, trying to figure out what was wrong, then he looked over at Lunise and said, *I'm gonna say something,* be-cause when the band first formed he used to rap into the mike—social commentary, insights into the "situation," in a kind of joking way though he knew sometimes the jokes weren't funny, they were absurdly real, and he began to realize he was scaring people so he figured just shut up and play, that had become the concept, just play and if somebody wanted to interpret shit in the music, that was their business but he wasn't going to say anything himself.

He waited for his wife's response but Lunise only looked at him, big-eyed, trying to measure his motivation. She had a sixth sense about things, she was instinctive, natural, and didn't feel compelled to constantly analyze and balance the way her husband did, yet whenever the omens got weird she'd speak up, and Richard would go along with it. But now she didn't open her mouth and they played on until after the next song, when he said again, *I'm gonna say something,* Lunise pursued her lips and looked away, he thought he was wasting his time, but finally she turned back to him and said, *What are you going to say?*

Carte blanche.

Let's find out, he said. *Let's rock.*

Before they went on stage, the club owner had not only reminded him to steer clear of "Fey," but said don't sing anything else that has any kind of social message in it, either. Considering RAM's repertoire, that left about one-half of one song. *Don't play anything that makes commentary,* the club owner warned, and Richard could only reply, *I don't know what you mean.* The cops were at the gate, the club owner was censoring their song list and Richard stood at the microphone glaring at the crowd, letting the anticipation build, finally admitting to himself what everybody in Jacmel already knew.

I didn't come here to do politics, he said. Immediately, several people stood up and moved toward the back of the club. *I didn't come here to do politics,* he repeated, slowly walking out toward the middle of where the swimming pool would be, this empty, ominous space, surrounded by a thunderstruck audience who didn't know if they were attending a rally, a massacre or a dance. He began threatening them, squatting down to slap his hand on the floor, demanding they get up and dance, he wanted them to stand up, *right now!* but of course no one dared move, and in Richard's exasperation the scene at the checkpoint popped back into his head and triggered a rant.

You people invited me to come here, he started saying, *if you didn't invite me I wouldn't be here, I've been here many times and what I know about the provinces, what I like about them,*

Bob Shacochis

*is that etiquette and courtesy are important to the people in
Jacmel, and here I am coming into town, on invitation, and you've
got some sergeant on the road being disrespectful to my wife, and
being disrespectful to the band . . .*

Lunise was at her microphone — *Richard! Richard!* — imploring
him to come back on stage. Three minutes into the soliloquy and
he'd gotten to the sergeant who, lurching out of the shadows at
the front of the club, had decided he'd heard enough. The sergeant,
the police commandant and two thugs started coming after him,
screaming all the way across the huge dance floor, empty but for
Richard, *Who the hell are you! You have no right to mention our
names, you have no right to talk about us,* frothing, walking
as fast as they could without running, the crackdown team. To
Richard it looked like instant replay slow motion, four guys coming at him, one grabbed his arm but he yanked it away, turned his
back to them and walked toward the stage, only three members of
the band were left, the rest had scrambled left and right and were
trying to mingle with the crowd, be invisible. Richard jabbed his
mike in the stand and beelined for the dressing room, the band
sliding in behind him, the cops elbowing through, and then out of
nowhere came an army officer, yelling *Evacué!* — Evacuate! — and
the police froze in their tracks, saluting — *At your order!* — and
retreated.

In the dressing room, the girls were moving fast; anything that
had anything to do with RAM, take it off. They had already changed
out of their colorful stage costumes and they'd gone into an automatic Haitian thing — Everything's fucked up, let's just disappear,
be nobody and disappear. The army officer stepped through the
door and started hugging Richard, saying *Rich, calm down, everything's okay, man. Go back on stage, you're going to say whatever
you want, you're going to sing whatever song you want to sing.
I'm here to give you protection all night long.* When they went
back out, the people, who had come to the Samba that night not
to dance but for the theater of the showdown between the band,
the army and the police, erupted with uproarious cheers, because
if RAM had won it meant they had also won, a small and meaning-
less victory against the police they so hated, and at the expense
of further allegiance to the military, who in fact commanded
the police, and so although the band played two more songs —
neither of them "Fey" — the crowd was still too intimidated to
dance, which in Haiti meant too intimidated to even think about

183

being themselves, and Richard said, *We're leaving,* and the army officer said, *Go ahead.*

Every day now on the television, the tyrants were broadcasting a Creole-dubbed documentary about the Panama invasion, the Americans plunging out of the sky like the Last Judgement, shooting up Panama City, the slums afire and reduced to ashes, the rows of civilian corpses. Usually you could get through the day without feeling crippled by fear, but every once in a while the paranoia came in waves, Richard would wonder what the hell was he doing, was he out of his fucking mind, the band had become a symbolic target and he asked himself, *What's the thing we haven't done yet, the thing that takes it to the next level, and are we on track for doing it?*

Up in the heights of Petionville there was a club, The Garage, owned by Michel Martelli, a popular singer who had a band called Sweet Mickey, and Sweet Mickey was *the* Macoute band, Michel Francois's — the notorious chief of police — favorite group, and so The Garage was a thug hangout, a playground for Macoutes and their prostitutes, the second most nasty place in the capital that advertised good times (first place relegated to a downtown bar called the Normandie, next to FRAPH headquarters, its walls pasted with trophy snapshots of the terrorist group's victims).

It was August, no one knew which way the "situation" was going to go, Sweet Mickey had left the country for New York and his wife was running the club. The Garage was no place for a band like RAM, but Richard was Michel Martelli's cousin — that's Haiti — and his wife had been trying to book Richard into the club for a year. Richard had fended her off, but now she sent her father down to the Oloffson and the guy wouldn't leave until Richard agreed to bring the band up the mountain the following Saturday.

That Saturday night, the crowd in The Garage had a predatorial reek — Haitian military and police, French gendarmes, the bodybuilder types from the American embassy, a table full of journalists too prudent to mingle. No MREs — none. Here we are, Richard thought, in Babylon. While the band opened with their introductory number, Richard walked through the crowd, checking out the genetics, making a mental note of two heavyset dudes, each with a whore, their tables next to each other; they had that look, military big shots in civilian — *chefs.*

The gig was flat, even Richard's appearance on stage seemed to make little difference, which meant he had to reach into his bag of tricks. Trick number one: If it's not happening, send the girls — the back-up vocalists — out into the audience. The first two bounced out, little queenies pulling guys off their seats. Richard was about to send a third girl down when, glancing over to the side entrance of the stage, he saw two cops in uniform and thought, send the girl after one of the cops, get him to dance, it would be like a semi-coup, just bring them all in and get everyone cooled out. So the girl went over to one of the cops and asked him if he was happy, took his hand and brought him across the stage to get to the dance floor, then Richard started fretting about what he was doing and looked at one of the two guys he had noticed earlier in the crowd and mouthed, *Is it all right if he dances?* and the guy mouthed back, *Yeah, that's all right.* Richard had guessed correctly because the cop went straight for the guy's table, whipped off his hat and gaily placed it on the fellow's table, then danced away with the girl, the crowd warmed instantly, even the journalists were jumping up. Eventually the band went into "Fey" and the shit started happening.

Six Macoutes — military in civilian — plowed through the front door, one of them beckoned at the cops and demanded they arrest the band, but the cop who'd been dancing balked, protesting that RAM had done nothing wrong. The guy shoved past him, hopped on the stage, focusing on the dreadlocked musician, and said, *Stop playing now.* It was like someone pulled the plug out of the wall — *eeeeerrhhhh* — the music died and Richard was pissed, no one had the right to stop the band but him. He walked over to the guy and said, *What the hell's up?* and the guy replied, *You can play any song but you can't play this song.* Richard told him if he had a problem, go talk to the club owner; the guy went off, the audience was wondering what the fuck and the guy came back with Sweet Mickey's father-in-law, who said, *Rich, what's wrong with the song?*

I dunno, said Richard, thinking if you can play dumb, I can play dumb. Martelli's wife's father said, *Well, shit, skip it, don't play it and we'll talk about it later.* Richard said, *Fine,* the owner nodded gratefully and walked away, but it wasn't fine, who the fuck were these people to tell him what to play, he was sick of the pathology, the compromises and subterfuge and obfuscations and games, sick of being a caged prop for the generals and their malignant smiles, the blather they fed the Americans about democracy, and he

remembered Jacmel, how the fellow who rescued them had identified himself as the *officer du jour,* so he stepped back to the microphone and started throwing stuff out and, to his bewilderment,
somebody answered.

Is there an officer du jour here?

It's me, said one of the heavyset guys, the same one who had
assented to let the cop dance.

Nooo! You're kidding. It's you? Richard said, not even certain
what an *officer du jour* was, what sort of status such a title carried,
but he gambled on it anyway. *Can I play the song?* The man hesitated for a second and said yes, looked over at his twin at the next
table for confirmation, who shouted out *Play the song!* so Richard
turned around to the band and said, *Gimme the song.*

Which was stupid. The band started playing the opening bars of
"Fey" and Lunise, the song's lead vocalist, looked at Richard and
said, *I'm not singing.* Richard waved the band silent, there they
were on stage, *tête-à-tête,* the two of them arguing about it in restrained voices, the band huddled around, Richard was proud of
himself for coming up with the whole *officer du jour* bluff, pulling
rank on the asshole who had tried to shut them down, but Lunise
had dug in her heels, she thought Richard was out of his mind to
even think about playing "Fey" in the middle of a Macoute pissing
contest, she kept insisting he was crazy and she wouldn't sing the
song, the discussion continued on for about forty-five seconds
until Richard deferred to her better judgement, they played two
more songs and went home, but there would be untold hell to pay
for Richard's brinkmanship at The Garage.

The next day, the story got back to police headquarters, Michel
Francois considered the incident an affront to his almighty power
and personally reprimanded the *officer du jour* for interfering with
the cops, going so far as to question the officer's sympathies —
Perhaps, Francois insinuated, *he was Lavalas, eh?* — so now the
fellow had no choice but to prove himself, reestablish his loyalties
in the fraternity of snakes. Thursday night there they were at the
Oloffson, the same *officer du jour* and a selection of goons, and
the plan was, when RAM goes into "Fey," bust up the joint. The
band held meetings, fire drills, about the possibility of just such a
thing happening, what to do if the shit went down, and Richard
kept telling them to stay on track, focus on the music, *We're playing music music music music — that's it, period,* but of course
there was more to it than that, Richard himself had lost a half-dozen

186

close friends since the coup, you lose one, you lose another; every day the band members would duck into the Oloffson's enclave with fresh horror stories, the attachés were swallowing up neighborhoods wholesale, you couldn't walk past Cite Soleil or La Saline without spotting gore, some poor disemboweled soul, someone slashed into grisly chunks, headless people, shotgun-blasted brains, the city had turned gangrenous, rotting on the hoof, and stank of death and dying, the population hunkered down in extreme fear praying for the goddamn Americans to come save them from damnation and still the Thursday nights proceeded, an eerie bubble of grace, people packing in in their doomsday wildness to vent the tension.

From the stage, Richard scoped the crowd, as was his habit, checking for weapons; he noticed the guy from The Garage, the *officer du jour,* and didn't think anything of it, but suddenly he's surrounded by a creepy throng of attachés clamoring for him to play "Fey," hissing *Play "Fey," play "Fey," please,* guys were walking across the stage whispering, *I hear they're giving you a hard time about "Fey"— don't worry, I've got your back-up,* everything's backwards, the people asking for "Fey" were the people who shouldn't want it, the band finished "Ibo Lele," the crowd was at as high a pitch as you could get it, screaming, singing, at the point when, normally, RAM would segue into "Fey" and send it over the edge. Instead, unable to overcome his misgivings, Richard walked off the stage, everything was too backwards so he just left, one of the goons blocking the exit grabbed him but he twisted away into the crowd, everyone chanting *"Fey!" "Fey!" "Fey!" "Fey!"*— the attachés were doing it between songs but now the entire audience was calling for it — and the sound man, sitting across the room at the mixer, had overhead the conspiratorial mutterings of the three Macoutes and, realizing the band was in jeopardy, preemptively shoved a cassette into the deck, Richard still had been deluding himself with visions of an encore but now, hearing *compas* pump through the system, he looked at the sound man and thought, *Damn, he blew it, we could have done "Fey" and gone off into rock-and-roll ecstasy.* One by one the band slipped away and regathered at the family residence attached to the Oloffson, half the members were in a rage over skipping the encore, saying *We're punks,* Richard himself fell into a fury, one of the back-up singers had cut his locks in the aftermath of The Garage, afraid he had been singled out by the cops, and Richard, whipping off the guy's cap, suspended him on the spot, the singer was endangering the band because in Haiti if you buckled to the pressure they came after you hard, if you were scared it meant your conscience wasn't clear, that you were doing something wrong. *If you die, you're guilty* — that was a Creole proverb.

The inevitable had merely been postponed for another week. Richard was on the phone daily with the embassy, telling one of the political officers, *Hey, man, you've got to get people over here,* and the guy was saying, *Well, have you thought about not playing, have you thought about switching songs?* It was the first week in September, the airport's closed, you couldn't get in or out, the Americans have ceased being coy about an invasion, the FAHD were pretending they could handle it, FRAPH was boasting they'd kill GI's *à la Somalia* and the tyrants' puppet in the palace, President Jonaissant, was saying we're going to fight this down to the last man. The country felt like it was being microwaved, cooked from the inside, incubating lunacy, and here came Thursday night, RAM's on stage, standing room only, two hundred people crammed front to back, half of them armed but not everyone for the same reason, the band's in the middle of a song . . . and the fucking lights go out.

It's pitch black, no one could see shit, Richard expected little yellow-blue flames of gunfire any second, the attachés frantic that Richard maybe doused the lights to hit *them*, the CIA guys were backing up against the walls — they're big, they're bad, they're embassy . . . but it was dark — people were waiting to get stabbed, people were waiting for shots, pants were being stained it's so godawful scary inside the Oloffson, and then the drums started, *petro* rhythms battering through the hysteria, Champs Mars *déjà vu*, the weirdest thing because there was Richard in the middle of the stage without the slightest fucking idea what was going on, nobody could see him, but the drums were lifting him up, lifting him beyond the vortex, he spread his arms like some deranged healer and started singing, he figured the girls had disappeared, because that's what they were supposed to do if something happened, but they're behind the stage, tucked into a corner, and suddenly there were their voices, harmonizing, it sounded to Richard like angels, they were singing what were called "points" — messages — old *voudou* songs, very meaningful, very antagonistic despite their beauty, very Fuck you: war drums and vocals resonating supernaturally — spiritually — in the pitch, pitch black.

People started lighting matches, the staff found candles, the hotel's handyman finally cranked the generator and Richard's thinking, *Fuck it, if the Macoutes don't have the balls to get us in the dark, we're just going to give it to them,* and off they galloped into "Fey," the audience exploded, rapturous, reeling, taken away to another sphere, and nothing whatsoever happened. Holed up afterwards in the living quarters, the band celebrated, giddy and laughing, drinking and horsing around, ready for next Thursday, thinking everything was over, they'd passed through the thing, the trial, whatever it was, and now they were invincible, the artful dodgers, fucking untouchable.

The *officer du jour* from The Garage, however, who had been to every RAM gig for five weeks straight, still had a big, big problem, still had to prove to his superiors that he wasn't Lavalas. Journalists had begun to shadow Richard, reasoning that when the Macoutes offed him, it was going to trigger the invasion. A British photographer was advised by the boys from the embassy not to take pictures around RAM gigs because she'd start a huge brawl and get herself killed. The more prudent members of the press were simply avoiding the Oloffson, moving up to Petionville to the well-guarded Montana — a safer place to be anyway, when the Americans started bombing the capital.

That final Thursday, the *officer du jour* was dressed all in black, like a gunfighter, and when the band launched "Fey," he removed the shirt from around his waist to wave it in the air, Richard saw him do it and thought, *This guy can't be dancing,* the malevolence in the officer's eyes was too intense, too intense, and Richard followed his gaze to a man sitting at a table, the men's eyes were locked, there's this diabolic telepathy between them like a red current; the political officer from the embassy had already split; uniformed cops, jigging with excitement, were scurrying out, he could feel everything slipping, sinking, and he spun around to the drummers and said, *Switch songs now,* which they did without skipping a beat, a little roll and they were in another song but here was the attaché on stage, bellowing *Stop playing! Stop playing! You can't play this song!*

Richard feigned innocence. *What song?*

The officer appeared dumbstruck, taking a second to realize what had happened, and then he started hollering back out to the audience, *It's not "Fey," it's not the song. Stop! Stop!* This wasn't Champs Mars, this wasn't Jacmel or The Garage, this was Richard's home, out of bounds, he'd had enough bullying and thuggery and fatuous intrigue and decided to find out who's behind this shit once and for all. Cordless microphone in hand, he worked his way through the dancers to the veranda, there were two *femmes blancs* at one of the tables, not your normal everyday Joanns from Omaha who would come for the buffet, listen to the first set and be off in bed by midnight. *Richard, is everything all right!* one of them asked, crisp-voiced, eyes like the end of forgiveness. *Who the fuck!* he thought, they were such a queer sight. *Embassy gals — ninjaettes!* Someone behind him was saying, *Go around the corner,* so he walked down the veranda, turning left toward his office and head-on into a viper pit. There was a nest of them — two uniformed cops, two lieutenants in the police, two slick guys in civilian, probably higher ranking, and a tribe of nasty-looking fuckers with Uzis and riot guns.

Everyone's surprised, everyone's blood was running high, the band was on stage playing and Richard just stood there staring recklessly at Michel Francois's assassins until one of them said, *Rich, what are you doing here!* and Richard answered, *What do you mean, what am I doing here! This is my house.*

Nothing's wrong, man. Everything's okay. Go back on stage.

I am on stage, Richard told him, raising the microphone to his lips. *Yeaaahhhhh* — his voice rumbled through the sound system. Suddenly he was off his feet, the attaché had come up behind, grabbed him low and started walking with him, Richard's shoes off the ground, they struggled and he broke free just as one of the lieutenants flipped a large mahogany table, smashing bottles and glasses, thugs were roughing up a photojournalist to get his camera, the officer grabbed Richard a second time trying to drag him out of there, the band played on, the guy's wrestlewalking Richard down the veranda and Richard, determined to get the band off stage, didn't know what to do but start singing.

Kadja bosou à ye ma pralé.

These were mystical lyrics, *Kadja bosou* was the *loa* of the crossroads, a Legba-type spirit — Richard had asked for safe passage, implying he was leaving, which so unnerved the attaché that he let go. The band couldn't see him but they heard, RAM was singing one song and here was a disembodied Richard singing the song they always finished with and they figured it out, brought the music to a slow stop and vanished, Richard's aunt had vanished, his mother who often helped at the gate had vanished, half the waiters were hiding out in the charcoal pits, the crowd was mobbing down the stairs to the parking lot and the attachés had grabbed a young man sitting at one of the tables, the muzzles of their Uzis shoved under his chin as they dragged him toward the steps. A girl with terrified eyes behind her glasses clutched at Richard, pleading for help because the Macoutes had taken her brother and Richard thought, *My God, maybe they'd gotten sufficient warning from the embassy not to grab me so they just grabbed anybody to get me to stop.* He'd been making decisions all along designed to keep people from dying, at the same time trying not to compromise what the band did, their essence, the rhythms and the old roots songs, but now it seemed he'd made a decision where someone was going to get fucked. These were his decisions, he was responsible, in a world gone mad he had used, however impetuously, however narrowly, his position of privilege to challenge the tyrants and they, in return, had let him buzz about like a bumblebee tied to a string, but now if ever a party was over it was this one at the Oloffson, Haiti's only DMZ throughout the time of the de factos. RAM was going on ice, and there was nothing left for Richard to do but take the deep breaths necessary to bring himself under control and walk down the steps to the fragrant palm-lined drive, where his guests negotiated for their lives.

There was no music at the Oloffson that next Thursday night. Richard sat at the bar, watching Clinton on CNN calling the regime the worst in the hemisphere, and when it was over, you could almost hear the entire country praying for salvation and yet fearing salvation's wrath, and then American planes droned over the city, parachutes fluttered and popped, and out of the balmy sky fell, not troops, but transistor radios and cartoons.

Several months later I was talking to the British photographer who had been warned by the embassy not to take pictures during RAM gigs at the Oloffson. "Can I tell you something about 'Fey'?" she said. "It was in October, the Committee Comme il Faut had organized a manifestation down south in Grand Goaves, so we went there for that, and it was basically a demonstration against the FAHD that was still in Grand Goaves. The manifestation went around, and we were all getting very nervous as it got closer to the police station, and everyone thought, *Oh God, if it goes down there it's really going to be a blowout,* but it didn't, and then the

191

people broke out into absolute glorious song — 'Fey'! — and I couldn't believe it, they went into that glorious chorus. And I just thought, *Fucking A*, because I had always thought RAM was just a phenomenon at the Oloffson, but no way, *this* was RAM, it's everywhere, and 'Fey' was an anthem for the movement, for freedom."

> *I'm a leaf.*
> *Look at me on my branch.*
> *A terrible storm came and knocked me off.*
> *The day you see me fall is not the day I die.*
> *And when they need me where are they going to find me?*
> *The good Lord, and St. Nicola,*
> *I only have one son*
> *And they made him leave the country.*

That was "Fey." Nothing much really, a harmless arrangement of folklore, traditional *voudou* lyrics for *petro* rhythm, twinned parables of death without dying and the hope of resurrection, the divine voice of a woman singing in ever fluid darkness, the necrotic skeletal hand of evil reaching for her throat.

That was "Fey," and that was Haiti — a paradox, a riddle: a song to sing if you wanted to live, but, depending on who you were, if you sang it, you died.

Two Poems
Merle Collins

CRICK CRACK

Crick!
crack!
Monkey break he back on a rotten pomerack
crick!
crack!
Monkey break he back on a rotten pomerack

What is the mirage and what reality?
Do we know what is truth and what is truly fiction?

When we were children the signals were clear
somebody say crick we say crack
and we know then was nanci-story time in the place
somebody was going to take a high fall on a slippery lie
so we say look at that eh
Monkey break he back on a rotten pomerack
monkey smash up he back on a rotten pomerack

But what is the mirage and what reality?
Do we know what is truth and what is truly fiction?

crick!
crack!
the little little spider defeat the lion
who thought he was king of the jungle
so we say but look at that!
monkey well smash up he back on a rotten pomerack!

crick!
crack!
you see that ball of fire tumbling down the hill?

pure spirit, you know, even though it looking like it real
monkey mashing up he back on a rotten pomerack!

crick!
crack!
Gentleman that person you walking with
in the long long dress
is really a la diablesse
devil woman with one good foot
and one goat foot

so monkey breaking he back on a rotten pomerack!
But what is the mirage and what reality?
Do we know what is truth and what is truly fiction?

crick!
crack!
come midnight tall tall cake
walking through the streets
all in white icing
Monkey break he back on a rotten pomerack

But some stories come
with no crick with no crack
and still monkey does well
break they back on a
rotten pomerack

no crick no crack
but they go west find India
so just call it West Indies
so we say, well

Look at that!
Not a crick or a crack
But sound like monkey well
breaking he back on some
rotten pomerack

no crick no crack
but 1992 they say

is five hundred years since
the discovery of America

We say
For true? But
look at that!
not a crick or a crack
but monkey well
smashing up he back
on a rotten pomerack

so what is the mirage and
what reality?
do we know what is truth
and what is truly fiction?

in South Africa de klerk
without a krick
without a krack
walking tall tall tall
through the streets
and they say he
freeing the Blacks

I say for true?
Where the blood?
Where the sweat?
Where the tears?
sound like monkey well
breaking he back
on some rotten pomerack

not a krick or a krack
but tall tall cake all in white icing
so what is the mirage and what reality?
Who knows what is truth and what is
truly fiction?

once an African child told me
a story she said she had learnt
at school

slavery, she said,
had been abolished by
a tall, tall, tall white man
in a tall, tall, hat
a man whose name she
couldn't remember

the name had gone
but the image remained
so what is the mirage and
what reality?
do you know what is truth
and what is truly fiction?

until lions have their own historians,
they say,
tales of hunting will always
glorify the hunter

tales of hunting will always
glorify the hunter
until the lioness
is her own
hiss-
-torian

NABEL STRING

The part of me
that is not there, not here
home, not wandering
not hey, how you doing?
but doodoo darling, you awright?

Not going up to this enclosed home
in the elevator, on stairs, in silent
unconcerned, instinctive hostility
with the neighbour I do not know
not turning the key for the umpteenth time

in the door of number 204 and suddenly
pausing, intent, attention on 203
I wonder who livin there? Not that
absence of you, of me, of warmth, of life,

but running outside with the piece of bread
Ay! Teacher Clearie! Shout the bus for me, nuh!
Ay! James! Wait! Take the kerosene pan!
I not taking no damn kerosene pan!
Eh! But he ignorant, eh!
Awright awright! Bring it! Ka dammit!

There, where neighbour is friend and enemy
to be cussed and caressed
so damn annoying you could scream sometimes
so blasted fast in you business
you could hate, most times
but when you're far away
hate is a memory of feeling
Loving and cussing and laughing and needing
is living. That blank stare from the unknown
next door neighbour kills something inside

And the sound that pulls
is of the heart beat, of the drum
beat. Is River Sallee, is a drummer
soaring, is Victoria, is Belmont,
those places that you, I, we left
Left to search, as always, for a better life
Left, sometimes, just because of a need to search
for the reason, the beginning, the end, the all.
So left, and will always be leaving
Left, too, to escape the lime
by the place they call the kwésé, by the L'anse
by the market. Left to find jobs, to chase education.

Go on child, take what I didn't get, you hear
I have no money to leave. All I have
is in you head. Left, too, because every year
more out of school, less work to get
because chemistry in fifth form this year

197

and standing on market hill straight
for the whole of next year
just didn't kind of make no sense.

Left, too, because love turned hate
is bitter, not sweet
Because the landless somehow becoming
more landless yet but still loving
some leader because of a memory
Left sometimes because things not so good
and something better is always somewhere else
Left because even if things going all right
the world big, and home is a feeling you're seeking

but in this new speaking, in the elevator, the lift
from over the sea there's the pull of the heart beat
of the drum voice. Ay! Bury the child nabel
string under the coconut tree, you know
by where I bury she father own!
So the nabel string there
and as the palm branch swaying

It pulling, it pulling, it pulling

From Marina 1936
Antonio Benítez-Rojo

— Translated from Spanish by James Maraniss

Bowsprit cracked with ice and paint cracked with heat.
I made this, I have forgotten
And remember.
The rigging weak and the canvas rotten
Between one June and another September . . .

— T.S. Eliot

. . . it was an old Cuban sloop, with mended sails
and ruinous appearance, that now was leaving
port at Santiago on a trip along a coast that kept
on getting steeper. It seemed to make no progress,
for it had to luff its course to push through the
opposing current . . .

— Alejo Carpentier

"TIN MARIN DE *dos pingués, cúcara mácara títere fue,*" Lucianito would have said on that morning of a special year (what do you call the year when memories start falling into place?) as he'd have to choose between two fists that I had clenched and crossed. I'd be there with the rusty wingnut in one palm, leant back above the starboard rail. I'd count to ten three times and listen as the clatter of bare feet and laughter spread out through the boat.

After noon had sounded, rung by mutinous Cisneros on the forward bell, Ana Zoila would appear at topside with her bilious long face, harried by the teasing wind inside her petticoat. She'd appear and start to hand out bumps and pinches, then she'd chase me weakly from the salt fish barrels piled up on the poopdeck over to the bow stays, moaning all the way that these damned nuisances that always held up lunch were inducing her attacks of migraine,

199

that she couldn't get the first idea of consideration through my skull and that the whole thing came from playing as I did with rotten kids, as if it didn't matter what she had to do to keep the fishing business above water and on top of that to keep my mama and my papa off her back.

In feigned exhaustion, I let her catch me by the coattails and then pull me back into the cabin, under my friends' mocking faces, as they scrambled up the ratlines like a band of longtailed monkeys — Ana Zoila's name for them — illustrated somewhere in *The Book of Knowledge.*

The table was drawn up under the skylight with its leaded glass: on the tablecloth there would be spread a worn-out silver service that for years had had a heavy ashen shine that it could scarcely hold. As soon as she had shaken out my knees and smoothed my cuffs, Ana Zoila would start tapping on the wall, and then Mama and Papa would emerge slowly from their dice game in the library; they'd come to lunch still arguing about the way to play a game that my grandparents invented at the turn of the century. Ambrosio, a courteous Negro with a tattered livery and a delicate tenor voice, would arrange the chairs for us deliberately, and stirring with his tongs inside a pot of murmuring brine above the cooking stove, he'd take out, for us to see, a steaming can of pork and beans or spaghetti with meatballs. The other dishes, except once a spoonful of syrupy fruit and maybe a bite of some fowl shot from our own crow's nest, were never products of the land: the basis of our sustenance was fish, and at dinner nothing else was ever tasted.

Our cabins took the best part of the upper deck, away from all the salting apparatus and the spinning drivewheels (not too present, actually: when the engine wasn't broken down we'd still be out of coal) stuck against the boat's ribs near the prow. The smartest cabin, which opened up below an overhanging roof, belonged at that time to Mama and Papa; the others, at one end of the passageway, housed Ana Zoila, plus a captain (that year there were three), Calleja (the first officer) and me.

My cabin was the smallest and its hatch opened to face the smokestack, which had been painted blue for luck. The furniture was just the following: a chest of drawers with bronze handles, a cracked mirror and — underneath the portrait of Don Fadrique Ocampo, my great uncle, oil oozing in the humid air, so faded that it showed nothing but a helmet with a greenish plume above one cloudy, persecuting eye — the rolltop desk, screwed like the chest into the floorboards; a Viennese chair, flexible and light as the albatross feathers that we sometimes found on deck in the morning; a basin, stuck to the wall by a rusted spiral stay, whose two inches of rainwater would be changed on alternate mornings by the decorous Ambrosio with bucket and sponge; above and to the right, on the shelf that hung inside the berth, there stood in line, protected by a vertical rim, a battery-powered radio (almost inaudible because it was a long-wave set and we sailed far offshore) and two ebony dolphins; their coiling tails held up two schoolbooks and a dozen novels; but no, all that was from another time, Padre Zacarías would not yet then have taken charge of my instruction and the mirror on the chest would not have cracked, and on the shelf, sitting sturdy and discolored, eternally forgotten, the picaroon Tribilín Cantore; beside him the little Mickey Mouse pitcher and the brand new box of hussars and grenadiers, then the horses, the covered wagons, the cannon that shot marbles and mothballs; and up on deck we'd play at hide and seek, and the forecastle was Bluebeard's; in time we'd storm it, having signed with Sandokan or Captain Blood; later, sword clenched in his teeth, Lucianito would scale it neither asking for nor giving quarter, as they used to say; but now we played hide and seek and seek and hide and had just begun a game of tag when George V died. Ana Zoila, on the verge of an attack, ran through the deck to spread the news, heard over the two-banded RCA with the strong battery that the Company had given her when she turned twenty.

Progress was a thing my parents measured by a radio's sophistication, by the number of bands and tubes a set would have, by the effectiveness of contacts, circuits (specifications printed inside the Christmas catalogues that Company ships supplied to our first officer Calleja), resistors, condensers. Of course, only portables mattered to them; it would be a while before they had electricity on board, that is, they'd die before it happened.

What we'd do is get together after supper in the library to listen to the music of the whole wide world. Between the static squalls and the messages in Morse code, while Papa lit a Larrañaga and slid its fragrant ring onto my thumb, Mama, tossing back her wig with a movement quite her own, would fish for European capitals; Roman fifes and tarantellas, epic slavic violins, cymbals in Berlin, gay French songs, marches, ballads, turbulent *paso dobles*; an entire continent trickling down the antenna to spill out on the dusky sharkskin then in service as a rug; *Europa,* mythic name.

Antonio Benítez-Rojo

Eu-ro-pa, a name that held its vowels together like a magic word, would find a passage every night through this resourceful cornucopia to storm us with ineffable froth, with sounds existing beyond good and evil, moving Papa to unroll old faded maps and scour geographies to find a more tangible reference, closer to our lonely, small, wandering reality. Where is Madrid?, here it is, that red star there is London, *Allemagne* means Germany, Russia is the great green bear, the wide blue space is the Atlantic and Christopher Columbus sailed along that thin black line.

Ana Zoila carried me half asleep to my cabin. Seated in the Viennese chair, I watched her light the oil lamp on the shelf by holding up her candlestick. Then she urged devotion in my prayers, especially the last one, the one most likely to reduce my years in purgatory. Before withdrawing to the passageway, to leave me in the semi-darkness face to face with Don Fadrique Ocampo's rheumy eye, she'd run her finger through my hair as though trying to erase the bumps that she'd given me at noon.

One or two times a week, and always on Saturdays, the noises woke me up: a shuffle of hoofbeats, curses, thuds and moans that beset my door and vanished down the corridor.

"That was the god Eshu himself, my child," Ambrosio would say, startled, pausing in the middle of an aria, signalizing with his sponge, spattering the mirror with a grayish dew that he wiped off quickly on his sleeve. He'd have to make him an *ecbó* with gills and guts so he'd eat by himself and not bother anyone.

"It's Satan riding with his devils," my sister would declare at breakfast time, crossing herself, bending her head down over her plate. "I heard them too this morning."

Mama and Papa never heard a thing; with the radio session over, daybreak found them still rolling dice on a gameboard, lost in a reverie that only Ambrosio could break by bringing in their seaweed broth.

One night, when Ana Zoila had just stopped her finger's forehead-stroking rite, the awful racket came through early. After a parade of curses not loud but deep, a dazzling shadow fell down next to the half-opened door.

Ana Zoila, dismayed, put her hand over her fishlike mouth and told me to be silent.

Grabbing the candlestick, she dragged me out into the hallway.

Spread out there on the planks, wrapped in his spangled cape, lay First Officer Calleja.

202

His eyes were shut and he had his head turned slightly toward the door; his braided, bicorned hat had fallen in the middle of the passageway. Escaping from his mouth there was a filament of vomit that ran down his beard.

Ana Zoila kneeled and pulled a handkerchief from her smock.

"Swear to me you won't tell anyone," she whispered, looking up. I leaned against the wall and nodded.

"Swear to God."

"I swear to God."

"Don't you dare say a thing, or your tongue will rot," she said, replacing the soiled handkerchief. "Now help me."

First Officer Calleja was only as tall as a fifth grader, but girded in a heavy shell of straps and weapons. I by one leg, and Ana Zoila by the other, dragged him slowly toward his cabin door. He smelled heavily of rum.

"Empty his pockets," she said.

Next to the candleholder, then, I laid out a string of coins, matchboxes, poker decks, squashed tickets, caramels, bullets, photographs of women, dice, cigarettes, holy images, colored pencils, amulets, chains, brass knuckles, razors, keys.

"Stop," she said, when I had almost emptied out the pocket. And she picked up the keys, which she began trying in the door.

We put him inside. Reaching up, I lit a candle.

Ana Zoila, hunched next to him, reminded me of what could happen to my tongue. Then she ordered me to take the candlestick back to my bunk.

But when I shut the door I blew the candle out and peeped through the keyhole.

*

There were mornings when we'd leap out from the marble boat and step on shore. The ship held back, her sails set, because back in Don Fadrique's time she had already lost her anchor. We rowed like madmen, under the flapping eagles and parrots, skirting violet reefs, green oyster beds, inferring the precise landscape from a labyrinth of simmering pools, red whittles and wedges at the surface, deep tunnels, spirals of amber, sargassum and jellyfish. The island was floating before us (it was always an island) walled in fog, mysterious, unmentioned in the charts that our captains and

First Officer Calleja scanned so often. We'd make our approach along the unbelievably narrow channel that would cut into a wall of breakers with the rumble of a lifting drawbridge. We rowed teetering above water flecked with scum, suspended, without railings, stuck to heavy bubbles of blue indigo. Crocodiles and long-tusked walruses were splashing on the banks; blinded in sunlight, they rooted in the sand. A stockade made of coconut and orange trees, royal palms, shore pines and breadfruit trees was growing, in the resplendent dunes, enmeshed in heliotrope and jasmine vines. In a rocky inlet, hundreds of penguins were collecting dry branches to be thrown diligently into bonfires; others, clutching flint hatchets, cracked open tiny turtles. From the cities surfacing upon the lilac mountain there came music made by little bells and triangles that delicately stirred the sea. We jumped out.

"I claim this island in the name of Il Duce, der Führer, el Generalísimo, Charles A. Lindbergh and the Dionne quintuplets," said Bartolomé Bartolomé, kneeling and deepening his voice to sound like his uncle Calleja.

We straightened up and looked round our viceroyalty in silence.

"What's this?" asked Isabel, pointing to a smokestack.

"The Eiffel Tower," I replied.

"And that down there?"

"That's London."

"Over there?"

"New York."

"What about the forecastle? What about Cisneros?"

"I don't see a forecastle," said Lucianito testily. "There isn't any forecastle and there's no Cisneros here."

"That's Bluebeard's castle," I explained. "The Abyssinians bring him virgins; when he's eaten one he'll notch it on the rail."

"What rail?"

"I mean the wall."

"Which ones are the Abyssinians?" inquired Pepe Luis.

"Those right there," I said.

"You said that they were penguins."

"They're Abyssinians," offered Lucianito in support. "Can't you see their spears? Don't you see the bows and arrows?"

"We've got to civilize them," said Bartolomé Bartolomé.

"And make them Christians," Melitón, the pious one, joined in.

"And that, what is it?" Isabel went on, and I reached out above her arm, reducing the world to a manageable void, a bottomless space that came alive and made its presence felt through the power of my breathing: and the crows' nests were cities; and the lookouts up there were their mayors; and the rigging's ropes were docksides and the canvas awning was made of gold. And after Lucianito dispatched us inland on heroic missions we could never complete, when we'd grown tired of discovering huge toy stores, famous battlefields interspersed with movie houses, soda fountains and amusement parks, we'd gather up again beside the marble lifeboat and Bartolomé Bartolomé would then propose another game of hide and seek while I rubbed my finger on the mainmast and pronounced the magic word that Ambrosio had taught me, and the contours of the island would fold up until some other morning and another call — like an intimate ghost — invoked it.

After a short while Ana Zoila would arrive to hand out pinches.

*

During those long Sunday breakfasts I never again mentioned the nocturnal noises. Whenever I opened my mouth, Ana Zoila, looking tired, would knock over the glass of water that Ambrosio had just filled, or perhaps she'd crack, with one blow of her spoon, the royal blue border of a china plate. I decided that I'd gulp my seaweed soup and run to the bathroom with a determined look on my face. From there I'd await the final call to eleven o'clock mass; Ana Zoila, pacified by my silence, informed me affably from outside the door that if I didn't hurry the Kyrie would be half over when we got there. In the stairway leading to the first between-deck we'd run into First Officer Calleja with his men. Papa and Mama would greet him frigidly, because everyone took it for granted that he hadn't made it to the quarterdeck without staining himself in blood. Sometimes we'd see the captain, and Papa, as he kept descending, talked about the recent law concerning women's suffrage, or the structure of the National Council on Tuberculosis, which Miñagorri would direct for several years.

The stairway opened to a spacious place, whose beams and bulkheads were dressed with posters, bills and bulletins. A system of deft mirrors caught the light that came down from the deck and threw it, pacified and bluish, along the thirty-two possible paths marked out on a compass rose. At the left of this locale, beyond the portico adorned with clusters of trumpeting angels, the broad and majestic cathedral of Our Lady of Fresh Water would hide another clean well-lighted space, with severe armchairs burnished to an orange glow by torches, candles, lights inlaid in capstans; circular patterns, drilled up and down with faded emanations from the rose window, a suffocating, waxy drizzle. Below this diurnal strife of rays and shining breasts, the heads of the faithful acquired a fleeting luster of copper and ash, which encouraged contemplation. On the opposite side, beside the busy corridor that came from the communal and domestic installations, lay the Great Theater, set into the hull — admirable in its marquee of Chinese lanterns, its vestibule of damasks, marble and coral, its spherical aquaria replete with jellyfish and seahorses — where twelve people standing and four more seated on a glorious couch of vermilion velvet would applaud, night after night, the songs of Lecuona that came streaming out from Borja, the beautiful, and the incomparable Rita Montaner, who wiggled her hips like no one else. Facing the stairway, across the open space, there stood the threshold of the Labyrinth. Its high façade, pocked with faux windows in the shape of Latin capitals — you could read: LIBERTY-EQUALITY-FRATERNITY — and worked in bronze with dozens of lemmas and allegorical figures, scurried along the plaza's lateral framework to run, secret and officious, toward the far reaches of the ship. Above the roof there lay, like a sweaty eel, the gutter, whose intakes opened up on deck to pick up water dripping from the canvases that were stretched between the yardarms. The chambers, halls and offices would offer every day their beat-up stools and benches to the troop of men — there were very few women, because certain acts of violence were allowed — who lined up at the foot of the façade. The business of the place was the immediate completion of the tasks laid out in the ship's Regulations. The pavilion was scarcely two meters deep. At the end of a bare entrance-hall, past a doorman who spouted gibberish as he hawked fried tidbits wrapped in brown paper, next to a greasy hanging emergency ladder, the elevator rose mechanically with its single passenger in a creak of cables, gears and pulleys. To the right and left, facing the shaft's open sides, were two slow passageways, lit by a lantern chained to the apparatus. It was enough to twist one's body, pick a direction and make a little jump to fall without much risk onto one of them. It would be something else again to go beyond the threshold's furtive penumbra, and move ahead feeling the wall to find an entrance to a ministry, the mayor's office, the magistracy, the upper or lower house, while walking into the narrowed gale that knocked off hats no matter how stuck on they were, and the scalding jets of steam that hissed out from the elbows of the pipes, and the filtrations from the aqueducts, intercut with the howling wind in a sweet, asphyxiating sprinkle, and trapdoors eating out the floorboards everywhere like hungry sharks, and one had to proceed without a lantern, and above all, never let one's hat be blown off, and the gale and the darkness never let up. But all that would have taken place on workdays, not on the Sundays when Ana Zoila, blushing beneath First Officer Calleja's look, pulled me along the deck by my fingers, then suddenly let them go to take advantage of a sudden spurt of breeze to straighten her skirt and find, out of the corner of her eye, the small, grim figure with the starry cape, to reproach him, perhaps, for the turbulent ambition that had moved him to install and then remove the captains just like fishes in a stewpot.

*

We played at discovering the island only on some mornings now. We'd meet at the poop taffrail by the little shrine that marked the Virgin's showing of herself to the Soyas brothers and to the dark Juan Joicos—in pictures they were always profiled kneeling in their fishing boat. There we'd yawn away our breakfast time with the wind at our backs, until Bartolomé Bartolomé arrived, and then, with no clear idea of how to play the best games, we would look out at the bustle under the canvas awning through kegs of porgies, roe and fishbellies: the workers who waited until the big globe of fish, hoisted in a net by a winch from the fish tank, would spill out on the platform before moving in with their clubs; the women in their bloody skirts and bonnets who bent over the tables and applied themselves at cleaning fish and salting it, their big knives whirring dizzily.

We wouldn't take off our shoes to play then, as we would have done before: we'd be ashamed. Now we'd spread out over the whole ship, squeaking up a racket with our U.S. Keds, jumping over pools of sunlight written on the deck by wind and tackle, running first helter-skelter on the old planks but then describing circles, intersections, sketching S shapes and the other letters with our arms spread out like wings on the airplane that pulled COCA-COLA

207

through Manhattan's upper sky that we had heard of on the news. Sometimes we'd lie down on deck and use our hands as visors to explore the clouds, cut through the air more quickly looking for the China Clipper or the Hindenburg's resplendent panels, and we'd spend those mornings furrowing our eyebrows, with a painful bright spot somewhere in our eyes because – and that was what Cisneros shouted at us when he saw us there face up – there was nothing really worthwhile happening in our sky, far from it.

Little by little we'd approach the marble boat – the boat that-couldn't-that-couldn't-that-couldn't-sail that Columbia had sung about to me a century earlier persuading me to swallow porridge from my little Mickey Mouse jar – it was hanging near the drive wheel from some chains that had been painted white. On a bronze plaque screwed to one of the davits a kind of epitaph was written. The pilot Ismael Sencillo, a revolutionary, a beloved man, a poet, had lowered starboard boat No. 5 during a spring squall, and, armed with a compass and a dueling pistol, and with almost no farewell to anyone, had disappeared forever over the horizon. Ancient eyewitnesses had heard him shout: "I'll show you now, you sons of bitches!" as he rode out over the waves. But – as sometimes is the case with final words and drowned events – the phrase was *comme il faut* on the inscription. Since the reason for his departure was a mystery or perhaps had not been examined in depth, some people – a minority – held that he had meant to find land all by himself at his own risk and then steer the boat toward it; others – also a minority – their opinions based on one or another of the contradictory papers that had been put together as his testament, as well as on one of Jonah's adventures and on an immortal novel, were sure that he had glimpsed the infamous White Whale, the monster who had been stalking us since Genesis along the dark route, and that it would have to be destroyed if we were ever to reach land; but there also were those who never bothered with conjecture: the pilot's name might surface randomly at a birthday celebration or a christening, there to be shamefully associated with Matías Pérez, a talkative balloonist who one afternoon had launched himself toward Halley's Comet.

Except for me, everyone on the quarterdeck had seen Sencillo's ghost seated at the poopdeck of his marble monument. He made his appearances after midnight, when the taverns by the smokestack had all rolled down their metal curtains and only spirits stayed above the deck. Mama and Papa used to see him often on the hot nights when they put down the dice cup and went out for air. Ana Zoila, returning from under the canvas awning on the laborious days of settling the accounts, would often hear him praying; nonetheless, according to Ambrosio, who kept her company up to the door of the quarterdeck, the pilot's stationary shadow would quietly intone the ballad "great as the wide ocean, and as great the sorrow," his rowdy moustache quivering in the night air beneath the gleaming constellations.

We still pretended that we rowed the boat. But the island didn't come up quickly anymore; along the route we'd try to reconstruct the color plates we'd seen inside a truculent anthology entitled *Storms and Shipwrecks* that Columbia used to read, along with fairy tales of Perrault and the Brothers Grimm, in whose acted-out version Isabel, the object of a touching courtesy, would stuff herself, dying with laughter, with the choicest morsels of our arms and legs, which had been amputated by the dexterous Pepe Luis. Of course we knew already that the word *"coño,"* uttered just like that, in a quick, vulgar way, had no magical properties anymore, not even if you laced your fingers together — Ambrosio's latest recommendation — for some reason its sonorous spell had worn itself out, and now, if I wanted to use it for something, it had to be written in the air in green fire, hung from the yards like a perforated shining curtain, and then, shutting eyes and teeth, I had to picture myself jumping a good distance through the center of the letters; and sometimes on the portside there appeared the narrow trail of bubbles creeping above the jetty, and while Lucianito found the nascent course in a magisterial rudder-stroke I unveiled the great lilac mountain's peak and set the music of the little bells and silver triangles afloat above the stamping breakers.

For several months I set out what we'd do on land, but in time my forehead's arrogant scar was fading, toasted by the sun of one day following another, and after a malevolent declaration made by Ana Zoila upon leaving church one Sunday, Bartolomé Bartolomé had blurted to my face that I had lied, I never had been in the fish tank. My friendship with the mutinous Cisneros, moreover, was not by then a sign of daring: his shabby figure, his notorious vagrancy, his link to the unruly rabble that, according to Mama and Papa, had disturbed the climate of normality that had ensued upon the opening of the university, plus the absurd visages and bows that he put on whenever anyone of quality passed by had gradually undone the awe we had for him, to the point that when we acted out the *Treasure Island* episodes that radio brought us we adopted without argument Isabel's suggestion that henceforward we forget about Bluebeard and adopt Ben Gunn, the misshapen hermit who kept watch on Flint's unburied treasure. With things being as they were, the expeditions over land, which kept getting rarer, would be commanded by Lucianito or Bartolomé Bartolomé, though my role as the discoverer was still respected up until the morning when the island stopped appearing.

But I haven't been entirely sincere in writing down these recollections. At the beginning of that year I was a protagonist in a strange scene, which, maybe from timidity or reserve, I first intended to pass over. After a rereading, however, I have decided to include it — I'd rather not say why — to end this manuscript.

We'd have been sailing somewhere close to Ecuador, in a winter of such heat and doldrums as to put the almanac in doubt. Columbia would come in flushed, accompanied in her advance by the creaking ribs of her parasol — always unwilling to fold up — which Ambrosio would hold by the door, and tossing writing book and primer on the sofa, she would admire her long, extremely red fingernails, then fan herself with her smooth straw leghorn hat and say: "How hot it is, Julián Ocampo! What will it be like when summer comes if we're barely into February?" and on the sofa now, her parasol swinging from the first hook on the hat rack, with the door closed behind Ambrosio's good afternoon, she cast her glance over the knocked-down covered wagons, dead hussars and grenadiers that lay out on the planks, the artillery deployed to aid the soldiers' final charge, at Austerlitz, perhaps, or Jena, even at Ligny, because above those fields a lucky star had shone down on French arms, and then she'd open up the primer on her lap, seat me to her right, stiff, dignified, almost sunken in the sofa's velvet, clutching in my hand the little drummer boy who had a bandaged forehead and half-opened mouth, repeating slowly PE A, PA, PE A, PA, PAPA, following the fingernail that traversed the page like a polished flame, EME A, MA, EME A, MA, MAMA, laying the drummer down beside the primer — impossible to stand him up, the folds, the pleats — to have her shove him when she underscored the last letter, send him falling from her thigh into the sofa, see her smile and hear her say: "He looks like you," and then I'd raise my hand to touch the bandage Dr. Miñagorri had applied to me, try to adjust it, flushed with pride, make a mistake on ENE I, NI, EÑE O, ÑO, NIÑO, reading hurriedly NIÑA, actually not meaning to, thrown off by gratitude and pleasure because she also knew my blood was beating underneath the lead and the enamel, and slowly she would pass her arm behind my neck and press me to her quilted breast, hurting me a little, saying "Learn all you can, Julián Ocampo, when you grow up we'll be married," and she'd say it with a voice both soft and low, and broken, as if she were going to cry; and there we'd be, she complaining of the heat, murmuring that she couldn't breathe, that in Paris women went out on the streets not wearing corsets, maybe they would put one on for a night at the opera or the Eiffel Tower restaurant, and as for New York women, enough said, and suddenly, still squeezing me, she'd tell me that perhaps she'd give hers up that very afternoon, at least until the weather freshened up, for she was suffocating, couldn't take it any longer, and leaning forward with her elbow on the sofa and the buttons on her blouse undone, she'd ask me to let go of her and keep going on the lesson, but beforehand I should bolt the door and shut the curtains on the sky-light, and I'd stick the soldier in my pocket, carry out the mission and then go back to the sofa to confront an intricacy of flesh, hems and laces soaked in sweat, she urging me, explaining how one had to pull the cords so that the silver arrow would go through the eyelets, then her back appeared, much whiter than you'd think, the skin indented by her seams and stays, crisscrossed by reddish stringlines, a little like the penitents whipped to a drumroll on the deck, and she herself, now standing, would unhitch the other buttons of her blouse, and turned around to face the curtains she'd remove her corset with the pale silk ribbons sliding on her shoulders, to let it drop while twisting windward, there being almost no transition, her skirt eddying, her eyes lost in the upheaval, her breasts whipped back like canvas in the wind; now fixed upon a course, haughty, enigmatic, she would navigate back toward the sofa, her ankle nudging aside the long siege cannon Ana Zoila gave to me, knocking it against the grenadier who lunged out madly with his bayonet, I watching as she neared, stopped, snatched up the primer from the burning velvet and then sat beside me murmuring that we would resume the lesson now, and naturally the class resumed, but now beneath a different emblem, different flag, perhaps the one that flew upon the island I discovered every morning after I'd erased the ship with one deep breath, and it would be so easy now to jump above the ENE I, NI, EÑE O, ÑO, NIÑO, fix my vision on the letters' center and read CE O, CO, EÑE O, ÑO,

COÑO, the magic word Ambrosio used to raise and lower the drawbridge resting on the edges of all things, and she'd embrace me once again, listening surely also to the little bells whose music gleamed onshore, and I'd take out the little soldier from my pocket, make him march carefully between the dunes and penguin bonfires, then inch by inch he'd climb up to the jasmine fence, I'd order him to sink his forehead in the brown and almost lilac-colored crown of the enchanted mountain, which a profoundly sweet and submerged voice would pose as JOTA U A, JUA, ENE A, NA, JUANA — the other one, the one trembling in my half-opened mouth, would be in a second "her sister," although just as tender, soft and fragrant as the pillow stuffed with albatross down that Mama rested on whenever she was suffering from headache — and there we'd be, she loosening my pigtail, smoothing out my hair above the gauze, conjecturing, after a sigh, that when the summer came the heat would kill us, and I, attentive, silent, scared to open up my eyes, my face sepulchred in the languid scent of talcum powder and cologne, the soldier's head sepulchred likewise in the other mountain's peak, more yet, the epaulettes, the torso, hand that hung above the drumstick, drum beating on his thigh, stiff blue coattail that rolled up when gaiters pushed against it, she muttering that the sofa's velvet burned her, that her skirt was boiling as though on a stove, and I would be the one who felt around her waist to find the buttons, pull her ruffles, making them roll to her feet in a crackle of stretched seams, she saying nothing to me, her body arched, letting her salmon-colored bloomers slide above the hollow curves, so I'd take them, with her stockings, and her skirt, out from between her ankle boots, I on my knees, stretching out my hand now with the soldier on it, fingering the lead nub over his left heel — the right leg would be flexed, suspended midstrike — moving his bare head toward the mystery that floated on the sofa, sticking it firmly in the spongy patch, pink, palpitating, that would break apart in an agony of bloody foam, and she'd jump up from the sofa howling and fall on the deck, spoil the deployment of a lancer squadron, and I'd give her a long look, as if I'd seen the queen in chains brought low in an engraving printed in the *Book of Heroic Deeds*, the axe blade to her neck, and suddenly the urge to get it over with, to cut the wailing and the tears, rescue her forever from that misery of distressing, cloudy liquids, and I'd reach behind the cannon, aim its mouth, and load it with a green glass bomb, and snap the spring to shoot and make it burst against her flank, then reload with a fat, yellow bomb to stagger the more conspicuous of her breasts, and dip my hand into the box again to find a red bomb, and then another that had purple veins, and another one, especially malign, rolled up with spit and scraps of newsprint, she moaning at each impact, lifting at intervals her startled head, inflamed, her lips all chewed and her eyes all whipped, in shock, and finally, after a mothball's lethal impact, she'd collapse, plugged full of holes, grave, stiff, and she would have to wriggle on her spine like a covered wagon blown down by the cannonade, its canvas shredded, horses gone, axles broken, and I'd start crawling toward her, smell the mysterious wetness of her wound and without knowing why I'd run my tongue along her thighs to dry them off before I left her to the soldiers and ran up on the deck to find a disconcerting scene of trees and trollies, and Cisneros laughing, dressed in white linen and a Panama hat, smoking a cigar while seated on a park bench, telling me to wipe that scared look off my face, that soon enough there'd be an end to letter books and primers and the stories of Perrault and Ana Zoila's noontime persecutions, that there'd be an end to many things and others would begin, because I'd neared the age of common sense, which — and he'd say this just before he disappeared — was the least common of the senses.

From Eccentric Neighborhoods
Rosario Ferré

FORDING RÍO LOCO

Río Loco got its name precisely because it was so temperamental; when it rained in the valley and the other rivers stampeded towards the sea like runaway horses, Río Loco was always dry. But when the sun was nailed to the sky like a hot coal, charring the cane fields and forcing the scorpions out of their burrows looking for water, it reared up like a muddy demon and tumbled this way and that over the dusty plain, enraged at everything that stood in its way. The river's source was far away in the mountains and when it rained the floods rose, even when there was fair weather in the valley.

Río Loco always reminded Elvira of Clarissa. The family would all be sitting peacefully in the pantry having breakfast, Aurelio would be reading the paper and Elvira would be reviewing her homework before leaving for school when all of a sudden Clarissa would rise and run to her room, Aurelio walking hurriedly behind her. As Elvira left for school she could hear Clarissa's sobs behind closed doors, mingled with the apologetic murmur of her father's voice.

Clarissa never explained to Elvira why she cried, and if Elvira insisted on asking, she risked putting herself at the mercy of one of Clarissa's sharp pinches, or she would angrily yank a tuft of hair from her head. Clarissa reminded Elvira of Río Loco. It was as if it rained in the back of her head, in its hidden crevices, when all around her the sun was shining.

Once a month Clarissa and her sisters all journeyed to Emajaguas from different parts of the island to visit Abuela Valeria, and Elvira used to accompany her mother on these trips. Family was important then; it wasn't like it is today, when relatives have become shadows moving across a darkened stage. Today one sees one's cousins and brothers only from month to month, and instead of feeling happy and rushing to embrace them, rubbing each other's

214

antennae as if one came from the same anthill and were simply out on an errand, one greets them affectionately but at a distance, careful not to forgive old grudges.

Elvira always knew when they were driving to Emajaguas because Carmelo Bocachica, the family's black chauffeur, would start whistling softly as soon as he was told of the trip. Carmelo had a good-looking girlfriend in Güayamés, and when they travelled there he spent the night with her and got away from his wife.

Crossing Río Loco was one of the high points of the journey to Emajaguas. The old, winding road from La Concordia to Güayamés had been built by the Spaniards, and although the towns were really not that far apart — twenty miles at the most — the journey took two and a half hours, much longer than it should have. Elvira's father always said the Spaniards had followed the "burro method" when they built the road: they took a burro from La Concordia to Güayamés, let it loose and followed it as it ran back home down the quickest path.

Río Loco remained without a bridge throughout the forties; it was the last important river on the island to be spanned by an overpass. The government was too poor to afford one, and it wouldn't be able to build one until the fifties, when a human wave rose from the island and thousands of Puerto Rican immigrants crashed into New York. This was good for the government's budget, and soon it began to invest in public works.

Río Loco was shallow, and ninety percent of the time one could drive across its dry gully without any problem, skirting the huge boulders that lay on the bottom like dinosaur eggs and the tree trunks left there by intermittent floods. When September arrived, however, Río Loco was often flooded, and pulled along with it everything that clung to its banks. The poor peasants who worked the *central* Eureka's cane fields had built shacks along the riverbank, as none could afford a plot of land. Most of them lived at the *central's* barracks, where they could cook outside on coal stoves and shit in the latrines the owners had built for them. This gave them the advantage of having the company store near at hand, where they could buy food on credit when they ran out of money, as well as medical supplies and services, but they were also more closely supervised by the overseer and fell into debt. For this reason, some preferred the dangerous freedom of the riverbank to the convenience of living at the *central*. Riverbanks, like beaches, are all public property by law on the island.

Río Loco was dry most of the year. The earth was black and fertile along its shore, as it was periodically covered with silt, and the peasants grew splendid plantains, manioc roots and corn stalks there. But when it flooded, the river reclaimed with a vengeance the terrain it had temporarily ceded to the squatters. You could see doors, corrugated zinc ceilings, rocking chairs, tables, cooking pots, mattresses, all floating slowly towards the sea; as well as dogs, pigs, goats and even cows, already swollen and floating legs up, pulled along by the brown mass of toffee.

Elvira loved crossing Río Loco when it was flooded, and as the family car set out for Emajaguas she always prayed for a *crecida*, never thinking about the havoc the river created for the peasants. It broke the monotony of the trip, the silence that inevitably sat like a block of ice between her mother and herself. As they neared it, Elvira's heart began to pound faster and faster. One never knew if the current would be high or not, and if the river couldn't be crossed, they inevitably had to turn back to La Concordia with her mother in tears.

As soon as they neared Río Loco's banks, Clarissa instructed Carmelo to drive the white Pontiac up to the river's edge, and Elvira would stick her head out the window to see what was going on. If the current was high, Clarissa would order him to pull up close to the river, and they would wait in silence under a mango tree, to see if the waters came down. Clarissa could never wait very long, however. Without a quiver of fear in her voice, she would command Carmelo to drive the Pontiac into the murky current. The car was soon bobbing and half-floating over the river bed, maneuvering its way over the invisible boulders. Carmelo hardly dared touch the accelerator with the tip of his shoe because any surge would flood the motor and the engine would choke. Then they would find themselves stranded in the middle of the river, the dangerous mass of toffee flowing by on each side, and they would *never* be able to get out.

This is precisely what happened one day. Carmelo followed in the wake of some hardy soul who had plunged his car into the water ahead of them, when all of a sudden the Pontiac had an attack of *delirium tremens* and died in the middle of the river. Clarissa ordered Carmelo and Elvira to roll up their windows, and for twenty minutes the three of them sat in silence, watching the brown waters rise inch by inch until it was licking the window-panes, carrying with it the debris from upstream. The car was full of good things to eat the cook at La Concordia had prepared: a leg of lamb, a roasted turkey, a cauldron of *arroz con gandures,* and soon the smell became stifling inside the car's interior. A basket full of oranges, pineapples and breadfruits had been picked fresh that morning from the garden and lay on the seat beside Clarissa and Elvira. It was like sitting inside a water-tight paradise: mother and daughter dressed in their Sunday best, Clarissa in a silk georgette printed gown and high-heeled Saks Fifth Avenue shoes, and Elvira in her white organdy dress with a satin bow on her head, watching all hell break loose around them.

Clarissa looked at her diamond Bulova wristwatch on its black elastic band and saw that it was already half past eleven. If they didn't hurry, they would be late for lunch at Emajaguas and she wouldn't be able to sit down at the table with her mother and sisters. She ordered Carmelo to start up the car, he turned the ignition key, the car gave a couple of lurches and died on them again. Clarissa then commanded him to honk the horn. Soon four barefoot peasants dressed in faded khakis and wearing scraggly straw hats on their heads who had been standing on the shore next to a pair of oxen watching this predicament waded silently into the river.

Rushing water up to their waists, they approached the car with their yoked animals in tow, Clarissa opened her handbag, took out a dollar and waved it at them from inside the window. The peasants tied the beasts to the Pontiac's front bumper with a thick hemp rope, and slowly the car began to inch forward. The smell of mud became stronger and Elvira stared in horror as a thin line of water began to seep in through the bottom of the door. Clarissa waved emphatically at the men to poke the oxen more sharply so the car would increase speed, until they finally reached the bank. Once back on shore Clarissa slipped the dollar bill to the peasants through a crack at the top of the window and ordered Carmelo to start the car up again. The white Pontiac jumped forward, its shiny surface dripping with mud, and took off at full speed, an anxious Pegasus flying down the road towards Emajaguas.

Rosario Ferré

BOFFIL AND RIVAS DE SANTILLANA

> *— We're all dead, children of the dead,*
> *the first man said.*
> *— No one dies, the second man answered.*
>
> — Naguib Mahfuz

In Güayamés it rains a lot from July to November; gray clouds are always rubbing their bellies against the roofs of houses and easing themselves over them like stray dogs marking their territory so the sun can't take over completely. Rain influenced Clarissa's life from the start. She was born in Güayamés during the rainy season, on January 6, 1914, when people in Güayamés stay inside much of the time. Anything can happen then: a sudden gust of wind may bring a tree branch down on your head like a punishment from God, or a wave of mud from the nearby Emajaguas River may roll down the street and whisk you away. Every year, from July to November, Abuelo Alvaro stayed in Güayamés with his family instead of moving to Emajaguas, from where he could easily supervise his cane fields. He always got bored in town, and for that reason Abuela Valeria got pregnant at the end of each July and gave birth at the end of each March. Clarissa was the first of their six children. As a child she was bitten by a mosquito bred in a pool of stagnant rain water and she developed rheumatic fever, which caused a *soplo* in her heart. So I suppose one could say Clarissa was born because of the rains of Güayamés, and also that she died because of them.

The house in Güayamés had a balcony that opened on to the main plaza, from which Clarissa watched the Lent procession every year, next to her four sisters — Siglinda, Dido, Artemisa and Lakhmé. Wearing white lace mantillas, the five girls would lean their elbows on the rail and admire the purple silk platform where Jesus carried the cross on his back, and the black velvet one where the Verónica, with her tear-streaked face, swayed to and fro over a sea of heads. Nevertheless, the Lent procession didn't elicit any special feelings of piety in them, since the Rivas de Santillana religious drama and pagan celebration were all part of the same play.

Around the middle of December, when it stopped raining and the cane had ripened in the fields, the family moved to Emajaguas, which stood three miles down the coast. Abuelo Alvaro had been born there in 1882, and both his parents had died young. He was brought up by two maiden aunts, Alicia and Elisa Rivas de Santillana. Sixteen years later, in 1898, his aunts bought a house in town. With the arrival of the Americans, the quality of life in Güayamés had greatly improved: streets were paved, and running water, a sewage system and sanitary drainpipes were installed.

Abuelo Alvaro's aunts had always pampered him, and in spite of the fact that they were only moderately well off, they spared no expense in his education. He was taught French by private tutors, and could do his arithmetic competently enough. But he didn't like to read and was a little bit afraid of people who read a lot because they always seemed to think they were above the rest.

Abuelo Alvaro, Clarissa said, learned everything there was to know about the sugar industry firsthand, struggling to keep his cane fields well tended. His aunts trusted him and put everything in his hands; with their combined fortunes Alvaro was able to keep Emajaguas in working order. Alicia and Elisa died in 1913, during a typhus epidemic which ravaged Güayamés. Abuelo Alvaro and Abuela Valeria were married that same year — she was eighteen and he was twenty-five — so that when the couple moved to Emajaguas, they had the whole house to themselves. Abuelo was saddened by his aunts' passing, but he had been so pampered, he thought it was only natural they should do so. They were only being considerate of him in his newly married state and didn't want to intrude on his privacy.

Abuelo Alvaro always remained a man of simple tastes; he was used to country life and mistrusted city ways. After he married Abuela Valeria the only time he traveled to Europe was in 1931 — the same year Tía Siglinda married Tío Venancio — because Valeria dragged him there by the hair. In Paris he moped around the whole time because he couldn't order *ropa vieja* — stringy beef stewed with onions — and *tostones* — crushed green plantains fried in oil — in any of the local restaurants. Abuela Valeria, on the other hand, loved to travel and took her children to Europe several times. She would spend a month in Paris, a month in Rome or a month in Madrid, installing herself in one of the best hotels with her children, a nanny, her personal maid and valet. She would go to the opera almost every night, as well as to concerts and museums, and always insisted that a trip to a foreign country was worth as much as a college degree.

Valeria was the youngest daughter of Bartolomeo Boffil, a

Corsican merchant nicknamed *mano negra,* who made a fortune at the end of the nineteenth century smuggling merchandise from Saint Thomas and Curaçao. Both of these islands belonged to the Dutch at the time and had a long tradition of smuggling and illegal trading. One could buy perfumes, shoes, fine linens and laces from France there, and all sorts of farming tools. Machinery for the sugar haciendas, not then manufactured on the island, was much sought after and was smuggled in from England and Scotland.

Bartolomeo Boffil was a rough man with no education, but he was proud of his business and considered it in character with the rebel nature of his ancestors. "The origin of the word 'corsair' comes from 'Corsican,' which means a native of the island Corsica," he used to say to his friends before the Americans arrived in Puerto Rico. "If we Corsicans hadn't managed to dodge the embargo the Spanish authorities placed on the island for three hundred years, these people would be so poor they wouldn't have shoes to put on their feet." Commerce with the rest of the world was banned by Spain, who wanted to benefit from it exclusively. The island had no choice but to depend on Spanish ships coming in through San Marcos, the island's capital and port city to the north, for all its imports.

Bartolomeo had been born in Sisco, Corsica's most inhospitable peninsula — a veritable tongue of rock where only billy goats prospered. He was a small, evil-tempered man who lived alone with his two daughters, Elvira and Valeria. His wife had died giving birth to his youngest daughter, and for that reason he was often cruel to Valeria, as if wanting her to pay for her mother's untimely death. He loved her dearly, but he couldn't help thinking that if she hadn't been born, his wife would still be alive and he wouldn't be alone.

Bartolomeo's farm was on the outskirts of Güayamés and he tended it himself. He grew ginger, tobacco, cotton and cacao, but it was a cover for his real business: smuggling. His farm had several protected coves where fishing sloops coming in from Saint Thomas, Curaçao and other places dropped anchor at night. Then a dozen rowboats would silently skim the waters and unload the crushing mills, iron winches and centrifugal steel pumps for which the sugar hacienda owners paid a handsome price.

Bartolomeo loved to go up to the mountains to hunt blackbirds with his shotgun in the company of his dog. Blackbird pâté was his favorite dish because he was sure it had magical qualities, and he used to make Valeria eat some of it every day. As with the story

220

of the Chinese emperor who fed his daughter nightingale tongues so that she would sing more sweetly, Bartolomeo was convinced that blackbird pâté would refine his daughter's voice, as well as make her more dainty and beautiful. Valeria felt terribly sorry for the birds but she was an obedient daughter and dutifully ate what her father served her. Brought up practically a prisoner, she was never permitted to go out of the house by herself to visit the neighbors and was always accompanied by a chaperone. At home she was taught the arts of embroidery and music by a governess; she could sing in French, English and Italian, and play the piano, but she couldn't read or write. Her father had forbidden the governess to teach her how, so that when Valeria turned nineteen she was illiterate. Bartolomeo hoped that this way Valeria would never leave him and would take care of him in his old age.

Valeria went to Güayamés to visit her sister, Elvira, who had married a man of means and lived in a beautiful house at the entrance of town. Bartolomeo had had no misgivings in letting Elvira leave; it meant one mouth less to feed. It was the youngest daughter who was supposed to stay home and take care of the widowed father in his old age. It was at Elvira's home that Abuela Valeria met Abuelo Alvaro. When he heard her sing and play the piano, Abuelo Alvaro fell head over heels in love with Valeria and asked her to marry him, but she refused. "I can't get married because I can't read or write," she said, with tears in her eyes. "What will you do when I sign the marriage license in front of the judge with an X? You'll be so ashamed of me you'll change your mind." "That won't make any difference to me at all," Abuelo Alvaro answered, laughing. "If you can cook as well as you can sing, everything will turn out all right." And that very night they eloped and asked the judge in Güayamés to marry them.

Bartolomeo found out the next day. Rumor has it that he ran to his son-in-law's house and tried to batter down the door with the butt of his rifle. When his daughter wouldn't open it, he began to hurl insults at them, calling them traitors and panderers, until he was so beside himself he suffered a heart attack and died. But Clarissa insisted that story wasn't true at all. What really happened was that he was caught in a shootout with the American coastal patrol, who kept a stricter eye than the Spanish Guardia Civil on the coconut groves of his farm. When he died Abuela Valeria inherited half his fortune, and this made it possible for Abuelo Alvaro to consolidate the family's economic situation.

The first thing Abuela Valeria did when she could afford it was have the schoolmaster from Güayamés's public school come to her house to give her private lessons, so she could learn how to read and write. Soon she became a passionate reader — she practically devoured the best Latin American novels of her time: Jorge Isaac's *María;* José Eustasio Rivera's *La Vorágine,* Rómulo Gallego's *Doña Bárbara* and sometimes she even read them out loud at dinnertime. Abuelo Alvaro, on the contrary, didn't care for literature at all; novels bored him, and he preferred books which dealt with life on the island as it really was. After their wedding, however, Valeria refused to make love if he didn't read at least one novel a week, and in this way she managed to educate him.

The Rivas de Santillana family lived at Güayamés during the sweltering season of heavy rains, when hurricanes like San Ciriaco and San Felipe were more likely to ravage the island. The town was a safe place to be during these storms, which uprooted trees and left the hills strewn with gabled roofs, which whirled away from the houses like zinc discs in the wind. They returned to Emajaguas at the time of the *zafra,* however, for the harvesting of the sugarcane which began in the first days of December. During the next six months there were sparse rains and cool breezes. April brought scattered showers (*"las lluvias de abril caben en un barril,"* Abuelo Alvaro used to say), May brought thunderstorms (*"las lluvias de mayo se las bebe un caballo"*), and June, July and August were dry as cane husks (*"junio, julio y agosto — marota seca para los cerdos"*).

After the First World War the family became very prosperous, thanks to the rise of the price of sugar in the world market. Abuelo Alvaro sold the house at Güayamés and the family stayed at Emajaguas the whole year round. Abuelo added several rooms to the house, and the kitchen and bathrooms were modernized. Clarissa and her sisters didn't have to go to public elementary school like they did in Güayamés but took lessons with a tutor — a skinny, bald man who drove every day from town in his old Model T Ford. This meant they could spend the afternoons horseback riding or swimming in the nearby river without having to wear a uniform or even shoes. This is why, when Clarissa talked to Elvira about her childhood at Emajaguas, it was as if she talked of a lost paradise, a timeless space where days and nights chased each other merrily around on the tin sphere of the grandfather clock that stood against the dining-room wall.

The Other

Arturo Uslar Pietri

— Translated from Spanish by Anabella Paiz

HE HAD HEARD the dry sound of a broken branch. It wasn't one of the thousand confused and mixed sounds of the night in the jungle teeming with the rumor of insects, the croak of frogs, of agitated branches and dead leaves stirred by the wind. It was the unmistakable sound of a man's footstep. Not an animal's. Of a man who has stepped cautiously and who stops at the sound.

"They won't get me in my sleep," Checho thought, sitting astride the hammock that hung high, close to the thatched roof of the hut.

Groping with his hand, he grabbed the machete he kept ready on the storage box and lay waiting.

It was easy to see in the semi-darkness of the night. The ashen brightness of the moon sifted from among the trees. The six bare poles that supported the thatched roof, with no walls, didn't hinder his sight.

Right there the jungle started, near the poles and the path. First there were briers and weeds, then shrubs and reeds, and farther away the dense crowd of the thick straight trunks of the big trees, branches and vines intertwined.

There, right in front of him, was the enormous ceiba with thick roots jutting out like tails of caimans. And among the roots, the spot where he hid the diamonds.

He fixed his eyes there, and then looked attentively from side to side.

There was nothing unusual in sight. The sound of the broken branch had not returned. Nothing moved underneath the quiet, rustling shade.

If it was a thief, it would have been a man alone. And he would have crept quietly over him, waylaying him asleep in the hammock. Checho smiled. It wasn't easy to surprise him. Or he would have gone to the roots of the ceiba, had he known where the diamonds were. Not that there were many. A scant dozen of cloudy

223

crystallines, broken.

If it was the police, they wouldn't have been so careful. It wouldn't have been a single man, but three or four, well armed. They would have surrounded the hut quickly, aiming at him with their rifles, "You are Checho, the one who killed the woman in Anaco."

That's it. But it could also be a single one, sent ahead, as far as he was, deep down in the jungle, to locate and identify him before sending down the rest of the agents.

If it was only one, he was not concerned. After a while he stretched back in the hammock without leaving the machete. If it was only one sent to spy on him, he would have had to walk a long time. From Anaco to Soledad. Asking all the time, "Haven't you seen a medium-sized man with such and such features?" Later he would have had to cross the Orinoco to Ciudad Bolívar. And later, by road and by bongo, up the Caroní, up the Paragua, searching for the small tributary branches where the diamond alluvion is buried with sand. Asking all the time.

It was far and they wouldn't find him. Lost behind so many rivers, so much woodland, so many deserted miles and miles and miles away. He began to fall asleep.

The dead branch creaked. Again. This time Checho jumped from the hammock with the machete in his hand. They wouldn't surprise him. He went out to the blurred path, slender in the grass like a trickle of lime. Looked on all sides.

Not a single human trace. Nevertheless, someone, who had stepped twice on a dead branch, could be hiding in the foliage. Hiding, spying, waiting to ambush him.

He thought, if I make him believe I have seen him, he might come out.

"Don't hide anymore because I've seen you. Come out!" he yelled.

Nothing moved.

"Come out, or do you want me to chase you out with the machete?" he shouted even louder.

Apparently no one was there.

He advanced along the path. It was a meandering path weaving among the sturdy groves searching for a narrow passage to reach the river. It took more than an hour to get to the river on that path.

Who would dare come that far at night to look for him? If it was to capture him, they would have better waited for him to come down to the river to search for the diamonds. He came down with the iron rod, the shovel, the sieve to sift the sand. The cover and the bag of provisions. And he began to stir the sand upstream, far away, where no one ever came. Almost half an hour away from the closest store. And he seldom saw the storekeeper and spoke to him even less. He handed him a list of what he needed.

They would have had to get to that storekeeper to ask, "Have you seen a man of medium height, black mustache, so and so?" The storekeeper couldn't remember him well because he hadn't seen him much. And furthermore, he did not know where he had his hut. Nor where he took the path or where he arrived.

Nor did anyone know his name or where he came from. There was neither hut nor house in all that immensity. Who would dare come that far at night to look for him? A branch brushed his back and he jumped back fearful.

"Epa!"

Nobody. There was nobody.

He returned slowly to the hut. He hopped back into the hammock. He placed the machete on the storage box within reach. And he stretched, searching for sleep.

"I will go down to the river tomorrow."

Rocking, he fell asleep. There was nobody. Maybe tomorrow he would find a piece of diamond in the river, big, cloudy and sparkling like the moonlit night.

He arrived at the river later than he had thought. He lost time marauding in the jungle in search of other dwellings. He had taken animal trails that thinned between the trunks and the shrubs, turning into narrow tunnels where a wild cat or tapir could barely pass. But he had found nothing.

The river was deserted in that narrow and torrential part upstream. The diamond hunters didn't come that far. Only a man like him could persist in washing in such a place.

He decided to go down to the store to search for supplies before beginning the task because it was late. He carried the list on paper in order to talk less.

The storekeeper was alone in the thatched hut of the store; the two benches in front of the counter were empty.

He gave the paper to the storekeeper.

The man seemed to look at him amazed.

"You came back so soon?"

There was no doubt he was talking to him.

225

"Me?"

"Yes, you."

"You must be mistaken. I just arrived."

"Arrived? But you were here a while ago."

"Not me."

"Not you?"

The storekeeper continued to look at him amazed. He seemed fully perplexed.

"Aren't you Chucho? The new guy who just arrived. The one who told me he lived nearby, in the woods."

"You are mistaken. My name is Checho."

"Almost the same."

"And I live nearby, in the woods."

"Same thing."

He thought he shouldn't have said that much.

The storekeeper couldn't shake his surprise.

"If it's not the same man, then you look alike. This seems like the work of the devil. Look, the same face, the same mustache. You're even dressed the same. The same striped drill, the same sash and buckle, the same cloth. Even the same dark hat. Are you sure he's not your brother?"

He didn't like the storekeeper's insistence. By means of so much comparing and so many questions, he would end up memorizing his appearance and learning things.

"Look, my friend. You better hand me over what I have here on the list."

He gave him the paper.

The storekeeper took it, but he continued to stare back with the same curiosity.

"What a strange thing! Nobody is going to believe me when I tell them about this."

He would start telling about this. To the men who came to the store he would say he had seen two guys who were exactly alike. That one of them washed diamonds upstream, and that he lived in the mountain. And he would describe each feature, the size, the voice, the gestures, the clothes. Even the name.

"One of them is called Checho, and he lives right here."

The news would roll from mouth to mouth. Everyone would want to see and compare them. He would be no longer safe in his hiding place.

"Give me what I asked for, quickly."

While the storekeeper was gathering the goods, he took the opportunity to urinate behind the hut, near the plantain. He hadn't finished when he heard the voice of the storekeeper calling him.

"Hurry up, my friend. Come and take a look."

He returned quickly. There was the other one standing near the window of the store. He had the immediate sensation that he was exactly like him. The broad face, the mustache, the heavy eyelids, the hat over the eyebrows, the hands on the sash.

He was speechless. The other one didn't speak either. The storekeeper looked from one to the other, nervous and perplexed.

"I don't believe it!" the storekeeper said. "They are like two drops of water. It's impossible to tell them apart. Anyone can make a mistake. It is as if they were twins. More than twins."

They looked at each other for a while with the suspicion of two animals that bump into each other for the first time. Checho passed his hand over his face as if he were trying to recognize by touch the same features he was contemplating in the other.

"You have never met?"

Neither of the two answered. They continued to stare at each other as if arrested by an unexpected revelation. Little by little the two countenances softened. Something between a grimace and a smile began to appear on their faces.

"At your service," both had said, almost simultaneously.

And almost simultaneously they said then,

"Checho."

"Chucho."

They laughed.

"It seems we look alike."

"That's what the storekeeper says."

"And it's true; we look alike. Down to the clothes."

"Maybe my old man passed by your village."

"Or your old woman."

"Uhú . . . Aggressive, are you?"

"Not aggressive, but not tame either."

They sat on one of the trunks that served as a bench and looked over their shoulders.

Checho spoke first. "Have you been here long?"

"Not long. How about you?"

"Neither."

"Do you wash in the river?"

"Yes. And you?"

227

"Also."

And almost in unison they said,

"But nothing comes out."

"Just a few little things that look like shards of glass."

"What's that?"

"Do you want something to drink? I'm toasting to this strange incident."

"Thank you," the two men replied, annoyed.

The storekeeper served two rums in two short glasses. The other one stood up and brought one back to Checho.

The other man had hands just like his, heavy, with dark grooves from drippings and machine grease. The hands of a mechanic and a driller like him. Maybe he had worked with a drilling crew.

"Are you new at this?"

"Yes."

"And before?"

"Before."

He looked at him, distrustful.

"I was something else before."

"I can tell you what you were."

"How could you know?"

"I don't know, but I can tell."

"Say it, let's see!"

"Driller on a rig."

The other one looked at his hands as he observed his own.

"You too."

"Yes."

"From around . . ."

"Around where?"

"From around Anaco. Campo . . ."

It was the other one who was finding out about him.

He could be a man sent down by the police to search him out. They found someone who looked just like him. That made things easier. It was easier to arrive and ask, "Have you seen a man who looks just like me?" It was easier than giving personal descriptions. The rest he knew because they had told him before sending him down.

"Do you come from over there?"

"Yes. I have been there."

Now it was his turn to ask to make things clear.

"And why did you leave?"

228

"Well, for the same reason . . ."

"For the same reason I . . ."

"Could be the same reason . . ."

"What do you know?"

"That's what I'm asking."

That's what he asked, the wise guy, because he wanted to find out. He wanted to confirm what he already knew. But he wouldn't tell him anything. He drank the rum in one gulp.

"I had to leave."

"So did I."

"One doesn't leave a good job to come to this woods without reason."

"That's right."

"One comes when one can no longer stay there."

"When one is no longer able."

"They won't let you."

"That's it, they won't let you."

Was he thinking the same, or was he repeating like an echo everything he said?

"Why did you come?"

"Had some difficulties."

"Difficulties with the authorities?"

"Also."

"You must have gotten into some mischief."

"Did you?"

He would not talk anymore. Trying to find out about the other, he was denouncing himself. In trying to keep my eyes open, I'm poking out my own.

But now it was the other who was speaking.

"You had a wife? And you left her? How did you leave her?"

He was afraid and kept silent. He thought, son of a bitch. Do you want to know, or do you know already? If you do, there's nothing else to say. I must get out of here now, the sooner the better, and tonight, pick up my stuff and disappear.

Could it be that the other one expected him to be as stupid as to tell him everything? Maybe he would let out he had killed his wife, María Rosa, on the night of San Juan, because he found her with another man.

"Women are fools." It was the other one who was speaking.

"Uhú."

"You can never be off guard around them."

"Uhú."

"One leaves for a job at night, and when one returns early, one finds a man inside the house. And what else can one do with a machete on hand?"

He knew about it. Otherwise, he would not have mentioned those things with such certainty. Unless the same had happened to him. Unless he had a wife and had found her at home with a man, and the man had run away, and he had killed his wife. And then, like him, had left before he could be caught. Could be. Things happen. It was better to continue talking as if he gave the matter no importance.

"That's right. What else can one do?"

"What did you do?"

"Well, the same thing you would have done. What about you?"

"Well, the same."

He grew silent. If it were true, it would be a big coincidence.

It was stupid to keep submitting to this game so that he found out what he did not want to disclose. He got angry.

"You seem to be trying to pull things out of me."

"You are the one who's trying to pull things out of me."

He took a risk. "It seems you killed your wife."

"You are the one saying it."

"Do you think I would be saying it if I had done it?"

"Nor would I."

"That's it."

"That's it."

They fell back in a mistrustful, hostile silence. From the corner of his eyes he watched the hands, the shirt, the head bent down over the chest of the other. He also had his head bent down, staring at the floor. He mumbled furiously. He had to say it.

"I don't like policemen. One needs to be a son of a bitch . . ."

"Nor do I."

They couldn't go on speaking like that. He thought about other ways of continuing the conversation. He could simply stand up and go off. But it would seem suspicious to leave that way. He would try to change the subject to bury what had been said.

"Are you thinking of staying here long?"

"It all depends. How about you?"

"It depends too."

They were silent. It depends on many things. I know, Checho thought. It depends on your coming to look for me to take me

230

prisoner. It depends on your being a policeman. There was a police station in Anaco. Ugly-looking people always standing at the door. With knife and revolver beneath the shirt. Staring at people who walked by, looking for trouble. If he were not a policeman, why would he be so interested in him? Unless he was a thief. He could be the one who approached by night to steal diamonds. There are people who believe it is easier to steal than to wash the sand in the river.

"To whom do you sell what you get?"

The other one looked back distrustfully. "I bring the small ones to this one . . ." and he pointed with his hand at the storekeeper.

"And the big ones?"

There had to be big ones. Sometimes washing coarse sand, a man had gotten a diamond the size of a bean.

"I haven't found any of those yet."

He could think he had found some. It would be better to erase all suspicion.

"Nor have I. If I had gotten any, I wouldn't be here."

"Where would you be?"

He was nosy. He wouldn't tell him, nor did he really know where he would be if he had money.

"Somewhere else."

"Far?"

"Yes, far."

"This is also far."

"It is far, but . . ."

He wanted to say that here he could still bump into someone looking for him, while there, in a place really far away, nobody would find him.

"But what?"

He wanted to know everything, but he wouldn't find out.

"He who gets a good diamond will not stay here for long. He will go to enjoy his riches in a better place."

A better place would be a distant city. With wide streets, and stores, and bars, a plaza and a cinema. And women.

"That's true. You know everything that can be done with money."

They stopped for a moment as if thinking about all that. It was the other one who began speaking.

"Do you want another drink? I invite you."

It was better not to accept. If he drank, he would need to offer another, then another one would come. And once drunk, which

was what the other one wanted, he would draw out everything he
didn't want to say.

"No thank you. I don't want any more."

"What a shame."

The other one went to the counter and ordered another rum.
Now with this drink he would become even more talkative, and
would not let him go. If he started towards the river, he would
surely follow him. And if he went home, he would come along.

The best would be to wait until the other one left. He had swallowed the rum in one gulp, sort of roared with satisfaction and
spit loudly in the middle of the worn path. The star of saliva began
to cloud with dust.

The other one seemed to be talking to himself, but in a loud
voice.

"When one drinks, it's as if it were a holiday."

If he continued to drink he would get drunk, and it would be
harder to get away, so he said as if casually, "But it's not a holiday."

The other one tried to reply as if he were looking intently for
something.

"I know it's no holiday. The holiday is San Juan, there."

That's what he wanted to get out. The memory of the night of
San Juan in Anaco. The sly one knew what he wanted. He knew
the holiday and he knew the time, and he even probably knew the
number of blows with the machete.

He dared to say: "It's getting late."

"It's still early."

"There's work to be done."

"There is always time to work."

He had returned to sit beside him on the bench. He could feel
the rum's smell on him. He decided to stand up.

"What's the matter?"

"Nothing. It's late."

"Heading home?"

"Maybe."

"Where do you live?"

He made a vague gesture towards the dark, thick wood.

"There."

The other one answered right away.

"I do, too. We can go together."

That was precisely what he didn't want.

"It's long, you know?"

"It doesn't matter. I also live far. We can walk together for a long while."

There was no other way. The man wanted to find out where he had his hut to return late at night. To rob him or to capture him with the police. He would have rather accompanied him to know if he really had a hut and if he was a man like him. Or if he was a policeman. Or if he was a thief and was lying.

"I'd rather accompany you."

"It's all the same. We take the trail, and whoever arrives first arrives first."

He could use a trick. Start walking on a different trail than the one leading to his hut. That would be the best way. Then pretend to be lost and turn back.

The other one paid the storekeeper and said, "Let's go." The storekeeper, staring at them, said again: "As if they were twins. Unbelievable. Like two drops of water."

"Let's go, then," he said.

He took a trail he had never entered before. It was narrower and more tortuous than the one he usually took, and it led in a different direction.

He felt insecure with the other one behind. It gave him a big advantage in case he wanted to attack him. He would have the blow on him before he realized it. He tried to look back, over his shoulder. The other one walked close to him.

After a few steps, the man following said: "Are you sure this is the way?"

"Don't you think it is?"

"I don't think so."

There was no doubt he knew the way.

"Do you think I made a mistake?"

"Maybe."

"Then, it would be better if you lead and I follow."

"If you wish."

The other one led. They backtracked and then, confidently, he took the path that really led to the hut.

He knows the way like the back of his hands, he thought; he has been here before. He has come looking for me without my seeing him. He must be the one who approached last night. If I hadn't waked up, who knows what would have happened? I heard the noise, and I settled in the hammock with the machete. Who knows if he was spying on me from behind the shrubs. He must have left.

Otherwise he would have gotten me in my sleep.

He could start straggling, inconspicuously, until the other was so far ahead, he would get lost at a bend. But whenever they separated, the other one turned around.

"If you're tired, we can rest for a while."

"No, I'm not tired."

"Let's go, then."

They would pair off again.

He would not let him go. It was clear he would not let him loose. He had come to look for him, he had found him, and he would not let him go.

"I don't like having people at my back. Walk beside me."

"It's true."

He said this, and he seemed to glance at Checho's machete, but then he looked at his own and continued walking.

He doesn't seem to feel safe, he thought. He's scared of me. Thinks I may take advantage of him when least expected.

They walked another stretch without saying a word. There was no sound other than their steps. That man walked stooped over, as if he were tied and dragged along. He wasn't tied, but it felt as if he were. And the more they walked and moved away, the more difficult it would be to get loose. It was clear he would not turn him loose.

He could turn around and get lost, running down the path. But the other one would follow. He hadn't gone that far just to let him escape without putting up a fight. He would start running behind him until he caught up with him. He was strong and was surely fit for the run. And when he caught up, he would have nothing to tell him. It would be like confessing everything he did not want to confess.

He would call on his reserves of cunning.

"Chucho," he said.

The other one stopped.

"What?"

What was he going to say?

"It's nothing. Just that there's still a long way."

"Not much."

No doubt he knew the road. He was going to say he had forgotten to pick up something at the store.

"I forgot to pick up the candles at the store."

But the other one had a reply.

"I have some, and I can lend them to you."

He had to insist to take advantage of the crossroads.

"You are very kind, but as it happens, I also forgot other stuff. I better go back."

He knew what was coming: "I'll go back with you."

He had taken into account that possibility and would not give in.

"No. No way. You go on, and I'll go back. I'll go with you another day."

Another day. Never. Another day would be when the frog grows hair. When the turtle climbs the tree. When the dogs meow and the cats bark. Never, because I'm leaving now.

"Don't say that! I'll go back with you."

"No. It can't be."

"Fine. If you don't want me to accompany you."

He could not believe he had said it. He had to take advantage.

"Good-bye, then. See you soon."

The other one said also, "Good-bye, then."

It was true that he could go alone. He felt a relief and happiness that must have been visible on his face.

He turned around and began to go back. The other one stood still and watched him as he moved away.

As he reached the first bend of the path, he stopped to look back, hiding behind a tree.

The other one was returning. He had increased his pace as if to catch up with him.

He thought of running. But running would be as if confessing to the other that he was fleeing. And if he did not run, the other would catch up with him. The man didn't want to turn him loose. He had found him, and he wouldn't let him escape.

The best would be to hide in the woods and let him go by. Hide among the trunks, the shrubs and the vines, and let him go by. That was the right thing to do, but it had to be done right away. There wasn't much time left. He brushed the reeds and the shrubs at the edge of the path. It was lush. He should have been able to use his machete, but it wasn't possible. He couldn't make noise, nor could he leave cutting marks. He would crouch and cover himself with branches and leaves. The other one would not see him. He would not think he was hiding there, but would think he had continued down the path. He would see him go by. He crouched, shrunken, without moving, almost without breathing.

He could hear the quick steps of the other one approaching. He was almost there. He stepped hurriedly and purposefully. He had almost reached the bend. He could see him. Fast, resolved, with the machete in his hand. He was about to pass by. He would let him pass by and wait a long while before coming out. He was coming so fast, he would pass quickly. He was bolting after him. But, suddenly, he stopped. Checho felt a cold terror running through his body. He stood. Had he seen something? What could he have seen? He had stopped. He paused for a while. Checho held his breath.

He felt him coming back slowly, as if he were searching for something. He seemed to search. He could see him from behind the foliage. He was looking from side to side, turning his head quickly. He seemed to talk or mumble. He was getting closer. He had stopped. He had stopped right in front of him and was looking at him. He had seen him and was talking to him. He snapped as if he wanted to bite him: "You were hunting for me, but you didn't dare, you coward!"

His eyes sparkled, and he had the machete brandished in his hand. Checho stood up. There was no point in hiding now. He stood up, grasped the machete and came out, walking carefully at a distance from the other to the middle of the path.

"You're the one who has been hunting me . . ."

"You have been looking for me, following me. Falling behind to take advantage of me . . . Lying . . . Hiding there to ambush me."

Each word was like a fist. Clenched, shiny, copper-colored, like the face of the man talking to him. Hard and cold like his machete, brandished in the air.

"If you were looking for me, you found me."

"You are the one who knows what he has found. I've seen you coming all the time."

"I'm the one who saw you coming."

They were getting closer with each word. They seemed to be within reach of their tight hands. The air of the harsh words hit their faces.

"I wasn't looking for you . . . You are the one who has been looking for me, following me. Why were you searching for me at the store?"

"You were the one searching for me . . ."

"No, damn it."

He had seized his neck and was shaking it harshly. Checho kicked him, trying to free himself, and after the kick dealt him a quick blow with the machete. The other one jumped aside, and the machete hissed in the air without wounding.

Now they were on guard, ready to attack with the machetes. Panting, tense, steady in the eyes.

"Don't move around. Stand still."

"I'm standing still."

They wielded the machetes, dealing blows, halting and dodging with their bodies. Checho felt a sharp blow on his shoulder and a slight sting.

"You hurt me, policeman. You piece of shit."

With all his force, he hurled the machete at the middle of his body. He felt it strike the flesh at his side. The other one moaned. They had drawn near and were united in a rasping panting. They rubbed their faces together and spoke in broken voices mouth to ear.

"You fucked me, policeman. They sent you to fuck me."

"Police . . ."

"Because of the woman . . ."

"Because of the woman. You came looking for me."

"A man can kill a woman who is unfaithful . . ."

"A woman who is unfaithful, and the policeman who wants to trap him . . . You trapped me . . ."

"Policeman . . ."

"Policeman . . ."

Their voices were becoming weak and detached, and he felt the heat of the slippery blood, coagulating on his flesh.

They walked arm in arm, stumbling like two drunkards:

"Why did you have to come and fool me . . ."

"It was you who did . . ."

"No, you."

They were on the ground, among the leaves on the narrow path, shady and quiet, face to face. Checho didn't know if it was too dark to see or if he could not see well anymore. He could see his eyes, his mustache, his nose. He could hear his panting.

"Foolishly we fooled ourselves."

The other one was not answering, or he couldn't hear what he was answering.

The storekeeper had said they had the same eyes and the same face.

"What a strange thing!"

It seemed he could not hear anymore.

"Are you listening to me?"

And then he said: "He can't hear anymore."

And then he said or heard the other one saying: "Brother . . ."

"Brother . . ." What a strange thing! He would never have called him that before. But he had said it now.

"Brother."

They were lying on the ground with no strength left to talk. Feeling the darkness of the night and of sleep.

"Damn the hour."

The last one spoke.

The other one did not hear. Had he heard him, and had he been conscious of it, he would have sensed that all returned to being alone.

Three Poems
Adrian Castro

MOKONGO Y TO' ESA GENTE

Eyibaríba eyibaríba enkamá
Wá   [*chorus*]
Eyibaríba eyibaríba enkamá
Wá   [*chorus*]
Sounds that spread through past wombs
those before Mokongo y toda esa gente
sound too much like thumps
like the procession of feet from Abakuá
on that day carrying casket y bailando la caja
teetering on bounce of 6/8 rhythm
like an incomplete thought between bone & spirit —
we were born on such a day
on such a day we kneeled before certain clouds
& chose our calabash full of destiny
The hardest thing to remember
is sounds from those wombs before Mokongo —
Eyibaríba eyibaríba enkamá
Wá   [*chorus*]

4 years he wandered streets in Regla
lingering like delicate webs of tabaco smoke
or inside vacant bottle de aguardiente
(That's why bottles should be layed to rest while empty)
Even two miscarriages our mother had
So they clipped a bit of ear from the stillborn
to identify him indelibly upon return
y to assure he did not leave again
fastened small chain around left ankle

Abakuá: Secret society of men in Cuba. Formed by descendents of slaves from the Calabar.

239

Adrian Castro

After 4 years Mokongo y toda esa gente
decided to help
On such a day
we sealed the pact with death/ikú
ikú would have to filter through thick curtains of mariwó
though the sounds thumped like a procession of feet
against the ear missing a snap —
Eyibaríba eyibaríba enkamá
Wá   [*chorus*]

*

What about Feyo, Frank, Emilio, Luis, y Mongo
their hair their platinum teeth
how they were men y mostly fathers
one young guerillero leaning on steel bars
shot in Santo Domingo
They keep waving flags of rainbow
asking for glass of water
flores y perfume
claiming they're still here —
though de vez en cuando
some café spills prior to being served
or a plate with morsels of platanos arroz y pollo asado
cracks in approval like an offered eucharist

And how can we forget Alfonsa —
placed like a dune of stone on the shore
smiling like someone whose known you for a while
dress of blue gingham/guinga flapping
like waves of laughter

*

In an isolated house
a father remains alone wearing
milky silky slacks y guayabera
watching the mediterranean stucco & tile

---

mariwó: Palm fronds.

asking certain stones & ceiba
wind & streams who animate things through the other world
to deliver this message to his son
We need the skull of a ram carnero o sheep —
just like bone is past memorized
just like blood is life actualized
so is spirit time humanized

Eyibaríba eyibaríba enkamá
Wá   [*chorus*]
Eyibaríba eyibaríba enkamá
Wá   [*chorus*]
Tó Egúngún!

CANTO OF THE TYRANT WHO HANGS HIMSELF

We purchased a piece of thunder
a ki-lack-um of ilú/tambor
We caught the thundercelt
in its rapid descension to
the dance of flames

We've seen the face of power
inside the inverted pilón
mortar con(secretos)
There were certain shadows
of caudillos on white horses —
Trujillo before his last date with the mistress
Batista entering one of his casinos
Barrientos posing with el Ché
Diaz Ordáz & corpses of 300 students
Videla surrounded by Plaza de Mayo mothers
Somoza slipping on a banana from United Fruit
Rios Montt wearing the cloth of countless massacred indios
Fidel is surfing the Gulf on a raft with his favorite cow
There were certain shadows
of the ceiba tree where they hung themselves
within the inverted pilón

241

mortar con(secretos)
After the tyranny
there are so few places to go
places to sing
eat gourds of quimbombó y kalalú
kalalú y quimbombó

We purchased a pinch of
ka-ki-li-ka-ki-li-ka-ki-li-kack
Who would be struck by red thunder
being summoned by goatskin?
And how would the first flame
arrive at the throne?

A palma showed us its kingdom —
We were smiling like red-vested mummies
like dancing worms
in a puddle of stones
pile of water
streams of smoke
smoke of streams sending signs
estamos vivito y coleando
this culture is still burning fresco
cool y caliente like guaguancó/columbia/yambú
Muñequitos de Matanzas style
like bomba y plena
Cepeda style
like merengue
Ventura style

There were certain shadows
of the imprisonment of Masayá
of the day he found Olufina's horse
on the path to the big mortar
on his way to greet him
The horse had been missing for some time
But just as Masayá was approaching the throne
Olufina's guards saw him riding the stolen horse
(ki-ti-tack ki-ti-tack ki-ti-tack)
saw him as a thief
(ki-ti-tack ki-ti-tack)

saw him prisoner
(ko-ko-koooo)
Don Masayá stated his case to small burned stones
He remained prisoner with a pen as a pillow
& white cloth
Yet mothers were giving birth to death
crops wilted the river
was now a snake of clay

A poet with yellow n' green tongue & wrists beaded
told Olufina there was someone
wrongly wrapped in iron boxes
someone of some relation
This retribution
was the source of much trouble
Masayá would later brand a poem
unto the turtle's shell
offer it to Olufina —
". . . so long you kept me hidden
& never saw my face
When would you've realized that I
did not steal yr horse
that I came to yr land to greet you
& bring you a gift . . ."

El pueblo dice: Masayá Obakosó o
& drums summon thunder
dicen: Obakosó o
& stones rain from the sky
dicen: Obakosó o
& the caudillo dangles from a ceiba
dicen: Obakosó o
& the old memory is the new
dicen: Obakosó o
& the new memory crackles
dice Masayá: Obakosó o
& odu burns beyond

---

odu: Divination verse in Yoruba religion.

Adrian Castro

PARA LA INSTALLATION DE JOSÉ BEDIA

Que tu son Kongo
emi ni son Yoruba
canto en inglés —

The marriage of spirit & history
is often like a dance of streams
dance of rainbows
like sending smoke signals yes there is hope
& yes we can resist the urge to forget

The brick boat
with its shadow about to speak
tells the story
So we gather bits of myth —
something like balsas
Something like torn cloth
armed with little war instruments
Shovel & hoe to erect roots
(they can be amuletos so long you keep them
    in yr pocket necklace yr head)
Something like rope
like white headtie
to provoke stability & peace of mind
Something like a strewn slipper de niño
we call this chancleta
we call this sorrow

Que tu son Kongo
emi ni son Yoruba
canto en español —

E yo hala garabato mi Kongo
mi Kongo Kongo real
hala garabato halo

We who are born from river water
sea water
tambor y trueno
repique de brisa & stones

244

We who circle clouds of cotton
with a certain chant
We who choose el canto —
in Spanish or Kongo Biyumba
Osha Lukumí
Monina nkamá
in Arara kwero Dahomey e e
We who build shrines to migration
We who die with
river water sea water
tambor y trueno
repique de brisa & stones

Those who cast the first balsa
in the bombardment of boats
who cast a desperate wail
Pablo, Antonio, Miguel
maybe even Raquel
They said one throws the rock
but it's the people who get blamed
it's the people who get blamed
when one throws the rock
(*Oye basta de cuento*
llego el momento de —)
Those who cast the first balsa
even though they've seen empty
even bitten innertubes
lying softly on a breezy shore
even though they've seen the iron rudder
with the signature of Zarabanda Kimbansa
strewn on a pile of stones
strewn like dead fish

*

He who struts con crutches
but dances without them
has a body of trembles
but inside has signs of infinity —
a dog can be his messenger

Adrian Castro

San Lao San Lao
Kobayende San Lao

He who sits at crossroads
changing destinies with a funny dance
sometimes from pebble to sugar
from sugar to pebble

*

Que tu son Kongo
emi ni son Yoruba
canto en Lukumí —

Eshu odara
Elegba kó soro odá ni ofo
kó soro ofo ni odá
Osha re o
Adashé
Four twins spin a hymn —
something about opening yr eyes
to what is before you
(Irosun meyi)
about being led into a trap
(Irosun meyi)
They said no one knows what's at the bottom of the sea
They said you must be careful
There's someone with big boots
standing on a shore
& yes there's a hole just ahead
You must be careful
the ocean seems to be hungry these days —

Two Prose Pieces
Severo Sarduy

JOURNAL OF THE PLAGUE

— Translated from Spanish by Suzanne Jill Levine

I.   19.I.91

TODAY WAR BROKE out. Why I'm beginning with this sentence I'm not sure, but after months of being blocked, I'm attempting to write a journal of the new plague. In order to do this, and to transmit my everyday life, I am abandoning my fourth novel *Cayman*, the last body of the zoological tetralogy formed by *Cobra*, *Colibrí* (hummingbird), *Cocuyo* (firefly) and *Cayman*. The insular cayman, or alligator — Cuba seems to have the shape of a cayman stretching into the Caribbean sea — would have swallowed the undulating cobra who would have devoured the hummingbird, fixed flyer, who would have gulped down the phosphorescent firefly. Cayman would be the last one left, alone, but with the other animals intermingling, embodied inside. Mute emblems of the devouring chain, a hieroglyph that becomes a question: who will eat Cayman?

The war has something in common with the present-day plague, as if a programmed apocalypse needed symmetry. Both hover above the planet like the threat of extinction, both are gaining ground, man after man, mile after mile. And yet one can be completely detached from them, absent. It's enough not to have access, in the case of war, or to renounce voluntarily all means of communication for everything to be the same as before. At least for the time being and in the west. You can go to work, wander the streets or your dreams, go shopping or make love without the slightest material sign of deflagration, unconcerned, almost unconscious.

The same happens with AIDS. If you are withdrawn and don't make the decision to take the fateful test, you might die an old man, lulled in your apparent health, just another innocent.

Unless, as in war, in the middle of the night . . .

II.   27.I.91

In the hospital, I point out to the male nurse passing by, or to an indifferent Antillian scrubwoman, the presence of cockroaches in the bathroom. "As soon as I can," he responds without the slightest sarcasm, concerned and professional, "I'll report it to the management . . ."

III.   27.I.91

The preceding is a memory. There will be many from my almost month-long stay at L. Beach, as I call that Parisian hospital. I was first admitted for seventeen days for a serious case of pleurisy. I had to return when I understood — in a paradoxical way that proves one's blindness to one's own body, I hadn't understood it despite my rudimentary studies of medicine, which I always exaggerate or protract in my memories — I was allergic to the antibiotics which were, precisely, my cure.

A terrible contradiction of the diseased body: it rejects its salvation.

"I didn't think I'd see you again so soon," the doctor on duty stated in surprise.

IV.   27.I.91

But all that has already become a memory, a recent limbo. A moment lived whose remains blossom like a morbid archeology, but only when exhumed by something. And so a garish signal on the television which, in the hospital without any other occupation or interest, I would watch several times a day, revives a chill similar to fever in me each time I see it now: not yet diagnosed I felt the same disquiet when I first saw it, but almost unconsciously.

What worries me now are the sequels. It's been two months since I left L. Beach — upon leaving I looked so healthy, many thought it was as if I'd come back from the beach — and I still have pulmonary pains. The pleura are neither forming scars, it seems, nor recovering their elasticity. I continue with my breathing exercises.

But maybe I'm just a white-collar marginal, an irresponsible masquerader, someone incapable, throughout his already long life, of taking care of himself, of avoiding danger, of surviving. *I do stupid things.* Almost under the snow I go out on the street in a raincoat, I frequent damp and unhealthy places, I go out till late at night, I drink to create that moment of blackout in which the plague and the war and everything is oblivion, nocturnal drifting, sex and respite.

Something in me is self-punishing. For some arbitrary reason. For example, some furtive, anonymous bliss, in the middle of the night.

V.   28.I.91

Reinaldo Arenas: three rebellions. In Cuba, very young, against the family, against poverty and the unbearable mediocrity of life in the country — I remember the melancholy, the sadness of the sunsets, as if death were approaching. Then, rebellion in Havana against the arbitrary revolution, the persecution of the homosexuals, the confiscation of his royalties, organized chaos. Finally, in exile, he ends his life rebelling against God's will, against AIDS.

That was his last freedom, to choose his death. Not to leave it in the hands of nothingness. Nor of that Nobody who dictated it.

VI.   28.I.91

Upon seeing the newscast, last night, chills down my spine. It's the gravity of the news — the dangers of a chemical bomb, the biological warfare paralyzing all life and leaving the rest intact, the silent landscape of the fallout, in short, the millennium — of those purely denotative words, spoken in a neutral tone, which pass over the body like a cold sweat. Or rather — terror of the same intensity, the same texture — it's the return of the pleurisy, one more sequel. The pleura, rejecting maximum magnitude, the normal rhythm of breathing, full breathing.

"You exhale fine," the doctor told me. "But you seem to lack the inspiration to inhale."

A lack of inspiration: a fatal diagnosis for a writer.

FIRE AT THE LAENNEC HOSPITAL. Now those images return, generated by television, but in disorder, shredded, burnt. A fire broke out in one of the pavilions, General Medicine, and progressed along the corridor destroying ancient installations — the hospital dates from the seventeenth century: damp or worm-eaten walls — charring the immobilized patients: old, infirm people, AIDS victims, trapped in the web of plastic tubes that perforate and nourish them. A few more hours of breathing. One more day of urine and excrement. A plate of food without salt. A glass of water. Any guarantee that life goes on, that death, waiting patiently, waiting to spring in the diagnoses and soiled sheets, in the intravenous vessels and in the cotton balls stained with blood and pus, has not yet arrived completely, has not yet struck, bluntly. At least not tonight, at least not today.

I recognize immediately, in the midst of the scorched medical machinery, the architecture of the building, the exterior gothic-inspired buttresses, and then, as the camera pulls away, the signs indicating the different pavilions.

The fantasy is inevitable: I see myself in the midst of the fire, unable to get out, trying to pull off the transfusion needles. Or rather — the worst-case scenario — in the midst of an injection. A needle puncturing my lungs streaming toward a recipient that I don't look at on purpose, a liquid the nurses judge by its color; the tones of painting return: coffee, light coffee, wine dark water, opaline, till shading into the mother of wine or the dregs of coffee. Hues that measure the degree of morbidity, the gold — so the golden staphylococci virus has been described — that clings to the walls of the pleura. Overworked or clumsy, the attendants disappear from the room while the liquid flows, no doubt fed up with this banal emptying. François watches over this repugnant flow.

Until the assistants return and take out the needle. They shout, exhilarated: "Almost a liter!"

Now those charred images mix with others in the same newscast, which follow them without respite, as if they formed part of the same secret sequence, or were destined to the same end. Fawn-colored, ochre, grayish, immobile, as if all movement and color had been expelled. There is a storm in the Saudi Arabian desert. The tanks have gathered near the border. Seen from the plane transmitting the images they form a strange geometric figure, the letter of an archaic or future alphabet, the hieroglyphics of death. The sand erases everything, as do the ashes the burnt hospital.

The foreseeable signal reaches its end, like the musical version, the open vowel of a suffocation.

It is followed by the fire, announced by the commercial which I associate with death or a fever: a ballet couple, sketching a figure in faded, yellowish, vomitive colors, tubercular-spit pink. Tones of dirty blue and menstrual purple border that horrendous *pas de deux*.

VIII.   18.II.91

Pleurisy, in French, contains weeping — *pleure* — so that now the unforeseeable weeping that lasted for a month has turned into sobs. Sobbing assaults me in my sleep, the sobbing of a person who has cried a lot, without being able to translate this sensation into French: the word, or the notion, has no precise equivalent in that language.

But perhaps there's more in pleurisy: the trauma of my birth, my desire — I slowly discover as life moves on — not to be born, not to encounter air. I was born choking. In the intrauterine fetal state the walls of the pleura touch, are closed: the air of birth opens them. Written in the sequels of the sickness I suffer is the pulse of my return to the only happy prenatal state which, why I don't know, I identify with the posthumous state, as if I had to finish as I began, choking.

To be born choking; to die choking. Aren't all deaths, however they may appear, a disguised form of suffocation?

Equivalence of the prenatal and the posthumous. The obsession of Cocuyo, a character in my last novel. Life appears then as an interlude, a vigil between two infinite absences. Sudden spark of being.

The presence, the awake state of life: does it imply a telos, a conscious purpose, or not?

For some reason I was saved from pleurisy. I sensed one night that a particular *orisha*, Oyá, the guardian at the gate of the cemetery — and who is identified in Catholic syncretism with Santa Teresa de Avila — rejected me or brusquely signalled to me that the moment had not yet arrived. The next day I inexplicably awoke without a fever.

What's certain is that for some reason I was saved, but why, I don't know.

Severo Sarduy

IX.   18.II.91

Yesterday my father died in Havana. I had just written the previous paragraph when my sister called to give me the news. I already knew that something was happening. In the morning I had seen a shadow, some disembodied thing that passed by, as always occurs when someone near me is about to pass away. I was ready.

"He didn't suffer," my mother said to me when I dared to phone her to assume the name, the role of patriarch of the family which genetics had now assigned me. "He died with his face in my hands." My sister thinks he realized that everybody was around him, taking care of him, loving him.

I am comforted by the faithfulness of some men: all the Cuban writers, my old friends, went to the funeral.

LADY S.S.

— Translated from Spanish by Esther Allen

According to Severo Sarduy's own statements — no birth certificate was ever found, despite persistent research by scholars in the sacristies of her native city — she was born in Camagüey, Cuba, on February 25, 1937. It appears that she was christened Eleanora, though to her family she was always Nora, and later, to Gustavo Guerrero, Juana Pérez. To herself, she was, in succession, María Antonieta Pons, Blanquita Amaro, Rosa Carmina, Tongolele or Ninón Sevilla, as her preferences in movies or rumbas changed over time.

Very little is known of her childhood, aside from what she recounts in her autobiography: a painful litany of banal anecdotes and terrible injustices in a context of poverty and the racial discrimination characteristic of small and insular provincial cities. In her own undoubtedly apocryphal testimony, she presents herself as a modern Justine whose outraged virtue could only transform her into a helpless being, forever and by definition frustrated.

To tell the truth, there are details in her polemic against consumer society that would only be repeated a few years later in the document which is the pride of our Letters and a model of syntax: *The Right To Be Born*. A father who abandons the home; a pregnant, unwed mother who loses her work as a servant for that reason; ill treatment; jobs that are beyond humble; rapes; and finally the correction center — the periphrasis that designated the jail for juveniles, the mitigated madhouse she lived through. In short, all "the ingredients of *la tragédie humaine,*" to borrow a typical phrase from Jacques Lacan . . .

In payment for the errands and cleaning she did for the proprietress of an equitable house of assignations in the neighborhood, frequented by the bishop and the local police — Raquel Vega's house (pity that amid so much order there were still cigar butts on the floor and a light no one ever switched off; it's plain to see how easily they were making money . . .) — the madame gave her permission to play a few records on the phonograph that decorated the parlor. She got to know her greatest idols that way: Daniel Santos, Lucho Gatica and especially Mirta Silva, the Fat Lady with the Voice of Gold, in whom she admired, above and beyond her repertory and the lyrics written by the greatest poets, the "immense sonorous volume and *le feeling* that was so particular."

Beyond all the speculations that a biography with such obscure origins can give rise to, one thing is certain: if Severo Sarduy became a singer it was by chance, or because, to cite Claude Lévi-Strauss, "everything is written out in destiny and the human being can do no more than *read*" — in the sense the famous French graphologist gives to this word, obviously.[1]

It all happened in Havana, when she went to meet her mother who was then living in the Cuban megalopolis. She had just left the prison on the Isla de Pinos where she had spent four months for illegal possession of marijuana with an aggravating factor of prostitution. They had to pay — though only a niggling trifle — for the room they rented in a prestigious area of Guanabacoa. One night as she went past the Mars and Bellona, she caught sight of a discreet little sign that, with impeccable spelling, sought dancers and waitresses for that distinguished locale.

This casual speakeasy was particularly famous for the pianists who enlivened it from late in the night to the dawn's twilight. The most popular of them was Chapotín, whose brassy style enchanted the dancing couples and who, with his party hat, the "bowler," the little black bow tie he wore at all hours and the cigar in his mouth, chatted with the clientele while playing the arpeggios which,

---

[1] In his volume, *De la grafología como una de las bellas artes,* Ed. du Seuil, col. Tel Quel, 1950, pp. 20–21 and, if you can stand it, 22.

Severo Sarduy

fortunately for musicologists and rumba fans, *La Voix de Son Maître* had the good sense to capture.

Before the first number of her audition was through, the owner stood up and with a gesture appropriate to Versailles, though drastic, told the young aspirant it was useless for her to go on wasting her time because she didn't have the slightest talent for dancing and couldn't take a single step that wasn't false.

The pianist took pity. Seeing her dashed down, passed over, *fânée*, washed up, given the run-around and told to get lost, he asked her if she knew how to sing.

She answered that she knew only one song by heart: *"Un chorizo na má queda, bombo camará."* She sang it, achieving notes of exquisite coloratura, vocal arabesques and a vibrato that hadn't been heard since la Malibrán.

That night she reached her lyric and vocal zenith, and forever.

Or, as the Barbarian of Rhythm would write years later, "That night, the phonetic/nomad signifier had its first and/or last anagnorisis with the criollo episteme."

But let's get back to Severo. At that point, she was earning eighteen pesos a week, in addition to the prodigious tips that the already nascent class of committed extortocrats — starched linen, Panama hat, diamond on the pinky and big cigar — slipped into her plunging neckline or under her garter belt when she went crooning from table to table after the seventh daiquiri. But this method of attracting the increasingly numerous masculine clientele becomes humiliating to her. She decides to stop once and for all and adopts the stance that others would deem arrogant and that would earn her the nickname of the Duchess or Lady S.S.

She makes her first record. She enters a bright period of her life since, after the shortages of Machado's reign of stupidity, the country is enjoying a dance of millions so unimaginable that the cabarets are multiplying; there's one on every corner. The Tropicana bedazzles the whole world and jukeboxes play their first records for a five centavo coin. Overnight, she becomes the great rival of Rita Montaner. Hollywood is clamoring for her. She travels to California to appear in the Paramount short film *Symphony in Black*, in which she performs one of the rare blues songs of her career.

I would prefer not to record the rest of her life.

Which is long and drawn-out.

And I'll tell you more about it later.

254

From Condolences
E*dwidge* D*anticat*

J*OAQUÍN SAT WITH* a hurricane lamp in the yard. He used his hat to fan the fire under Señor Pico's bath water. As the flames grew, the night breeze teased them, making black shadows dance on the sides of the tin bucket.

Pinta walked over to her husband and handed him a bowl of stew. To warm it, Joaquín placed the bowl near the bucket. He cleared a spot on the ground and spread a small rag next to him for Pinta to sit on.

I watched them from a rocking chair that faced a small arc of calabash trees in front of my room. I was tired and sleepy but I couldn't go to bed until everyone else had.

I had strung a few of Señora Valencia's empty perfume bottles on the lowest branches of the calabash trees. My parents had always said that the trees were our original temples, the first places where we blessed our children. The bottles were guardian eyes, vessels for visiting spirits, souls who knew when babies were born and stood watchful guard against danger on their first night in this world.

As the wind whisked through the large calabash leaves I thought of little Caterina. She had nearly died during her birth with the umbilical cord curled around her neck and a caul clinging to her face. Like a tiny warrior woman, she had fought and battled for her first breath.

When I was a child, my parents had strung bottles on all their calabash trees. My parents were considered rain makers. People came to them during droughts and asked them to make it rain. They had a collection of bottles that they used to talk with the weather. Orange bottles for sunshine. Black ones for clouds. Red bottles for lightning and thunder. And crystal clear bottles for rain. The farmers would point in the direction of their fields and my parents would pray to make it rain for them.

Were there spirits in the perfume bottles that I had hung? Did little Caterina have a guardian for her soul?

"How was the car ride?" Pinta asked her husband.

"Too fast," Joaquín reported. "Papi drove too fast going to the barracks. Señor Pico went too fast coming back."

"At least you returned in one piece. Saint Christopher, we thank you."

"I thought you'd have to go and plant a white cross on the side of a mountain for me," said Joaquín.

"They were anxious, both of them, to get back."

"I was more anxious than them," he said. "When Señor Pico was at the wheel he struck a goat and a man, not far from here. The car nearly overturned. The goat I know is dead. It's over there under the flame tree."

"He took it?" Pinta asked, peering at a lump beneath a burlap blanket that lay under the flame tree.

"It was more cruel to leave it on the road, dying. He shot it mercifully, with just one bullet."

"And the man?" Pinta held her head with both hands. "Blessed Mother who gives life, forgive us."

"Señor Pico thought there were two of them. It was pitch black. I was squeezed into the back seat and could see nothing. Someone yelled in Creole when the car hit him, but when we got out to look, they were gone. We thought they were *braceros*. They must have run into the ravine not far from here."

My heart jumped up to my throat. It could have been any one of the cane workers who toiled in the nearby fields. It could have been Sebastien.

Sebastien and I occasionally kept each other company. Sometimes I escaped to his shack in the cane cutters' lot. Other times he came to my room in the middle of the night, always leaving before dawn.

It was too late now for me to go walking through the fields. I hoped Sebastien would come and visit me after everyone was in bed. I wanted to know that he was all right. I also knew he'd take great pleasure in hearing of the birth of the twins.

"Holy Saint John, please look after that poor man," Pinta said.

There was a rustling under the flame tree. I jumped to my feet, expecting to see the dead goat rise. Instead, it was Doctor Berto. He was waiting for two other people to climb the last stretch of the hill.

Pinta stood to greet Doctor Berto, who was with his friend Noche and Noche's sister, Blanca. Blanca was carrying a covered plate that smelled like cinnamon-drenched rice pudding.

Nodding hello to Joaquín, Doctor Berto asked, "Has Pico arrived?"

"Yes, Señor Pico has come," Pinta said. "Good evening, Señor, Señorita Blanca."

Pinta dusted the dirt off the back of her dress. She took the dish of rice pudding from Blanca.

"You will wish to go inside," she said.

I couldn't stop worrying about Sebastien. As the greetings and laughter echoed from the parlor and Señora Valencia's bedroom upstairs, I walked over to the flame tree and peered at the dead goat.

In this valley Haitian blood — my blood — was as cheap as goat's blood. What if Sebastien had been the man on the road? What if he had ended up suffering the same fate?

Near the goat's bloody head was my sewing basket. I had dropped it at that spot when I heard Señora Valencia first screaming in labor. I picked up the basket and took it back to the rocker with me.

The joyful reunion continued upstairs while Joaquín carefully fanned the flames to keep Señor Pico's bath water warm.

Señor Pico was finally ready for his bath. Joaquín carried the water over to the house. I dozed off in the rocking chair in spite of my efforts to stay awake.

Pinta tapped my shoulder. "The Señora would like to see you."

Señora Valencia was in her room alone with her sleeping infants.

"Amabelle, you look extremely tired," she said. "You worked so hard today. I hope you'll sleep very soundly tonight."

"Thank you, Señora."

"Amabelle, I hope you'll understand what I'm about to say." She moved her lips very close to my ear.

"I had to tell my husband an ant-size lie. I didn't tell him how much you helped me with the births because I know he'd see this as bad when we all see it as good."

"You do what you think is correct, Señora."

"Actually, it was Papi who decided this. He thought it best. I'm simply following along."

"Papi knows best then, Señora."

"I'm very grateful to you, Amabelle, for what you did today."

"Anyone could have done it, Señora."

"I promise you, I will show my gratitude."

"There is no need."

She reached over and squeezed my hands. When her husband walked in, wearing his pajamas, she quickly dropped my hands.

"Amabelle, you can return to your room," she said. "Pinta will stay here tonight."

Señora Valencia stood in the doorway. Her husband stood behind her, his arms wrapped around her waist. Then he pulled her inside and closed the door.

"Good night, Señor, Señora," I said.

They didn't hear me.

I found Pinta piling up blankets on the floor of one of the empty rooms. I waved good night to her as she lay down on the pile to sleep. She blew out her lamp, leaving me in complete darkness.

Down in the parlor, Papi sat alone in a corner near the house radio. He placed his right ear next to the trumpet-shaped speaker, straining to make out the news announcer's voice without raising the volume and disturbing the others.

Papi was an exiled patriot fighting a year-and-a-half-old civil war in Spain from afar. On his lap were maps showing the location of different Spanish cities which he consulted as he listened.

"How is the fighting?" I asked, while walking past him. "Is your side winning today?"

"The good side doesn't always win," he said.

"Do you wish you were there?"

"In the war, an old man like me?"

"Do you need anything?"

He shook his head.

"Did my daughter speak to you?"

"Yes," I said.

"Good night then."

"Good night, Papi."

Joaquín had skinned and chopped up the goat. He was piling up the legs in a white plastic pail and covering them with handfuls of coarse salt.

When I was a little girl, I used to play a game using the small bones from a goat's leg joints. These bones are like dominoes except they have a curved back and three hollow sides. I'd spend hours trying to get a handful to land on the same side. I never succeeded.

I asked Joaquín to cut up the small bones for me. Wiping off the blood, I took them to my room.

I undressed, taking off my gray housedress and the matching square of cloth that covered my head. Everything I had was something Señora Valencia had once owned and no longer wanted.

I spread an old sisal mat on the floor next to the castor oil lamp and a conch shell that Sebastien had given me, saying that within it was the sound that fishes hear when they swim deep inside the ocean's caves.

On the wall was a seven-year-old calendar from the year of the great hurricane when so many houses were flattened and so many people were killed that the Generalissimo had to torch their corpses in public bonfires which burned for days, filling the air with so much ash that everyone was forced to walk around with their eyes streaming, their handkerchiefs pressed to their noses and their parasols held close to their heads.

I lay on my mat on the floor, hoping Sebastien would come.

When I closed my eyes I could see my home in Caco. I imagined my fingers sifting through the rusty golden soil, the wind whipping through the red and yellow croton leaves that grew everywhere.

I saw myself as a child, hiding in the tiny spaces between the mango trees which lined the road leading to the sea. I smelled the dark, wet coffee grains, still hot and sticky, laid out in the sun to dry. I saw the husks of violet corn and the unripe bananas suspended from tree branches beyond my reach.

In our house my parents' voices bounced from the palm frond walls to the wood shingles on the ceiling. Imperceptibly, their murmurs—"Amabelle, come quick. We need you"—became Sebastien's.

I got up and went to the door. Sebastien was standing there. He handed me two large yams with the roots and dirt still clinging to them. The yams were from his garden. Sometimes I cooked them for him and, whenever we could, we ate together.

"I was dreaming about you," I said. "I was home, and you were with me."

"I thought you were asleep," he said. He had a large gap between his two front teeth which made him hiss a little when he talked. "I've been waiting outside, watching for the right moment. People were coming and going all night and then Joaquín killed that goat. Is there a celebration?"

"The goat was already dead," I said, remembering that he, Sebastien, was not. I grabbed hold of him, my head barely reaching the center of his chest. His arms were steel, hardened by ten cane harvests, five years of chopping in the fields.

Sebastien seemed lavishly handsome by the light of my castor oil lamp even though the cane stalks had ripped apart most of the skin on his shiny black face, leaving him with some deep scars.

"Señora Valencia gave birth today. She had twins," I said.

He gently pushed me away as he removed a piece of burlap sacking which was wrapped around his head. He didn't ask about the children.

"Have you eaten?"

"I won't be able to stay." He tugged at a scruffy beard, too gray for his twenty-seven years. "Old Congo's waiting for me at my house. His son, Wilner, was hit by a car and sent flying into a ravine."

Sebastien's forehead was sweating. He brushed the drops off with a single swipe of his hand.

"Your boss killed Wilner," he said. "I saw the blood on the front of his car. I keep asking myself what should be done about this death. The first thing is to put the body in the ground. And then?"

"Does Congo know it was Señor Pico?"

"Right now all he knows is what hurts him, that his son is dead. He needs wood to build his boy a coffin and he can't buy any. The cane bosses hardly pay anything at all. They certainly don't pay for funerals."

Joaquín had gone to bed. I led Sebastien behind the latrines. There Papi had a stack of cedar wood that he occasionally used for his hobbies, making furniture and building miniature houses.

Sebastien took four long planks, just enough to make a coffin for a grown man.

"I'll come see you when I can," I said.

I heard him puffing away, struggling with the weight of the wood. I went back to my room, ready to put an end to a very long day.

"Poor Congo." I whispered the words to myself. "My heart aches for you, Congo. Condolences from far away, Congo. Two new children came into the world today while you have to put yours into the ground."

Prologue from The War of Knives
Madison Smartt Bell

CITIZEN BAILLE, commandant of the Fort de Joux, crossed the courtyard of the mountain fortress, climbed a set of twelve steps and knocked on the outer door of the guardhouse. When there was no reply he hitched up the basket he carried over his left arm and rapped again more smartly with his right fist. A sentry opened to him, stood aside and held his salute. Baille acknowledged him, then turned and locked the door with his own hand.

"*Les clefs,*" said Baille, and the sentry presented him with a large iron keyring.

"In the future," Baille announced, "I will keep these keys in my own possession. Whoever has need of them must come to me. But there will be no need."

Citizen Baille unlocked the inner door and pulled, throwing a part of his considerable weight against the pull-ring to set the heavy door turning on its hinges. He stooped and picked up a sack of clothing from the floor, and carrying both sack and basket, passed through the doorway and turned and locked it behind himself.

The vaulted corridor was dimly lit through narrow loopholes that penetrated the twelve-foot stone walls. Baille walked the length of it, aware of the echo of his footfalls. At the far end he set down the basket and the sack and unlocked another door, passed through and relocked it after him.

Two steps down brought him to the floor of the second vaulted corridor, which was six inches deep in the water that came imperceptibly, ceaselessly seeping from the raw face of the wall to the left — the living stone of the mountain. Baille muttered under his breath as he traversed the vault; his trousers were bloused into his boots, which had been freshly waxed, but still they leaked around the seams of the uppers. Opening the next door was an awkward affair, for Baille must balance the sack and basket as he worked the key; there was no place on the flooded floor to lay them down.

Ordinarily he might have brought a soldier or a junior officer to bear those burdens for him, but the situation was not ordinary, and Baille was afraid — no (he stopped himself) he was not *afraid*, but. . . . He could not rid his mind of Suzannet and Dandigné, the two officers of the Vendée who had lately evaded their captivity here. It was an embarrassment, a scandal, a disgrace, and Baille might well have lost his command, he thought, except that to be relieved of this miserable, frozen, isolate post might almost have been taken as a reward rather than a punishment. Baille still had little notion how the escape had been possible. There was none among his of-cers or men whom he distrusted, and yet none could give a satis-factory explanation of what had taken place. The prisoners could not have slipped through the keyholes or melted into the massive stone walls, and the heavy mesh which covered the cell windows (beyond their bars) was not wide enough to pass a grown man's finger.

And Baille's current prisoner was vastly more important than Suzannet or Dandigné could ever dream to be — although he was a negro, and a slave. From halfway around the world the First Con-sul's brother-in-law, Captain-General Leclerc, had written that this man had so inflamed the rebel slaves of Saint Domingue that the merest hint of his return there would overthrow all the progress Leclerc and his army had made toward the suppression of the re-volt and the restoration of slavery. Perhaps only the whisper of the name of Baille's prisoner on the lips of the blacks of Saint Domingue would be sufficient cause for that Jewel of the Antilles, so recently France's richest possession overseas, to be purged yet another time with fire and blood. So wrote the Captain-General to his brother-in-law, and it seemed that the First Consul himself took the live-liest interest in the situation, reinforcing with his direct order Leclerc's nervous request that the prisoner be kept in the straitest possible security, and as far away as possible from any seaport that might provide a route for his return.

The Fort de Joux, perched high in the Alps near the Swiss border, met this second condition most exactly. One could hardly go further from the sea while still remaining within French borders. As for security, well, the walls were thick and the doors heavy, the windows almost hermetically sealed. Yet the walls had failed to contain Suzannet and Dandigné — yes, well, there had most certainly been betrayal. The officers had somehow obtained the files they used to cut their bars, and probably had enjoyed other aid from some unknown person in the fort. For this reason Baille had chosen to wait upon his new prisoner himself and alone, at least for the present, despite the inconvenience it occasioned.

While pursuing this uneasy rumination, he had crossed the third corridor, which was set at a higher level than the one before and therefore was less damp. He opened and relocked the final door and turned to face the openings of two cells. Clearing his throat, he walked to the second door and called out to announce himself. After a moment, a voice returned the call, but it was low and indistinct through the iron-bound door.

Baille turned the key in the lock and went in. The cell, vaulted like the passages leading to it, was illuminated only by coals of the small fire. Baille's heart quivered like a jelly, for it seemed there was no one in the room — he saw with his frantically darting eyes the low bed, stool, the table . . . but no human being. He dropped the sack and clapped a hand over his mouth. But now the man was standing before him after all, not five paces distant, as if he had been dropped from the ceiling — or spun himself down, like a spider on its silk. Indeed the barrel vault overhead was filled with dismal shadows, so that Baille could not make out the height of its curve. The vault dwarfed the prisoner, a small negro unremarkable at first glance, except that he was slightly bandylegged. Baille swallowed; his tongue was thick.

"Let us light the candle," he said. When there was no response he went to the table and did so himself, then turned to inspect the prisoner in the improved light. This was Toussaint Louverture, who had thought to make the island colony of Saint Domingue independent of France. He had written and proclaimed a constitution; he had, so rumor ran, written to the First Consul with this arrogant address: "To the first of the whites from the first of the blacks." But now, by explicit order of the First Consul, he was to be called nothing but "Toussaint," without any honorific whatsoever; he was to be parted from his uniform and from any other tokens which might recall his former status in the colony.

Baille faced his guest with a smile, feeling his lips curve on his face like clay. "I have brought your rations," he said.

Toussaint did not even glance at the basket, which Baille had set down on the table when he struck the light. He looked at the commandant with a cool intensity which Baille found rather unnerving, though he did his best to hold . . . after all, it was not quite a stare. Toussaint's head was disproportionately large for his body, with a long lower jaw and brown irregular teeth. His eyes, however, were clear and intelligent. He wore a madras cloth bound around his head and the uniform of a French general, which was, however, limp and soiled. Apparently he had had no change of his outer garments since he first was made prisoner and deported from Saint Domingue.

"I have brought you fresh clothing," Baille said, and indicated the sack he had dropped on the floor in his first surprise. Toussaint did not shift his gaze to acknowledge it. Presently Baille picked up the sack himself and stooped to lay out the contents on the low bed.

"This clothing is not correct," Toussaint said.

Baille swallowed. "You must accept it." Somehow he could not manage to phrase the sentence with greater force.

Toussaint looked briefly at the coals in the fire.

"Your uniform is soiled and worn, and too light for the weather," Baille said. "It is already cold here, and soon it will be winter, sir —" This *sir* escaped him involuntarily. He stopped and looked at the woolen clothes he had unfolded on the bed. *"Acceptez-les, je vous en prie."*

Toussaint at last inclined his head. Baille sighed.

"I must also ask that you surrender any money you may have, or any. . ." He let the sentence trail. He waited but nothing else happened at all.

"Do you understand me?" This time Baille suppressed the *sir*.

"Yes, of course," Toussaint said, and he turned his head and shoulder toward the door. Baille had already begun walking in that direction before he recognized that he had been dismissed, that he should not permit himself to be so dismissed, that it was his clear duty to remain and watch the prisoner disrobe and see with his own eyes that he held nothing back. However, he soon found himself against the outside of the door, unreeling in his mind long strings of words that stood for curses, although he did not know for certain if it was the prisoner or the assigned procedures he meant to curse.

After a few minutes he called out. The same indistinct mutter returned through the door, and Baille opened it and went back in. Toussaint stood in the fresh clothes that had been given him; his feet, incongruously, were bare. Or rather Baille felt that he himself would have looked absurd and foolish standing barefoot in such a situation, but it detracted in no way from the dignity of the prisoner. Toussaint motioned toward the table with a slight movement of his left hand.

Baille approached. On the table lay some banknotes and coins, a couple of documents of some sort, a watch with a gold chain.

"I will keep my watch," Toussaint said, and already his hand had gathered it up and put it into a pocket, chain and all. There seemed nothing to do but assent; Baille nodded and scooped up the money and papers without looking at them, feeling a stir of shame. Toussaint had stuffed the dirty uniform into the sack in which the other clothes had come. Baille picked up the sack and also collected Toussaint's high-topped military boots — he had furnished a pair of ordinary shoes, but it was not his concern whether the prisoner chose to put them on.

"I have need of pen and ink and paper," Toussaint said. "I must write letters — I must make my report to the First Consul."

"I shall look into the matter," Baille said, and thought of notes somehow forwarded through mesh, through keyholes, folded into minute pellets and passed to the confederates of Suzannet and Dandigné. No, he would not furnish the writing supplies on his own authority.

"As quickly as possible." A hint of a smile on Toussaint's face, but only a flicker, and his look was stern, commanding. "My duty is urgent."

Baille undertook no direct reply. "Good evening," he said, and swallowed the *sir*, as he made his retreat from the cell.

Toussaint stood near the door of the cell, listening to the lock springs snapping, hinges groaning in succession, each sound somewhat fainter than the one before, as Baille receded down the series of passageways. He could hear the commandant's feet splashing in the middle corridor, or thought that he could. Then nothing. He moved from the doorway, his bare feet splaying over the flagstones of the floor. The bell of the castle clock rang with a grating of discontent. Toussaint pulled his watch from the pocket of the coat he had been furnished, and opened the case. It was a quarter past seven. Darkness had come early, or at any rate there was no light at the barred window, but the embrasure had been bricked over two-thirds of the way to the top, and the mesh beyond the bars never strained much daylight through itself, regardless of the hour.

He had learned that now. He replaced the watch and felt the other pockets of the coat from the outside, here and there; he had in fact kept back a few gold coins and a couple of letters from Baille's lackadaisical inspection. The wool coat and trousers fit him loosely, but were warm enough. The uniform of a private soldier, with all insignia cut away. Toussaint coughed thickly, and held his hand over the center of his chest, hoping to suppress another spasm. He had caught a heavy cold on his journey from Brest across France to the Fort de Joux, and the cough was lingering. His whole ribcage felt bruised by it. He did not like what Baille had said of the approach of winter ... which seemed to prove this cell would be no temporary waystation. He expected an interview with the First Consul — the opportunity to speak on his own behalf, explain his conduct — he expected, at the least, a trial. It must be a military tribunal before which he would appear in the uniform of his rank in the French Army, and therefore he also misliked the clothes he had been given, though they were perfectly serviceable otherwise. Their coarse quality, even their previous use, was no great matter to him; he had known worse.

He walked to the table and turned back the wooden lid of the basket. Salt meat (already cut), a pale hard crumbly cheese, a supply of biscuit. Ship's rations, more or less. There was a flagon of red wine and what struck him as a meager sack of sugar. Some ground coffee had been included, along with implements for brewing it and some other utensils with which he might warm the food. There were two spoons, but of course no knife. He touched the meat — a corner of it crumbled between his thumb and forefinger. Water had been brought to him separately beforehand, in a clay pitcher; he might prepare a sort of stew. Toussaint hesitated. In Saint Domingue, he had been careful of poisoning. Among any company he did not entirely trust (and there was little company he trusted absolutely), he would eat only uncut fruit, a piece of cheese sliced by his own hand from the center of the round, a whole roll or uncut loaf of bread — and drink plain water, never wine.

He raised a scrap of the salt meat and sniffed it, nostrils flaring, then let it fall back into the basket. Turning his head at an angle, he smiled slightly to himself. In this predicament, he would of course be unable to sustain his former precautions. Unless he elected to starve himself, his jailers might poison him whenever they would. Therefore it was useless for him to concern himself about it. He would eat as his appetite demanded him, and without concern. But for the moment he was not hungry.

He took out the wine jug and poured a measure into the cup, then added a small amount of water and drank — red wine, slightly sour. He shook in some sugar from the bag, revolved the cup and drained the mixture. The treacly warmth of the wine seemed to coat his throat against the cough. He closed the lid of the basket and then blew out the candle that Baille had lit when he came in. Firelight spread yellowly, pulsing on the stones of the floor. Toussaint went to the fireplace. The hearthstone was warm to his bare feet, and thoroughly dry. He stooped and added a piece of wood to the glow of coals.

More distant from the fireside, the flagstones were clammy, not quite damp. He sat on the edge of the bed and drew on the woolen stockings which had been given him. Cautiously he raised his legs onto the bed and lay back, holding his breath. The cough thrust up in the back of his throat but he swallowed it back and managed to exhale without coughing. When he touched the raw stone wall above the bed, his fingers came away moist and slightly chilled. He turned his head away from the wall and looked into the room, lying partly on his side, his legs slightly bent, his palm cupped under the left side of his jaw. An observer might have thought he slept, but he was not sleeping. He watched the fire through slitted eyes and thought of one thing and another: his valet, Mars Plaisir, under lock and key in the neighboring cell; his wife and sons, confined in some other region of France under conditions of which he knew little; the accounting he would make, when pen and paper were brought to him, for the eyes of the First Consul, Napoleon Bonaparte. (And why had Baille been so evasive about this matter? — a flick of worry touched Toussaint, but he let it pass.) The work of writing would require some skill, some artifice. He tried to think how he would begin, but it was difficult without his secretaries, without pen or paper. The words of which his case must be constructed stood apart from him, as if the pen's nib would mine them from the paper; they were not part of his mind.

The castle clock struck another quarter hour, without Toussaint much remarking it. His concentration was imperfect, and he felt warm and blurry. Perhaps he had a touch of fever, with the cough. The firelight on the hearth narrowed and flattened into a low red horizon . . . sunrise or sunset. From the red-glowing slit expanded a featureless plain, whether of land or water was unclear. A dot interrupted the red horizon; Toussaint blinked his eyes, but the dot persisted. It sprouted spidery limbs, like an insect or stick figure of a man. The form grew larger by imperceptible degrees, as it came over the bare plain and toward him.

Reggae Fi Bernard
Linton Kwesi Johnson

wi nevah come fram di same blood-line
but wi pawt kriss-kraas an jaine
an alldow wid wananadah
wi wozn dat familiah
all di same
wi woz family

dats why mi a beg pawdn an tek dis libahty
an phudung a couple rime to yu mehmahry

it come een like a jus di addah day
yu lef school an jaine di railway
wid nuff ambishan an a fewcha plan
yu wozn drawin big pay
but yu woz well an yu way
an jus wen yu ready fi staat
fi goh choo-choo choo-boogie
train cut yu journey shaat

di day yu get yu laas send-awf
fram yu bawn-groun
before dem fly yu bady
doun to jamdoun
di sun stay away fram work dat day
an di slate grey january day
a sing a silent dirge
as daak clouds daat
callide an canverge
merge an re-emerge
inna blustah a emoeshan
inna di church grey sky

an di rain it a fall inna squal
tear-tip arrows piercin di awt a di mounah dem

di baptiss church
full-up to di brim
        owevah-flow
                pan di steps to di street
                langtime-noh-si family an fren
                meet an greet
                taakin bout yu hayste retreat
inside mounful vices a sing
dem familiah bittah-sweet hymn
an it is well
it is well
wid yu soul

rude boyz bruk doun in tears
mini-skirted girls weep an wail
deres a passi a black an white workaz
fram british rail
yu calleeg dem fram yu shaat workin years

an dere woz testimony awftah testimony
fram yu age mate dem
punctuated by spantaneous applauz
bout ow yu did tall an slim an good-lookin
wid yu lang chin an yu captivatin grin
bout yu kineness
bout yu carin
bout yu tautfulness
bout ow big an ow broad in love yu woz

up to now wi still noh get noh prapah explanaeshan
no witness at di stayshan no police investigaeshan
as to ow yu get fi en up pan di wrang side a di track
ow yu face get fi tun fram front to back
an a who yu did a taak to pan yu mobile
dem jus call it hacksident an close yu file

jamdoun woz yu true dream i-lan
noh deh soh yu did a plan
fi mek yu final destinaeshan
now yu dream come tru an yu touch doun
hashis to hashis
dus to dus
inna sent elizabet sile

Axe and Anancy

Fred D'Aguiar

RED HEAD GOT his name and visionary capacity at age nine when he ran behind an uncle chopping wood and caught the back of the axe on his forehead. His uncle, Beanstalk, feeling the reverberations of a soft wood as it yielded to the blade he'd swung back, looked over his shoulder and saw his favourite nephew half-run, half-walk in a wobbly line, do an about-turn, then flop to the ground in a heap. This was the uncle who, when leading a party hunting for the unbelievably sweet young shoots of coconut plants they'd christened 'growee,' began to cross a trench on a log that bucked and flung him off, and who, as everyone scattered and fought to climb the nearest tree, lassoed the log's head and tail before the word 'alligator' had formed on anyone's lips.

The child saw red. Red in the earth and clouds and sky, a red dye making visible the air he could only feel until now and drink too, in confirmation of all he felt, red, in the trees and in the ripe fruit and red behind his shut eyes. Red, then black. Beanstalk dearly wanted the whole thing to be a mischievous joke. Like the time his nephew emptied a half-bottle of rum in one long headback slake and tumbled headfirst down the thirty-eight steps from the house into the back yard in such a state of absolute relaxation that he didn't incur so much as a graze. Something made the uncle stare at the boy's forehead as if he were watching a miniature screen. The ruptured screen resembled a door blown off its hinges. Out stepped a white body of fluid in one boneless move. As if surprised by the sudden recognition that it was naked, the nubile body gathered about itself a flowing red gown which ran in ceaseless yards, covering all of the boy's face in seconds.

Beanstalk dropped the axe, produced a scream that shook the birds like gravity defying fruits from the trees, bolted in a complete circle around the reddening heap of his nephew, then collapsed next to him. The shriek that emptied the trees also woke the house sleeping to the grandfather clock of his axe splitting wood. Doors and shuttered windows sprang open. So many souls materialised from the house, it was as if the scream were a foot that had stepped on an ant nest. Another uncle, younger brother to the one now prone, was the first to reach them. He leapt from the window he looked out of, one floor up, while everyone else took the more conventional route down the stairs. He ran from one body to the next, settling on the smallest and bloodiest since it looked most in need. He opened Red Head's mouth. It was empty. 'Find his tongue,' he shouted between gorging air and expelling it into Red Head's mouth. Cousins and nephews scrambled around the area hunting for a rubbery organ, caked with the recent lunch of roti and curry. Beanstalk stirred, raised his head in the direction of the unconscious nephew he was sure he'd unwittingly beheaded, since his last image of him was of a headless chicken running around, and fainted again. The child had turned as pale as a cloud. Blood drained from him. Then, as if his body did not like the idea of becoming white, it darkened into progressively deeper shades of blue, like the brewing of a storm.

It dawned on the uncle giving resuscitation (more like lightning than a dawning) that the air he was blowing into his nephew's mouth was serving merely to bloat the boy's cheeks; he was playing the instrument of his nephew's face, exhaling into its geometry as he was taught but without success: the child had swallowed his tongue. A neat swipe by the uncle's index finger cleared Red Head's windpipe. Red Head coughed and gasped. The storm that was whipping itself up behind his eyelids evaporated. Instead of blue sky and daylight greeting his opened eyes, he looked up through a pool of red. He saw figures move in slow motion through this red liquid. He identified one of the figures in this parade behind the screen of his forehead as himself. The other was a presidential figure dressed entirely in purple riding a white stallion. Both the President's purple regalia and the white hide and mane of the horse resisted the red stain that permeated the tilted field of Red Head's perspective. Red Head was perched on a russet horse with a draughts board flying in the air between him and the President. Though both horses were in full gallop, the entire scene was undisturbed and the two concentrated on the board as if they were in an airless drawing room instead of sprinting on horseback near the red rim of surf on a red beach.

Next, in this private parade, came a man wrecked by polio. His arms and shoulders were huge and barred and striped with muscles, in shocking contrast to his shrivelled, bony waist and matchstick legs. This broken man was riding a bicycle twice his size. He rode to the end of a jetty and dived off his bike directly into the sea. The wheels of the fallen bike spinning on greased ball bearings and the ticking of the sprocket, with no rider in sight, made it look like the scene of a suicide. The broken man did not sink as one might expect, but zoomed away fluently, his pointed rugby ball of a head floating on the water, his arms rotating like twin propellers, his body submerged like the hull of a ship.

The third image was that of a kite flying without a hand to guide it. A long S-shaped tail made of coins strung together waved under the kite's slow pendulum swing. Both sides of the coins appeared to be a portrait of the same face. A noise akin to the lowest note from a baritone saxophone came from the kite's tongue as the wind blasted it. Under the hard gaze of the sun the kite seemed to be a rainbow in the sky. Each part of the child-high frame, modelled in the shape of a giant hand, was covered in paper of a different primary colour.

All three passed: purple President, broken man and kite. 'There were four,' piped a small, insistent voice. Red Head cut in quickly, 'No, three. I should know. Now get out of my head, you're trespassing.' The little voice obeyed, dissolving with a puff. Film on the projector ran out, leaving a tilted, pitch-black screen as Red Head plummeted into unconsciousness.

Granny was the last one out the door. She appeared to float down towards the commotion as a breeze rushing up the stairs fingered its way under her floor-length dress, causing it to billow like a sail up to her hips, where the muscled breeze gripped her, raised her off her feet and bore her down the stairs, even though the dress was as heavy as the cloth of flour sacks that had been ripped out, dyed and stitched into a simple, tentlike design to sit on her six-foot frame, covering her bones in utilitarian fashion, warding off the heat and retaining pockets of cool air, its pleated fringes used for mopping perspiration from her brow, its dark colour disguising the sweat patches under her arms from her constant meanderings of toil that defined her day and that of the house and everyone in it from sunrise to sunset.

The whirlpool of uncles, aunts, nephews and cousins surrounding Red Head and Beanstalk parted before the grandmother the second she reached its perimeter and closed behind her again as she made her way to its still centre. She knelt beside Red Head. Worry traversed her face, like the shadow of an aeroplane rippling across a field, and disappeared, as if denied permission to settle on it. Granny plastered a dam of a poultice in the split on his forehead and stemmed the tide of blood. Next she turned to Beanstalk, raised his head in her right hand, delicately, as if holding a precious crystal to the light, and with the open palm of her left hand delivered two slaps to his face, one to each cheek, in rapid strokes. Beanstalk sat bolt upright. She returned her attention to Red Head, pulling from her apron the long white flag of a bandage which she used to strap the poultice in place. Red Head groaned. Whispers that Beanstalk might have been spellbound by a pernicious strain of guava circulated among the children.

Wheels was the natural choice to ride the big black fixed-wheel bike the five miles to the hospital with his patient balanced on the crossbar. Had it not been lunchtime, they would have used the mule and cart for an ambulance. But the mule was out grazing and would have taken too long to round up, cajole into a harness, strap to the cart and whip from a trot to a full gallop.

Wheels sat on the bicycle with his left foot on the pedal. The saddle was so high the toes of his right foot just reached the ground. He opened his right arm to receive the dazed Red Head and steadied the handlebar with his left. There was a slowness in the way he propped the slumped child on the crossbar, allowing the lolling head to cradle in the crook between his left shoulder and neck. He inclined his head so that the side of his jaw braced the child's head where it rested against him. Once he'd grabbed the handlebar with his right hand, with Red Head's legs draped over his arm, he nodded to no one and everyone that he was ready.

'Give me a push' were his parting words. His two brothers, the big-headed Bounce and a tearful Beanstalk, gave him the initial running start he required. Wheels broke into an immediate sprint, pulling away from them. A trail of sand from the red road fanned out and up. Everyone looked away and shielded their faces. Wheels, Red Head and the bicycle were lost in the voluminous cloud that followed the road out of town as if a route had been predetermined for their tornado. When the storm brewed by Wheels swooped round the corner and could still dimly be seen above the houses and the trees, only then did the twenty-six uncles, aunts, nephews and cousins with Grandmother dismantle the human roadblock they'd erected across the road.

They had been oblivious to the honking of horns by tractors and the ringing of a dozen bicycle bells that had merged into a huge alarm clock some sleeping giant was ignoring. They had blocked out the church-summoning loudness of the bells on carts, mooing cattle on the drive to the abattoir or market, and bleating sheep. Sheep had gotten mixed with cows, some of whom had butted and kicked them. The minders of both quarrelled among themselves and gesticulated at anyone whose eye they managed to catch, as if to say, 'What did I do to deserve this?'

Jammed behind all these were the big-axled, sixteen-wheeled, fuming, growling, articulated trucks, which reputedly never stopped for anyone or anything they hit. Laden down with their excess payload of rock, sand, wood, broken bottles, tar, water, new billiard cues carved from smoke-cured greenheart wood watered by the Orinoco, billiard balls made from the ground bones of the manatee, food, mainly basmati rice, known throughout the interior and even among the Waiyaku of the upper reaches of the Amazon as the best rice for boiling with coconut milk, and fuel from the oil fields of Surinam, they were all destined for the thousand-strong road gang stationed outside the capital. The road gang was rumoured to be paving the sand road with seamless bitumen, the result so smooth an aeroplane could land or take off on it. These men travelled at a quarter of a mile a day, accompanied by a colony of Chinese and Kashmiri cooks, Ghanaian seamstresses and laun-dresses, barbers whose ancestors were from Karachi and the ancient city of Lahore, Cuban doctors and nurses who relied on the sur-rounding vegetation for whatever medicines they prescribed and Amerindian prostitutes who floated between four ad hoc bars: one for cocktails, run by an Italian from the north corner of Lake Garda; another peddling frothy beers and managed by a six hun-dred–pound German wrestler; a third dealing exclusively in wines pressed from grapes grown in the Dordogne but owned by a male couple from Brittany with their own language and swearwords for anyone who dared to tell them they should speak patois; and a fourth, specialising in the overproof spirits of the Windward Islands of the Caribbean, run by four Jamaicans. The Jamaicans also man-aged the two coffee huts whose beans came from the Blue Moun-tains of their island's heartland and were as valuable as gold bullion; in fact, used as such by the government on more than one occasion to pay the contractors who had lost faith in the bonds issued to them and threatened to withhold their expertise unless the treasured beans were made available to them in several hun-dred bushels ready for export. Added to these were a comedy theatre of six Englishmen in their late forties who were foremen of the road gang during the day but whose commedia dell'arte at night consisted of cross-dressing with coconut shells as breasts, kente cloth from Accra for elaborate headdresses and moccasins from Oklahoma, drawing catcalls, wolf whistles and applause from the same men they had been ordering around a few hours earlier and would be in charge of again after a night's sleep; a cinema that was really only a projector and a white sheet stitched to two poles for outdoor screening on dry, insect-ridden nights, which showed Hindi films made in the cavernous studios of Bombay, with their countless love songs which the men committed to their hearts and mouthed during their labour; and an American supermarket with fifty varieties of cereal, all under tarpaulin, which competed with the trading stalls set up on carts owned by Venezuelans. Spontaneous stick fights, stone throwing, arm wrestling, boxing and cricket matches would break out between the rowdy or sporting contingent in the road gang and the inhabitants of whatever locality the red road they were converting to an airstrip happened to pass. Soldiers and police, tax collectors and moneylenders, lawyers and psychics were always camping nearby, some to maintain law and order, others to corrupt it, in this nomadic city trundling towards the house where Red Head lived with his twenty-six relatives and Granny and Grandad, all of whom swore they would not let the road gang's city enter Ariel.

'There were four.'

Red Head woke to the small voice he'd banished from inside his head what seemed like only a second earlier, but from his surroundings must have been hours, perhaps days ago.

'There will be red, then there will be black.'

The voice increased in volume as light intensified in the room. Red Head thought of lifting his arm and flattening into an asterisk whatever it was on his forehead that bugged him, but his arms were two cement blocks by his side, obedient to a will other than the one he mustered.

'You will listen. There were four.'

The voice did a thumping march across his forehead. His eyes watered. A flashbulb flickered though his lids were pressed tight. Each flicker was triggered by a syllable from that voice. Each syllable delivered a hammer blow to his nerves. And every strand of his nervous system seemed strung into a wet mop being wrung tighter and tighter by two powerful hands.

'Red, then black. I know you can hear.'

There had been a fourth image in the parade behind his skull witnessed moments after the bolt of lightning from the axe. But what he saw had scared him so much he had censored it, cut it from the film he had viewed and put it at the back of a bottom drawer in an attic room he'd locked with a key he'd thrown far away.

'There were four. Red, then black.'

The voice grew to a deafening boom. Light flickered so fast the flashes became a glare. Red Head felt the water run from his eyes and collect in his ears. He allowed the attic room to surface. The hands that wrung the mop released their grip immediately and allowed the strands to shake loose. The flicker behind his eyes lessened to something a little slower than the second hand of a clock.

'There were four,' he admitted to himself.

'All right!' the small torturer's voice shrieked, accelerating the flickering and the thumps for two drawn-out seconds before they became a dull, intermittent ache once more. Red Head conjured a picture of the attic door and willed it to open. 'Open sesame' were the only words he could think of. A career at picking locks suggested itself to him but he was swift to push it to the edge of his mind, afraid he might invite again the voice that made him cry like a baby. Just as he was about to open the drawer and reach in to retrieve whatever he'd hidden there, he made one last effort to banish from his head the attic, the bottom drawer and, he hoped, the pernicious little voice as well, by summoning a fact.

'Ariel, formerly Percival, Cooperative Republic Village number — One windowless government school run by a teacher with a class of forty-nine, ages ranging from six to sixteen. One rum shop. One baker. Countless guava, guinep, sapodilla, mango, downs, tamarind and coconut trees . . .'

The intruder in Red Head's skull, put there, he thought, by the surgeon who had stitched the opening made by the axe, resumed his torture of Red Head.

'There were four! Red, then black!'

The slow flicker went straight to a glare, followed by a thumping across his forehead so rapid it would have made an hour pass in a few seconds if it had been keeping time. Again, two big hands gathered the straggly mop of Red Head's nervous constitution and twisted it. Tears stung Red Head's eyes. Instead of giving in to the voice and attic and contents of the bottom drawer, Red Head summoned more facts to help him in his fight, this time a story the teacher told to his class one rainy day at recess when they were all stuck inside and rain blew in the portholes that served as windows.

'Anancy the spider had one hand of bananas which he brought home to his wife and four children for their first meal that day – '

'There were four, damn you!'

'How many bananas make a hand? He gave each of his children one banana. How many did he have left? Anancy offered the last banana to his wife. She refused to accept it. She begged him to eat it. She said he needed the strength to go out and find the next meal – '

'Four! Red, then black!' The little intruder emphasised each word by jumping four times on the wound on Red Head's forehead. A near-colourless fluid began to seep out despite the ten tight stitches.

'Anancy the spider insisted until his wife accepted. They sat round the table. Anancy took his usual place. His empty plate stood out next to the plates with bananas that belonged to his wife and children. Anancy's wife cut her banana in half and put one half on her husband's plate. A small light appeared in Anancy's eyes – '

The little devil repeated his athletic exercise. 'Four!' Jump. 'Red!' Jump. 'Then!' Jump. 'Black!' Jump. Red Head bit his tongue but found the interruption only served to make him want to get to the end of his Anancy story.

'Anancy looked at the banana on the plate of his eldest son. His son followed his father's gaze, cut a third off his banana and put it on his father's plate. Anancy's eyes grew wider and brighter as his gaze travelled to the plate of his second child. She too saw his eyes and did exactly what her brother had done. She cut a third off her banana and put it on her father's plate. How much banana has Anancy collected so far?'

The little devil jumped on the wound and began to twist on it as he sang, 'There were four! Red, then black!' to a rock-and-roll tune. Red Head coiled and squirmed, pulled at his bed sheets and cried but continued his Anancy story.

'Anancy's third and fourth children followed their father's gaze as it crept up to their plates, then they copied their brother's and sister's example by slicing a third off their bananas and placing the pieces on their father's full plate. Anancy's eyes grew so wide his

face became two headlights on full beam. How many bananas did
Anancy end up with?'

'There!' Twist. 'Were!' Twist. 'Four!' Twist and jump.

The diminutive devil was ankle-deep in blood, ruptured flesh
and severed nerves. He paused to look at Red Head. He saw that
the boy's face was a series of crags and ridges, while his teeth were
bared (though no sound escaped his wide mouth) and bloody from
a bitten tongue. Pint Size, the name that occurred to Red Head for
his tormentor, stepped out of the wound, shook the muck from
his boots and settled down next to the suppurating mass in a half-
lotus. Red Head allowed the door to the attic to swing open. He
reached to the back of the bottom drawer. The forbidden fourth
image flickered to life. Red Head was shuddering, yet he was
covered in sweat. He found it hard to bring the image on the screen
into focus. Whatever it was, it looked much like the kite of the
previous image. Red Head thought it might be a mistake, that it
was indeed the third image being replayed, but before he could do
anything to sharpen what he saw so poorly into something recog-
nisable, the light faded, then reddened, then went black. Pint Size
punched the air with his fist, considered jumping into Red Head's
wound again to twist for a bit, but thought better of it, and said
very quietly into Red Head's left ear, so that Red Head heard even
though he had slipped into unconsciousness, 'Another day, Axe-
features. There will be another day.'

'The doctor said he had to strap your hands to your side.'

'What did I ever do to him?'

'He said you destroyed his neat stitches.'

'Why would I do a stupid thing like that?'

'Delirium.'

'You let a strange man tie me down and sew me up?'

Wheels smiled because this was the Red Head he knew and
loved, with a tongue in his mouth more like a whip for one so
young. He pedalled as if out on an afternoon jaunt. Even this far
inland a cool sea breeze nudged them from behind. At the S-bend,
on Ariel's outskirts, two police motorcycles pulled up and waved
Wheels to the side of the road. Soon a black limousine approached.
Wheels thought of covering Red Head's bandaged head to protect
it from the dust the car would raise as it flew past but Red Head
wanted to see. Instead of splashing red sand in their faces and dis-
appearing in a cloud, the car slowed to a crawl. A window in the

Fred D'Aguiar

back seat glided down and sprouted an arm, then a face, masked in a pair of silver-tinted sunglasses with massive lenses — just like the ones his father wore propped up on his skull when indoors and dropped over his eyes with a sharp nod as he ducked into sunlight. The arm waved, the face smiled. Red Head saw himself reflected twice in the sunglasses with two astounded copies of Wheels trying to salute and keep the two Red Heads stable on the crossbar at the same time. When the eyes behind the glasses made four with Red Head's eyes and winked, Red Head winked back. The police motorcycles accelerated away, followed by the limousine, whose open window retrieved the arm and face and glided up, shutting out the sun and dust.

'Did you see yourself in double karate-chopping the air?'

'The thought of three of you frighten me more than him. One bad enough.' Both laughed.

The encounter with the President spurred on the legs of Wheels. He raised himself off the saddle and made a dust cloud of his own to rival the President's limousine. Red Head leaned with Wheels into both corners of the S-bend. His bandaged head felt weightless. He closed his eyes and listened to the bicycle tyres eating up the yards of sand between them and the house. Each time Wheels pressed down on the pedals Red Head heard the teeth of a saw being pulled and pushed through wood. Soon the sawing lost the little pauses between each stroke as Wheels reached a sprint. It became the continuous whirr of propellers. Wind sang in their ears. They were flying. The frequent little bumps were turbulence.

Wheels drew up in front of the house. Everyone came out. Some-one shouted, 'Axe-man back!' Beanstalk lifted Red Head off the bike, hugged him and showered him with apologies. Beanstalk's head was inches above the six-foot paling fence. He loved to impress the children by vaulting it in a peculiar backwards dive. As Beanstalk bounced along the path from the road to the house with Red Head in his arms, the boy rested his chin on his uncle's right shoulder and tried to count the individual slats of the paling fence as they bobbed up and down.

'Boy, I thought I chop off your head!'

His uncle's casual strides were so long Red Head fell further and further behind in his count. He skipped some palings until his eyes drew level with his uncle's legs but found as he resumed counting that he immediately fell behind again.

'You make a big man like me faint!'

Instead of skipping a few palings as before, Red Head gave up counting and watched the pattern of light and shade made by the spaces between the palings and his uncle's deft pace.

'Nothing ever scare me so!'

'I sorry I make you faint, Uncle. I sorry I scare you.'

Beanstalk gave Red Head a little squeeze. His nephew squeezed him back.

'Guava had nothing to do with it.'

'I know, Uncle.'

He climbed the few steps to the porch with Red Head in his arms and met his mother at the door. He handed Red Head over to her. Whereas Beanstalk was solid and hot, Red Head's grandmother felt soft and cool. Beanstalk had smelled of the sun; Granny, on the other hand, smelled of soap.

'I see the President, first in purple on a white stallion, then in a limousine. He had dark glasses like Daddy's and I beat him at draughts.'

'You beat everybody at draughts.'

Someone shouted from the yard, 'In your dreams.'

'Ask Wheels.'

Wheels nodded. 'Is true what Red Head saying. I don't know about a white stallion but our great benefactor did pass us in his black limo.'

Not everyone was impressed by the attention Red Head was receiving. Someone who sounded like Red Head's elder brother shouted, 'You're Axe-man now.'

'I am no Axe-man. I is Red Head. He should be Axe-man.' Red Head pointed with his chin to Beanstalk, who looked away with a broad smile. But a second voice, this time belonging to Bounce, the youngest of his three uncles, with a huge head that was harder than a coconut stripped of its husk and who could butt anyone on any part of their body and make them cry without his eyes so much as watering, shouted, 'Is too late, once you get name that is it, Axe-man!'

'Go butt down a tree, Hammerhead!'

Bounce shook his concrete block in amusement and delivered a quick rejoinder, 'Your head blunt the axe, not mine!' This raised a big laugh from everyone.

Red Head tried to match the smiling paving stone. 'That same axe would have bounced off your mallethead and chopped Beanstalk!'

There were wolf whistles as everyone prepared for a slanging match. His grandmother turned away from them with him and pulled the door shut behind her. Red Head heard someone shout, 'When is an axe not an axe?' The question made him cork his ears with his fingers. He did not want to hear the reply to a riddle he had no part in solving. But he still caught the raucous laughter that erupted in response to a muffled voice that sounded like his brother's.

'Never mind, child. You still my little Red Head.'

Granny led him into a bedroom designated for his convalescence. He felt giddy. She eased him onto the bed.

'So you saw our President?'

Red Head nodded. He let his head drop onto the cool white ironed cotton pillowcase, shut his eyes and pondered when an axe was not an axe. He wished he'd heard the answer because now he would have to make one up.

'He only stop because election coming up.'

'I know, but he stop for just Wheels and me.'

'You don't know, Red Head. We can't afford to have any losers in this election.' Granny put a damp cloth on his bandaged forehead. The cloth's coldness made him suck on the air. His mind emptied of everything except the lime-grove scent and mesmeric cool of the cloth. This strip of cloth was bleached. Though he could not smell it, he could tell from its stark whiteness. And it resembled several others he'd seen drying on the line every few weeks or so but whose function he'd never believed when told by his girlfriend Sten that the cloths were used by the grown women to stem a monthly flow of blood.

'Does that mean that you will bleed?'

'Yes, one day.'

He had changed the subject after a moment's silence and pushed the information to the back of his mind.

'When can I get up, Granny?'

'What do you mean, when can I get up? You just lie down!'

'I was only wondering.'

'Well, you wonder and stay in that bed!'

'All I want is to know.'

'Soon, soon.'

When his mother had gone abroad with his three younger brothers and left him in Ariel with his elder brother, she too had told him soon. She would return soon. That was six months ago. He missed her. She was bony but her skin was soft. She was sweeter than any fruit or flower, whereas Granny carried the odour of soap and, when she'd just brought clothes in off the line, of the sun. At his age every desire was soon. And his father had gone away. Just like that, he'd dived into the hot afternoon, his eyes hidden with a nod just in time to avoid the sun. The last time Red Head had talked with Bash Man Goady about missing their mother, father and brothers, they were having a walk-race to school. His brother was breathless but he'd paused to draw hard on the air and had spoken as if they had been swinging in the hammock at the bottom of the house.

'If you don't think about it, it won't hurt.'

He had taken his brother's advice as a necessary gospel. So far it seemed to work when he was awake, but when he slept all he saw was his three brothers and his mother, just out of earshot of him. And no matter how hard he ran towards them, they always maintained the same distance from him even though they did not move. But his father, who was never in these dreams, was simply gone. Red Head would wake up with his heart pounding, angry and ready to cry, but because he was not alone, he could not cry. The others would see and they'd call him a crybaby and laugh at him.

Red Head woke up to a bowl of soup, three pieces of buttered bread and his friend Raj smiling at him. He sat up in bed and ate fast. The bread was oven-warm. Melted butter had to be balanced on the slice as he lifted it to his face. He inhaled deeply, then took a big bite and chewed with his eyes closed. He drained the bowl of rice and pea soup and would have used his bread to wipe the bowl had Raj not been there. All this time Raj stood and watched him and smiled. Once Red Head was finished, Raj took the tray from his lap and placed it on the floor. Red Head propped himself up some more but his grandmother cast him such a look when she came to collect the empty tray that he slid down under the bed-clothes until his head was resting on the pillow again.

'Granny, your soup and bread is the best in the whole wide world.'

'Child, what do you know about the world?'

She rested the back of her hand on his forehead, squinted at the bandage and exited. The hem of her long dress swept the floor clean of any prints she might have left.

'Raj! What you got to tell me?'

'Boy, something boss!'

Raj had a photographic memory for Westerns. He didn't tell you what happened in a film, he showed you. He spoke all the parts and drew an imaginary pistol from an imaginary holster and made a pistol shot with his pursed lips in rough synchronisation to his cocked thumb hitting his pointed index finger. His weak sphincter muscle interrupted his show several times. As a result he tended to shorten any long panning shots or rides into and out of towns. Despite wads of tissue stuffed down his trousers, there remained a permanent wet patch on his crotch. A strong smell of urine emanated from him, earning him the name Pissy-missy. Were it not for this affliction, his Westerns would have made him many more friends. Once Raj got going, the smell around him evaporated and his wet patch vanished. Granny came into the room and opened the window. Raj had got to the point where the star boy, as all the heroic cowboys were called, had an arm pumped full of lead and he was in the process of crawling off to his hideout to be nursed back to health by an Indian woman. Granny placed the back of her hand on Red Head's forehead.

'That's enough for today, Raj. You killing him with all the excitement.'

Raj waved from the door. Granny twitched her nose. Red Head knew it was because of the rancid smell, but he said nothing and did everything in his power not to twitch his nose too. She changed his bandage. Neither spoke. Towards the end of dressing his head, she began to hum a calypso. He knew the words and smiled.

'What tickle you?'

'I know that song. It rude.'

'If you know it rude, you better don't let me catch you singing it.'

Instead of the words to the calypso, the solution to the axe puzzle leapt from his mind onto his tongue like one of those fishes in the trench that sometimes shot clear of the muddy water and ended up on the bank in an epileptic frenzy as they drowned in air.

'Axe! Ask! When is an axe not an axe? When it is a request! When you ask for something!'

'Boy, you too bright for your own good.'

'Can I play draughts with someone? I won't sit up.'

'All right, but only a couple of games, no more.'

Bash Man Goady hovered with the board and the draughts as if waiting for an invitation. They nodded and set about erecting the black and white round pieces on opposing squares. Red Head glanced at Bash Man Goady and caught him scrutinising his damaged forehead out of the corner of his eye.

'Does it hurt?'

'Not a lot.'

'Boy, I never see so much blood in my life.'

'Did you think I was going to die?'

'No. You're a Santos. We're tough.'

They looked at each other and smiled in a rare offering of kindness. The departure, first of their father and then their mother and younger brothers, had driven a wedge between them. Whenever there was a dispute in the house they found themselves on opposing sides. In school they never spoke to each other and when they went on day trips, people were often surprised to learn they were related, never mind brothers. Red Head had overheard his mother trying to explain the rivalry between them to her alarmed mother-in-law, after their first terrible fight at Ariel in which they'd exchanged punches until their eyes were closed.

'I don't know,' she'd said in stubborn bewilderment. 'Is like the second one born too soon when he born at seven months, and the first one feel he get push out of the way.'

His grandmother began to offer some remedy in her usual method of contradicting everything Red Head's mother said or did, but he had heard enough and had already bolted from the kitchen door convinced that his premature appearance into the world was solely responsible for his brother's short temper and grouchy demeanour.

'Hello? Wake up! I said, What's this about beating the President at draughts?'

'Boy, I wash his gall! It was only a dream but it was real as you and me talking now.'

'You think you will win the National Draughts Championships?'

'You want me to?'

'What kind of question is that? Of course!'

'I wasn't sure.'

'Look, you is my brother, right? We fight and things, but you is my blood. Put our name on the map!'

Red Head hopped over three of Bash Man Goady's pieces and gained a king.

'Man! I can't play you, you too good!'

Granny came in and from her knitted brows he knew it was time to rest. His brother packed up the game, proffered that rare smile again and left. Granny tucked him in so tightly he had to strain to loosen the sheets. Then she dropped the mosquito net over his bed. To him the net was like the lid of a casket, sealed with him inside. Had the axe been one inch lower to the left or right this would have been his fate; except it would have been dark with less room to manoeuvre. He shuddered. His grandmother's tone was neither admonishing nor sarcastic when she watched his struggle with the sheets and asked him whether he thought he'd turned into a man. He still felt weak and any sudden move made his head throb.

He lost track of the days. Everyone was at school or in the rice fields or minding the cows or attending to the pigs or the chickens or preparing some meal in the kitchen. Everyone was everywhere but in the room with him. They were kind enough to leave him a draughts set but playing against himself only revealed the futility of any attempt to fool or trick his mind. They brought him a slate from school on which he practised his writing, which was better than usual without the teacher looking over his shoulder. He wrote the alphabet with a flourish as if his name consisted of all twenty-six letters, pretending that his chalk was really a quill and that he was signing the Declaration of Independence of his country from British rule or the unification of all the land's seven peoples. He also made up words by haphazardly juxtaposing letters plucked from his head or suggested by a portion of the wall that had caught his eye. Some mornings he'd be dreaming, something he couldn't recount when awake, and the smell of Granny's baked bread that filled the house at dawn would work its way into his dream, causing his mouth to water, stirring the desire for food and nudging him from sleep with its promise of fresh bread, melted butter and tea.

Raj visited once more, armed with the story of a new Western he'd seen. His sound effects of gunfights involving up to a dozen gunslingers with an array of six-shooters and rifles produced foam at the corners of his mouth, imbued with a urinous air acrid as sulphur. After Raj departed, Granny opened the window and left in a hurry without a word. Red Head was sure she was holding her breath throughout. Bash Man Goady looked in now and again too, sometimes with a message from Sten, other times for a quick game of draughts. Grandad's visits were the most important of all. He'd sit on the end of the bed and ask Red Head to imagine a draughts board on the sheet between them. Then he would talk what he called 'tactics' with his grandson. Red Head never saw Grandad leave because without fail he'd fall asleep at some point during these tactical lectures. Grandad kept returning so Red Head reasoned that he couldn't have minded.

One morning Granny came in to change his bandage. He sat up. She circled his head with her hand as she unwound the cloth. He thought he was being blessed, but the sign was a circle, not a cross. Somehow the Crucifixion had occurred and the most important motif that had emerged from the event was a circle. He pictured the front of churches and Bibles with a circle on them and light radiating out from the edges of the circles. Perhaps Jesus had been tied to a wheel he had to carry in public to jeers and taunts and then lowered into water repeatedly until he drowned. What about the two thieves? Where would he place them? On two more wheels with all three being lowered head first periodically into the water?

He inclined his head for a new bandage in vain. Granny pointed to the door. Red Head hugged her and headed straight for the voices he could hear splashing in the shell pond. At the pond the others were so pleased to see him, they stopped their game of trying to escape the touch of whoever was the last to be touched and clapped and cheered. Most called him Red Head; a few, Axe-man. He saw reflected in the mirror of the shell pond a path on his forehead much like the red sand road in its wavering but the ten stitches across the gash made it look like a single railway line with sleepers across it. Someone splashed near him and the image shimmered. Now his face softened just as the red sand did after rain when the cars got stuck in it but he knew the road on his forehead would be impervious to water. As he shaped up for a belly-splashing dive, he remembered a finger waving a warning in his face, so close it displaced the air there. He was not to go near the shell pond and get his head wet. He dismissed his dive as a bad idea under the circumstances and waded in. A cool stocking rode up his legs. At crotch level he gasped, pulled in his stomach and straightened to his full height. At chest level he stood still for a moment, allowing the pleasant shock of the ring climbing his body to be warmed by the sun. He swam like a dog, keeping his head high out of the water and paddling his hands below the water in front of him. The others resumed their game. Everyone took care not to splash around him.

There were shells on the bottom, though he could not recall when he had last looked down with his face pressed through the skin of the pond's surface to witness their magnified clarity. He automatically responded to the thought by lowering his chin but checked himself, jerking his head back. His eyes shut out the light and the water went very cold. The mirror of the pond he now located in the sky. According to this logic all he needed to do to see the bed of the shell pond was to raise his eyes. The sheet of lightning he'd missed for weeks struck and blackened his sight. He swallowed. Copper sprang to mind. Trees and sky were shells laid out on this black background for inspection. The whole arrangement was tilted at an angle. He took this as an invitation for him to ponder its detail.

'There will be red, then there will be black. The red sand road will be a river of blood. The river will dry but the red sand will not reappear. A hard black road will run through the heart of the land.' The small, unshakable voice was familiar to Red Head. He struggled to focus on the shells but they remained blurred. The tilted display receded from him or he from it.

The others did not miss Red Head. They'd grown accustomed to playing around him and then had proceeded to ignore him. Beanstalk was watching the children playing in the shell pond from a first-floor window he habitually sat beside as he smoked and talked to whoever was in the kitchen. He sounded as if he was shouting at someone because the entrance to the kitchen was at the far end of the room. Perhaps it was hard to register the fact that one of the heads, the least frantic of them, had lowered itself in the water and had not surfaced for some time. He stopped shouting in mid-sentence and placed his cigarette on the edge of the table with the lit end hanging but without taking his eyes off the pond. Whoever was in the kitchen heard him exclaim, 'Jesus!', and if they had had time to enter the room he was in, they would have seen him leap from the window to the ground and run at the fence that was a few inches short of his six feet five inches and take the fence in a backward flip which he simply pointed into a dive as he entered the shell pond. When Beanstalk surfaced, Red Head was in his arms. He depressed Red Head's stomach and blew air into his lungs. Red Head spluttered.

A small, close, truly wicked voice whispered, 'There were four.'

Later that day Beanstalk carried Red Head across the field of tall razor grass separating Grandmother's house from the mud hut of the reclusive Miss Metage, who administered natural remedies for children's aches and pains. Her hands had delivered Red Head's youngest brother, whose sudden birth was brought on when his mother chased Bash Man Goady to lock him in the brush pen for his bad behaviour. The exertion, though successful since she was the fastest sprinter in the village, nevertheless made her double up with labour pains. The children called Miss Metage Ole Higue because they were sure she flew on a broom at night and sucked the life out of babies in their cots. Whenever they saw her they ran from her, all except Red Head's youngest brother, and she reserved her smile just for him.

She pointed to a rug on the floor of her mud hut. The second Beanstalk released him, Red Head sat up and peered at the stooped, short body of the woman. He was afraid to look into her eyes. She motioned at Red Head to lie on his back but he obeyed only when Beanstalk raised his eyebrows at him. She passed a string over an open flame burning in a small spherical metal dish and allowed the wax running off the string to fall on her open palm as she moved, swiftly for her years, from the one small table in the hut to where Red Head lay. Her hand came away from the bottom of the string and the hot wax dripped on Red Head's bare chest. He bawled. Beanstalk winced but he knew it was fear more than pain that had caused the child to scream. When she asked Beanstalk to hold the whimpering Red Head as still as possible, the child's sobbing renewed. 'This will not hurt.' She reached for the metal dish with the single flame. Shielding the flame with her hand and body so that Red Head could only see her back as she drew near and stooped next to him, she thrust it at his eyes. Red Head tried to pull his head back but his uncle's grip was too strong. He clamped his eyelids and saw lightning. His tongue was instantly coated with copper. 'Let him go.'

Beanstalk eased his twitching nephew onto the mat and looked at Miss Metage for an explanation. But she was busy placing a folded piece of cloth under the child's head and peering into his mouth to ensure he had not bitten or swallowed his tongue. When Red Head's shuddering stopped and he opened his eyes but did not seem to know where he was, Miss Metage took the cap off a dark bottle, waved the open neck near his nose and his head cleared. She held the bottle at arm's length from herself and Red Head, and Beanstalk took it and replaced the cap.

'Don't screw it too tight or I'll have to call you next time I want to open it.' She tried to mop Red Head's brow but he recoiled. When she smiled at him and tried again, he let her. 'You had a fit. You are young, you might grow out of it. Never stare at the sun or any flickering bright light. Always keep a lump of sugar in your pocket in case you feel hungry. Never stand on your head or dive head-first into water. Avoid sudden noise and don't let anyone hit you on the head again.' She looked at Beanstalk when she said the part about avoiding knocks to the head, and he examined his feet. 'Why you never bring the boy to me when you chop his head? Whoever stitch this must have been drunk.' She selected a jar from a row lined up against the wall on the floor, lifted a feather in it and daubed Red Head's cut with a brown, viscous liquid. This time he kept his head very still for her. She blew on the cut and it felt cool and the skin around the cut stiffened a little as the liquid dried. It reminded him of how mud felt after he crossed a trench and the mud on his feet went dry. Miss Metage ruffled his hair and broadened her smile and gave him a cake made from pieces of coconut covered in brown sugar.

'Thank you, Ole — Miss Metage.'

Beanstalk gave her two small bags; one contained rice, the other flour.

'Feed him with the heart of young coconut trees. That will mend his mind.' She told Red Head if he blurted 'thank you' once more, he would induce a fit. 'Say howdy to your mother.'

Beanstalk gave him a piggyback along a winding path across the field to their house. Red Head decided never to run from Miss Metage again and never to hide from her and pelt her with the red sand stones that exploded on impact. He asked Beanstalk if she really flew on a broom and turned into a ball of fire in order to get through keyholes to babies' cots. His uncle said Miss Metage wouldn't hurt a fly.

'Boy, it looks like we have to find you some growee.'

'Would that be like trying to find guava?'

'Much easier, I think.'

Red Head speculated whether a fit would hinder or help his game in the coming draughts championships. Beanstalk was sure fits would prove useful, if Red Head could summon them at will.

'What if I could touch someone's head during a fit and pass it on to them?'

'Or when you touch them you could read their thoughts!'

'Now that's what I call power!'

From Island Liturgies
Marlene Nourbese Philip

Sinon l'enfance, qu'y avait-it alors qu'il n'y a plus?
— *Pour Féter un Enfance*, St. John Perse

Childhood of an island orphaned in cut-loose time
adrift in the memory of history:
a sudden threat of islands nuclear and racial
from Toronto four, six hours to London
close by too far to the States and Russia;
islands strung past tense
plucked as if by some giant hand
in the gestation of forever in held
pregnant with curve and possibility and brinked
on the threnody of always
release the resonance of never.
Island of hip-roofed houses eyed red with weeping
for centuries alien to belonging,
whose grass was never greener or sun ever hotter
where a spendthrift sun of constancies reigned over a childhood
reckless with wish and whim and spur:
sun and sun, sun and rain, rain and rain, rain and sun and sun and
where now and no, continental plates of a past collide
and webbed beginnings of truth spun taut
webs a mind sticky with memory.
Tobacco and myth of a crusoed island wreathe blue smoke
around the SpanishFrenchDutchEnglishDutchSpanishFrenchEnglish
the names of many — Belaforma, Asuncion, Tabago, Tavago, Tobago
stolengiftedpassedheldhandled and handed
in the cradle of history to and fro, back and forth rocked —

Isle of child!
where the sun's ledger holds night and day in perfect balance
exacts from each fruit payment of ripe
today cashew, tomorrow mango, day after sapodilla, in one week

chenette and plum
and fireflies ferry sunlight on the black back of night;
abandoned place of faith and place of abandoned faith
childhood chorus!
Resurrected life of an orphaned island,
wild runs the green of a child's lifehood
small wanderings through a pink of pigeon peas
to capture the honey in the window with
    the wishbone of childhood.

Would they lie — the memories?
Did they?

Coco's Palace
Glenville Lovell

POLITICAL DEBATE AND LAUGHTER, inspired by the alcohol that flowed freely there, prevailed in Coco's Palace. Perched on a hill, the Palace was nothing more than a wooden two-room structure; one room served as a bedroom, living room and general debate area for the many "light-livers" who congregated morning, noon and night; the other contained a tiny kerosene stove and a plastic-covered table with sprained legs propped on brown bricks. It was called the Palace because the owner, Reynold McKintosh, a six-footer with a thick beard, known as Coco, had once pronounced himself king of the village. He'd fashioned a crown from bamboo leaves and cane-stalks, designed and executed a staff in rough mahogany and set about acquiring five more "wives." His legal wife deserted him, taking the children, the minute she heard mention of other "wives." He quit his job as a grave-digger, declaring, "There's more to life than dead people," and instituted a series of taxes to support himself and his new family, promising in return to provide spiritual advice to help the villagers lead better lives. Well, no one paid the taxes and, after two months of going from house to house begging for food, Coco's five "wives," by then in various stages of pregnancy, left him.

All day long, men and women, young and old — some boys as young as ten, mostly used as runners to fetch rum from the shop — attended Coco's court at the Palace. There they found food, drink and debate; a place to drown their sorrows, start a fleeting romance or sever difficult relationships. Always noisy, it was the liveliest place in the village with the human traffic heaviest around midday and midnight. Sometimes fights broke out between friends, lovers, or between lovers and friends, but never between strangers; for strangers, except politicians laden with money, were never allowed in the Palace.

An untrained eye, at first glance, might be tempted to dismiss the people who filled the Palace as misfits, because at some point in their lives most of them had been beggars, prostitutes or thieves;

Glenville Lovell

even Devil, convicted of murder at seventeen, was welcomed back and feted after he'd done his ten years in jail. But that would be a mistake. Politicians in search of votes found the Palace a fit place to test their new ideas. For, despite its outward appearance, the Palace was a hotbed for change, and a challenge to the status quo. The outcome of the Palace debates could swing the village for or against a particular party.

The resident political expert was Pappy-Boy, a Harrison College dropout who'd decided he was brighter than his teachers and left school six months before graduation. Attempting to burn his books in the backyard, he set his grandmother's house on fire, which landed him in the mental hospital for a year. He spent the time teaching the patients Latin, his language of choice. "The brightest boy in Buhbaydus," his grandmother used to brag before half her house went up in flames. After that she just called him mad. On his release from Jenkins, Pappy-Boy sat his G.C.E.'s and passed all nine of the subjects. He was now studying economics at the university. His ability to memorize facts and dates and repeat them with accuracy made him a natural debater. His arguments, stated in a voice which boomed from his chest, could always swing the village's sentiment.

That afternoon, Tavian found Coco sitting on a window sill, rum glass in hand. From the way Coco was holding the glass Tavian knew it was empty. Coco's right-hand man, Devil, was seated on the floor. Tall and baby-faced, Pappy-Boy, dressed in tattered shirtjack and cut-off jeans, was leaning against the doorpost playing with Coco's gray cat. Three women were seated around the kitchen table: Millie, a waif who always sounded as if she had a chest cold and whose deep laugh rattled like thunder whenever she became drunk (which was seldom because she could hold liquor with any man twice her size); Carla, a buxom, middle-aged woman whose excessively thick lips made her the butt of jokes (told behind her back, for Carla carried a knife in her bosom, as did Millie); and Juanita, a petite beauty with almond-shaped eyes and delicately balanced ears, who only visited the Palace to escape the boredom of a failing marriage. The others in the Palace were Race-Horse and Devil's twelve-year-old son, the runner of the day.

Race-Horse had the floor when Tavian walked in. "I believe a woman poison him. I hear that from reliable sources. Everybody know he had nuff women. And I personally believe a jealous

294

woman poison him."

"What proof you got? Leh me hear," Coco said. Then, "Ah Tavvy, jus' the man I want to see. Come man, pour one."

"After you," Tavian replied puckishly. "Everybody know you' glass empty, man. If my gran'mother was here she would hear the emptiness in that glass. Pour one if yuh drinkin'. You expect to trick big men all the time walkin' 'round with a big empty glass?"

Coco picked up the rum bottle sheepishly. "Tavian, boy, you too smart for yuh own good sometimes, yuh know." They slapped hands. "But how yuh doin' though, yuh lucky son of a gun."

"Not bad," said Tavian, pouring a glass half-full of rum. "Who that Race-Horse talkin' 'bout that get poison?"

"Scandal Broome. Our late departed MP. May his soul rest in peace," declared Race-Horse mockingly.

"Yuh better don't let nobody hear you wid that," Tavian cautioned. "Yuh could get lock up for sayin' them t'ings."

"Lock up? For sayin' wha' I know is true? Wha' this ain't Russia." Race-Horse sucked his teeth loudly, poured a drink and swallowed hard. "Ain't a man alive could shut me mouth when it begin to rattle. I, myself, sleep with one of his outside women. Nearly bre'k she in two with the bamboo stick. She was so happy to get a real man, she tell me all the she secrets. Tell me he used to beat she up. If he wasn't such a old man I woulda put some licks in he ass meself, but I don't like unfairing people."

The women heard this and brought their conversation to a halt. Race-Horse was forever talking about sharing licks. At least two of them could confirm that the only licks Race-Horse ever shared were with his tongue glued between their legs, and he wasn't too good at that. If they mentioned it in the Palace they knew for sure he would deny it. After all, no self-respecting Bajan man would ever admit to putting his face, far less his tongue, near a woman's sex. They left the kitchen and found seats on the floor of the court.

"I don't open me mouth unless I got something to say. You know that, Tavian," Race-Horse continued.

"That ain't what I hear," Millie said with a laugh. The other two women chuckled.

"Who talkin' to you? Yuh hard-faced fool."

"Yuh still ain't tell we who give you this information," Devil said.

"Man, you think I so foolish? Wunna expect me to give names, especially with these women 'bout here? The way these women does lick dem mout', how long you think it go take for me name to get back to Scandal family? I will say what I have to say when these women gone."

Pappy-Boy stepped to the center of the room, still holding Coco's cat, and in his most professorial manner, looked around slowly with a cock-sure smile.

"Yuh know sometimes wunna does get on so silly it does make me want to puke," he began. "Anybody would think wunna ain't got no sense, that every day I don't come in here and analyse facts fuh wunna. Anybody would think I don't explain and expound on the different social and economic factors that make up the fabric of this society, why so many people sittin' down on a rock stone under some tree skinnin' their mouth, while a rich few basking on the decks of fancy yachts sipping drinks with a smile, so that wunna could understand what is important and what wunna should just discard. Here it is, a by-election go be contested in this constituency and before wunna concern wunna-self with the candidates and what they plan to do to improve wunna lives, wunna discussing if Scandal get poison and why. All that is irrelevant to your situation, don't you understand? Yuh all need to be lookin' at where this government leading the country, whether wunna see any real improvement in wunna lives since this government was in power, and if not wunna need to decide if it ain't time to send the government a message, a message them would be foolish to ignore."

"Look, Pappy," Race-Horse interjected, "you does take life too serious sometimes, yuh know. That is why yuh ass went to Jenkins. I, for one, gettin' a little tired of you tryin' to treat big men like them in primary school. If we want to have some fun at Scandal expense, what the ass wrong with that? Politicians does be laughin' at we every blessed day. If you look carefully on them yachts you does be talkin' bout you go find a politician lickin' somebody ass. All you' brains and education can't change that. So sit down and cool yuh ass, man. Or go and look for some real pussy and stop playing with that blasted cat."

If it were any other two people, Coco would've let the argument continue. Over the years he had found that the best debates were between people who were passionate about the topic, not about each other. That wasn't the situation with Race-Horse and Pappy-Boy. Pappy's father had taken up with Race-Horse's mother a few years back. Fate stepped in and took care of Pappy's father a short time later when he slipped into the well he was digging just after he'd lit the fuse of an explosive charge. Since then, any exchange between Pappy-Boy and Race-Horse, from a simple "How-de-do" to a debate, had the potential to break into blows.

"Listen here, Tavvy," Coco began, hoping to change the subject, "we been hearing you got a high-society woman lickin' yuh feet."

Tavian shot a glance in Race-Horse's direction. "You should know better than to listen to Race-Horse. Remember Oscar Waldron who tell so much lie and had so many names, one day he wake up and didn't know who he was? Same thing go happen to our friend here one day."

"You sayin' it ain't true?" Coco asked.

"I ain't sayin' nothin' til I pounce 'pon another one of these fowl-cocks." He poured a Cockspur, gulped it down and set the glass upside-down beside the bottle to thwart the buzzing flies. Tavian looked around the room. All eyes were pinned on him. The blank eyes of naked white women pasted to the wall next to the tearful eyes of defeated paperweight politicians beneath headlines illuminating their failures; the wonder-filled eyes of Gary Sobers in a life-sized poster, the greatest cricketer to ever drink a rum (as declared by Coco); the hungry, anxious eyes of the Palace regulars waiting to breathe something real, something new. He wondered what they saw in his eyes.

"As far as I concern, I's a free man. My woman left me and I can see whoever I please, don't you agree, Coco?"

"As a man, yes. So who's this woman?"

"That's all I have to say right now."

Millie poured a drink using Tavian's glass, then lit a cigarette. Up close to his face, she put a wedge of smoke between them, waited for it to decay, then with a sad, sly smile said, "Why you's a good one though, Tavian. How come you' woman left you and yuh ain't come and look for me?" She touched her chest, right around her heart. "Yuh know I been holding this thing in me chest for you for the longest time."

"Yuh betta mek sure it ain't a cold," Devil quipped.

Tavian knew better than to answer Millie. She looked like she'd been drinking all day. A glazed, flushed look had already taken over her face. She was the spitting image of a cat. And in this half-drunk state, with her tiny, black eyes half-shut, she was liable to do and say anything. Every man in that room must've taken advantage of Millie in this state at one time or another, at least that's what they said and Millie never bothered to deny it. Tavian was the only one never to make that claim, and though a long time ago he'd found himself in bed with her, they were both too drunk to do anything. For that reason, it seemed, Millie was always offering herself to him.

"You need to get yuhself a man, Millie," Race-Horse said.

"Guess that won't be you, 'cause you ain't much of one."

The occupants of the room burst into laughter with Devil's sounding high above the rest.

"You let she talk to you like that, man?" said Devil, living up to his name.

"I don't pay she no mind," Race-Horse said, "I tired skinnin' she up all 'bout the bush."

"You ain't know who want skinnin' up? Yuh old wuffless mother."

Race-Horse sprang to the center of the room a few feet from where Millie was slinging her bony frame around Tavian. Like lightning, the knife appeared in her hand as she turned to face him. Tavian jumped between the two combatants. Putting his arm around Millie, he led her toward the kitchen.

Race-Horse screamed at her back, "And yuh betta stop walkin' 'bout givin' people the clap."

Millie spun round eager to return to the fray but Tavian held her firm. Gradually she relaxed, allowed herself to be comforted by him, liking it more and more each second. Tavian released his hold. She continued to lean on him. He moved away to stand against the stove.

"Millie, you know better than to talk 'bout Race-Horse mother. You know how sensitive he is on that subject."

"I don't give a rass 'bout Race-Horse. He jus' vex 'cause I won't let him screw me. He want every woman his blasted eyes see. I can't stand him."

Tavian moved to return to the main group. Millie reached out and held his hand intently.

"You got any money, Tavian? I need to borrow twenty dollars."

"What for?"

"I have to go to the doctor tomorrow."

"What's wrong?"

"I don't know. Been having some shooting pains in me side of late."

Tavian followed her eyes to the floor. Cracks were beginning to appear between the floorboards where the linoleum had been ripped away. Bits of food, cigarette butts and mango skins glossed with dirt made a shiny mosaic on the floor.

When Millie looked up her eyes were wet. But he'd been fooled before by Millie's watery eyes. Her sunken jaws made her dome-like cheekbones spread half across her face, appearing even more prominent, and in the sun-drenched kitchen they stood out like mountain ridges against the sunset.

"Why you can't borrow money from Juanita or Carla?"

"You know how them is, too. If I borrow money from them, next week the whole village know."

"You don't care 'bout that."

"Now how you go say something like that, Tavian? That is how you think 'bout me? Worth nothin', not even a smidgin of pride?"

"That ain't what I mean, Millie."

"That is how it sound. I gots my pride, Tavian. I don't always show it but one day you will believe me. I come to you 'cause I know you would keep it secret between we. And look, I ain't asking you to give me for nothin', ya know. Like, maybe tonight I could come by your place and give you something in return."

"Something like what?"

"Anything you want. Anything at all."

He reached into his pocket, pulled out two bills, a twenty and a five; he gave her the twenty. She smiled. The money disappeared into her bosom.

"Yuh know, you should stop knockin' 'bout the place and find somet'ing to do," Tavian advised.

He'd always liked Millie's infectious high spirits despite her reputation of being slack and easy. Looking at her now, Tavian still saw traces of the beautiful young girl she must have been.

"What I go find to do now, Tavian? Who go give me a job?"

"Yeah, it tough, I know. My situation ain't no better than yours. I could use a job too."

"I don't know why you don't go back to Saint Andrew and work with your gran'mother. Them things wunna does make real beautiful. If I still had me voice I won't be 'sociating with these wuffless, own-way men 'bout here. Don't get like them, Tavian. Go back and help yuh gran'mother."

He suddenly felt very brotherly toward her. Maybe this was what he'd felt for her all along. Brotherly love. Or something like that. He touched her hair gently, a touch which transmitted his concern, at the same time reinforcing the distance between them.

"Should I come by you tonight, Tavian?"

He shook his head. "Maybe some other time."

She turned and went out the side door, her cat steps soundless on the linoleum.

Tavian went back to the raucous gathering in the next room.

"I bet she beg you for money," Race-Horse pounced.

"Man, why you don't mind yuh own blasted business?"

"Why you always sticking up for that whore?"

"Maybe you should just leave her 'lone."

"Leave her 'lone? Wha' I do she? She always borrowin' money from you and never pay back a red cent. And what you does get for it? Nothin'. That's why women would always take advantage of you, man. Yuh trust them too much. Man, I bet she goin' down the road laughin' at you. And she go probably buy some man a bottle of rum, get drunk and get fuck, and tomorrow she go be broke and beggin' for money again."

Tavian remained silent.

"He right, yuh know, Tavvy," Coco said.

"So what, man? What's the big effin' deal? Sometimes I does come here and spend a hundred dollars on rum and food, and I don't hear nobody complainin'. So what if she take the money and spend it on a man? I don't care, yuh understand? I give her the money, she can do whatever she want with it." Tavian felt assaulted from all sides. "Maybe if we had something better to do than sit around here drinkin' rum and talkin' shite, we won't worry so much 'bout what Millie do and don't do."

He looked at the other two women, expecting them to help him out, to defend their friend. But they sat, amused, even a bit elated, with no intention of defending Millie.

"So now you sayin' we lazy and ain't got nothin' better to do," Race-Horse challenged. "All of a sudden you become somebody 'cause you smellin' up under a society-woman."

"Sound like Race-Horse jealous," Coco laughed.

"Jealous of what? I don't need no society-woman. Them ain't got nothin' any of the women 'bout here ain't got. And the women I know ten times better than any of them society-women. Them so does only want a man them could twist 'round them finger. She go use up Tavian and then throw he 'way like a dirty Modess."

This brought guffaws of laughter from Coco and Devil.

Right then Tavian felt alien in that place. This house which had almost become his place of worship, these friends, were about to toss him onto the dump heap, about to do to him what they would do to Millie. For what? Because his new girlfriend was light-skinned, a lawyer, and came from a well-to-do family? He'd known these people a long time. He'd expected them to appreciate his newfound importance in the world. But how could they? They'd never met Spring. She was just another "society-woman" to them. Perhaps they knew better than he the true nature of his newfound self-importance. If pressed, he would have to admit that Spring's social status increased his hunger for her. He thrilled at the thought of being caressed by her expensively manicured hands, of putting his own rough, callused fingers in places so soft and receptive he could've been playing in water. Spring made him feel more alive than he'd ever felt. That was why Race-Horse's pronouncement that it took a woman like her to make him feel he was "somebody" troubled him.

His affair with Spring was beginning to change him. He looked around the room at the group. The emptiness in their eyes was blinding. That was something he'd never noticed before. Race-Horse, with his gluttonous need for women, looked like a man who'd given up hope, who'd resigned himself to just another life. That would never happen to him.

Tavian could not stay there any longer. He deserved more than this. He picked up his hat and slipped out the door.

Coco's voice pursued him. "Where you goin', man?"

He didn't answer. The truth was he didn't know.

From Flickering Shadows
K*wadwo* Agymah K*amau*

I WAS THERE THE SATURDAY NIGHT the police raided the Brethren here on the Hill, with the lamps flickering in the lamp-holders up on the church walls, walls that my two old hands had helped put up with the other men in the village even though the rheumatism was turning my joints into knots.

The church wasn't no shack like the newspaper said. It wasn't big and fancy like the cathedral and them other big churches in town, but it was a church, we "own-own church," like Clemmie used to say, God rest her in her grave. The best wife I ever had, Clementina.

But like I was saying, even the shadows was dancing that Saturday night.

The drum skins feel tight and smooth. My hands feeling like they working by theyself, pounding out the rhythm. And the sound bouncing off the walls and echoing inside the church. The women clapping, dancing, singing. Their tambourines bupping and rattling. The men rocking and jerking. The women voices high and the men bass voices low, low, low: like oil flowing beneath clear water.

My grandson Cephus playing the drum with his head cock one-side and his eyes shut. Young Boysie, his friend, leaning over his drum, working it, his hands in a blur, a frown on his face, naked to his waist, like the rest of young men sitting with their drums between their legs and the sweat glistening on their bodies.

Me? I had a robe sling over my shoulders, covering my old bones from the chill of the night.

Young Estelle collapse and fall down on the floor rolling around, in the power. And young Cephus eyes like two balls in his eye sockets, staring at Estelle puff-leg bloomers.

But Sister Wiggins pulling down Estelle dress to cover her nakedness. And disappointment pulling down Cephus young face.

I had to lower my head so nobody wouldn't see me smiling.

Sister Wiggins and Sister Scantlebury helping up Estelle, and Estelle reigning back and shaking; her eyes shut and her face screw

302

up. And she talking in tongues, sounding like, "Ahumalumaluh . . . a-chimumalumaluh . . . hmmmmm!"

Sister Scantlebury is a tall woman, tough from working the ground by herself and raising a young boy-child ever since her man fall in a toilet pit and dead. She old enough to be Estelle mother. But the power got hold of Estelle, so Sister Scantlebury struggling, strong as she is.

Old Sister Wiggins, short and with the fat jiggling loose on her arms, trying to help Sister Scantlebury wrestle with Estelle. Sister Wiggins just like me, always complaining for rheumatism, but she grabbing on to Estelle right arm and en letting go. Every time Estelle shake, Sister Wiggins stumbling. But she determined. Her forehead crease up and her mouth set. One of her gray plaits unwinding from her head and hanging like thick rope, whipping back and forth every time Estelle move.

And Estelle big gold hoops glistening against her black skin in the light from the lanterns on the walls.

Brother Joseph, with his beard almost down to his chest, standing in front of the drummers in his white robe, pounding the ground with his snake staff and stretching his other hand straight up in the air. "Yesss, sister! Yesss . . ."

All of a sudden, *brug-a-dung!* Is like a hurricane battering the front door. People heads swing around. Even Sister Wiggins and Sister Scantlebury eyes fastened on the church door.

Estelle still shaking like she in a epileptic fit.

Old Brother Oxley and his wife still holding hands, moaning and rocking with their eyes shut, as usual, as if they in a world by themselves.

My hands stop. One of the drummers give a couple more beats — *whabap!* — on his drum and stop.

Look like the whole police station standing in the door, and the sergeant clomping down the aisle with his big-guts self. Big Joe.

Everybody quiet now. Everybody know Big Joe, with his two little marble-eyes, his small bullet-head and his slant-back forehead. All Big Joe know to do is to beat people.

Big Joe standing up in front Brother Joseph, smacking the club in his palm, with his manager belly push out, his shoulders throw back, rocking backward and forward on his two bandy-legs.

"Unna can't keep no more meetings here," Big Joe saying. Big Joe got a small voice for such a big man.

Brother Joseph standing up straight, with his snake staff at his

303

side. The snake carved on the staff, with the tip of its tail resting on the floor, the body winding up around the staff, and its two heads staring full in Big Joe face.

"WHY?" The voice booming deep, echoing in the church.

For years after that, people swear that it is the snake that ask Big Joe "why"—why they can't keep no more meetings in the church.

Big Joe jump; his eyes open wide; he gulp; he smack the club in his palm extra hard; he take a deep breath. "Cause the guvment say so," he say at last. "And *I* say so. That is all you got to know. The guvment say shut unna down, and I come to shut unna down." His little-boy voice is the only sound in the church building.

I throw a quick glance at Cephus. Cephus looking at his father and mother — Granville and Violet — standing couple rows back: Granville in his stiff-starch-and-iron short-sleeve white shirt — people say Granville is the image of me, but I don't know about that — I always thought he look more like his mother, Clemmie; Violet beside him in her white dress and white head-tie — she is a nice daughter-in-law. I can't complain.

Everybody eyes fasten on Big Joe and Brother Joseph.

Big Joe raise his hand and signaling the rest of policemen at the door to come in. "We taking the drums and all the rest of this," he say. He looking at the masks and the pictures of Garvey and Nkrumah on the walls, and the painting of a African woman holding a baby that hang up right behind the pulpit. And his face screw up like he smell a fart.

A young policeman coming for my drum, but I en letting go. I stubborn in my old age. I wrap my arms around the drum, looking up in the face of the young constable. The boy en even start shaving yet.

I see when he raise the club, but en had time to raise my hand to block before . . . *whacks!*

Is like something explode in my head. Talk about seeing stars! Is like the whole galaxy inside my head. I falling down off my bench, still trying to hold on to the drum; blood beginning to run down my forehead — warm; I crouch over and scrunch up to protect my head and my balls — I know this young generation spiteful; you never know what they would do even to an old man like me.

My drum rolling away. And my head hurting, hurting to rass.

My daughter-in-law voice bawling out: "Daduh! Cephus! . . . Oh Lord have 'is mercy! . . . Cephus!" And Granville deep voice saying: "God blimmuh! Unna hit my father!" He saying this like he surprised.

A bench tumbling over and women voices hollering,

"Mr. Cudgoe . . . !"

"Oh Lord Jesus . . . !"

"Hold he! Don' let he get heself in trouble!"

And a man voice: "Woman, shut up your mouth! Lef the man lone!"

And more benches knocking over. Blows raining, sounding like how bag flour does sound when you cuff it: *buff! . . . buff!* Heavy boots tramping down the aisle. Hands grabbing me up rough under my armpits and hauling me; my feet dragging on the ground. I open my eyes and the red carpet sliding past under my face; blood dropping off my head and making darker red spots on the carpet.

When they reach the front door and my shinbone hit the top step, I try to twist round so that they wouldn't drag all the skin off my old shinbones dragging me down the church steps. But I en as young as I used to be.

Through all the pain, I squint open my eyes.

A white inspector standing up longside the Land Rover in front of the church. A bony-face white man with a moustache, in a peak cap, khaki tunic, short pants and long socks nearly up to his knees, standing upright like he got a bamboo spine, tapping the Land Rover fender with a cane, not doing a thing, while Big Joe and them in there busting people ass.

I en last too long after that—after police break in a church and beat up old people; Dolphus Blackman losing his finger when the police slam the door of the police van shut, and them brutes keeping him at the guardhouse with the blood dripping on the floor and Boysie just staring at his father finger hanging by a little piece of skin; Miss Blackman sitting on the bench between Dolphus and Boysie at the police station, big with child, and losing the baby later in the courthouse, with the judge banging his hammer and bawling, "Order in court! Order in court, I say!" and one of the Brethren jumping up and hollering "Order your fucking self!" and asking the judge if he en got a mother, and turning to the crowd in the courtroom and saying, "Look him! Look him! With a curly white wig on his head like a blasted sissy," and turning back to the judge and saying, "You lucky all these policemens in the court or I would come up there and knock that blasted wig off your kiss-me-ass head." And people gasping and their eyes popping open.

And the judge pointing his finger at the man and hollering, "Thirty days! For contempt of court!" and ordering the policemen, "Take him out! Take this man out of my court!"

And a whole gang of policemen rushing at the man right there in the courthouse and raining blows on him like peas, and the man bawling, "Loose me! Loose me! So help me, I go kill all you today!"

But his voice getting softer as the batons beating him down and the boots kicking him like he is a football, till after a while all you can hear is the kicks, the baton blows and the man grunting and groaning like a sow in labor.

And the judge hunched like a vulture in his black robes, staring over his glasses and tapping a pencil on his desk.

My heart couldn't take it. It couldn't take it. I drop down right there in the court room. Dead.

Well, that cause a whole new set of commotion in the courtroom.

They buried me right next to my Clementina in the cemetery up on the Hill.

Things settle down on the Hill after I pass away, although life was never the same again.

The man that cause a disturbance in the court living in town now, roaming the street, walking up to people and barking in their faces, "ORDER IN COURT!" And people jumping with fright.

A lot of people stop going to Brethren meetings, and the few stubborn ones that hanging on with Brother Joseph peeping and dodging to hold their meetings down in the gully, with a little boy up in a tree looking out to see if the police coming.

Around that same time, Anthony Roachford, little brown-skinned Anthony that born and raised on the Hill, come back from study-ing law in Away, but he never set foot back on the Hill. He open a little law office in town.

Then the next thing the people on the Hill hear, he and a set of young lawyers start a political party — the People's Labor Party. People calling it the People's Lawyers Party.

Leaflets start appearing on electric poles, shop doors, even on the big evergreen tree in the square in town. The leaflets saying,

DOWN WITH COLONIALISM!

INDEPENDENCE NOW!

The Parliamentary Council in an uproar. The white men in the Council — plantation owners, merchants, the governor from

Away — pounding the table with their fists and saying things like, "over my dead body," calling Roachford and his party "bloody upstarts" and "colored bastards."

Two black men in the Parliamentary Council: Dr. Bostick and Dr. Greaves. But all Dr. Bostick doing is standing with one hand in his waistcoat and playing with his watch chain and saying, "I object most strenuously!"

Dr. Greaves sitting with his gray-haired head down.

And through the windows they can hear shouts, glass breaking, running footsteps. People rioting.

A policeman catch a fella pasting a leaflet on a bench in the botanical gardens.

A crowd gathered around the policeman and the fella, and a rumor spread that a policeman kill a man just for handing out leaflets.

So now, people roaming the streets, breaking store windows and saying, "We want independence!"

But some fellas in the crowd only feeling up the white clerks in the stores. One of these fellas smelling his finger every couple minutes with a big smile on his face.

A bottle whiz through a window of the parliamentary building.

Dr. Bostick sticking one finger in the air, pushing out his chest and bellowing, "The day of revolution is at hand!"

Dr. Greaves still hunched over with his head down.

The plantation owners and merchants looking frightened and the president of the council — the governor from Away — a robust, red-faced man in short sleeves, striding to the door and bawling for the police. "I say! I say!"

Well, to make a long story short, the king in the Mother Country (that is what even the educated ones that should know better does call it) send down a man to investigate.

And the investigator going around talking to people, asking questions, even going to the prison to talk to the rioters the police arrest.

The investigator gone back to Away. Things quiet in the country. But it is an uneasy kind of calm, like the stillness you get the day before a hurricane — a slow, heavy, oppressive passing of time.

Then the news is like sudden flashes of lightning — a big headline on the front page of the newspaper say, "Mother Country to Grant Independence"; the governor announce elections; the

Council pass a law saying everybody over twenty-one can vote; and a delegation going to the Mother Country to make arrangements for independence.

Meanwhile Dribbly Joe, who does walk around town, sometimes with his fly open, with dribble dripping from his mouth and wetting the front of his shirt, having a flash of enlightenment and drawling, "How . . . anybody . . . can . . . give . . . we . . . in-de-pen-dence?" And he going on to say something about the king in Away tying a string to a bird leg, opening the cage door and flying the bird like a kite, and the bird think it free because it en feeling the string around its leg, but if the bird ever try to fly too far it going get a sudden shock when the king yank the string.

Hearing so many words coming from Dribbly Joe is like hearing a baby fart. People mouth dropping open at first, then they laughing at the foolishness "that half-idiot" Dribbly Joe talking, forgetting what the old people always say: every fool got his own sense.

Not long after that, Roachford come back on the Hill. First time he set foot on the Hill in all the time since he come back from studying law in Away.

He and two carloads of men stop at Mr. Thorne rum shop.

A crowd gather. Inside the shop, Roachford done order rum. Two bottles on the counter. Estelle opening a tin of corned beef and setting it on a plate next to a packet of biscuits.

Roachford head towering above the crowd. "There's more where that come from," he saying.

Roachford slapping fellas on their back and talking about if the Lawyers Party win the elections, things going be different. "Massa days done wid," he saying. And it sound out of place the way he say it.

Ever since he come back from "my sojourn in the Mother Country," as he like to put it, he talking like he born and bred over there. So now when he trying to talk like everybody else, he en sound right.

The fellas laughing and tossing back the free rum and eating the free corned beef and biscuits. As long as Roachford standing the drinks and the eats, they don't care; he alright with them. So when he say, "Massa days done wid," everybody laughing and saying "Yeah!" Everybody except Boysie and Claude — Boysie with his full beard covering his face and looking serious, with one elbow resting on the counter and a bottle of stout in his hand; Claude, tall

308

and lanky and leaning against the side of the shop.

"And what that mean in concrete terms? 'Massa days done with'?" Boysie asking.

Roachford turn to face Boysie.

"Give me some *specifics*, cuz," Boysie saying. "Some *specifics.*"

Roachford looking around at the crowd. Everybody watching him to hear what he going say.

He take a deep breath. "Well, for one thing," he say, "we plan to take away the land from the old plantocracy and give it to the people." He look around with this big grin, like he feel he do something.

But Boysie saying, "You forget where you come from? All of us up here own our own land."

Which is true. Years ago, when the plantation owner decide to move back to the Mother Country, he divide the land into plots and sell it out.

Some people only buy sufficient land for a house spot. Others, like Boysie grandfather (Roachford great-uncle), buy piece-by-piece till they got enough to support themself.

Roachford looking around the crowd, still confident. "Of *course* I know. Hill people independent fuh so. I is one of all you, remember? Gimme a break, man."

Somebody in the crowd snicker.

"He should stick to talking great," a low voice saying. "He sound like a real assbeetle when he trying to talk like we."

The crowd gone quiet.

Roachford start sweating, pulling a kerchief from his pants pocket and wiping his face.

He look around the shop, sizing up the people. Then he force a smile. "Anyhow, why spoil a good rum with talk, huh?" he say. He raise his glass. "Drink up, man. Drink up."

The other party, the Doctors Party, en do much better when they decide to hold a meeting on the Hill.

Dr. Bostick, the leader of the party, sticking his finger in his waistcoat and reminding people that he and his "colleagues have been fighting the colonial rulers" before these "young Turks" in the Lawyers Party were born.

But the people start booing and heckling, saying that since the governor give them two seats in the Council, they just like the plantation owners.

Somebody start pelting rocks, and Dr. Bostick and the other doctors in the party fleeing down the hill.

Good luck for them a lorry driver spot Dr. Bostick as the doctor that take out his son tonsils. He stop his lorry and lean out the window, but he barely had time to say, "Hey, doc . . ." before all the doctors clamber up on the back of the lorry and Dr. Bostick jump in next to the driver, slam the door and hollering, "Drive, man! Drive!"

Pyramid Chapel
Mark McMorris

- for Peter Gizzi

1.
It was raining, the clear doze of being
comes back to me, of music in a thatched place —
no music, the globes of light out of step with the music
and below the swiveling dancers
falling in a circle that settles like a coin
the beautiful array unravels
till only a husk is left

Posing for the eye of a book that had sparrows in it
two faces of the same dancer
two faces of the same prospect of doubt

I walk through a door with a table in my pocket
as wood, as metaphor, as everything that leads up to me
the funnel as it flowers to let in the camels
perhaps the first step of music in the crossing
the field of goats, and rocks, and small hills
with goats on them, left to fend and devoured by a tiger
of these things I need not compose a treatise
the wooff of stories, and the warp of logs
other trails from the heads of experts in lore
make their own way upon the trail of the dancers

Posing for the eye of a book that had sparrows in it
the atoms cannot stand still, they swerve
and coalesce, and topple, and make a different
story from the particles of light
names are blossoms falling in a circle
in which we are two, in which we are the one
dwelling in space, adjusting vision, talking

311

of names on a map: Sligo, Vere, Oxford, Magotty
two faces of the one dancer
and the hills of music eroded like a coin whose face is lost
above the high flat sand of California
a terrible kiss in a dream

All of this ended, and we went back to the garden
hand in hand with steps to the music
ready for the trek cross-country when the garden gives up
with sun at my back that vectors in the particles
below the wings of a pigeon, trapped in flight
like him I am at the wall, my steps mark a perimeter
of solid rock, more than a line of trespass
the river whose names sit on the bottom like the eyes of a fish
at the utmost reach, thick with vines and unwilling
to acquiesce, and leave a clearer space for our walk

2.

You wake me, put me to work, take me home
and feed me from your pot of ox tails —
eating from a pot is something I wanted to do
a cast iron thing squatting in mud, and here it is finally
the eye connected to the mouth, my mouth
not of the great-house but of the small, not of the ship
but of windows where the light, once admitted,
cracks with surfeit of itself
a pause, a frame of white wood onto the yard

"Today opens and closes
never moves and never stops."

A spit of land on which the words break
and beneath it, the weed patch we walk in
pass and bewilder two sentinel owls in the branches
and make our own way to the clearing

we stand at the edge of the circle
and look at the cost of being outside the circle
the dead bat, old machinery in the grass, a coil of rope
put on a shelf, a handkerchief like sea, and queues

of workers and mules loaded with wealth
destined for the port —
hard to classify this much labour

what's more, all of this ended long ago
the circle gets big with too much, too many allegories
and the factory still wired for electric light
and burnt crops still burning beside the reservoir
till only the stupid whap of the sea
is audible

    3.
The blaze of gun with its teeth of fire
a play ring scratched in the dirt

opens to a funnel as it defines
the exit and fracas of the hour

    the mixing and the power
    the power and the swift

a flash of light on its wing won't answer to the black
and then it vanishes, the bird is ended

storm cloud begins with the homily
to bare signs in a clinch of fire
a dwelling across a ditch never can be finished
see the bodies are coming
swaying
see the caravans of purpose
serial headlines that pour out their grief
how else to say "sun"

the beach house porous in the night wind
and to think of this as part of our speech

take us over the ford, a boy asks the keeper of gaps
of crossing, with rough seas, and wind

4.

If a truck comes with soldiers or melons
with one road in and out

one
one

some of them are dancing in a blaze
of double-vowel cities
some sprawl at the door-step
some wear a head-tie of pitch and kerosene
a match struck in a fight
some live where the bees come
to map spaces for standing
or windows onto wind

I seem to see a ceremony of drum
and catch at my own head feeling the drizzle
of liquid down the throat, over my legs
one invigorated morning

I heard it said that this is to be our legacy
these spaces in our head
a forked wheel from a wagon
hitched to a wagon and a mule to haul them both
over the backs of workers in pottery
these are your gifts to me
songs that the young boys drop
like weighted fish-line to the foot of the tree
names are blossoms falling in a circle

and so we come out to the patio
morning glory bush, ixora, cup of gold, jacaranda
everywhere the backs of grasses with some thing to keep

5.

The smoke continued from the killing fields, the noises
were days in advance of the profitable refugees
some were forced to drink piss from a sky hung crowded with silver
they filled up their palms, they turned savage, they protected the routes

everyone arriving at the coast, in time to ship out
— nothing was certain

we had license to speak the words *ganja* and *physis,* to drink rum
to dismiss the notions we didn't invent or put into speech
the Latin heart of the Law, a post of sentries
scattered on the islands, brought in and left —
some others went back to the east

this month, when the sea soft, under an eyelash of palm tree

there was dancing:
puffs of smoke where the ginko tree grows high
in a dark place with a multitude of leaf
a celebration or heaps of the black

   6.
Out on the water

out of the salt with the driftwood piling up
the fascinating dream ends, and a storm cloud
comes to our thatched house
looking for its rest — a tray of coffee for the master? —
I go out to meet them, a single mind
peering at creases made by sun and furious wind
and coax them into birds of meaning
which say, "Come back to me
I have a house close to the beach — I have blueprints for a skiff —
and this sea is a text, to be shared by more than one"
and stopped there as the rain began, our syllables

went over the sea wall
chills up our sleeves told us of the far-off mass
the blast of it, and sun mixed in
— we couldn't get back

And so I found myself, that morning,
sitting with my legs twined up in a body of feathers,
blank-chested, mystified, smelling of old sweat, pronouncing
words with sand in them, awake to the width of the basin,

315

there was a level sea and a wedding of continents,
other things to say to each other

a village with a few seeds left
fertilizer, telegram, logs for the kiln
the cool of the bottle on our tongues

From Palm of Darkness
*M*ayra *M*ontero

— Translated from Spanish by Edith Grossman

BLUE SHEEP

A TIBETAN ASTROLOGER told Martha I would die by fire.

I thought of it as soon as Thierry began talking about the feasts of his childhood. It was a gratuitous association, since he was really trying to tell me the name of a fruit he had tasted only once in his life, when he was still a little boy and had suffered an attack of what I think was malaria, and to comfort him his father brought this rare treat to his bed. From the description I assumed it was a pear. Thierry chuckled quietly: that fruit reminded him of a young girl's flesh, and he had never again held anything like it between his lips.

We were lying in the underbrush and I let him talk a while. It's impossible to keep a man like Thierry quiet for long. We had just recorded the voice of a superb specimen, a tiny frog with a blue abdomen that lets itself be seen only one week during the year, and I was thinking that the joy of having captured the sound helped me to be tolerant. Perhaps it was joy and not the story about the pear that forced me to think of death, *my death*, and what Martha had been told in Dharamsala. "He said my husband would be burned to death"— I could hear her voice, furious because I had suggested there must have been some misunderstanding — "and as far as I know, you're the only husband I have."

Thierry was still waxing nostalgic about how well you could eat in Jérémie thirty or forty years ago, and I concluded it was pretty ironic for anyone to prophesy that kind of death for me, considering how much time I spent submerged in ponds and lagoons, drenched by downpours in the swamp, crawling along riverbanks, my mouth full of mud and my eyelids rimmed with mosquitoes. I said as much to Martha.

"That's no guarantee," she replied, happy to contradict me. "A

317

person can burn to death in an airplane, a hotel room, even on a boat, you know, when you're right on the water . . ."

Martha brought the coat home from Dharamsala. It was a gift from Barbara, the friend who made the trip with her. It was too coarse for my taste, but she claimed it was made from the wool of the blue sheep, and had I ever heard of that sheep? It was the favorite meal of the snow leopard. I stared at her and she returned my gaze: the coat was the best proof that Martha herself had become Barbara's favorite meal.

When you're in a profession like mine, it's very easy to catch certain signals, identify certain odors, recognize the movements that announce imminent *amplexus* (the term used for sexual embrace between frogs). Martha refused to have me go with her on that trip — years before, when we were first married, we often talked about traveling to India someday — but she didn't say it like that, she calculated first and said it with even greater cruelty, if that's possible: since I had to fly to Nashville for my conference — she said "your conference" — she'd take off a couple of weeks and travel with her best friend. She avoided mentioning the place they'd be going to, and I went along with it, swearing to myself I wouldn't ask a single question, and gradually my suspicions were confirmed: by the brochures that suddenly appeared in the house, by a couple of books on the Hindustanic Plate — Barbara is a geologist — and finally by the plane tickets. Martha kept them in her briefcase, then one night decided to take them out and leave them on the big table in the study; she obviously intended for me to find them there, look at them without saying a word and understand. One needs a lot of understanding.

Thierry often says that the bad thing isn't if a man feels afraid to die, the really bad thing is if a man never thinks about death at all. He doesn't say it in those words, he uses other words, probably better ones. Thierry's eloquence is solemn, profound, almost biblical. When Martha returned, much later than planned, she brought back the blue sheep coat as if it were a trophy, along with a smoldering certainty about the kind of death awaiting me in my present life — she emphasized the phrase "your present life." Then I realized that during the whole time we had been separated, the possibility that she was somehow leaving me had never entered my mind. Just to be polite, she asked about the response to my paper, but I didn't have a chance to answer, there was an interruption, a telephone call for her, she talked briefly and came back, even felt obliged to try a second time: how did it go in Nashville?

The idea for this expedition had, in fact, surfaced in Nashville, but I didn't tell her so. A few hours before I was due to leave for home, I received a dinner invitation, a white card with an engraved drawing of a small gray frog: Professor Vaughan Patterson, the eminent Australian herpetologist, would expect me at eight at the Mère Bulles restaurant, and would I please be punctual.

I was so flattered that I did something extraordinary: I rummaged through my suitcase to see if I had a clean shirt and jacket. At seven sharp I walked out of the hotel and started down Commerce Street, which leads directly to Second Avenue right across from the restaurant. It was a short distance, it wouldn't take me more than fifteen or twenty minutes, but I wanted to be there before Patterson arrived. He was known as an impatient man with a short temper and sheer contempt for colleagues who talked to him about anything but amphibians. Yet all of them would have fought for the privilege of sitting at his table. Patterson was the greatest living authority on everything having to do with the African anurans; his work with the Tasmanian axolotl was legendary, and he boasted of keeping alive, when the species was already considered extinct, the last specimen of *Taudactylus diurnus*, sole survivor of the colony that he himself had bred in his laboratory in Adelaide.

When I walked into the restaurant, forty minutes early, Patterson was already there. He smiled timidly, you might almost say sadly, congratulated me on my paper and offered me a seat beside him. I noticed that he had skin like cellophane, and frail, small, rather stiff hands. With one of them he began to draw on his napkin, I watched him become engrossed in sketching a frog, he didn't even look up when the waiter brought his drink. *Eleutherodactylus sanguineus* he wrote in small letters when he was finished, framing the name between the animal's paws. He handed me the drawing.

"Help me look for it," he whispered. "If there are any left they're on the Mont des Infants Perdus in Haiti."

Then he fell silent and began to look at the river. From the windows of the Mère Bulles you can see the waters of the Cumberland River and, from time to time, a nostalgic steamboat. One of them, called the *Belle Carol*, sailed past just then. I was so astonished that I deliberately concentrated on the drawing. Patterson became aware of this and took back the napkin.

"I don't have the time or the health to search for it," he murmured. "Did you hear that I have leukemia?"

Patterson folded the napkin and patted his lips, ruining the sketch, of course. Then he made his offer: if I agreed to undertake the expedition in the fall, the biology department at his university would cover all the costs. And as soon as I brought him a specimen of *Eleutherodactylus sanguineus* ("I'll settle for one") they would grant me a two-year fellowship for research on the subject of my choice, anywhere I wanted to go. It went without saying, he emphasized, that he expected an immediate reply.

At this point I ought to mention that Martha is a very suspicious woman, her profession also allows her to detect the smallest, most fleeting sign of instability or danger. She slowly realized that something significant had happened in Nashville, perhaps something having to do with my paper, and the danger lay in my not telling her about it.

From then on her interest stopped being merely polite and took on all the ferocity of a siege: she questioned me about every detail of the conference, about the other speakers and the subjects under discussion; she tried to find out if something important had been said, an unexpected announcement, one of those bombs that are suddenly dropped in the middle of a paper and leave everyone speechless. Did I remember the time Corben seemed so circumspect and then came out with his findings on the incubation of *Rheobatrachus silus*?

Of course I remembered. Martha was capable of resorting to any kind of trick to get the secret out of me. She knew the allusion to Corben touched certain coiled springs of memory, memory and rivalry, things that are sometimes confused in the heart of a frog hunter, a researcher who wants to get there first, get in the first shot, before anybody else. She was trying to find out what had happened in Nashville, and to do that she would play dirty, root through my jealousies, search out my petty disappointments and failures. Corben was a genius who had been lucky.

On the other hand, her interest obviously did not come as a complete surprise to me: Martha was also what you could call a woman of science. We had already chosen different fields before we were married; she had decided on marine biology. "Instead of a division of property," she would say to her friends, "Victor and I are making a division of fauna." But she always kept up with my work, and was a meticulous collaborator from the time I began to accumulate data regarding the disappearances.

At first we avoided calling it by that name and used less violent words: "decline" was my favorite, amphibian populations were "declining"; entire colonies of healthy toads went into permanent hiding; the same frogs we had grown tired of hearing only a season earlier fell silent and became rare; they sickened and died, or simply fled, no one could explain where or why.

But her questions about what had happened in Nashville revealed a different kind of interest, a perverse delight in trivial details that went beyond simple scientific curiosity. Of course I didn't mention my meeting with Patterson, she was the one who asked if I had seen the Australian. I was careful to ask which Australian she meant, which of the dozens of herpetologists who had come from Melbourne, Sidney, Canberra. Yet it made no sense to carry it too far. I had to be aware that the Australian, the only possible Australian she was interested in, was the venerated Vaughan Patterson.

Two months later she accidentally learned about the upcoming expedition. The professor who was going to replace me at the laboratory called to give me some information about another Haitian species that hadn't been seen for many years. Martha wrote down the name of the frog: *Eleutherodactylus lamprotes,* carefully noted all the data and typed them on a small card. Across the bottom she wrote in longhand: "Don't you think Haiti is a dangerous place for field trips?"

I copied the information for my files and gave her back the card with another sentence written below hers: "Your astrologer already said I would die over a slow fire somewhere in the world."

*

Between 1974 and 1982, the toad *Bufo boreas boreas,* better known as the Western Toad, disappeared from the Colorado mountains and from almost all its other American habitats.

According to studies carried out by Dr. Cynthia Carey, professor of biology at the University of Colorado, the cause of its disappearance was a massive infection attributed to the bacteria *Aeromonas hidrophila.* The infection produces acute hemorrhaging, especially in the legs, which take on a reddish coloring, giving rise to the name of the disease: Red-Leg Disease.

A healthy toad should not succumb to an *Aeromonas* infection.

But in the case of *Bufo boreas boreas,* there was a failure of the immune system.

The cause of the failure is not yet known.

BOMBARDOPOLIS

My father never called me by name. What you love you respect, he said, and there is no need to name what you love.

He learned this from his father, who did not call him by name either. It was an ancient custom, something that came with the first man, with the first father of a father of my father who came to this land from Guinea.

My father was named Thierry, like me, and he had a very difficult job, the most difficult one ever known: he was a hunter, he was what they call a *pwazon rat,* that is what those hunters were called.

My mother, whose name was Claudine, had her hands full taking care of us, her five children. We lived in Jérémie, not right in the city but in a shantytown near the port. We learned to swim there, that was where we learned to fish. Haiti was a different place in those days. The sea too was wider, or deeper, or more loved by the fish, and from that sea we took our food, white-fleshed fish with short spines that brought joy to the entire family. We also had a pen for pigs, the kind they call brown devil pigs, and when a litter was born we feasted in our house. One suckling was set aside and sacrificed to the Baron. My mother was a devotee of Baron-la-Croix, and my father had to be one too because of his profession.

You want to know where the frogs go. I cannot say, Sir, but let me ask you a question: where did our fish go? Almost all of them left this sea, and in the forest the wild pigs disappeared, and the migratory ducks, and even the iguanas for eating, they went too. Just take a look at what's left of humans, take a careful look: you can see the bones pushing out under their skins as if they wanted to escape, to leave behind that weak flesh where they are so battered and go into hiding someplace else.

At times I think, but keep it to myself, I think that one day a man like you will come here, someone who crosses the ocean to look for a couple of frogs, and when I say frogs I mean any creature, and he will only find a great hill of bones on the shore, a hill higher than the peak of Tête Boeuf. Then he will say to himself, "Haiti is finished, God Almighty, those bones are all that remain."

On Sundays Papa would bring us sweets. He bought them at a drugstore that used to be in Jérémie, a place filled with odds and ends and smells, it was called Pharmacie du Bord de Mer and sold more candy than medicine, nobody took medicine in those days. The owner was a skinny man with sunken eyes, and ears that faced forward like a sick dog's, and a tiny, fleshy mouth, a mouth like a chicken's ass that never opened even to say good morning. He inherited the drugstore from his mother, who was scalded to death in syrup. This happened before I was born, but I know that everybody in Jérémie mourned her, brought candles and drums to the funeral, took down the *loas*, the fire spirits, and the mourning lasted many days.

This is how the accident happened: a woman who worked for Madame Christine, for that was the owner's name, was walking back and forth carrying sacks of bottles, and she happened to trip on one of them, tried to steady herself on the edge of the stove, but instead she grabbed onto the big pot where that day's syrups were cooking. Madame Christine was squatting next to the stove, pouring some milk for her cat. They were both bathed in disaster: she did not move, she was cooked on the spot, she didn't even drop the pitcher of milk that must have boiled in the heat; the cat ran off to die in the underbrush.

The first time they told me that story I was very little, but the first thing I asked was what had happened to the woman carrying the sack of bottles. That's a defect of mine when people tell me something: I always keep track of the ones in the background, the ones who disappear for no reason, the forgotten ones. Everybody talked about Madame Christine and her kitty, but let me see, whatever happened to the woman who worked for her? Did she fall down too and burn her back? Did she get up and run after the cat, or did she slowly creep over to her dead employer, take the pitcher from her hands and blow on the milk to separate the cream?

My older brother was named Jean Pierre, and he was born a little lame. In fact we were born together, we were twins, but the midwife took Jean Pierre out first and was in such a hurry she hurt one of his ankles. A year later Yoyotte came into the world, the only girl my mother had, and they gave her that name in honor of her godmother, who was a cook from Bombardopolis, a town up north where my father used to spend a lot of time. A little while later my brother Etienne was born, and it wasn't until many more years had gone by that Paul, our youngest brother, finally made his appearance.

When my sister's godmother came to see us, we had the feasts I told you about. My father invited his brothers; my mother invited her female cousins, because her brothers and sisters were all dead; and the cousins brought their own children, who were our age, and the house filled with music and dancing and shouting, and Yoyotte Placide, the most famous cook in Bombardopolis, began to sing and beat egg whites for merengues. I still remember her song:

> *Solèy, ò, Moin pa moun isit o, solèy,*
> *Moin sé nég ginin, solèy,*
> *M'pa kab travèsé, solèy,*
> *Min batiman-m chaviré, solèy.*

It was a very sad song: "Oh, Sun, I'm not from here, Sun, I was born in Guinea and can never go back, oh, Sun, my boat sank," but she sang it as if it were the most joyful thing. Yoyotte Placide always said there was no way to make a good merengue if you didn't sing to the yolks that had been left behind, saved for the omelette. You had to keep the rooster's seed happy, then she showed us a red dot in the middle of the yolk: that's where the song went in, that's where the order came back for the whites, mixed together in a separate bowl, to let themselves be whipped into foam: that's how you made merengue.

My father's brothers drank the rum called Barbancourt, and from time to time my mother's cousins raised the bottle too. One of them, named Frou-Frou, lifted her skirt and began to dance. My mother scolded her but she paid no attention, we children sat on the floor facing her and applauded when Frou-Frou twirled around. My father applauded too, sometimes he would dance with her, he grabbed her by the waist and they spun around together, but then my mother would come out of the kitchen and separate them, and we children would applaud some more because by then Frou-Frou's blouse had opened and suddenly out popped her two breasts, so big and lightskinned. The other cousins came running to stop my

BUSINESS REPLY MAIL

FIRST CLASS MAIL   PERMIT NO. 1 ANNANDALE-ON-HUDSON, NY

POSTAGE WILL BE PAID BY ADDRESSEE

CONJUNCTIONS

Bard College

Annandale-on-Hudson

P.O. Box 9911

Red Hook, NY 12571-9911

NO POSTAGE
NECESSARY
IF MAILED
IN THE
UNITED STATES

CONJUNCTIONS Give a subscription to yourself and a friend!

Your subscription:

Gift subscription (with a gift card from you enclosed):

Name _____

Name _____

Address _____

Address _____

City _____

City _____

State _____ Zip _____

State _____ Zip _____

☐ One year (2 issues) **$18**

☐ One year (2 issues) **$18**

☐ Two years (4 issues) **$32**

☐ Two years (4 issues) **$32**

☐ Renewal ☐ New order

☐ Renewal ☐ New order

All foreign and institutional orders $25 per year, payable in U.S. funds.

☐ Payment enclosed ☐ Bill me   Charge my: ☐ Mastercard ☐ Visa

Account number _____ Expiration date _____

Signature _____

mother from hitting her, and Frou-Frou fell down, she lay on the floor on her back and began to moan, then we saw something jump around in her stomach and go down to her belly and we children thought she had eaten a toad — excuse me, I know you don't like jokes about those creatures — and the women held her down and shook her a little to keep her from taking off all her clothes.

My father would get angry because he hated for my mother to scold him in front of his brothers, he left the house in a rage and walked around for a while looking at the ocean and swallowing mouthfuls of rum. After a while Frou-Frou began to calm down, she had a little girl named Carmelite who put cold cloths on her forehead and helped her comb her hair. My mother swore she would never invite her to our house again, but the months would go by and when my sister's godmother sent word that she was coming, everything was forgotten and Frou-Frou arrived for the feast.

As time passed, she stopped putting on a show, we children would ask her to dance and she would shake her head and smile. Instead she would go to peel vegetables by the pigpens, she would toss the parings to the brown devil pigs and grow dreamy as she watched them eat.

Yoyotte, my sister, wanted to be a cook just like her godmother and set up a business in Jérémie like the one the other Yoyotte had in Bombardopolis. Yoyotte Placide was not opposed to her goddaughter learning the trade, but instead of opening a business in Jérémie, she encouraged her to come to Bombardopolis and help at her own foodstand. "Sooner or later it will be yours," she would say, because Yoyotte Placide had no children and was too old by then to ever have any.

All of this was talked about at the table while we ate our fish soup, and my mother fumed because she didn't want them to take her only daughter away to Bombardopolis. Nobody wants to lose her little girl, she would say, who would take care of her and her husband later on? My brother Etienne, who was a very sweet-natured boy, put down his spoon and promised that he would take care of them both. Jean Pierre, my older brother, burst out laughing and called him a faggot, my mother finally gave vent to her feelings and smacked each of us, even me, though I hadn't said anything, while she glared at Yoyotte's godmother with hatred. Sometimes the discussion grew heated and my father would stand up, kick away his chair and bite his lips, a sign that at any moment he would put an end to the feast. Since nobody wanted that to happen, we were all quiet except Frou-Frou, who walked in and out of the kitchen chirping like a little bird, asking my father if he'd like more squash, or asking my mother if it was time to serve the dessert, which was almost always papaya in syrup or pan sugar with guava.

One afternoon during Holy Week, while we were still sitting at the table, Frou-Frou went out to the pen to feed scraps to the pigs, and her little girl Carmelite announced that soon she would have a brother, just like we did. The other women made a great fuss, and my mother barely managed to bring her hands up to her chest. My father's brothers stood to ask him if it was true, then they began to laugh and embrace him, patting him on the back to congratulate him. My father laughed too, but in a very strange way, with his eyes fixed on Yoyotte Placide, his cook from Bombardopolis, who had lowered her head and looked grief-stricken.

Frou-Frou never came back to our house. My mother invited her, but Yoyotte Placide threatened to scratch out her eyes if she ever saw her again. And no one dared to doubt Yoyotte Placide's threats, much less defy her orders: she was the one who brought the food, she was the one who cooked it, without Yoyotte Placide there was no party and my father and mother both knew it. But Carmelite, Frou-Frou's daughter, still came by. My mother, who was a fair woman when she wasn't angry, told us all that the little girl was not to blame for what her lunatic mother did, and she invited her, like always, and treated her the same, or almost the same, except she never allowed her to speak of the baby that was on the way.

The last feast I remember was a farewell banquet for my sister. She had just turned eleven, and following the wishes of her godmother, she was going to live in Bombardopolis to learn the trade and work at the foodstand that would one day be hers. My mother cried all night, but then she became very happy at the table, especially when she saw Carmelite carrying in her little brother so we all could meet him. My father told Jean Pierre and me, because we were the oldest, that the infant was also our brother and would be living with us from now on.

When Yoyotte Placide finally left for Bombardopolis with her goddaughter, my father ran over to Carmelite, snatched the baby out of her arms and put him down on my sister's bed, which was now free. Carmelite didn't seem very sad, just the opposite, she told Jean Pierre and me that the child cried too much and it was a relief to give him away.

Later we found out it had all been arranged before the feast. My mother began to care for the infant as if he was her own, though Frou-Frou came by from time to time and helped her wash diapers and prepare his pap.

They named the boy Julien, but my father never called him by name.

PEOPLE WITHOUT FACES

I tried to maintain a cordial tone. Writing that first letter to Martha, after everything that had happened between us, required a dual effort entailing caution on the one hand, boldness on the other. I told her about the sudden end to our expedition on the Mont des Enfants Perdus, including the theft of my field tent. I told the story in a rather cold, objective way, as if it had happened to someone else. I also told her about Thierry, and about his father who had been a hunter. I didn't mention what it was he hunted for.

Although I hadn't found a single trace of *Eleutherodactylus sanguineus,* I assured her that in a couple of weeks I'd try again on the same mountain, and in the meanwhile I would stay in Port-au-Prince and use the time to locate the only Haitian who had become seriously interested in declining populations, someone who was not even a herpetologist but a physician, a surgeon named Emile Boukaka.

I avoided talking about the city. I told her that the pool at the Oloffson was empty, that it was cleaned occasionally. Two men in shorts would jump in and sweep up the dry leaves, palm fronds, the half-rotten fruit, some scraps of paper, and stuff it all into plastic bags, then climb up the ladder, drenched in perspiration that ran down their backs as if they were really coming out of water. Then a handful of guests would lie on lounge chairs and read the French newspapers that arrived three or four days late.

And I didn't mention the dead bodies, I assumed Martha knew about them through the press. There was always a small swarm of photographers on the streets of Port-au-Prince, and every morning I saw them milling around the bodies. The corpses, generally young men, were found everywhere, but one morning the body of a woman showed up almost at the doors of the hotel. I went over to look with the rest of the curious crowd, I couldn't see her face, she was lying on her stomach, and then I realized her hands were gone. I had no idea that the corpse of a woman missing both hands could make so strong an impression on me: I felt nauseated, and closed my eyes.

My letter to Martha ended with several requests. In the same envelope I included some papers and memos for my colleagues; there was also a report for Vaughan Patterson, written in longhand, and I asked her if she would have time to type it.

My next move was to inform the embassy that I would be in Haiti indefinitely, and to ask them if they could include my correspondence in the diplomatic pouch. It was not just any correspondence, after all, but documents, notes and photographs addressed to laboratories and universities.

That afternoon, as I was about to go out, a hotel employee stopped me in the lobby: some people were waiting to see me, he said, and pointed at two men in uniform who had stationed themselves in different locations; when they saw me they began to move in my direction. They identified themselves as police and asked for my passport. They stank of sweat. One of them had a broken nose, his upper lip had also been cut and the swelling reached all the way to his right cheek, and his right eye was swollen too; he was the one who did the talking. He wanted to know how long I planned to stay in Port-au-Prince.

My impulse was to be pleasant, I asked them to sit down, but they shook their heads and remained standing, waiting.

"I'm a biologist," I said finally, "and I'm looking for a certain frog, not here, but on the Mont des Enfants Perdus."

I took a small sheet of paper from my pocket: it was the little frog I had sketched for Thierry at our first meeting. I didn't even use the scientific name, I called it the *grenouille du sang*, there it was, that was the only thing I was interested in.

"I have a permit from the foreign office," I added.

One passed the drawing to the other, and I realized they were scarcely looking at it. Still, they soiled the edges, I could see dirty fingerprints on the onionskin, black, perfect fingerprints. "Those permits aren't valid anymore," the one with the broken nose said abruptly. "All permits were cancelled in September."

The other one handed back the drawing.

"You can't stay longer than thirty days."

They bit off their words when they spoke, and it occurred to me they might be impostors. I was about to ask them to show me their papers again, I had only seen a couple of wrinkled, damp-looking cards, I hadn't even checked the photographs. I stopped myself just in time, but I suppose my attitude must have changed.

"I plan to stay about three months," I said.

"No longer than thirty days," the man repeated, and he handed me a paper as dirty as the edges of my picture: it was a subpoena.

"Bring your passport," he added, "and that permit from the foreign office."

I read the paper and folded it along with the drawing, turned and walked slowly toward the door; the two men stayed where they were, watching me move away, I walked faster and went out onto the smoke-filled streets. For a variety of reasons there was always dense smoke on the streets of Port-au-Prince; if they weren't burning piles of trash they burned old furniture or tires, sometimes the bodies of dead animals were set on fire. That afternoon it was a burro, and I had the strange impression that the animal was moving its legs while it burned. I stopped to watch, a boy standing beside me laughed, a woman passed and shouted a few words at him that I couldn't understand, they were harsh words, then the legs stopped moving and I continued on my way.

At the embassy I had to fill out a form that asked for my personal data, the reason for my presence in Haiti and the person to be notified in case of sickness or death. I hesitated before writing down Martha's name, and beneath it I added my father's. The official who took care of me asked if I had a definite itinerary and I told him no, that my work depended on a series of expeditions, and they depended in turn on other factors such as rain, clouds, fog and even the phases of the moon. When the moon was full, anurans were much less active and possibly went into hiding, which was the reason so many expeditions failed.

The man listened attentively but refused to accept my correspondence, he first had to find out if it could be sent by pouch. In any event, he would have to fill out some other papers and suggested I call the next day when he could give me a definitive answer. I left the embassy, and when I was on the street I checked in my wallet for the address of the Haitian professor who had recommended Thierry, I wanted to ask him for the name of another guide. I thought I would tell him what had happened, some people just don't have the right chemistry and Thierry and I hadn't taken to each other. It would be difficult for me to work with him again after what had occurred on the first expedition.

I asked a passerby how to get to the address on the card. He told me it was some distance away, and I thought the best thing was to go back to the hotel and drive there in my car, the same Renault I had used to travel to the Mont des Enfants Perdus. One of the hotel employees who washed it had advised me to fill the tank; you never knew when gasoline would be unavailable.

I walked a few blocks and was back in the middle of a cloud of smoke, this time I couldn't tell the source but guessed it was an animal again. I decided to take another street, and when I turned the corner I felt my arm being pulled, I thought it was a peddler, I tried to shake loose, and that's when I was hit the first time, near my eyes, almost at the temple; the second punch landed right in my stomach. I fell down, tried to get up, but then I was kicked in the side, so hard I was afraid I'd been stabbed.

Two men held me down, somebody put his boot on my shoulder, a black, unpolished boot. Out of the corner of my eye I saw his other boot, and I saw two more boots, I thought they would kick me again, then I felt the tug, my hand was still holding the envelope with my correspondence, a large padded envelope addressed to Martha. I tried to hold on to it and discovered that my fingers still responded, I tried to call for help, they pulled harder, another kick, and I passed out.

I believe I came to right away, because I was still sprawled in the middle of the sidewalk and people were standing around me. Then I thought of the corpses at dawn. Somebody helped me up, but no one was brave enough to ask if I was all right or needed assistance. My left eye hurt and I could barely open it, my face burned and I had trouble breathing. I walked the rest of the way to the hotel, holding myself up against the walls of buildings, but in the lobby I collapsed and two employees came to help me, I asked them to take me to my room and call a doctor. A third person came up behind me and tried to support my head: it was Thierry.

That night he stayed with me. The ice packs that the doctor prescribed for my eye had to be changed constantly, there was the possibility of a broken rib and the slightest movement was painful, but even so I refused to go to a hospital. Every four hours I had to take two pills; Thierry placed them in the palm of my hand and I swallowed with difficulty, washing them down with some kind of warm infusion that he had prepared and brought in a thermos.

The pain grew worse in the middle of the night, I complained and Thierry attempted to comfort me: "Wait till dawn. Daybreak brings relief."

Neither of us slept that night; I nodded off, sometimes I was delirious, I had no fever but the sedatives gave me a feeling of unreality, it seemed to me that other people were walking in and out of the room, people without faces who came out of nothingness and dissolved back into nothingness.

Thierry was right: at first light my eye grew numb, the pain in my ribs eased, I fell into a deeper sleep and dreamed that my mother was trying to sketch the *grenouille du sang* and I was beside her, showing her the exact color she had to use.

The sound of voices woke me, and I could see with my good eye that a waiter was bringing in a breakfast tray. The doctor who had treated me the night before was also there, doing something to my left arm, he said good morning and asked if I was feeling better. I didn't answer right away, and he said my blood pressure was still very high.

"Perhaps it's due to the shock," he declared. "Do you want us to notify anyone?"

I shook my head, closed what was, for the moment, the one eye at my disposal — the other had been bandaged — and tried to remember the dream about my mother. I had the feeling that perhaps at this very moment, so many miles away, she was working on the only decent oil painting of her life: a little red frog looking out at the world from its bed of lilies. Variegated brown lilies, that's what they had to be.

After breakfast I felt more energetic, I mentioned taking a shower and the doctor recommended waiting until the next day, prescribed more pills and then Thierry walked with him to the door. When he came back, he stopped to look out the window.

"They're still there," he said.

I realized I had lost the letter to Martha, the notes for my colleagues and the report for Vaughan Patterson. A handwritten report documented with drawings and tapes recorded in the field.

Thierry closed the curtains and the room darkened.

331

The Sleeping Zemis
Lorna Goodison

He kept the zemis under his bed for years.
One day he came upon them in a cave
which resembled the head of a great stone god
the zemis placed like weights at the tip of its tongue.

Arawaks had hidden them there when they fled,
or maybe the stone god's head was really a temple.
Now under his bed slept three zemis,
wrought from enduring wood of ebony.

The first was a man god who stood erect, his arms
folded below his belly. The second was a bird god
in flight. The third was fashioned in the form
of a spade, in the handle a face was carved.

A planting of the crops zemi,
a god for the blessing of the corn,
for the digging of the sweet cassava
which requires good science

to render its roots safe food.
And over the fields the john crows wheel
and the women wait for the fishermen
to return to sea in boats hollowed from trees.

Under his bed the zemis slept.
Where were they when Columbus
and his men, goldfever and quicksilver
on the brain, came visiting destruction?

Man god we gave them meat, fish and cassava.
Silent deity we mended their sails, their leaking
ships, their endless needs we filled even with
our own lives, our own deaths.

Bird god we flew to the hills,
their tin bells tolling the deaths
of our children, their mirrors
foreshadowing annihilation to follow.

Spade god we perished.
Our spirits wander wild and restless.
There was no one left to dig our graves,
no guides to point us the way to Coyaba.

He turned them over to the keepers of history,
they housed them in glass-sided caves.
Then he went home to sleep without the gods
who had slumbered under his bed for years.

A World of Canes

Robert Antoni

WE BEGIN WITH love? Doudou, I ain't know what we begin with. What you call that? *Bullying.* You call that bullying. We begin with bullying, meet up with little love. Maybe little bit. Una could suppose.

I could remember the first time. I did had but thirteen years then, and Berry, he did had about sixteen. Thirteen and sixteen, two children, nothing more. We wasn't nothing more than two children then. I did just finish at the elementary school. I got to look for work now. I can't go at high school, ain't got nobody to send me at high school. Buy me books and different things. I got to look for work. So my grandmother, she arrange for me to go by a woman does do needleworks. I go by this woman to learn the needleworks from she, Mistress Bethel. But to get from Sherman to Mistress Bethel house now, I got to pass crossroads, you know, got to pass *he* house, where he living, this Berry. Well that ain't nothing. Ain't nothing in that. I ain't fraid for the man, I ain't thinking nothing about the man. I just keeping to myself, go long about my business. My grandmother, she buy couple dresses for me, you know, to go at needleworks, I press them and I make them neat and thing. So I walking, my little bag, my clasp and my ear-ring. Looking pretty, real pretty now, and I pass this Berry sitting relaxing pon he gallery. Big wide porch front the house. Well this Berry stand up and he watch at me, you know, ogle me every time whilst I pass. I was thinking, *What this man watching at you for? What he watching at you for like that?* But he ain't tell me nothing, and I ain't saying nothing to he neither.

Then one time I had to go up crossroads in the night, there where he was living. I had to go up with a cousin of mine to meet with she friend. She friend uses to work at this shop, grocery shop, selling groceries. This shop close at seven o'clock, you know seven o'clock *dark.* This girl *fraid* to walk home by sheself come seven o'clock. So we gone to meet with she, you know, keep she with company. We leave home about six, six o'clock come already you can't *see* you hand front you face. So we gone over. We making plenty noise, bunch of we walking together must be about five-six, we going over to bring my cousin friend. You know must be two-three miles from Sherman to crossroads, but all is canes. Canes canes and more canes. That place. And so dark. So we got to pass by this man house, coming *and* going.

When we get there now, when we approaching this Berry house, you know he got a lot of little pups. Lot of little pups. Like he had a slut-dog or something, uses to got pups all the time. And he just keep the pups, raise up the pups. But anyway, he must be had about a dozen pups. We did frighten enough for them dogs, oh yes, but long as he there, you would think, *Well he would call them back. If he there he would call them back, them dogs ain't going be out in the road.* Well anyway you more scared of he than the dogs. You prefer the dogs to he! Cause you could ring a rock in the dogs, you could do that, but you couldn't ring a rock in *he.* He more dangerous than the dogs! So we approaching now, little before where the house is. I see he light on, I say, cause we uses to call he *the beast,* that's the name we did call he by. I say, "The beast, the beast light *on.*" So we, we shut we mouth now, easy, we passing to this side he living to this side, you know how *frighten* we is for he? Oh, yes! And he there *a-waiting.* The beast there a-waiting we.

We going quiet now we tipping, we tipping so silent them dogs can't even hear. All in a sudden I feel somebody grab on me, my arm, grab my arm tight tight. I say, *"Wha?"* When I look, is the beast-*self* grab me. I say to myself, *Oh my Jesus what this man want with you now? What he going do with you now?* He make the rest a sign like that, he fist in the air. You know, go-long! get! So they all gone a-running. They take-off! Gone a-running and left me, poor me, left me there with this beast, this trap-man. I say, *My sweet Jesus don't let this man kill me! Don't let this man murder me tonight!* I say, and I talking up aloud to he now, I say, "What you? What you *want* with me?" He did pushing me forward, shoving me like that, big tall red-man. You know, red-skin negro and tall. He say, "Una walk. Una just walk. Or I going let go *all* these pon una." This time he got he pockets full with bombs, *full.* Cause it was getting to November now, Guy Fawkes time. And you know before Guy Fawkes they does start to selling the rockets, and the starlights, and the bombs and different things. Well we got to settle for little pack of starlights, maybe a bandit, pack of bandit, but this Berry, he got the works. He aunt bring it from town for he. This Berry got he pockets *full* with these bombs. You know the bombs you does hit down? The ones with the flint? When you hit them down that flint hit you all up in you foot. And I did frighten for them things so *bad*, so *harsh!* I say, "What you going do with me? When them children come back, you would let me go home? You would let me go home with them?" Cause I know they had to come back going the next way. He say, "Don't ask me nothing. Don't ask me what I going do with you, you just wait and see." I say, "If you kill me they would find me tomorrow, and them children know you is the body carry me!" I start to wriggle now, wriggle-out, he say, "Don't you wriggle neither. Don't you wriggle neither or you going wriggle in two of these. *In* you backside I going put two of these bombs!" Bombs with the flint, oh my Jesus that thing does hurt so, scorch you all up in you foot.

I just want to get way. I did fraid so bad when them other children leave me, and I just want get home. I say, "What you going do better start doing now, cause it getting late." He say, "Got to do in the patient." I say, *"What!"* He say, "Got to do in the patient now." I say, "You, you wouldn't patient with me already! What you going do, do *now.* And let me go. Cause when them children reach home they would tell my grandmother where I gone, and she would call police pon you!" He say, "I ain't killing nobody." I say, "Look how you got me holding! I ain't give you consent to touch-up me!" He was walking me straight, direction of them canes. So we reach in the dark now, this where the canes start. He say, "Stop." I say, "What you stopping for? You going shoot me?" He say, "You see I got gun?" I say, "I ain't know what you got, nor I ain't *want* to know neither." He say, "You know what I want." I say, "I ain't know what you want, and you better, you better don't *touch* me!" He say, "You done touch already." I say, "Done touch already, but never by no vagabond like you. Never by no beast!"

Cause, doudou, I didn't had much of experience, not much, but I had enough to know sex is the firstest thing they does go for. The firstest thing. I accustom to that already. But truth is, I didn't think that's what Berry did want from me. I didn't think that for minute, not one second. Amount of bright-skin girls going at the high school would give he that? And anyway you don't does fraid for that. You more fraid for he to do you some *meanness,* cut you up beat you. Cause you know them people with money, always want to beat up the poor ones like that. They always doing like that. Berry say now, "You going give me trouble tonight?" I say, "I ain't going to give you no trouble. But if I give you anything, make this the first and the last. Cause me and you ain't no company." He say, "Oh, yes. You very easy to say make it the first and the last. You want to get way." I say, "Yes, I want to get way." He say, "Why you want to get way from me?" I say, "You is no good, you does beat up people, you unfair!"

Well we reach in the canes now. Deep in the deep of them canes. I can't see where I going, just walking in the blind wherever he push me, shove me. I say to myself, *Ain't no cause to fight he. Big tall red-man. Just let he do what he want, then you could go home.* So then, then he stop. He lie me down, lie me down in them canes. You know, things happen, he just do he business and that is that. Wasn't no pain, that terrible pain searing. Wasn't nothing. Nothing to not-like nor like neither. Just what you got to put up with. What you got to bear. And you getting accustom to that already anyway.

So he finish, he get up, I get up, I want run now. But still he holding me, holding my arm. He say, "Where you run and going?" I say, "I going home." He say, "You expecting to go cross that road by youself?" I say, "More happy going by myself than going with you." He say, "After what happen you ain't trust me?" I say, "No. That could happen to anybody. That ain't nothing. That's just something *got* to happen." He say, "You's a stupid woman." Just like that. I say, "Well I like to be stupid." That's all I did answer he, "Well I just like to be stupid."

So we walk. We walk in them canes, he holding my arm. He ain't saying nothing, nor I ain't saying nothing neither, only, "When I get home I going tell my grandmother, that's all." He say, "Well you tell you grandmother and let *all* you cousins hear what you do, then you name going be out in the street. Ain't nobody would bother with me, but they all going talk about *you.*" And that's the truth. Cause you know when a girl do anything like that, when people hear, they call you *nasty.* Oh Lord they does call you so bad! You got to keep that thing in the secret. I say, "But if I don't tell them, if I don't tell nobody, *you* would tell them. You would tell them cause you's a *slut.*" He say, "You ain't got nothing to say to hit me with, who you calling a slut?" I say, "You." Just like that. He say, "When I going see you again?" I say, "You ain't *never* going see me again. Never. Me and you ain't no company." I say, "Why *me?* All we going up crossroads together, other girls there and thing, why me? Why you *picking* pon me? Is cause my family can't, cause we can't come up? Cause we poor?" He say, "It ain't money.

It is people. People. You understand?" I say, "That ain't true you know better than that. You and me ain't no company. And you ain't *never* going see me again." He say, "When you going up crossroads tomorrow, going at needleworks, you stop me from seeing you. Try and stop." I say, "All right, see you tomorrow. Just let me go home, and I would see you tomorrow."

So he left me go now, left my arm go. I run home. I gone. And I ain't tell nobody, not my grandmother nor nobody. I too shame to tell. I *can't* tell. Just like he say, I can't afford for my name to be out in the street. I just go to the pipe for water and I bathe. I bathe and I scrub that piece of soap so hard, wash he out from my skin. Next morning I got to go at needleworks, I play sick. I tell my grandmother something, my belly bad or something. I play sick for two weeks. Cause, doudou, I ain't going back at needleworks for he to hold me again. Mistress Bethel send to ask my grandmother what happen with me, how I just start out and learning the needleworks so good and thing, what happen that I stop so quick? My grandmother say I claim sick, but she ain't know what happen, cause I ain't sick. She did know wasn't nothing wrong with me. Onliest thing is, I can't *tell* she that. How I fraid to go at needleworks cause fraid for this man to hold me again.

I get a job ironing out the clothes with my Uncle Arrows. He father is Mr. Bootman the Panama Man, and Mr. Bootman got he business to wash out the clothes for the sailors. Sailors that come in off the ships. American and English ships. Cause whole lot of American and English ships uses to come in in Corpus Christi then, come in from the war. Mr. Bootman would pick up the nuniforms from off the ships in the harbor, and he bring them back in he car for Arrows to wash them out. So Uncle Arrows would mind the machines turning to wash and dry the clothes, but then he got to iron out the seams. I tell he I could do that. I say, "*Chups!* Arrows, man, I could do that!" Was one of them heater-irons he had, you know, the kind with the coals. So pon my way in the morning I just buy up two pound of coals, light the coals, and when them catch up good, cover it down. Cover that iron down tight tight. Cause it could go a long time like that. That's one them *big* iron I could tell you, with handle, and *heavy*. I could scarce even pick up that thing. Doudou, you know the amount of pants and thing I scorch and had to throw down in the toilet before my uncle miss them, and Mr. Bootman!

So I ain't seeing Berry again. Must be about three-four months.

I ain't going at crossroads so ain't *got* to see he. But this Berry making it he business to come in now, come in by Sherman where I living. He get to know a fellow name of Lewey, this Lewey live facing my grandmother house. So Berry, he would come early pon evenings, you know, cook and different things with Lewey. They playing draughts and thing. Making a racket. But still I ain't had no confrontation with the beast as yet, not since the first time. I didn't even uses to be at home most the time pon evenings.

Cause my grandmother, she uses to go at church regular pon evenings. Church meeting, or choir practice, something so. You know she always doing something in that church. My grandmother go with she boyfriend, Lambert, and I uses to go with them and visit with my cousin whilst they in the church. Cause my cousin living cross from the big Baptist church, and I could visit with she. So when ten o'clock come, and my grandmother and Lambert going home, they call me out from my cousin house, I just run and catch the bike and I go long. Cause Lambert uses to drive bicycle, and he would, you know, put my grandmother to sit pon the front, pon the crossbars, and he riding the pedals and they going long like that.

So I there talking with my cousin, it getting late, past ten now, and I hear, *glerring! glerring!* Lambert pon he bell. My grandmother call, "Time to go home!" I was just waiting to hear she voice, and I bawl, "I coming!" and I run out to catch, you know, hold the fender and running behind. I ain't notice nothing particular, my grandmother sitting pon the crossbar, she wearing she broad-hat that she uses to wear at church, and Lambert driving the pedals. Onliest thing is, they moving a speed tonight, *fast,* but I could run fast too, so I just catch the fender and running behind. Quick now Lambert shift in the dark. Shift in the dark quick quick like that, dark of them canes side the road. I say to myself, *This very strange, that he shifting in the canes! What Lambert going in them canes for!* Because una could suppose maybe my grandmother want to use the toilet, you know, something like that. But una ain't thinking nothing particular, just hold pon that fender and running behind. All in a sudden I notice, I say, *Well my grandmother looking very big tonight. She looking very big and tall tonight.* When Lambert stop, and my granny hold, hold pon my arm tight tight. Doudou, when I look up in my granny face, I see this vagabond. Is Berry *self* dress up ganga! And there driving the bike is he friend Lewey. I say to Berry, "Wait! Is you, you again!" Berry was wearing he own grandmother broad-hat, he had on this wig that he get from some place. He got on earrings, and bracelet, rings pon he fingers. He wearing he grandmother long-dress, oldfashion long-dress with them big pump-sleeves, big apron, so that could fit he like that. Big tall red-man like he, dress up in he grandmother clothes *ganga!*

Well I say to Lewey now, cause I know Lewey he living cross the street from me, I say, "Lewey, man, why you drive this man bike for me to hold on like that? You know I ain't want nothing to do with this beast." Lewey say, "He pay me to do it. He give me money pay me and you know with money, anything goes. You *know* that!" Berry jump off the crossbar now and Lewey gone, was Berry bike Lewey did driving. Lewey gone and he take off like that, left me there with this vagabond. I think to myself, *This man gone and hold you again? You got to go through this thing again?* I say, "I ain't talking with you. Ain't talking with you no matter *what* you do me." He say, "Wait! I go through all this to get to you, dress up myself in ganga, and you ain't going talk with me?" He say, "You think that I would go through all this, and let you go so easy?" This time I thinking, *Well you can't fight with he, big tall man like he, and strong.* I say, "Talk then. Talk then what you want cause I can't fight with you."

So then he talk talk talk. He talk. But I ain't answering he nothing. I ain't speaking a good time. Last I say, "You does bully everybody to talk with you like this?" He say, "No. I don't does bully people." I say, "Well what you doing with me now then? You don't call this bullying? This is bullying, this ain't love." He say, "I does feel something for you." I say, "Well I ain't feel nothing for you. I just feel when I look in you face hatred like I want *kill* you! Or you going kill me!" He say, "You just keep quiet, or let me cuff you in you mouth." I say, "I know you going cuff me in my mouth that's all you could do is cuff." He say, "Why you keep telling me them things? Why you keep telling me them things make me mad, and running from me? Why you keep running from me for?" So I say, "I fraid for you to cuff me." He say, "Not so easy. Not so easy." I say, "What you going do with me now?" He say, "I ain't going do nothing more than I ain't do already." So I say, say like the last time, "Well you just do it quick and let me go. Cause onliest thing I want is to get way from you." He didn't answering nothing to that, and I didn't talking nothing no more neither. He just pushing me walking through them canes, push me deeper in them canes. So now I thinking, *Well look, you could just give up. Cause he so tall, and strong, you can't do nothing to get way from he.* And plus I was thinking, *Well if he could put heself so low, so low as that to dress up heself as woman, dress up heself as ganga, only to get to you, maybe something there? Maybe something there in that?*

Then he lie me down again pon some dead canes, he find someplace soft in them canes for we to lie. Now he start to feeling me up, but not so rough, more gentle this time, and I kind of relax. I say, "Leastest thing you could do is take off that wig. That broad-hat and them earring. You look like a *fool.*" He did embarrassed now, so he take off he ganga-clothes, he start up again. I just relax more into it, don't fight with he too much, and I did start to like it this time. You know, he was feeling me up but gentle, gentle now, and I just go soft inside. Down there. I just go all to waters. Deep blue and purple warm *wistful* waters, and he raise up and he go inside, he, whole of he warm deep inside, and I just melt down soft into it like that. Easy. Not fighting now. And it did feel good this time. And he did know I was liking it too.

When he finish, you know, he laugh and thing, I laugh, I feeling good now. Not so bad. We talk and thing, we laugh little bit, he ain't holding me no more but I ain't running neither. We say, well he ask me if I want to go in town. I say, "No. I can't go in town. I ain't got no money to go in town. What little few cents I could catch from the ironing got to give my granny. Or take and buy the things that I need. I ain't got no money to go in town. You know how it is?" He say, "Well I could give you money to go in town. You could be my girlfriend." I say, "Don't you, don't you *laugh* at me!" He say, "Ain't laughing at nobody." I say, "You and me is different kind of people. Where you come from and where I come from is different kind of people. So you got to look for you kind of people, and I got to look for my kind of people. That's just the way." He say, "Who is my kind of people?" I say, "People that got money. Got education. People that go at high school and got car and big house and thing." He say, "It don't be money. It *don't.* Is just people, understand?" He say, "Just let we, just tell me if you would be my girlfriend, and you could see me. I ain't want to dress up in ganga-clothes all the time to come looking for you." Well I laugh at that. I just *had* to laugh at that. He laugh too. We laugh so hard! We laugh till we belly hurt. Now we ain't saying nothing a time. A long time. Just sitting there in the silent. Listen in the silent to them breeze brushing through the canes, all them canes a-creeking, *kerrack, kerrack-kak,* and smelling green, and earth wet. And feeling the cool. Feeling far off. Like we did far off from everybody. Last he say, "Man, do, say something!" I say, "All right. All right then. I could be you girlfriend. You ain't got to walk behind me dress up ganga, but you, don't you *bully* me!" He say, "I ain't going bully you. I ain't. You going see. I going be all right." So then we, we do it again. He ain't hold me this time and I ain't run this time neither. We do it again and I hold *he.* Hold on tight to melt in them warm, wistful waters. And I did like it good enough this time.

So he tell me where to meet he and I go. We meet. Time to time. You know, I still did doubt, I still did had it pon my mind. I ain't in love with the man so good as yet. But then he did behaving heself ok. The beast did behaving heself ok. I start to like he. Well, *more* than like, and he too. Time come when I just couldn't miss he out from my eyesight. Nor he couldn't miss me out from he eyesight neither. We did going together, a time, we go in town a Saturday evening, take in a picture-show, things like that. And we go in the canes, always in the canes.

But then my grandmother get to find out, find out about we. Sweet Jesus! My grandmother give me so much of *struggle,* so much of struggle over this man. Tell me I hang my hat too high, and when I go to reach it down it going fall and hit me pon my head. I trying to come up too much, I should mind my station. All them kind of thing. My grandmother say, you know, he too big for me and thing. And then he father get to find out, Berry father did. Well he was more worse than my grandmother. He tell Berry I ain't no good, no class, I ain't no class for he. Berry father say I's low-down people, call me monkey, molasses-monkey, all them kind of thing. Oh Lord we get the *works.* So much of struggle. He get it from he side and I get it from my side. When I go in the canes at night with Berry, my grandmother shut me out the house. Lock me out. I got to sleep under the cellar. You know that house was standing pon posts, groundsills, and underneath open. We call that the cellar. And that place so damp, and so cold. When I sleep under the cellar my eyes swell up. Catch cold in my face.

So when Berry come to see me the next morning, he bathe and dress and walk over to see me, come from crossroads, you know I can't come out. My eyes swell too much! And then my little cousin, my little cousin Clive run out and he say, "She sleep under the cellar last night!" Thing like that. I can't see Berry no more, I too shame. But then one time Clive run out and he tell Berry, "She sleep under the cellar last night and she face swell!" But Berry call me still. He call me to come out and he standing there waiting till I come. He say, "You must *tell* me. When she shut you out like that." I say, "What I going tell you? I can't go telling you things that happen to me about my family. I got to *bear* with it. Cause you and me ain't no company." I say, "If you treat me bad, kick me or anything so, you know what they going say? They going say how I *deserve* that. How I hang my hat and thing. And they going be right. I can't bring my troubles before you. Cause I ain't got no *right* to be with you!" Berry just stand there and he shaking he head, say, "Just you tell me when she shut you out. Just you tell me so."

We meeting in the canes about every night now, sexing all the time, and feeling good. Reach a point we ain't want to go home not for nothing, he to hear from he father, me from my grandmother. One night we stay out most the whole night, and didn't get scarce no sleep neither. That morning I scorch up must be about a dozen the sailor pants. You know I was working two heater-irons now, two going at the same time, steaming up, ironing out the seams. I smell this thing scorching and I turn round, I throw off the iron quick quick and sprinkling water pon this pants, time as I turn round again, *next* pants a-scorching. On and on again and again till I must be scorch up about the entire American Navy! Me one. And is not Uncle Arrows come in that morning to find me, is *Mr. Bootman the Panama Man.* When that Mr. Bootman the Panama Man come in to find me with all these sailor pants a-scorching, near went after *me* with them iron! He say, "Man, you know who nuniform this is? You know who nuniform you got the privilege to hold in you hands? This garment near *sacred.* You don't play with Uncle Samson like that already!" I just take-off and I running. Take-off and I ain't looking back.

Now I got to find more work. I say to myself, *What you could do? Ain't nothing you could do.* So then I watch at my grandmother. She does work estate, work in the fields doing labor. Not cutting canes. She work pulling grass, pulling grasses from between the canes, keeping the canes clean. So I say to myself, *You strong as she. You could do that good as she.* I ask my granny, "I want to help you in the field." Granny Ansin say, "I ain't want you coming behind me. I ain't want you nowhere *near* behind me. I ain't even want you in my house!"

But I go behind she still. I was thinking, *Them's the whitepeople canes. Them don't belong to she. I got as much right to work them*

343

canes as she. So I follow behind, and when she look back, I dodge in the canes. I watch at she how she doing, and I doing just the same, and when she look back I dodge in the canes again. Time as lunch come I near fall down about four times. That work so *hard!* I so tired, and mouth so dry! But I keep on. I just keep on the whole day. When I reach home that evening. Well Ansin, she reach before me, and when I reach home Ansin was there waiting, she say, "Girl, you look like a ghost, you turn black like a ghost. Look you face black already and you turn more black still, black like a ghost!" She say, "You go outside and you bathe before you come in here." I say, "I too tired to bathe. I going rest awhile, and when night come I would bathe." Ansin say, "You get pay?" I say, "No." She say, *"What?"* I say, "Ain't sign so ain't get pay. Ain't nobody tell me to sign." Granny Ansin say, "Girl, I ain't know if you more black or more stupid. I ain't know *what* you is." I say, "Well you don't worry cause I know what I is. I is human being. And tomorrow morning I going sign and I going get pay."

So things carry on like that. I work two weeks and then I rest awhile. Cause that's hard work you working them canes, you can't go like that all the time. I rest and I work some more. They pay me sometimes three dollars, three-fifty for two weeks. That can't buy you scarce nothing that three-fifty. Maybe couple yards of cloth to make a dress. Jar of cream, Pons cold cream, something like that. Two weeks for jar of cream. But that's the only work you could get, so you got to do it. Berry, he ain't want to hear nothing about me working in them canes. Cause that's poor people work, that's the work for poor people. And plus, he know when I in the canes working all the day like that, I ain't going back in the night. I say, *"Chups!* Man, next thing I be *living* in them canes." I say, "I tired, man. I too tired!" But he know I still like it good in them canes. Like it good enough.

Then one time my grandmother went pon excursion, church excursion. You know how the church have excursion to visit some other church and thing? We call that mission day. Well this mission day was my grandmother turn to cook. You know, preacher give she money to make the picnic. So my grandmother bake and cook and all kind of thing, and she make this big picnic basket for this excursion. *Big* basket. I wasn't going, but I tell my grandmother that I would carry the basket for she, with all these cokes and food and different things. I know me and Berry would get chance to be together the whole day cause my grandmother ain't going be there. I say, "Ansin, let me carry the basket. This a big basket, and I could carry it I stronger than you. Let me carry the basket up the hill." So she say I could carry the basket. I raise it up pon my head to carry, we walking with them other women going up crossroads to catch the bus. I tell my grandmother, "You go-long. Go-long up in front and catch the, you know that bus would come soon so you go-long and catch and I would come up fast behind."

So I walking long and I reach up my hand throwing out the cokes now, two for him and one for me. I throw out some sandwich, about six-eight sandwich, cakes, about three different kind of cakes I throw out, coconut cakes and chocolate, different fruits and thing. He did hiding in the canes, following behind me but sticking to the canes, and when I throw out, he just run and he collect-up. The things I throwing out. One time like my grandmother, like she catch me, she wait for me to come up and she say, "What happen with you? You very far back." I say, "Feel so *tired.*" She say, "You go-long home! Give my basket and you go-long home." I say, "No. I going carry it to the bus." Cause I did feel so shame now to give she back that basket. She say, "I feel something going happen with you today. I got a presentiment for that." I say, "Ain't nothing going happen with me. You go-long have youself a nice time in the picnic." Anyway, bus come, my grandmother gone, she climb up in the bus and she gone. Ain't even notice the basket empty. Near empty. But when this man come out the canes now! So many things I throw out, near about *everything* was in that basket. Well we running we can't scarce carry all this food and cokes and different things, can't scarce wait to get weself inside them canes. So then we sit down and we start and we eat. We *eat eat eat.* Eat cakes and different things, eat banana, we must be eat about six banana each. Now we take a break and we do little something, we do little something and then we eat some more, eat some sandwich and drink a coke, take a break and do little something more, eat some more, eat a coconut cake, or chocolate, off and on and off and on like that *whole* morning long. My sweet Jesus *that* was picnic we make that day! We did start from early morning, about eight o'clock, we doing just how we feel. *Everything!* So reach now about two o'clock, I say I going home and bathe and change, he say he going home and bathe too, and he would meet me back there in the canes about four o'clock.

So I going home now, but before I go and bathe I pass by a friend of mine cause I did feel so *thirsty*. After we eat so early and so much, eat till all finish, cause we ain't stopping till ain't nothing more to eat. So this girlfriend of mine, where she living had plenty coconut trees, *tall* coconut trees. Coconut trees with water-coconuts. Them trees so tall the coconuts stand and get big big, you know everybody fraid to pick them coconuts cause they fraid to climb up so high. But doudou, this day I feeling I is boss. I is *boss*, and I going climb up them tree. I put this big ladder up in the tree, and I start to climbing up in that tree till the ladder get a belly like, a belly of sinking, but I keep climbing. I keep climbing, and just when I get at the center, just when I reach in the center of that belly, *plaks!* the ladder break, and all I know now is I flying. Doudou, I *flying!* Flying through the air. Ain't even know when I hit, when I hit the ground. Cause all I could remember is that flying.

When I wake up must be about three-four days later. I ain't even know how I reach in the bed. All I know is my body so stiff, so stiff. I couldn't even raise up my head off the pillow. But he come and he stand pon me. Berry did. He come and he stand pon me every day, and soon I start to feeling better, getting back pon my feet. You know he bring eggs, and malt, iron, build back up my nerves. He buy block of iron, you know that black thing? He just chip off some in the milk, and milk start and turn just like iron. Taste, *shew!* real bad, but it good for you, good for the nerves. I lie there in the bed, he looking down pon me, I looking up pon he face, I say to myself, *Well let you look and he real good now. Look at he good, cause you only ever see this rat mostly in the night, darkness of them canes.* And he was handsome too. He with he long nose, and them freckles on it. That man handsome in truth. Then my grandmother, one morning she come to me and she say, "Like he a nice boy. Like I did treating he wrong." I say, "I know he gavering nice to me. He gavering nice to me a time."

So I start to getting back pon my feet now. Everybody saying like I pregnant and gone up in that tree cause I gone crazy, I want to throw the child. Berry father say I did want to kill myself, cause I pregnant and he family don't like me. Say he feel sorry, he feel sorry for doing that. But truth is, I wasn't pregnant then. I sure about that. I sure I wasn't pregnant then. Cause that come *after*. Maybe about three, that came about three-four months after the tree. After that fall. And when I start and find myself pregnant now, when I find myself now with baby in truth, doudou, that's when everything turn to bad. Not for Berry. He did happy enough. For everybody else. Granny Ansin and he father. For them two things turn straight to bad.

My grandmother turn bad pon me again. Treat me so harsh. Worse even than when she uses to lock me out the house, and I got to sleep under the cellar. Worse even than that. Then one day I went up crossroads, catch the bus, and Berry father hold me front everybody. Hold me and curse me front everybody. Say, "I would give you one kick in you belly kick that child through you mouth! Get you whoreself way from my son!" Say worse than that. Oh my Jesus I did feel so *bad*, so shame. And, doudou, I did crying. I cry so much for that. I say to myself, *Lord, what I gone and do? What I gone and do to get this?* I tell Berry, I say, "Look, man, you just go about you business, and forget, let me go about my business." Berry say, "You can't tell me that. You *can't*. Cause that what you got in you belly that belong to me too. We just got to make out. We just got to make out together."

So Berry gone now and he apply for fireman. Gone and apply for fire service. You know you got to sit exam to do that, cause that's government thing. So Berry sit exam and he come out all A's. All *A's!* Cause he very very smart, he very smart and he could write so *pretty*. They tell he he come out all A's. So he gone and he drop from the high school, cause he going join in the fire service now. Hat and cape and everything. We find weself this little house to rent. Pay down the first month. Six dollars. Only a little one-room board-house, but it got in the bed, and two chairs, and little table.

We had it plan. How we did do. You know Berry gone and he buy the bucket, water bucket, and I gone and I buy you the cup. Little white metal cup for you. And little spoon. Cup and spoon and water bucket. And we own house to live in. Doudou, that afternoon we did think we own the sky! We own the sky and earth both, so much of things we had! So next morning when Ansin go in church, and Berry father out driving the bus, we move in all we things inside the house. Yesterday. That was only yesterday we movin' here. Seem like a month! This little house. But, doudou, ain't so small. Cause you know what you daddy tell me? He say, "Vel, the thing I like mostest of this house is the yard." I say, *"Yard?"* I say, "Onliest thing we got for yard is the street. Pothole and puddle!" Berry say, "I talking about the *back* yard. You ain't notice the back yard?" He say, "We got the whole world of canes for we back yard."

NOTES ON CONTRIBUTORS

ESTHER ALLEN's most recent translation, *The Book of Lamentations* by Rosario Castellanos, was published by Marsilio in October.

JULIA ALVAREZ is originally from the Dominican Republic. She is the author of two books of poems, *Homecoming* (Plume/Penguin) and *The Other Side* (Dutton). Her two novels, *How the Garcia Girls Lost Their Accents* and *In the Time of the Butterflies*, were both published by Algonquin Books of Chapel Hill, as is her new novel, *¡Yo!*, which will be published in 1997.

ROBERT ANTONI's *Divina Trace* (Overlook) won the 1992 Commonwealth Prize for Best First Novel. His second novel, *Blessed is the Fruit*, will be published by Henry Holt this spring. He teaches fiction writing and Magical Realism in the MFA program at the University of Miami, and is the associate director of its Caribbean Writers Summer Institute.

GAGE AVERILL has written extensively on Caribbean popular music, specializing in Haiti, and is the author of *A Day for the Hunter, A Day for the Prey: Popular Music and Power in Haiti* (University of Chicago Press, 1996).

JOSÉ BEDIA was born in Havana, immigrated first to Mexico and then to the United States and now lives and works in Miami. A painter who works in various media, including painting and installation, his work is included in the collections of the Whitney Museum of American Art, the Spencer Museum, the Philadelphia Museum of Art and the Museum of Art of the Rhode Island School of Design, among many others. In 1996, his work has been exhibited at the Hyde Gallery, Trinity College in Dublin as well as at the George Adams Gallery in New York.

MADISON SMARTT BELL is the author of nine novels, including *The Washington Square Ensemble* (Viking) and *Waiting for the End of the World* (Ticknor & Fields). He has also published two collections of short stories: *Zero db* (Ticknor & Fields) and *Barking Man* (Ticknor & Fields). His novel *All Souls' Rising* (Pantheon) was a finalist for the 1995 National Book Award and the 1996 PEN/ Faulkner Award. *Ten Indians* will be published by Pantheon in November 1997.

ANTONIO BENÍTEZ-ROJO teaches Latin American and Caribbean literature at Amherst College. Several of his books have been translated into English: *The Repeating Island* (Duke University Press), winner of the 1993 MLA Katherine Singer Kovacs Prize; *Sea of Lentils* (University of Massachusetts Press), a novel; and *The Magic Dog and Other Stories* (Ediciones del Norte).

Born in 1910, JUAN BOSCH, the Dominican Republic's most respected and prestigious author, has published more than fifty works of fiction and collections of essays. He has also been a political activist, founding the first revolutionary party of the Dominican Republic. While exiled in Cuba in 1931, he organized and trained soldiers to lead an unsuccessful expedition against the dictator

Rafael Leónidas Trujillo Molina. After Trujillo's assassination in 1961, Bosch became president. He has lectured at various universities, and among the students of his course "Techniques of the Short Story," given at the Universidad Central de Venezuela, was the youthful Gabriel García Márquez. Together with Alejo Carpentier, Miguel Angel Asturias and Arturo Uslar Pietri, he is recognized as a precursor and founder of the Magical Realist movement.

KAMAU BRATHWAITE was born in Barbados in 1930. He is a professor of comparative literature at New York University and the author of *MiddlePassages* and *Black + Blues*, both published by New Directions.

ADRIAN CASTRO has been published in several anthologies, including *Paper Dance: 55 Latino Poets* (Persea Books) and *Little Havana Blues* (Arte Publico). He frequently performs in Miami, where he lives, in various venues, often with music. In the fall of 1997, Coffee House Press will publish his *Cantos to Blood & Honey*.

CLARE CAVANAGH recently published *Osip Mandelstam and the Modernist Creation of Tradition*. She is co-translator on two books of Polish poetry with Stanislaw Baranczak. Their most recent collection, of Wislawa Szymborska's *View With a Grain of Sand*, won the PEN/Book of the Month Club Translation Prize for 1996.

MANNO CHARLEMAGNE is the mayor of Port-au-Prince and Haiti's best-known singer/songwriter. His albums include *Manno et Marco* (1979), *Konviksyon* (1984), *Fini les Colonies* (1985), *Nou nan Malè ak Oganizasyon Mondyal* (1988) and *La Fimen* (1994).

THOMAS CHRISTENSEN's translations include works by Alejo Carpentier, Carlos Fuentes and Julio Cortázar, among others. His translation of *Ballets without Music, without Dancers, without Anything* by Louis-Ferdinand Céline is forthcoming later this year from Sun & Moon Press. As a translator he often collaborates with Carol Christensen, as on their translation of Laura Esquivel's *Like Water for Chocolate*.

MERLE COLLINS is a fiction writer and poet. Her most recent poetry collection, *Rotten Pomerack*, was published in London in 1990. Born in Grenada, she teaches creative writing and Caribbean literature at the University of Maryland.

NILO CRUZ is the author of *Night Train to Bolina, A Park in Our House* and many other plays. The scenes published in this issue of *Conjunctions* are from *Dancing on Her Knees*, which was directed by Graciela Daniele and produced at The Public Theatre in New York.

Guyanese-born FRED D'AGUIAR has written three books of poetry (the latest is *British Subjects*) and two novels, *The Longest Memory* (Avon) and *Dear Future* (Pantheon). He teaches in the MFA program at the University of Miami and in its Caribbean Writers Summer Institute.

EDWIDGE DANTICAT is the author of a collection of short stories, *Krik? Krak!*, which was a finalist for the 1995 National Book Award, and a novel, *Breath, Eyes, Memory*, both of which were published by Vintage. The piece in this issue of *Conjunctions* is from her novel in progress. She lives in Brooklyn, New York.

MARK DOW's poems have appeared in *Threepenny Review, Southern Review, Pequod* and *Crazyhorse,* among others. He has also published a variety of nonfiction pieces, including several articles on Haiti.

ROSARIO FERRÉ was born in Ponce, Puerto Rico, and writes both in Spanish and English. In Spanish she has published short stories; two novels, *Maldito Amor* and *La batalla de las vírgenes;* essays and poems. In English she has published a book of short stories, *The Youngest Doll,* and two novels, *Sweet Diamond Dust,* for which she received the Liberatur Prix in Frankfurt, Germany, and *The House on the Lagoon* (Farrar, Straus & Giroux), nominated for the National Book Award in 1995.

CRISTINA GARCÍA is the author of *Dreaming in Cuban.* "A Natural History," excerpted from her second novel, *The Agüero Sisters,* will be published in spring 1997 by Alfred A. Knopf.

GABRIEL GARCÍA MÁRQUEZ is the author of many novels and collections of stories including *One Hundred Years of Solitude, The Autumn of the Patriarch, Chronicle of a Death Foretold, Love in the Time of Cholera, The General in His Labyrinth* and, most recently, *Of Love and Other Demons* (Knopf), García Márquez was awarded the Nobel Prize for Literature in 1982. He lives in Mexico City and Bogotá.

Jamaican LORNA GOODISON is the author of *Selected Poems* (University of Michigan Press, 1993) and *To Us, All Flowers Are Roses* (University of Illinois Press, 1995). She teaches creative writing at the University of Michigan. She was awarded the Commonwealth Poetry Prize for the Americas of 1986.

EDITH GROSSMAN's most recent translations include *Death in the Andes* by Mario Vargas Llosa (Farrar, Straus & Giroux), *The Adventures of Magroll,* by Álvaro Mutis (HarperCollins) and *Of Love and Other Demons,* by Gabriel García Márquez (Alfred A. Knopf).

WILSON HARRIS's *Jonestown* was published by Faber & Faber in July 1996. His fiction includes *The Guyana Quartet* (1960–1963), *The Sleepers of Roraima* (1970), *Black Marsden* (1972), *The Angel at the Gate* (1982), *The Carnival Trilogy* (1985–1990) and *Resurrection at Sorrow Hill* (1993). He was awarded the Premio Mondello dei Cinque Continenti in 1992.

Born in Jamaica, LINTON KWESI JOHNSON has been called the world's first Dub poet. He has published four books of poems, among them *Inglan Is a Bitch* (Race Today) and *Tings an Times* (Bloodaxe Books and LKJ Music) and recorded seven albums.

KWADWO AGYMAH KAMAU's first novel, *Flickering Shadows,* was published by Coffee House Press in September 1996. Born in Barbados, he currently lives in Virginia.

SUZANNE JILL LEVINE, author of *The Subversive Scribe: Translating Latin American Fiction,* is currently writing a literary biography of Manuel Puig, to be published by Farrar, Straus & Giroux. She is recipient of the PEN Gregory Kolovakos Award for career achievement as a translator of Hispanic literature.

GLENVILLE LOVELL was born and raised in a tiny village on the island of Barbados. His first novel, *Fire in the Canes*, was published by Soho Press. "Coco's Palace" is from *Wade in the Water*, a novel in progress.

JAMES MARANISS is the author of *On Calderón* (University of Missouri Press, 1978). He translated the Antonio Benítez-Rojo novel *Sea of Lentils* and his book of essays, *The Repeating Island*.

IAN McDONALD was born in Trinidad, attended Cambridge University and has lived in Guyana since 1955. He is the author of the novel *The Hummingbird Tree*, published by Heinemann, and three collections of poems: *Mercy Ward* and *Essequibo*, published by Peterloo Press, and *Jaffo the Calypsonian*, published by Peepal Tree Press.

MARK McMORRIS is the author, most recently, of *Figures for a Hypothesis* (Leave Books, 1995) and *Moth-Wings* (Burning Deck, 1996). *The Black Reeds* is due out this fall from the University of Georgia Press. Born in Jamaica, he currently lives in Providence, Rhode Island.

MAYRA MONTERO is a Cuban writer and journalist who lives in Puerto Rico. She has written one collection of short stories, *Twenty-Three and a Turtle*, and four novels that have been translated into French, German and Italian. Her most recent novel, *Palm of Darkness*, will be published in a translation by Edith Grossman by HarperCollins in 1997.

ANABELLA PAIZ's translations have appeared or are forthcoming in *Mangrove* and *Prairie Schooner*. She was born in Guatemala and now lives in Miami with her husband and five children.

Originally published in Spanish in 1991, "The Wolf, the Forest and the New Man" brought SENEL PAZ worldwide acclaim. Fellow Cuban Tomás Gutierrez Alea asked Paz to prepare a screenplay that resulted in the film *Strawberry and Chocolate*, which won first prize at the Berlin Film Festival. This is the first publication of this work in America. Senel Paz lives in Havana.

MARLENE NOURBESE PHILIP is a poet, novelist and essayist. Her most recent work is *Showing Grit: Showboating North of the 44th Parallel*. Born in Cuba, she now lives in Toronto.

Novelist, short-story writer and journalist ARTURO USLAR PIETRI was born in Caracas, Venezuela, in 1906. Winner of many awards, among them the Rómulo Gallegos in 1991, he is the author of novels such as *Las Lanzas Coloradas*, *El Camino de El Dorado* and *La Isla de Robinson*. He is both precursor and contemporary of the Latin American boom and Magic Realism.

ZAIDA DEL RÍO is a Cuban artist living in Havana, whose illustrations were reproduced in the original Edición Homenaje edition of Senel Paz's *El lobo, el bosque y el hombre nuevo*.

During his lifetime, SEVERO SARDUY (1936–1993) published six novels, several volumes of poetry, plays and essays. An editor at Editions du Seuil in France, he was responsible for bringing much contemporary Latin American fiction to European readers.

351

MARK SCHAFER is a literary translator and visual artist living in Boston. He has translated *Mogador* by Alberto Ruy Sánchez, *The Book of Embraces* by Eduardo Galeano (with Cedric Belfrage) and *Cold Tales* and *René's Flesh* by Virgilio Piñera.

A Jamaican who lives in Canada, OLIVE SENIOR is the author of eight books, including three collections of short stories, two of poetry and nonfiction works on Caribbean culture. Her first collection of stories, *Summer Lightning* (Longman, 1986), won the Commonwealth Writers Prize in 1987. Her most recent collection of stories is *Discerner of Hearts* (McClelland and Stewart, 1995) and her latest book of poetry is *Gardening in the Tropics* (McClelland and Stewart, 1994.)

BOB SHACOCHIS is a novelist, essayist, journalist and educator. His fifth book, *The Immaculate Invasion*, a chronicle of the U.S. military intervention in Haiti, will be published in 1997 by Viking/Penguin.

Poet and playwright DEREK WALCOTT was born in the West Indies. He is the author of *In a Green Night: Poems 1948–1960*, *The Gulf* and the book-length poems *Another Life* and *Omeros*, among many others. He has also written some thirty plays, among them *Dream on Monkey Mountain*, *Ti-Jean and His Brothers* and *Pantomime*. He was awarded the Nobel Prize for Literature in 1992. His poem "Signs," which appears in this issue of *Conjunctions*, is part of his forthcoming book *The Bounty* (Farrar, Straus & Giroux).

ADAM ZAGAJEWSKI was born in Poland and now lives in Paris. He has four books in translation: two books of poetry, *Tremor* and *Canvas*, and two collections of essays, *Solidarity Solitude* and *Two Cities*.

In addition to the world's best
writers, we've also been recognized
by the U.S Government.

They attempted to burn issue 21.

*Until moving our offices to New York in 1972, a certain customs official over at the U.S. port of
entry was always an obstacle. Outraged by the appearance of a single scatological word, he ordered
issue 21 to be taken to the city dump and burned. Before the arrival of the U.S.
marshalls, a band of loyal followers spirited the crates away from the loading
docks to various basements in Greenwich Village. Eventually, much to the
delight of our subscription holders, the proper officials in Washington reviewed
the issue and decided that it shouldn't be subject to fire. Call (718) 539-7085
and you'll understand why back in 1959 a group of editors risked breaking the
law just so they wouldn't miss an issue.*

{4 issues (one year) $34, $8 Surcharge outside the U.S.A.}
http://www.voyagerco.com

THE PARIS REVIEW *The International Literary Quarterly.*

UNIVERSITY OF MIAMI
CARIBBEAN WRITERS INSTITUTE
1991-1996

Sponsored By:
DEPARTMENT OF ENGLISH

WORKSHOPS IN DRAMA, FICTION, AND POETRY
SEMINARS IN LITERATURE AND CULTURE
TRANSLATION INSTITUTE
VISITING WRITERS AND SCHOLARS
WRITERS AND SCHOLARS IN RESIDENCE
READINGS BY CARIBBEAN WRITERS

◆ **Writers-in-Residence:** Michael Anthony - Robert Antoni - Kamau Brathwaite - Fred D'Aguiar - Lorna Goodison - George Lamming - Mervyn Morris - Olive Senior - Earl Lovelace

◆ **Scholars-in-Residence:** Edward Baugh - Antonio Benitez-Rojo - Michael Dash - Lillian Manzor - Sandra Pouchet Paquet - Gordon Rohlehr

◆ **Visiting Writers and Scholars:** Michael Anthony - Brian Antoni - Giannina Braschi - Erna Brodber - Maryse Conde - Cyril Dabydeen - David Dabydeen - Edwidge Danticat - Joan Dayan - Zee Edgell - Lorna Goodison - Merle Hodge - James Maraniss - Tess O'Dwyer - Richard Philcox - Sam Selvon - Olive Senior - Derek Walcott - Ana Lydia Vega

———— •••• ————

WHILE THE CARIBBEAN WRITERS INSTITUTE ENJOYS
INSTITUTIONAL SUPPORT, ITS PROGRAMS RELY ON GIFTS FROM
INDIVIDUALS AND INSTITUTIONS
UPON WHOSE GENEROSITY THE FUTURE DEPENDS.

FOR FURTHER INFORMATION ABOUT HOW YOU CAN CONTRIBUTE,
CALL OR WRITE:
DR. SANDRA POUCHET PAQUET,
P.O. BOX 248145, UNIVERSITY OF MIAMI,
CORAL GABLES, FL. 33124-4632.
PHONE: 305-284-2182. FAX: 305-284-5635